I WAS JUST ABOUT TO CALL YOU!

And Other Mysteries

Content guidance: the matter within contains graphic descriptions of medical facilities and treatment, cancer, death, and bodily functions. Topics also include suicide, psychosis, and some mild homophobia.

This book is a work of autobiographical fiction and 44 years have gone by since the time of occurrence of the events depicted. Some characters are based on real persons, some are composites of several individuals, and some are completely fictitious. The key events depicted have a basis in real life while other lesser events are fabricated to extend the story line. All identities, names and places have been altered and their details removed or added for creative purposes.

All Bible verses quoted herein are from the New Revised Standard Version (NRSV), copyright 1952 [2nd edition, 1971] by the division of Christian Education of the National Council of Churches of Christ in the United States of America. Used by permission. All rights reserved.

The Holy Quran, 17:85 is from the Sahih International Translation.

ISBN: 979-8-9879761-0-4

LCCN: 2023904786

Remember the Joy! Publishing
rememberthejoy.com

I WAS JUST ABOUT TO CALL YOU!

AND OTHER MYSTERIES

A Novel

MEDICINE, FATHERHOOD, & QUANTUM ENTANGLEMENT

Roger W. Byhardt, MD &

Lydia Byhardt Bollinger, LCSW

RWB

ACKNOWLEDGMENTS

Thanks to Mom and Dad, Marilyn, "Bro," "Cuz," Erik, Hobbes, Grandma across the driveway, Marly, and Miss Oole for support, editing, and encouragement.

Thanks to Paul, Levi and Anya for tolerating my time away every Thursday afternoon to do epic three-hour writing calls with Dad. Maeven and Sophie, thanks for checking in—your purrs are very therapeutic.

Doris, we miss you. We really needed your particular skills.

CONTENTS

CHAPTER 1

———

WHIRLIGIG

"... it's much more interesting to live not knowing than to have answers which might be wrong."

— Richard P. Feynman

Rude Awakening

Zelda Biedermeier, the family's deepest sleeper, had charge of a "thunder-clap" alarm that could recall Lazarus from Hell, but the previous night, she forgot to set it. Working late into the night on a deadlined art design project, she hit the bed like a brick long after her husband, Randall, had given up the ghost. Randall was assigned the task of corralling their two grade-schoolers, Kyle and Addie, into bed so she could finish the project.

Randall got the kids overtired and sugar-hyped with an ill-advised, not Mom-approved, cookie bribe. Thankfully, the two hyper munch-kins finally settled for the night after a Dr. Seuss bedtime story. It was half-past bedtime when they, at last, succumbed to sleep. Had sleep not come, Randall was contemplating asphyxia. At least for himself.

Biedermeier's black-and-white tuxedo cat, Baldspot, usually slept on the floor on a cushioned cat bed under a south-facing window in the master bedroom. She was the family's default alarm system. A ded-icated "foodnatic," Baldspot's biologic kitty clock was in sync with the morning alarm. If the alarm didn't sound at the expected time, Baldspot prowled and yowled until someone on the service staff woke up to do a food fetch.

This Monday morning, January 10, 1977, with no alarm or backup alarm, the 06:30 wake-up time was reached and surpassed. At 06:35, the fickle finger of fate took command. The small metal catch holding the spring on the large roll-up window shade in the master bedroom decided it was tired of holding the stupid spring. The spring suddenly released and sent the shade rolling back up at warp speed. *Thwap thwap thwap!*

When it reached the top, the entire shade assembly popped out of its bracket and came crashing down onto the white ceramic lamp of a cherub holding a bowl on its head. Clear marbles embedded in the outside of the bowl simulated grapes, badly. Both bad art and insufficient light, the lamp crashed onto the window seat where Baldspot's cat bed cushioned it before Humpty-Cherub tumbled to the floor and shattered. Translucent marbles scattered across the carpet.

Randall responded to the cacophony of sound as though his on-call beeper had just gone off. He sat bolt upright in bed, rubbing his eyes, trying to discern the source of this rude awakening. Randall was deeply annoyed. He'd been having a "good" dream, one that would have made Zelda jealous. Now he'd never know if the dream would have met his grand expectations.

"What in holy smokes was that?" Randall yelled to no one in particular; since Zelda, still fast asleep and snoring, was completely unphased by the noise.

If sleeping were an Olympic event, Zelda would be a podium finisher. She once even fell asleep with her head in the kitchen towel drawer during a thunderstorm.

Randall, needing a bit more time to wake up, took a moment to take in his wife's sleeping form. Zelda was small, yet mighty, with curly red hair to match her fiery disposition. Randall thought of Zelda as his little fox. Some might imagine foxy as long-legged with low necklines. This little fox was sly and lithe; her freckles and blue eyes gave her a look of childlike innocence that belied her mischievous and mercurial nature.

Unblessed by the slumber gene, Randall could usually wake up on a dime. He did so countless times during his medical training years. While not born with the ability, he had acquired it by necessity.

Momentarily, Randall began to cognate at a semi-alert level and do a quick survey of the room. *Shade, lamp, crash. Didn't like that stupid lamp anyway.* His aunt had made the lamp in a ceramics class and "gifted" it to him. A true white elephant.

No big loss, he thought. *Its time had come. TIME! Oh, crap, what was the time?*

He glanced at his Timex and panicked. Already 07:10! Forty minutes past wake-up time. The kids would be late for school! He might be late for work! No time to clean up the cherub lamp mess now.

REST IN PIECES

Before Randall could sort out what to do first, Addie and Kyle ran into the bedroom, still in pajamas. "Daddy, Daddy, what was that big noise?" screeched five-year-old Addie, still holding her treasured but tattered blanket remnant.

When seven-year-old Kyle saw the downed shade and busted lamp, he went into reflexive self-defense mode. "I didn't do it, Dad! I was in bed the whole time!"

Despite being in crisis mode, Randall had to laugh. "No worries, Buddy. The window shade self-destructed all on its lonesome and took the lamp with it. Finally put that eyesore out of its misery. Be careful, you two, don't walk over there with bare feet until I can clean it up later. You guys hustle back to your rooms and get dressed for school."

Disregarding her father's warning, typically obstinate Addie took two steps closer to inspect the damage. She picked up a few of the sparkly marbles. "Oh, pretty!"

She slipped them in her pocket. "Daddy, are we late for school? I think the hands on my horse clock say it's late. Why didn't Mommy wake us up?"

Zelda snored on, dead to the world. Randall reached over and checked the alarm. "You're right, Rosebud. Looks like it wasn't set. Listen up. Just get dressed as quick as you can. I'll wake up Mom. It may take cold water."

Other fun options bubbled up from Randall's subconscious, but he dismissed them. Fun, but too consequential.

Kyle started off for his room but turned abruptly and came back. He pointed to the empty cat bed. "Hey, where's Baldspot? She's usually howling for food by now."

"I have no idea, son," said Randall. "You just get a move on and get dressed. I'm sure she'll turn up underfoot while we're trying to navigate the kitchen."

Randall looked over at Zelda, still zonked and sawing hardwood. Sure, things were on high alert, and he needed to hustle through his morning routine, but . . . .

Randall grabbed the bedcovers and slowly pulled them off Zelda's sleeping form, down to her knees. He took in the tantalizing sight. A stray curl of red hair poked out from under the elastic leg band of her white panties. Focused on geography below the Mason-Dixon line, Randall did not notice Zelda opening her eyes to see why she was suddenly so cold.

"Randy!" blurted Zelda. "Why are you just standing there, panty peeking? Are you now a total pervert?"

Randall shook his head. "Not 'total' yet, but I'm working on it. I rarely get to see Treasure Island in broad daylight, so I thought it a shame to miss the boat. Sorry. Had to wake you up, and this usually works best. Look at the clock."

Zelda did a "look at my tonsils" yawn, then a big exhale. "What are you doing up in the middle of the night? I just got to sleep. Did someone die?"

Randall picked up the alarm clock and held it in front of her bleary face. "Sorry, Sleeping Beauty. Look at the time, and the sunlight coming in the window. It's morning, and we all overslept. We're late! It's time for hyper-prep mode. 'Someone' forgot to set the alarm."

Zelda shook her head. "It wasn't me. I swear!"

"Well now I know one thing for sure," said Randall.

"What?"

"You are definitely your son's mother."

Randall ducked as a pillow flew his way. "If you're back among the living, maybe, together, we can get the Queen Mary out of the harbor before the tide goes out. It's already 07:15. The frosting on the cake is that it snowed overnight, and the outside thermometer reads 7 degrees."

"Above or below zero?" groaned Zelda.

"Does it matter?"

Zelda jumped out of bed and quickly donned her robe. "Shiver me timbers, Cap'n! I'll help ye heave to. You SSS, while I get the sprouts off to school. We usin' cars or dog sleds?"

"Cars. I forgot to feed the huskies. Now mush!" Randall headed for the bathroom to shave, shower and spit.

Zelda spotted the broken lamp on the floor. "And what in blazes is all this mess on the floor? Yippee! The stupid cherub lamp has passed on to cherub heaven. What happened?"

"I'll explain later. Right now, we have to get a move on." He hustled to the bathroom, then called through the door. "By the way, Baldspot is missing. Keep an eye out!"

By some miracle, Randall was out of the bathroom, dressed, and downstairs by 7:30. Zelda was putting away dirty cereal bowls and pushing the kids out the back door to get in the car. Addie opened the closet door to get her boots, and Baldspot erupted from the closet.

Just before bedtime the night before, Addie had accidently closed the closet door with Baldspot still inside, exploring some smelly cowboy boots. The cat had meowled and scratched, but the cacophony was not heard in the upstairs bedrooms.

Baldspot zoomed into the kitchen and ran in circles to celebrate her release from imprisonment. Zelda tripped over the cat and nearly dropped the cereal dishes.

Kyle caught Baldspot and picked her up. She began to lick Kyle's face.

"You poor thing! Nasty Addie locked you away. I know you're hungry. I'll get you some Meow Mix," said Kyle between wet kisses.

Zelda belayed that idea. "Kyle, put her down. We don't have time for feeding the cat. She's not going to starve. I'll feed her when I get back. Besides, it's the cat's fault we're all late!"

Addie started sniffling. "No, it's my fault, Mommy! I locked Baldy in the closet last night by accident! And it stinks in there. There's poop in your shoe."

"What?" yelped Zelda.

Addie went to the closet and came back with Zelda's outdoor loafers. The left one had what looked like a moist Hershey's kiss neatly deposited in the center of the heel space. A dried-out roller was in the right shoe.

Instead of being angry, Zelda started to laugh.

"Let me see," said Kyle, who also thought poop was laugh-worthy and started to guffaw.

"Mommy? You're not mad?" asked Addie.

"Nope," said Zelda, patting Addie on the shoulder. "You've got to appreciate talent when you see it. When it comes to shoe-poo, old Baldy is a van Gogh. Don't you worry your little head about it. It wasn't your fault. Accidents happen. Now get your boots and coat on. You too, laughing boy. Now get into the garage, and we can make the van Gogh."

They scattered out the door.

Zelda rushed to put her coat on over pajamas and robe, grabbed the keys to the orange VW campervan, and made a beeline for the garage. The kids were already waiting and buckled in.

As Zelda climbed into the driver's seat, the kids shouted that they didn't get lunches to take to school. Zelda promised she'd bring them to school later. She brought the VW to life and reversed down the driveway.

Kyle, in a rare show of brotherly love, put his hand on Addie's arm. "Actually, sis, you may have saved Baldy's life!"

Addie wiped her nose on her sleeve. "What do you mean?"

"It's simple, stupid." Kyle rolled his eyes. "If Baldy had been in her cat bed this morning, the lamp would have hit her."

Addie looked at Kyle wide-eyed. "You're right. Maybe it was magic."

Kyle laughed. "*Hah!* Don't kid yourself. It was just a lucky accident."

Randall, still in the house, was about to leave for work when he remembered their golden Lab, Polluto. The ding dong dog spent the night in his basement kennel, which kept him from howling all night, breaking into food supplies, and treating the cat box like his own personal buffet. By now the dog's teeth would be floating.

Randall dragged the dog upstairs and pushed him out the back door into the fenced back yard. Zelda would be back soon enough to let the big galoot back in from the cold once he made his mark on the territory. Randall gathered his gear and jetted out the back door. He threw his briefcase and backpack into the trunk of his VW Scirocco.

The Scirocco didn't like cold weather and balked at starting, but finally kicked over. With a roar and a screech of spinning tires, Randall skidded down the driveway.

On the way out, Randall spotted his septuagenarian neighbor, Flossie Bush, looking out her kitchen window. She shook her head in disapproval at his tire-squealing antics. It was 7:40 by the time he cleared the driveway. The kids would make it to school on time, but Randall had already missed the morning opening of his Radiation Oncology Department. He was sure there would be heck to pay.

RUSH TO JUDGMENT

Randall decided the six-mile drive to the VA Medical Center would have to be a road rally sprint. This late in the morning rush hour and with the new snowfall, he would be slipping and sliding. Was it city roads or the freeway? As he drove south on 84th Street, past Greenmount Ave, he looked ahead at the freeway overpass. Traffic was dead still.

He bit his lip, then made a quick U-turn and backtracked north to eastbound Greenmount. The roads had been plowed earlier in the morning, but new snow continued to fall and anoint the road with more. Many cars were having trouble navigating the compacted snow ice ruts. After several close calls at busy intersections, Randall mumbled a special blessing for the inventor of antilock brakes.

Approaching the VA from the north via Greenmount meant he had to enter from the back, using Hickam Drive. The VA hospital building was at the southernmost section of the large grounds. Hickam Drive was a winding, narrow two-lane road that meandered through a large veterans' cemetery and past multiple historic buildings dating to the 1800s. Fortunately, the back roads were usually kept clear of snow by a squadron of plows, snowblowers, and an overabundance of salt. Unfortunately, the sloth-like road crew had barely started.

Randall had always thought of Hickam Drive as his private road-racing course with its many S turns, elevation changes, blind corners, and old railroad tracks to bounce over. Snowy conditions made it even more "challenging." Randall checked his dash clock. He had seven minutes to complete the back course, find a parking spot, and get into his clinic. He almost clipped a snowplow but made it with a minute to spare to his designated parking spot. He thought it ironic that they always plowed the lot AFTER everyone was parked.

The main hospital parking lot to the east was reserved for patients, so staff had the unique privilege of parking in a remote lot accessible only with a pass card, when it worked. In cold weather the gate device was unpredictable. The lot was about two blocks north of the hospital and three blocks west. Staff climbed two flights of ice-covered stairs, navigated unshoveled walkways, and entered through the back entrance of the old hospital, a TB sanitarium dating back to the 1920s. The sanitarium had been converted to a research laboratory space when the ten-story main hospital was erected in 1968.

When asked why staff had to park so remotely, the Medical Center Director opined it was part of a program to provide daily aerobic exercise for the medical staff.

Yeah, right, thought Randall, as he trudged through the snow, *for your health. If I collapse right here in this snowbank, maybe they'll find my frozen carcass by spring.*

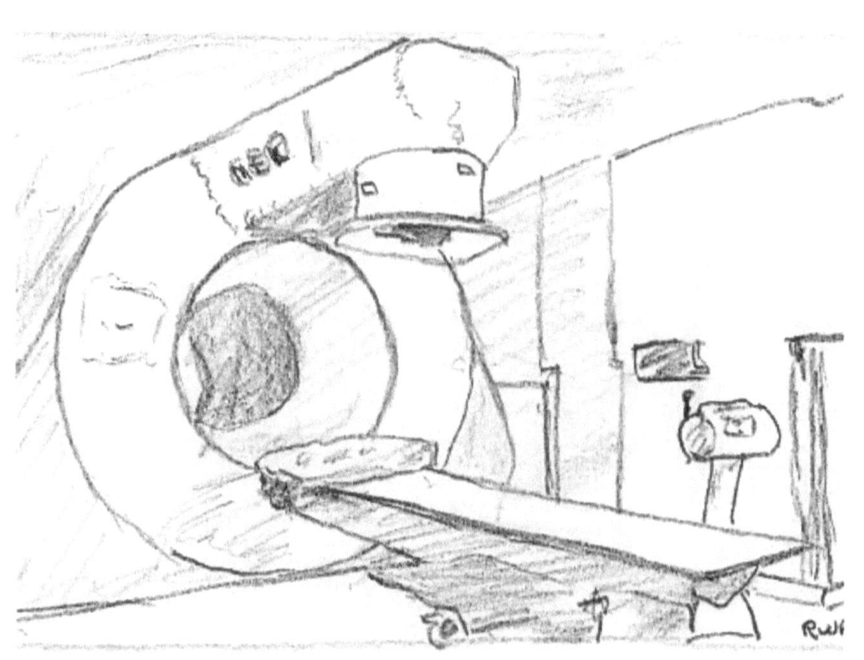

CHAPTER 2

VA SPA

"After my gastrectomy, I was hungry for pizza but didn't have the stomach for it."

— Gutless Wonder

TREK AND STALL

On the Iditarod-like trek from the parking area in winter, Randall carried half his gear in a backpack, and the rest in his briefcase. Brown-bagging lunch avoided eating the fare at the VA cafeteria. The food was passable, but the menu was recycled every week, and the common ingredient was mystery meat.

Shrugging into his backpack, Randall locked the Scirocco and lurched up the two flights of concrete stairs leading to the ground level of the old main building. The stairs passed a hissing twelve-foot diameter laundry steam pipe that looked to Randall like the building had a large rectal tube inserted in its behind.

Closer to the building, the strong north wind reflected off the wall with a wind tunnel effect that took his breath away and threatened to blow off his hat. Randall scanned his ID badge at the back entrance and the door lock clicked open. Relieved to get out of the cold wind, he stomped snow off his shoes. There remained a two-block walk through the old building to the main hospital. From there, it was down the east access stairs to the basement and further down the hall to the Radiation Oncology Department.

As Randall rushed through the double doors connecting the Research building to the main hospital, he passed the intersecting hall leading to the administrative offices, which included the Center Director's hideaway. That speeded up his pace, like walking past a cemetery. Often the times he had needed to use the administrative corridor had been unpleasant, like being called on the carpet for some deviation from arcane VA rules or begging, hat in hand, for equipment or staff.

Although it was a long walk from his department, he liked to use the "executive bathroom" because it was less crowded and cleaner than the more public facilities. It was rarely occupied and made him feel special to sit on the throne of the elites. On the occasions when he walked in to find the Center Director's wingtips visible behind the stall door, it was the great equalizer. As they say, all men put their pants on one leg at a time.

Randall was already five minutes late when he reached the intersection with the administrative hallway. At that point he had an acute bladder spasm. The choices were immediate action or wet pants. He turned right and pee-pee danced into the executive bathroom. His shy bladder shunned the urinals, and he shuffled into the stall. Fumbling with briefcase, backpack, and coat, he managed to get his pants down in the nick of time. Everything came out just fine.

Randall buttoned back up and left the stall to wash his hands. What he saw in the mirror resembled something the proverbial cat dragged in. His hair looked like he combed it with a Mixmaster. He tried to pat down the worst of it, but hands make imperfect combs.

Then Randall had a sudden attack of overwhelming lethargy. He felt like a man rushing to be tortured. *So what if I'm late? What's the hurry? All my work will still be there, and I'll be the only one to do it even if I'm five minutes late. Take a breath. Prepare for the pain.*

Resting his hands on the sink, he leaned forward, his chin sagging to his chest.

"Can't do any good for anybody unless I pull myself up by my own bootstraps," he muttered to himself. "Must pull self together." He closed his eyes in silent meditation and tried to take deep breaths to settle himself and reflect.

Take a Breather

Randall studied himself in the mirror. Just short of six feet, he looked like a taller drink of water than he actually was, because of his slender build. His mother called him a beanpole. At 150 pounds, he was no football player, but he had excelled in the cross-country team 5K. With a narrow face, his father's largish nose, and a somewhat weak chin, Randall was not traditionally handsome. Yet there was something impish about him. He had a ready wit that eased initial encounters. His mustache and black-rimmed glasses evoked a young Groucho Marx.

Randall loved to banter with his patients, but knew when it was time to be serious. A selective rule follower, Randall wore what hair he had somewhat long, liked to curl the ends of his mustache, and favored brightly colored ties to provide contrast with the stark white of his lab coat. He inadvertently offset any hint of white-coat elitism with the numerous coffee stains, red China marker blemishes, and embedded dirt he neglected to launder.

His secretary, Doris Hicks, often chided him about his aversion to laundry soap. She claimed it gave him an "absent-minded professor" persona. He said he wanted the dirty coat to reflect his hard work ethic and that he was just one of the proletariat. Doris asked why a person would work hard to achieve a position with status and then shun it. He had no response.

As Randall's mind wended its way down these garden pathways, the executive bathroom door flew open with a bang against the wall. Randall nearly jumped out of his backpack.

"Dr. Biedermeier!" intoned a deep voice that Randall immediately recognized as that of the Center Director. "You feeling sick or just praying to the sink gods? Sorry if I don't stop and chat. Need to make an urgent offering to the toilet gods."

Randall shuffled out of the Director's way. "No problem, sir. Be my guest. Uh, I don't feel bad enough to exactly qualify as sick. I was just seeking sink sanctification."

"Ah, yes. I've invoked those gods many times this past week," came the reply from behind the stall door, mingling with the sounds of a tinkling stream. "*Ahh*. Usually more helpful than my so-called staff assistants. Be a good man—I believe it best if you now get out of earshot. You have my blessings for the day. Have strength and move on."

Randall picked up his briefcase and made for the door. "Yes, sir. I now leave you in peace."

Randall was tempted to listen at the door, but it didn't seem right after being blessed by the man.

Grim and Bare It

The Center Director's intervention had overcome Randall's lethargy attack. He was once again braced for the day. By the time he reached the east end of the long first-floor hallway and took the stairs down to the basement, it was just past 8:15. He was certain there would be a non-welcoming committee awaiting him.

At the main entrance to the Radiation Therapy Department, Randall peeked around the doorframe. The department square footage was too small to have space for a waiting room. Patients awaiting treatment sat in plastic chairs lined along both sides of the main corridor, which ended at the treatment unit control console. A dogleg to the right of the console led to the Radiation Treatment Room and a smaller hallway branched off to the right and to the back door, which required a key for outside entry.

Inside the treatment room, a linear accelerator, made by Mullard Electronics Limited (MEL) generated the six-million-volt X-ray used for treatment. Randall had nicknamed the unit "Big MEL." Proper shielding to prevent scattered radiation from leaking out of the room required three-foot-thick, high-density concrete walls and ceiling, supplemented with sheets of one-inch-thick steel. The 15,000-pound lead-shielded entry door was opened with a chain-driven electric motor that slid the door on a rail mechanism. Randall imagined the equivalent of three Cadillacs hanging from their front bumpers.

Most radiation oncology departments in hospitals were located in the corner of a basement to avoid the need to shield the floor, but Randall always fantasized about mutant earthworms taking over control of the VA. He suspected no one would know the difference. First-floor spaces above the treatment unit were not popular, even though well shielded. Knowing radiation was "down there" was sort of like a superstition. "Step on a crack" and all that.

This day, Randall saw that every available chair in the waiting hall was occupied, and four patient-bearing gurneys were crowded in front of the chairs. A fifth gurney poked out into the main hallway outside the department. The radiation therapy technologists (RTTs) were standing, hands-on-hip, in front of the console looking frustrated. Randall did a quick lateral arabesque past the main entrance and came in through the department's back entrance to avoid running the gauntlet of waiting patients.

Randall unlocked the back entrance double doors and hauled his gear through. His two RTTs, Grace Lederman and Molly Sorensen, spotted him immediately with a quick glance to their right, but failed to pounce on him with the expected pleas for help. They weren't the best RTTs he'd ever worked with in terms of creative thinking, but they were certainly adequate. He wasn't sure what the problem was.

Grace was an odd duck. Randall thought her name was ironic. She looked about ten years older than her stated age of thirty, due more to nightly tippling than genetics. She described herself as "short-waisted." She had extravagant curves that had once been attractive in a floozy kind of way. Her chronically disheveled aura and contempt for "dirty old veterans" made for a high coefficient of friction. Extra effort was not a phrase in her lexicon.

Molly was a "past her prime" swan who had devolved into a goose. Of medium height and in her mid-fifties, her thinning hair had once been blonde. Divorced after a twenty-year alcohol-marred marriage, she had parlayed her background as a diagnostic radiology technician into further training to become an RTT. She struggled her way through an RTT training program, but had trouble finding work until applying at Hobbes VA.

Pleased to be momentarily ignored, Randall scooted into his office, shed his gear, and walked out to the console while donning his lab coat. Molly and Grace were still staring at Big MEL's control console. The audible timer clicked off monitor units and then unexpectedly stopped. It looked to Randall like they had been trying to complete the warmup routine, but it had defaulted.

As Randall observed, an attractive, white-uniformed young blonde emerged from the equipment room that housed the massive electrical components for Big MEL. He guessed she was an RTT student rotating through the department.

"You were right, Molly," said the blonde. "The main control safety switch unit has shut down. What do we do now?"

Grace was first to answer. "I don't know, Melinda. Let's ask the big boss here." She grunted and gestured toward Randall with her thumb.

Randall looked about, mystified, but recovered quickly. "*Umm.* Good morning to you guys too. Can't make a diagnosis without knowing symptoms and findings. What's been happening?"

Molly responded with a somewhat kinder tone. "Oh, sorry. Good morning, Dr. B, seems we have another water leak. The machine keeps shutting down when we try to go through the warmup cycle."

Randall was momentarily distracted by Melinda. "And just who is this young lady? We haven't been properly introduced."

"Oh, this is Melinda Moore, Dr. B," said Molly. "She's rotating here from the RTT program at the U. Melinda, this is Dr. Biedermeier."

Randall shook Melinda's delicate hand. "A pleasure, young lady. How long have you been in the program?"

Melinda tilted her head slightly and gave Randall a pert smile. "So you're the big boss, eh? Heard a lot about you down at the U. I've been in the program for three months now."

"Well, welcome aboard," said Randall, while he assessed what he saw. "We should discuss what they've been saying about me sometime later today."

Grace let out a grunt. "Much later. We've got bigger fish to fry right now."

Molly interrupted more politely to keep Randall on task. "Water is dripping all over the treatment couch. Probably the vinyl cooling tubing is brittled out and cracked again. We've tried doing the warmup routine, but it keeps defaulting out like it just did."

Red flashing lights lit up the monitor screen.

Randall nodded and clucked his tongue. "Looks like we need a physicist for this one. Is Bob Storch in yet?"

Grace grunted a response, "Not yet. He called in and said he's stuck at the U, helping them fix a blown primary power supply on their Betatron. Has to order a part from Allis-Chalmers and then he'll head back here. With the snow an' all, he thinks he'll get here no sooner than noon."

Randall shook his head ruefully. "Wonderful. Another day in paradise."

Molly pointed at the peanut gallery in the hall. "Yeah, and the natives are getting restless. They've been here since 7:30, waiting for their treatments to start. Do we cancel the day and send them away, or what?"

Randall was now grateful for the bathroom meditation break he took and the Center Director's blessing. He tried an alternate ploy. "Did you ask Mr. Kornberg to help? He is your supervisor."

"Are you kidding me?" retorted Grace, with two loud snorts.

Randall knew he'd asked a very silly question. Al Kornberg was the titular tech supervisor, but his training predated linear accelerators. He knew so little about operating them that, fortunately for everyone, he declined actually treating patients, arguing it was below his pay grade. He was the prototypical, dysfunctional VA employee protected from dismissal by seniority, outdated Civil Service rules and union protection. In reality, his default departmental tasks were ordering supplies, restocking exam rooms, and polluting the air with his pipe smoke.

Randall shook his head. "Sorry. Not sure what I was thinking. How about I take a look at leaky Pete?"

"You?" gasped Grace.

Randall winked at Grace "What am I, chopped liver? Don't bunch your undies. Won't hurt to look. Grace, before I go in, please shut down the power supply. I don't want a shocking experience in there."

The waiting patients got excited when they saw Randall giving orders. They began to mutter and gesture anxiously. Randall turned to address them. He promised the nervous vets that the machine would be up and running in a New York minute as soon as he applied his skills to the task. The complaints softened but did not stop.

"Never fear, Dr. B is here," offered Randall reassuringly as he turned toward the Linac Room entrance. He stopped halfway there and turned back to motion the techs forward. "Well, what are you guys waiting for? Come along and help me. Someone bring the stepladder. Time to work a little magic. You come too, Melinda, or would you prefer Ms. Moore?"

"My family name is Moore. But I'm not Ms. Moore – that's my mom! You can call me Melinda, I guess, if you let me call you Dr. B. My friends call me Mel."

Randall nodded. "Got it, Mel. *Hmm*, but that might be a bit confusing, since we call the machine Big MEL. Not saying you're big, of course. I mean, you're small. I mean, petite. Dainty? In a feminine way, of course, *um* . . . never mind! Let's fix this leaky Linac."

His cheeks flushed a little.

Randall had seen Bob Storch, the department's radiation physicist, repair the Linac often enough that he knew the first steps. He climbed up the stepladder to remove the marine-blue fiberglass housing covering the guts of the treatment head. As Randall began to remove the housing screws, Grace became alarmed. "Hey, why are *you* doing that?"

Randall replied calmly. "For the halibut. Where there's water . . ."

Grace reached for the stepladder and grabbed his pant leg. "This is no time for a fishing expedition."

Randall pushed away her hand, and the ladder wobbled. "Hands off the goods. If it's something simple, it could keep us from floundering around all morning with a shipload of patients and no way to treat. You got a better idea? We're on the same team here! Here, help me lift this panel down."

Molly took hold of the panel and helped Randall place it on the floor.

Melinda moved closer for a better look at the innards. "Why does the unit have water circulating in the treatment head anyway, Dr. B?"

Randall looked down, enjoying the view of Melinda from above. All the correct shapes were present and contained within her neckline. Her white skirt and blouse were wrinkle-free and almost looked tailored. She wore practical flats, but rather than clunky nurse's shoes, hers resembled delicate ballet slippers.

Randall's momentary pause prompted Melinda to ask her question again.

This time Randall responded. "Excellent question, Padawan. Electrons are accelerated down this long copper tube toward the platinum target here in the treatment head. When the electrons hit the platinum atoms in the target, they produce X-rays. The reaction also creates a lot of heat, so the water cools it. The vinyl tubing carrying the water attaches to the metal housing of the head by way of these brass nipples. That's usually where the leak occurs."

Melinda was awed by what she saw. "It's really complex in there. Wait. I think I see a drip coming from the nipple to your right." Melinda pointed excitedly, creating subclavicular tectonic activity.

Randall looked to where Melinda was pointing and jumping with enough excitement to wag her ponytail. "Holy cow, you're right, kid. You've got a sharp eye for nipples."

"Dr. B! Really!" exclaimed Molly.

Randall scoffed. "Well, she does. That's our leak."

Melinda was unperturbed. "Why do the leaks occur there?"

Randall nodded agreeably. "Another wise query. Prolonged exposure to X-rays makes the vinyl tubing brittle, especially in the spots it gets stretched around the attachment nipples. Mullard didn't know X-rays made vinyl brittle when the machine was first designed."

Melinda gave Randall a strange look. "What's a duck got to do with it?"

Randall laughed. "Not mallard. It's Mullard. The manufacturer's name is Mullard Electronics, Limited. Newer units use copper tubing to avoid nipple leakage."

Grace gave Randall a queer look and crossed her arms over her chest. Molly rolled her eyes.

Melinda was unphased and nodded her understanding. "Makes sense. And I am guessing that the VA doesn't have funds for an upgrade."

Randall whistled. "Right you are. Whenever I ask for the money to be put in the budget for us, the administration natters like nabobs of negativity."

Melinda laughed. "Those pusillanimous pussyfooters!"

Randall was shocked Melinda knew the reference. "You hit that nail dead center. Turns out that we're only a small part of Radiology's budget. Whatever is left, after they buy their stuff, trickles down to us in the basement. Barely keeps us afloat. The Radiology chief runs and hides whenever I come up and beg for a small piece of pie."

Grace grunted in agreement. "Tough titty said the kitty when the milk ran dry."

"True that," agreed Molly.

Randall returned his attention to the leak, running through possible solutions in his mind.

"So what's next, Boss?" asked Grace. "You gonna fix it with a nasty look?"

Randall clicked on an idea. "No, I'm saving nasty looks for employee insubordination. How about one of you gets me a scalpel from the wound repair kit, STAT?"

Grace started to protest. "But how will that . . ."

Randall cut her off. "I'll explain later . . . if it works."

Usually, Bob replaced the tubing branch when nipple leaks occurred, but that was beyond Randall's skill set. Plus he had no idea where the spare tubing was. There seemed to be enough slack in the tubing to cut off the split end and reattach it. When Grace returned with the scalpel, he pinched off the offending tube to prevent water leaking out, removed it from the nipple, and cut off the cracked end. He pushed the tube back on the nipple, but it still leaked a bit, having lost elasticity.

Grace was first with a discouraging word. "It's no good. The leak's not as bad, but it's still dripping. Admit it. You can't fix it."

Without responding, Randall pulled a small nylon zip tie out of his pants pocket and secured the tubing end with it.

"Where in the world did you get . . . ?" gasped Grace.

Randall waved off her temporary awe. "I'd like to claim I am Inspector Gadget, but I actually brought it in to secure some loose cables behind my desk today. Pure chance. Now I'm not going to put the cover back on the head until we test drive the repair. Go back outside, power up, and retry the warmup procedure. Run 200 monitor units, then we'll recheck for leaks."

After this was done without issues, Molly ran into the room to recheck the connection. She came back to report all was dry. After a brief output check proved to be correct, Randall gave the go ahead to start the morning treatments.

"Okay, team, you get the charts ready for the first patients. Then I'll do calculation checks with you while you're running through the first batch," offered Randall.

"Deal," responded Molly and Grace in unison.

Though somewhat impressed by his own resourcefulness, Randall tried to appear nonchalant. He was amazed he pulled it off on a day when he was at way less than his best. His father had often preached to him about this very thing. "Some days you win just by showing up."

Surely, that gave him license to feel self-satisfied in a quiet way.

Randall shouted out to get the attention of the waiting patients. "Good morning, gentlemen. I'm happy to report that I, Randall Biedermeier, MD, not a medical physicist, have, for your benefit, corrected the minor mechanical problem on our treatment unit that was preventing it from making X-rays. Through my beneficence, *we . . .* are now ready for liftoff."

Randall made a grand gesture of welcome. "Who's first in line?"

The Me's Have It

In response, came a "Me" duet. One "me" came from Clyde Dale, a rather large, long-faced man with a full mane of white hair, who occupied the closest gurney. The other "me" came from Jackie Stuart, a slight, middle-aged man, who sat perched on the edge of his seat like a jockey. Both insisted they were next. Jackie's green-striped pajamas and robe hung on his meager frame like a poncho. "Dr. B, I was here a-fore chattering Clyde over there. Why does he get to go before me?"

Randall raised his right index finger and pointed it accusingly at Mr. Stuart. "We have told you many times that your appointment is at 9:00. Do not come down from your ward until then. Mr. Dale's treatment is at 8:00 because he has to be brought down by escort. They've already set the machine up for him. If you jump the gun, and we treat you now, you'll get *his* dosage. You don't want that now, do you? If we have to reset the machine for you, we'll get even further behind all day."

Despite this logic, Mr. Stuart swore a blue streak and stomped on the floor with his hospital slippers. It wasn't nearly as effective as his colorful invective. Melinda interrupted Mr. Stuart's hissy fit. She took the man by the arm and turned on her 100-watt smile.

"My, my," said Mr. Stuart. "Just who might you be, dearie?"

Melinda gently led Mr. Stuart back to his seat. He didn't object. "My name is Melinda. I'm going to be a real tech soon, but I'm still in training. Come sit down. Let's get you comfortable!"

"Well, I'm sure you'll be a righteous good one when you're a-finished," said Mr. Stuart, giving her his best toothless grin.

"Now, about that swearing," said Melinda. "That's just not something we want to hear. It disturbs people with delicate constitutions. Don't you agree?"

Mr. Stuart did an aw-shucks shuffle and sat down. "Sorry, Miss Melinda. I jus' gets so nervous about gettin' the treatment. Jus' wanna get it over with. Skipped muh breakfast to get down here first thing."

Melinda nodded in sympathy. "Do you suppose your tray is still in your room?"

"Could be, they's pretty slow on the pickups," said Mr. Stuart.

"Here's a deal for you," said Melinda. "You stay right here, and I'll quick run upstairs. If your tray is still there, I'll bring it back down for you to eat here. But you have to promise me that, in the future, you won't come early."

"It's a deal. But my coffee's probably cold as a brass monkey by now," Mr. Stuart protested.

Melinda, unperturbed, offered to get Mr. Stuart fresh coffee from the department communal pot. As frosting, she suggested he could eat at a desk in the little-used orthovoltage treatment room.

Mr. Stuart lit up like a little boy at his first birthday party.

Clyde Dale chuckled. "Will you chew his food for him too, young lady?"

Melinda giggled and dashed off.

Grace, who'd just witnessed act one of the Melinda show, just harrumphed and pushed Clyde Dale's gurney into the Linac Room.

Gum Up the Works

With Mr. Dale's gurney out of the way, the traffic jam was freed up. Randall went to bring in the gurney from the outside hallway where Ira, the patient escort, had left it. The patient, Sammy Conklin, had dozed off despite the heavy elevator traffic just feet away.

Randall grabbed the frame of the gurney and shook Mr. Conklin's shoulder. "Rise and shine, Rip Van Winkle. Don't worry, I've got a license to drive this thing, and rock star parking inside for you. Would you like the *Wall Street Journal* to read while you wait?"

Mr. Conklin opened his eyes and coughed. "Yeah, right, and a good cigar."

Randall repositioned the gurneys in the department hallway then spotted Ira trying vainly to get 260-pound Ronny Rutherford's wheelchair out of the elevator. He was a thirty-five-year-old paraplegic with Hodgkin's disease. The elevator door slid shut and got jammed on the wheelchair footrests each time Ira just got the chair rolling.

Randall hustled over and held the door open long enough to get man and chair extricated.

Rutherford had been riding his motorcycle on a country road when one of Wisconsin's plentiful deer ran across the road in front of him. He swerved to avoid the deer, but the deer's hind foot kicked backward and hit the cycle. The kick sent the bike and rider skidding into a roadside ditch. Rutherford flew off the cycle, landing safely in some muck, but hit his head on a culvert pipe. He was stunned but remained conscious. The cycle lay in the ditch twenty yards behind him, in gear with the motor still running.

The cycle slid slowly down the side of the ditch. When it reached the bottom, the spinning rear wheel shot the bike forward, and it hit him in the back, fracturing his mid spine, paralyzing him below the waist. He lay for hours in cold ditchwater until a passing truck driver spotted and rescued him. He was stabilized at a local hospital, but X-rays of his spine revealed a mass in his chest that was later diagnosed as Hodgkin's disease. The irony was that although the accident had allowed discovery of the Hodgkin's at an early, treatable stage, the price of that discovery was lifelong lower extremity paralysis. Rutherford's wife, Catherine, a 110-pound dynamo, had quickly taken charge of overseeing his management to that point and was still on the job.

Ira was still looking jumpy and unsure of where to go with Rutherford's overloaded wheelchair in the crowded waiting hall, when Catherine emerged from the next elevator and came over to run interference.

Catherine waved her arms like a traffic cop. "Doctor, if you cluster some of those gurneys a little closer together, maybe we can squeeze Ronny in."

"No room at the inn, eh, Doc?" bellowed Mr. Conklin from his gurney.

"Looks that way," said Randall. "But I think the techs are about to take the next gurney, and that should clear a spot. If you all just wait here a sec, I think we'll have room."

In the nick of time, Grace and Molly pushed a gurney-bound patient from the treatment room after treatment and pushed in the next gurney patient who was waiting in the hallway.

Randall took over and shouted orders. "Ira, go grab the gurney the girls just brought out and wheel the patient back upstairs. I'll roll Mr.

Rutherford aside until you clear the hallway. Then I'll move him in after I move the last gurney forward."

Ira did as commanded.

Randall never tired of seeing Ira's awesome hair, which consisted of one five-inch patch on the back of his head. He'd let that patch grow to at least twenty inches and then combed it over the side and top of his head. It defied physics and looked like a swirl of hair frosting. It was a true hairspray marvel.

Melinda waved to Ira from down the hall and shouted. "Thank you, sir, for being so prompt in moving the carts around."

Ira did a double take. He wasn't used to the RTTs noticing him or calling him "sir." He patted his hair swirl, his cheeks reddening.

Randall watched the interchange and shook his head. *Melinda, Act Two. Well played, young lady!*

Randall helped Ira wheel the gurney through the hallway maze and onto the elevator. Walking back to the department, he peered up at the sign above the double doors that read: Department of Radiation Oncology. It was a typical government issue sign, made up of a layer of white over black plastic. Routing through the white layer created black lettering. Randall noted that today there was an added custom touch, a pink blob just in front of the "R" looked like a blotchy asterisk. Curious, he pulled an empty chair from the end office and stood on it to get a closer look. It was a wad of gum.

"Holy crap," Randall muttered to himself, "how in the world did anyone get gum up here? It's more than seven feet above the floor."

Randall pulled out his trusty pocketknife and pried the wad off the sign. The gum was fresh and smelled strongly of cinnamon. One brand came quickly to mind: Wrigley's Big Red. Randall knew smokers favored the brand to mask tobacco breath. He decided this defacement of government property was an insult to his department. It demanded deeper investigation. He would channel his inner Sherlock Holmes to compile a list of suspects. Several came to mind.

He put the evidence in a plastic sandwich bag from his lunch. Later, he *would* conduct a full analysis.

DEPARTMENT OF
RADIATION ONCOLOGY

CHAPTER 3

———

GUM CONUNDRUM

"Time flies like nothing; fruit flies like bananas."

— Uncle Peter Byhardt

HELLO, DORIS

After Randall finished playing musical gurneys in the department waiting hallway, he headed to his office to finish unpacking his gear. The hallway entrance to his office led through Doris's tiny office, which was initially intended to just be an anteroom to his office. Her large desk was jammed into the too-small space. There was barely room to get behind her desk and it made the walk-through space to Randall's office rather a one-way street. Doris served as a buffer between Randall and the outside world. She guarded the passageway zealously. It might as well have been a moat, though she was no dragon.

"Good mornin', Dr. B," said Doris. "I declare, I don't know how y'all tolerate this snow and ice. I still can't get used to it. My poor knees are barkin' at me." Doris's syrupy, but refined, Southern accent made everything she said sound sugarcoated.

"I know what you mean. I've abided this weather for most of my life, and I haven't fully adjusted yet. Summer doesn't come until about three to five months after winter is over. Then summers are so nice, you forget about winter, until it cycles back in and beats you over the head. Those who fail to learn from history are doomed to repeat it."

Doris nodded. "True that, Dr. B. Well, I'm sure some hot coffee will get you back in sorts. Oh, before I forget, Mr. Bob called, and he's still stuck at the U. He thinks he can leave by 10:00, but you know the drive from the U takes at least a half hour in the snow. He says as long as we're up an' runnin' and makin' X-rays, we can treat until he gets here and does the big fix."

"That sounds about right. The big U always takes priority," said Randall. "What do I have on for today besides further assaults by the thundering horde?"

Doris checked her prodigious appointment calendar. "*Hmm*, nothin' so far besides the headless chicken dance that passes for normal 'round here. I did notice that the patients in the hall are as close as a cat's breath! I can't recall when I've seen it so busy. Oh, it almost slipped my mind—you've got a meetin' with the VA compliance officer at 4:00."

"The who?" asked Randall.

"Rock band I don't much care for," said Doris with a grin.

"Very droll. What's a compliance officer? One of those guys who gives you the third degree?"

The VA was forever creating new and fancy names for its burgeoning but mostly useless administrative staff.

"Oh, it's a new VA program. He'll explain it to you. Don't you worry your shiny little head! He says we run the most efficient department in the hospital, so he wants to use us to pilot a new program." Doris held her hands to her heart, looking proud.

"That sounds delightful." Randall struggled to curb his 'enthusiasm.' "Call him and tell him we're closed today. That's it! We're having a snow day and we have to reschedule."

Randall had been around government facilities long enough to know that the department's efficiency would be duly punished.

"Sure thing, Dr. B. I'll have him wait in your office when he gets here. Maybe distract him with some sweet tea?" Doris always showed hospitality, even to administrative excess.

"Maybe switch that to a Long Island iced tea! Maybe he'll forget to 'reward' us. Now I've got chart calculations to check. Keep an eye out for Bob. If he doesn't show, we may need to send out the dog team to rescue him."

Doris waved a hand. "Okay, Dr. B. Don't you worry none about the meetin'! That compliance man is probably all hat and no cattle! By the way, what's that you're holdin'? It looks like an old gum wad."

"Very good. You're razor's edge today. It's not just a gum wad. It's evidence, my dear girl, evidence. I need to give it a more detailed study in the workshop."

Wad'ya Know?

Randall closely examined the gum wad on a clean workbench. He had placed it carefully on a Plexiglas sheet and pulled over a high intensity exam light. A Film Noir jazz soundtrack played in his head.

After Randall finished his gum wad evaluation, he came to several conclusions. First, the specimen was fairly fresh. TOD (time of deposit) was less than twenty-four hours earlier. Second, it had probably been cinnamon flavored, based on nasal flow analysis. Third, while DNA analysis was not possible, one tooth mark could be used if needed. Finally, he suspected it was an inside job and the placement of the gum outside the department was an intentional misdirection or false flag operation. Whatever the case, he silently vowed to track down and deal with the "perp."

"Dr. B! We need you out here! Lifting help in the treatment room!," one of the RTTs called from beyond his black and white scene.

Rats! Foiled by reality. Gratification would have to be delayed. There were more urgent fish to fry.

He joined the RTTs in hefting a patient onto the table, then headed for the treatment console to do chart and calculation checks. Grace and Molly scrambled to get back on schedule with treatments.

As Randall ran the numbers, he mused about what complete opposites his two techs were. Molly was a dogged worker and never shirked. She was guardedly upbeat the majority of days. Grace, on the other hand, had warts. She most frequently had the personality of Eeyore, the pessimistic donkey from *Winnie-the-Pooh*, and was a galloping grump. But they both got the job done in the end. The new student, Melinda, showed promise and was much more pleasant to be around. Maybe she could be convinced to stay on after completing training. That would truly be good fortune.

Randall was reminded of how often he thanked the secretary gods for providing Doris. Without her guarding the gate, he was certain he'd not survive the VA environment for long. That she was in Milwaukee, at all, was rather a miracle.

The year before Randall had come to Harry C. Hobbes VA, he had taken an assistant professor position at Duke University and was assigned to the Durham VA, an affiliate hospital. Doris, then fifty-two, worked as secretary/receptionist in the Durham VA Radiation Therapy Department. Doris and Randall were an "odd couple," but had hit it off from the start.

Doris, an only child, had lived at home, taking care of her disabled mother, who died shortly after Randall arrived. Doris, by her own description, had a "gland problem" that was the cause of her morbid obesity and *alopecia totalis*, a total absence of body hair. To mask the condition, she always wore a wig and painted on her eyebrows each morning. Though self-conscious about her appearance, she was comfortable in the VA environment. It had become her safe refuge.

Randall found Doris to be an excellent secretary, and they soon fell into a comfortable working relationship. After about three months at the Durham VA, Randall asked Doris how she thought things were going between the two of them.

Doris had replied, in her sweet North Carolina drawl. "Dr. B, things is goin' just fine, but . . . if you could just learn to slow down from 60 mph to 30 mph, like all good southerners, things would go even smoother. You northerners what comes to the south need to realize things move a tad bit slower down here because of the heat. No sense in gettin' all sweated up if you don't need to."

Randall had nodded. "*Ah*, the old mountains and molehills aphorism."

Doris had just nodded back "*Hmm . . .* indeed."

Grace interrupted Randall's musings. "Are you done checking calculations on that chart or dreaming about hot bodies? I need that chart. Right now."

Randall jerked a bit in his seat. "Not dreaming. No, just finished with this one. Here you go."

Grace took the chart and, as she walked away, had a parting joust. "*Hah*, and I bet I know just which hot body is on your little mind."

"You do not!" said a rattled Randall. Grace just chuckled loudly. Randall decided to calm himself and take a coffee break. He went back to the Ortho Room to fill his cup with the elixir of wakefulness from the communal coffee pot. His thoughts turned back to Doris's origin story.

After Doris's suggestion, Randall did manage to slow down to about 45 mph, and all had gone smoothly at the Durham VA until, several months later, a wrench was thrown into the works. The Duke Radiation Therapy Department chairman was caught *in flagrante delicto* in his office one night, delving a bit too deeply into an anatomy issue with the attractive lead tech. Leadership admonished the chairman with prejudice and dismissed him. Unable to recruit an adequate replacement rapidly, there was a mass exodus of staff.

Without senior staff mentorship, Randall decided it was time to leave the sinking ship. By coincidence, a visiting professor from the Medical University in Milwaukee had approached Randall in Durham, knowing he was an alumnus. He informed Randall there was an opening for a chief of Radiation Oncology at Milwaukee's Harry C. Hobbes VA, which was a teaching affiliate for the U. One door had closed and another opened. Randall's start date at Hobbes VA would be July 1, 1975.

When Doris learned Randall would be leaving Duke and Durham VA, she decided to transfer her VA employment to Hobbes VA to continue as his department secretary. This decision shocked everyone who knew Doris, since she had scarcely ventured away from Durham, and had almost never been outside of North Carolina. But she rationalized that with her dear mother now in the ground, it was due time to go off and see the world. She might have reconsidered her decision if she'd factored in the significant climate change. The day's weather was a stark reminder.

Randall slurped his fresh java, sat down at his desk, and triaged the mounds of paperwork that had accumulated on his desk in just several hours. He leaned back in his chair, closed his eyes, and put his head back. It was so tempting to take a little nap. *Too many choices: do paperwork, take a nap, or momentary diversion.* He chose the latter.

Look at anything but the paperwork.

He rotated his chair to the left and stared at his eight, wall-mounted, X-ray view boxes. Bad choice. Stacks of beam films needed to be compared to the corresponding simulation films to verify that the radiation target area had not shifted from the original setup. Usually, the ones already on view boxes had problems the RTTs had seen, and needed beam adjustments ASAP. Only he could authorize such adjustments. On the shelf below was an empty tomato soup can that served as the holder for China markers, rulers, and pens.

Look away before you get sucked into the vortex!

Swiveling his chair to the right, Randall took a moment to admire his diplomas and certificates. They reminded him that he actually had gotten his BS and MD degrees followed by Board Certification in Radiation Oncology. They weren't just a pigment of his imagination. But most importantly, there was the YMCA certificate for passing beginner's swimming. Randall hated water. He knew the display of paper meant nothing to his patients. They were mostly a morale booster for him.

Basking in the glow of past accomplishment was cut short when his gaze fell upon the prodigious stack of medical journals partially obscuring his Indian Guides badges. He was months behind. It was almost impossible to keep up. *Oh, not that. That's the seventh layer of hell. Better go back to the devil I know . . .*

Paperwork seemed like the best option. *Best to get it out of the way first. Dang stuff multiplied like rutting rabbits.*

Paperwork was inevitably part of radiation oncology, which required incessant quality control and double-checking to avoid potentially life-threatening mistakes. The specialty had, for Randall, been sort of a default career choice, but he had grown to enjoy it beyond his expectations. It was challenging enough to hold his interest and he kind of liked the necessary detail work. It fit his somewhat OCD personality.

The only peeve Randall had about radiation oncology was that it was almost always located in the basement of the hospital in the corner in the dark with no window to see outside. He realized that radiation oncology departments were unlikely to ever have windows, but that didn't stop him from incessantly complaining about it, even at home.

One night, Zelda had finally reached her limit. "Randall Biedermeier, you are the pickiest obsessive compulsive on our block! You keep blaming radiation oncology for landing you in the basement with no windows. You're just darn lucky you stumbled into it. It saved you from possibly dying in Vietnam like five of your fellow interns."

Randall raised both hands and backed away. "Sorry, precious. I promise I won't bring it up again."

"Oh, but you will," interrupted Zelda. "Here's my deal. If you promise never to bring it up again. I'll paint you a picture of a window to hang in your office. In fact, I'll do four of them. One for each season."

Randall smiled so widely that his ears almost disappeared. "*Ooo,* very cool. Can I hang the summer one up in the winter?"

Zelda waved an arm. "For all I care, you can take them out of their frames, roll them up and stick them where the sun never shines!"

"No need to get snotty about it!" laughed Randall.

Zelda just huffed and ignored the comment. After a week of work in her studio, she presented Randall with the promised four seasonal window paintings.

He chuckled at the memory and turned in his swivel chair to gaze at his window picture. It was remarkably realistic. It depicted a casement window with a view of a sunny meadow full of yellow flowers. Green trees filled in the background. He squinted and the simulation of reality was enhanced.

While momentarily convinced that he was looking outdoors, a forty-pound load of dirty sheets and pillowcases was launched down the laundry chute from the eighth floor and hit the concrete pad on the other side of his office wall. The bolus of dirty bedclothes hit the pad with a loud *thwop* that rattled the wall and jolted the picture off kilter about 15 degrees. The spell was broken.

"Sweet cheez-its!" blurted Randall. "Real windows don't tilt without earthquakes."

Randall had grown used to the intermittent deadfall of laundry dumps and mostly ignored the sound. He had grown tired of readjusting the tilted diplomas and certificates, so he just left them akimbo. But the window picture adjustments irked him. Though the laundry *thwomps* were irksome, they could provide some amusement. If the laundry hit the wall while he was interviewing a newcomer, he would show no visible reaction. If said newcomer asked about the noise, Randall responded with a benign sounding "What noise?" He knew it was mean, but . . .

Randall righted the window picture. *I wish it were this easy to fix the issues at home. Zelda has been so cranky lately. I never know if I'm in trouble and why!*

He ambled out of his office, past Doris's cubicle and into the hall.

Doris chirped up. "Hey, Dr. B. Your wife just called to remind you to be home by 5:30. She said you are not in trouble."

Randall's heart dropped. He knew that the olive branch she offered sometimes had sharpened tips.

Three waiting patients attempted to ambush him.

"Hey, Doc, just a minute. Can I ask ya somethin'?" blurted the fastest one.

Randall quickened his step. "Hold that thought, Mr. Dithers, I'll be seeing you after your treatment, and we can share war stories."

Randall called this particular patient behavior the "Heydoc syndrome." He tried to avoid it by ducking and dodging, but sometimes even the oldest vets buttonholed him. He had tried to perfect his "I am not here" walk, but it still needed work. Wishing the department had a real waiting room, he juked past two vets and made it cleanly to the treatment console. He considered lubing the elbow of his lab coat to create a "no grip" zone. A little elbow grease usually worked.

Randall cleared his throat loudly as he approached the techs working at the console. "Hey, guys, is Big MEL running okay? Any more leaks?"

Grace grunted, and Molly followed up with actual words. "The radiation output is good, Dr. B, and no more drips!"

"Yeah, except for some present company," added Grace. "MEL ain't incontinent anymore."

Randall tried to ignore the not-so-subtle dig and wondered what bug had wandered into which orifice. "Nothing more we can do about the leak until Bob gets here. If the zip tie fails, we can always try chewing gum, particularly Wrigley's Big Red. Anybody got some?"

Molly frowned. "Not me. We know how you hate chewing gum. Why Big Red, by the way?"

Randall stared at Grace until she replied. "I only chew spearmint."

"I've read Big Red has better adhesive qualities," said Randall. He sidled over to where Melinda was sitting on a work stool, watching Grace set up the console for the next treatment. "Hey, Melinda, can I borrow your seat for a few minutes? I need to check these next five charts before treatment."

"Sure, Dr. B," said Melinda, getting off the stool and pushing it toward Randall.

"She has it all warmed up for you, Chief," snarked Grace.

Randall just smiled at Grace. "Wonderful. I was feeling a bit of a chill."

Melinda interrupted with a question. "Dr. B? After you're done with the chart checks, can you explain to me how big MEL makes X-rays?"

Randall shook his head. "That's not a short story, Melinda. There's no time now. Maybe later."

Melinda looked rather disappointed. She had worked hard to get into the Radiation Therapy Technologist Training Program and was hoping she could charm the boss into speeding up the process. She was smart enough to realize that her pushing things was a bit premature. She would bide her time. There would be future opportunities to win friends and influence the right people.

Randall noticed Melinda's disappointment and, for a moment, felt bad about stifling her welcome interest. But he realized that one could be misled by a book's interesting cover into overlooking the underlying content. This was a girl not to be underestimated and perhaps to be a bit wary of. He'd already seen that Melinda seemed to really irk Grace. He wasn't quite sure why, but his risk detector suggested caution.

Myth of Ignorance

Randall turned his attention back to chart review as Melinda followed Grace and Molly back into the treatment room to set up the next patient. Thus he didn't notice Melinda stop halfway to the room, turn, and make a little pouty face. She had hoped he'd still be watching her walk away and see the pout, but no such luck. She muttered to herself and walked on.

While Randall scratched his head over the dose calculations, Grace and Molly set monitor units on the control console and ushered patients in and out of the treatment room. Melinda followed them around, just a bit behind the pace. She tried to inquire about the ongoing procedures, but her questions frequently went unanswered. Grace kept complaining that Melinda was just slowing them down.

After reviewing five charts and finding no issues, Randall found the next three charts to have minor dose calculation or addition errors. Sloppy mistakes really got his goat, and that possibility was the reason he double-checked everything, especially with these two techs. No matter how much he preached accuracy, Grace and Molly continued to be error prone. They got really annoyed every time he brought it up and pleaded not guilty by virtue of overwhelming workload.

When the two techs came back out to set monitor units for the next patient, Randall motioned them to stop. He plopped the chart he'd been working on down in front of them. "What's wrong with this picture?"

Molly and Grace looked at the chart and studied the console settings and cumulative dose. "Nothing I can see," said Molly.

"Me neither," echoed Grace. "You trying to pimp us again?"

"I don't have to try hard," replied Randall, rather undiplomatically. "Look again. Better yet, Melinda, you take a look."

Grace harrumphed. "Why you asking her? She doesn't know squat about what we do. She's a freshly minted copper penny."

Melinda pulled out a pencil and used it to scan the columns and rows. "I understand these numbers, but what are these little letters? GL and MS? I am not familiar with these abbreviations."

Grace huffed and rolled her eyes. "Those are the techs' initials, you bubblehead. We both have to sign off on the charts and doses before each daily treatment. It's called quality assurance."

Melinda looked unphased and continued her investigation. "Oh, right here. The daily dose was given, but not added to the total dose. Plus, the wrong monitor units were recorded the day before."

"What?" said Molly. "Let me see that." She grabbed the chart from Melinda. "Cheese is Kraft!" said Molly. "She's right."

Randall nodded. "And whose initials are next to both entries?"

Molly looked again. "*GL*. They're Grace's."

"That's right," said Randall. "Now if GL had taken thirty extra seconds to double-check these entries, not only could she have avoided a potential error, but spared us having to waste the time checking and correcting."

Grace crossed her arms and harrumphed.

"How could this happen?" asked Molly. "We do this every day. It's what we do. How could we miss it?"

Melinda saw her opening and took it. "Have you ever heard the saying: 'familiarity breeds contempt?'"

"I have," said Grace. "But that don't apply here."

Melinda smiled sweetly. "It just might. It means the more you do a routine and become familiar with it, the greater the chance will be that you'll get bored with it and less critical. Then you have to force yourself to pay attention to prevent errors."

"That makes sense," said Molly. "If you do the same thing thirty times, the chances for error increase, because you can lose your concentration, especially if you're rushing to get it done."

Grace harrumphed with even more umph.

Randall nodded. "Exactly. On a related topic, who can tell me the difference between an ignorant person and a stupid one?"

"I got that one too," offered Melinda. "Stupid means you're not smart enough to learn complex stuff. An ignorant person may or may not be smart, but if they are smart, they just haven't yet had the opportunity to learn."

Grace shrank back and screwed up her face. "Hey, kid. You calling me stupid?"

Melinda immediately regretted popping up with the answer. She thought it best to backpedal. After all, it was just her first day, and she didn't need to make an enemy right out of the gate. "Heavens no, Grace. That's not what I meant at all. Please don't take it the wrong way."

"Then how was I supposed to take it? *I* made the mistake."

Melinda adopted a puppy eyes look. "I only meant that nobody here is stupid. You guys are plenty smart, and I'm the ignorant one. You have so much experience, you make it look easy. I have a lot to learn from you on this rotation."

Grace nodded. "You sure do, sweetie! That ain't the half of it."

Melinda felt she had more to add. "The only thing you're guilty of, Grace, is being stuck with the monotony of what you do and so busy you don't have time to double-check things. What Dr. B does with his chart checks protects you from making errors of repetition. I've been on several rotations, and none of them had the doctors helping the techs prevent errors like he does."

Randall stood up a bit straighter. "*Hmm*, is that a fact?"

Molly put in her two cents. "The girl has a point, Gracie. I've missed stuff before too, and Dr. B. picked up the mistakes with chart checks. If he hadn't caught them, they could have led to overdosing a patient if they'd continued."

Randall took the ball. "That's exactly what I've been preaching. A small error can get even worse if it's not caught. I don't expect you guys to be perfect, and I'm certainly not perfect either. That's why we check each other's work. I'm your insurance policy, and you're mine. If you see something of mine that doesn't seem right, don't keep it a secret. Feel free to kick me."

Grace softened up a bit. "Alright. I guess I don't mind if you pick up my *little* errors. Just don't kick me."

Melinda laughed. "Grace, if I'm getting in the way observing, maybe I could help Dr. B with the chart checks. It looks like a bunch of patients are due to finish this week. I could shadow you guys next week."

Grace didn't like that idea at all. "Absolutely not. We need you to help with mustering the patients in and out. Just stop with all the questions. You'll pick up the details soon enough. Leave the nitpicking to the expert." Grace nodded toward Randall.

Melinda backed off. "Just a suggestion. Consider me at your disposal."

Grace almost cracked a smile. "Alrighty then. Let's get cracking. Tote that barge. Lift that bale. Melinda, you grab the next contestant. Molly and I'll get the room set up for him."

Molly and Grace walked together into the treatment room, whispering to each other as they walked. "Nice going, Grace. Having those two spend any quiet time together is a recipe for a distracted doctor. We need to keep a close watch on that little morsel."

Grace nodded conspiratorially. "True that. I was thinking we might have to fit him with a bib. From the way he's been acting, I figure he's been paddling up the Lackanooky Creek at home for a bit now."

"You think?" winked Molly as she brought the block cart over to the treatment table. "Besides, we're just following orders. If we can prevent a small error now from leading to a bigger one later on, we're just doing a good QA job."

"Yep," said Grace. "Just practicing good QA, like the doctor ordered."

BLOCKING GUARD

Randall had turned his attention back to finishing the last chart checks when the tech trio, led by Melinda, returned to the treatment console. Molly and Grace began setting up the console while Melinda sat behind them and dutifully watched.

Grace tasked Melinda with monitoring the CCTV image of the patient lying on the table in the treatment room to be sure he didn't move during treatment. The CCTV screen was mounted in the countertop next to the console. A microphone and speakers allowed two-way communication with the patient. If movement was detected, the techs could stop treatment and redo the setup.

The CCTV screen was mounted flat so that prying eyes couldn't see it unless they were very close. A yellow tape line marked off the area around the control console as restricted, but curious patients would still try to sneak a peek at the screen. So a warning sign was posted on the wall above the monitor that read: "*Achtung! No lookinspeepen. Keine augenblicken!*" For those who couldn't decipher the Germlish, there was an adjacent sign with a red circle and a slash mark over a pair of eyes.

Randall sat nearby the console, balancing several charts on his lap. He looked through the counter clutter for his pen. Not finding it, he fumbled through the pockets of his lab coat. Frustrated, he swore under his breath. No matter how many pens he picked up and pocketed, he'd always lose them.

"Now where in the heck did my pen go?" Randall asked no one in particular.

A female hand, holding a ballpoint, reached over his shoulder. The fingernails were adorned with ruby-red nail polish.

"Here you go, Dr. B," intoned Melinda. "Your wish is my command. By the way, your pen didn't go anywhere. Pens can't do anything on their own."

The proffered pen startled Randall. He had been deep in concentration and jumped a bit. "*Err*, thanks. I misspoke. How about 'where in the heck did I misplace my pen?'"

"That's better, Dr. B," said Melinda, smoothly. She was standing so close that Randall got a good whiff of her shampoo scent. It was Gee, Your Hair Smells Terrific, the same shampoo Zelda used.

The proximity made Randall a bit nervous, so he tried to throw a changeup. "*Err*, do you realize we've had nine new consults this week already? And it's only Monday." Randall pushed his chair back and pointed at the flickering X-ray viewing box to his left. "Will you look at that? Darn light box is acting up again. Just got the thing replaced. You'd think the VA could afford a working light box!"

The shampoo scent was suddenly overwhelmed by Old Spice and the vague smell of stale Vodka sweat as Grace swept in to grab a chart from Randall's lap.

"Were you saying something, Dr. B?" asked Grace, using her outdoor voice. "Best pay attention to the console, Little Miss Muffett, before the spider crawls up beside you."

Melinda got the not-so-subtle hint and scooted to her right. She'd learned a few key things in short order. One of them was not to underestimate Grace. Another was that Randall might have a few chinks in his armor, but the armor was thick. She decided it would be wise to pace herself. This day was just a baby step up the mountain. There was time, and time she would give it.

Jacobs
Tested
Feed Corn
30

CHAPTER 4

SWINDELL DOES A LAZARUS

"It is only through mystery and madness that the soul is revealed."

— Thomas Moore, *Care of the Soul*

TAKE YOUR LUMPS

As lunchtime approached, the logjam of patients waiting impatiently in the waiting hall had thinned out. The techs were in a groove, ushering patients in and out of the treatment room. Melinda's more passive manner suited the techs and Randall better. To them, observation meant "watch and learn," not "interrupt and obstruct." There weren't enough minutes in the day for that.

As Randall was finishing chart checks at the treatment console, Doris approached him with a sheaf of papers. "Dr. B, look what just showed up. We've gotten eleven new consultation requests since 8:00. You're goin' to have to go through them, and tell me how to prioritize them."

Randall was dumbfounded. "Sweet breezes, that's a new record!"

"It is, indeed, my captain. How are we goin' to fit them all in? Four of 'em are marked 'STAT.' I put those ones on top."

Randall took the papers from Doris. "Let me see that mess. Spinal cord compression, brain mets, airway obstruction, tongue cancer with bleeding..."

He scanned through the rest and heaved a big sigh. "Monkey mayhem!" he exclaimed. Nearly half of these need to be seen today, no question. These four, tomorrow, and the remainder can be fit in over the rest of the week."

Doris took the papers back from Randall. "Just how do you intend to see five consults today? There's already six follow-ups scheduled this afternoon."

"Good thing I brought my roller skates today," joked Randall without much enthusiasm.

Doris shook her head. "Seriously, how are you fixin' to get it done?"

Randall touched a forefinger to his temple. "Kidneys."

"Dr. B, kidneys is for piddlin', not for thinkin'! You sure about that, sweet cheeks?"

"I am," said Randall. "I'll drink lots of coffee so I have to piddle. Piddling gives me an excuse to run in and out of rooms. What's important is that I 'see' the consults today. All five are inpatients, so they're already here. The rest are outpatients and need scheduling. I see the five inpatients and get just enough information to write a progress note with recommendations. That makes the referring docs happy because the consult was addressed, and plans are in place. Then I stay late to fill in all the blanks and leave orders for simulation and treatment start. I'll go back up to the ward if I need more info or need to recheck an exam, if you know what I mean."

Randall held his invisible suspenders and rocked on his heels. "I 'gar-ron-tee' I can fit the follow-ups in between. They are all long-term prostate cancer patients doing well, and I can fast-waltz them."

Doris nodded in understanding. "I get it. You have a method, even if it may be a bit mad. This is where you go the northerner 60 miles per hour, like a thoroughbred catapulted out of the gate at the Kentucky derby."

"You got it!" said Randall with a big grin. He slapped his hip with an imaginary crop. "Now, giddy up! Get to work scheduling."

Doris trotted off to her office to get the ball rolling. The three techs came out to the console to treat the patient they had just positioned on the table.

Molly took a long look at the hallway. "Looks like we're finally getting caught up, Dr. B. With all the patients finishing this week, we should be able to get the number of on-treatments down below forty again. It's feast or famine here. When it's a feast, we complain. When it's famine, we worry that cancer has been wiped out, and we'll be out of jobs."

"So true," said Randall. "But I'd happily retire from radiation oncology if that ever happens. I could get used to laying around all day."

Molly shook her head. "Don't you mean lie around?"

"Huh?" asked Randall.

"The way I learned it, living beings lie down but you lay down an object," said Molly. "Where did you learn your grammar?"

"At my grandma's house, mostly," said Randall.

"Har de har," said Grace. "So which is it? Lie or lay?"

Randall just screwed up his face, turned his head to the side and stared at an imaginary audience rather like Groucho Marx on his '50's TV show *You Bet Your Life*. Sometimes Groucho got more laughs with the look than by actually saying anything.

After wiggling his eyebrows and completing the appropriate comedic pause, Randall turned his head back to the group. "Alright. How about this sentence, grammarians? 'As his wife lied in bed about how handsome he looked, the husband suspected a liar lay before him.'"

Molly shook her head. "That's just confusing, Dr. B! You're as clear as mud. As usual."

"Worse than usual," added Grace.

Melinda just smiled and kept quiet.

Randall ended the comedic break. "Rest assured, there'll be no drop off in patients any time soon. Cancer never takes a holiday."

Grace perked up her ears. "Is there something we should know about?"

Randall paused for effect. "We've gotten eleven new consults since opening bell. If they all start treatment, which seems likely, we'll easily hit near sixty patients under treatment by Friday."

Grace looked like she'd been slapped. "They can't *all* need treatment this week!"

Randall did a slow head nod. "Unfortunately, most of them do. Two of them are Vietnam vets with huge head and neck cancers. They also have PTSD. You know how time-consuming they are to set up."

"I hope those new head and neck cancers are not as bad as Mr. Swindell's goomba," said Molly.

Melinda looked confused, but then figured that it must be another one of Randall's made-up words. "Goomba? What? Is he Italian mafia?"

Randall was amused and chuckled a bit. He stood up from his stool and raised his arms like a Pentecostal minister about to expound on the afterlife.

"Let us be clear, sistren. It's a descriptor of magnitude. A small tumor is a goober, closer to a pea. A medium sized tumor is a 'three-mor.'" Randall allowed himself a chuckle.

Melinda took the bait. "So a larger tumor is a 'four-mor?'"

"Ah, such innocence! No, young one. The correct term for a larger tumor is a *goomba*. But Swindell's is not just goomba. It is . . . it is a *magoomba*," Randall said with a flourish. "That means the mother of all goombas. Though I've just been doing the work of radiation oncology for, lo, these past eight years, his lip cancer is the largest of its kind that I have seen to date."

Randall paused again for effect, then pointed at Melinda. "So you are in luck today, Ms. Melinda Moore. After Mr. Dithers, comes Swindell. He should appear any minute. Then you will have the great fortune to see your first magoomba. After that I will tell you the legend of the Great Turban Tumor, another epic tale . . ."

Randall looked off into the distance, as if preparing to launch into a shaggy dog story. Molly recognized the sign and tried to head it off at the pass. "What Dr. B said is mostly true, but as a student, you need to remember that Mr. Swindell is not just a tumor. He has the misfortune of having a terrible cancer. He is a veteran, and he is a person who deserves our respect. Treat him with kindness, and do not focus on the tumor. He's already self-conscious about it. Really, Dr. B, be careful what you say to virgin ears."

"That's what I was going to say next," offered Randall weakly.

"Sure you were," grunted Grace.

Randall backpedaled. "No, really. I was trying to prepare Melinda for the experience so she wouldn't freak out and I was going to explain our arrangement with him."

"What arrangement?" asked Melinda.

Molly chimed in. "Well, Mr. Swindell feels self-conscious about his tumor, so we figured it best to have him wait for treatment in the front office by the entrance. The other patients don't need to see that and get more scared. Plus, with him in the office, they can't stare at him and make him feel even more uncomfortable."

Grace pointed down the hall. "Speak of the devil . . ."

Randall turned to see Mr. Swindell waving to let them know he had arrived. Impossible to bandage, his huge cancer replaced the whole left half of his lower lip and extended down to his chin. Red and angry, the lesion shined like a beacon.

Grace, who avoided unnecessary exercise whenever possible, shouted down the hall to acknowledge Mr. Swindell's arrival and waved an arm to direct him to wait in the front office. He waved back and shuffled his thin frame out of view.

Melinda was somewhat overwhelmed by the sight of Swindell's lesion, even though she had expected it to be bad, but she tried her best not to show it. It hit her then that she still had a lot to get used to. She knew how exposure to new extremes could shift one's limits of acceptance, but she felt it would take more time before Swindell's appearance would seem routine.

LOSING PATIENTS

Mr. Dithers had been under treatment for weeks, but always complained when asked for his name and Social Security number before treatment. "Why do I have to tell you this stuff again? You asked me yesterday."

"Yeah, and I told you why yesterday, Dithers," chafed Grace. "Some of you are so deaf that when I call for Smith, Jones gets up and parades in here. Half of you are wearing the same green striped pajamas, and you all look the same to me. You want us to treat your head instead of your prostate?"

"Sure, why not? It'd probably do me about as much good," grumped Mr. Dithers.

Molly gently stepped in. "Okay, children, let's get on into the treatment room. Time's a wastin.'"

Somehow, Randall had gotten so used to the inane hallway banter that it was just ambient noise. He could tune it out and still concentrate on calculations. In fact, when things were too quiet, he had trouble concentrating. It was like having a comforting soap opera playing in the background. Randall figured he'd acquired selective hearing from his two grade schoolers. They seemed to match the average mental age of his patients.

When Dithers came back out of the room after treatment, Randall ducked in the Ortho Room to avoid a "Hey Doc" session. When the path was Dithers-free, Randall went back to the console to do an inverse square dose correction. Molly helped Melinda get Swindell's chart ready. Grace waddled down the hall to get Mr. Swindell from the office for his treatment.

She came back grumbling that she had wasted her dwindling energy, because he was not in the office sitting in his designated chair. "Crap, I had to walk all the way down the hall for nothing. He usually sits in the chair with his paper cup of weak coffee, but even the cup ain't there." Grace flopped down on her chair, breathing heavily. "I wish I had some gum. It's lunchtime. When are we ever going to break to eat?"

Molly was immune to Grace's grumbling. "Probably went to the men's room down the hall. I'll keep an eye out. Treat Jimmy in his place. He's been waiting a while and he's getting most perturbed. You know, he's got the patience of a New Yorker. Dr. B, would you mind just walking down to the men's room and see if Swindell is in there? For survival's sake, we don't go into man land."

"Sure. I need to visit the used coffee depot myself." Randall quickstepped down the hall.

While the search for Swindell continued, Jimmy Burdin groused about the delay. He was a gurney-bound, eighty-two-year-old World War II vet with paraplegia caused by a tumor pressing on the spinal cord at T6. He was not and had never been a happy camper. "I'm missin' my lunch. By the time I get back to my room, it'll be cold, or they'll take it away. Why can't you girls ever get to me in time?"

Melinda walked over to the gurney to settle him down. "Well, sir, we do have other patients to treat." That was a mistake.

The old man grabbed Melinda's arm and pulled her down with strength that belied his appearance. "I don't care about them other patients. I want my lunch! Get me in there now!"

Grace rushed to the rescue still carrying Swindell's chart in her left hand. With her right hand she squeezed Burdin's bicep hard enough that the man was forced to let go of Melinda's arm. "Shut up, old man, and lay off my student. Try to get this through your thick skull. We don't get to you late; the ward brings you early—before your appointment time." Ironically, Grace had little patience for belligerence.

Burdin snorted. "What appointment? You people do me when *you* feel like it. I have no say in it!" Even without the cancer problem, Jimmy was a guy who didn't feel alive unless he was complaining about something. The techs had that figured out, so they always gave back what he dealt. The rationale was that if he had the energy to quarrel, he had the energy to get better.

Grace softened just a bit. "Melinda, you better check and see if Swindell came back while we were dealing with this old reprobate."

Melinda skittered away, looking remarkably like a scared rabbit.

Burdin snorted again, waving a dismissive hand at Grace. "What are you talkin', Swindell?" He looked away. "That poor bastard died last night."

Grace rolled her eyes. "Aw, come on, Jimmy. How would you know anything about Swindell?"

Molly overheard the dialogue and walked up to the pair. "Does he know something about Swindell?"

"I sure do! I was his roommate upstairs!" Burdin pointed to the ceiling, exasperated. "His tumor opened an artery or somethin'. He bled out like a stuck pig. Blood everywhere. It was a slaughterhouse! They called a code. Commotion kept me up half the night. Must've been a dozen doctors and nurses in that room, hollerin' and pumpin' on his chest and whatnot. It weren't no use though, he just bled right on out. Sprayed blood on my slippers too." Burdin waved a hand, then got quiet. "I seen guys die before, you know, in service. Was like he'd been shot in the head. Plus, I knowed him from the VFW. We was friends, kindalike."

Molly saw tears well up in Burdin's eyes.

Grace turned as pale as her lab coat, which took some doing, because her face was usually suffused in red. Molly held her breath, her hands over her heart.

Melinda returned halfway through Burdin's narrative. "He . . . he wasn't there!" she announced.

Grace, refusing to believe Jimmy's tale and Melinda's report, ran to the console phone and dialed up Swindell's ward.

"Ward 8CS, how can I help you?" crackled the voice on the other end of the line.

"You can tell me why Mr. Swindell isn't down here in Radiation Therapy. We called for him an hour ago," babbled Grace, her pale face sweating profusely.

"I am good, but I don't do miracles," the ward nurse replied in a tired voice. "The poor man died last night at 3:00 a.m. Bled to death."

"Uh, th . . . that's too bad. He was a . . . nice guy," stuttered Grace.

"Yeah, he was. You'll excuse me, I've got meds to pass," said the nurse and hung up.

Grace froze, eyes wide. "Yeah, sure. Meds to pass. Must be constipated. Well, goodbye," Grace said to the dial tone and sank into a chair.

Molly and Melinda joined Grace at the console, looking spacey and disoriented.

Randall returned from his trip to the men's. "Hey, guys, good news and bad news. My bladder is flatter and gladder, but Mr. Swindell was not in the men's room."

"We know." Grace said flatly. Swindell's chart slipped out of her hand, sending loose papers scattering across the floor. No one moved to pick them up.

"What's wrong with you guys? You all look like somebody died," said Randall.

"Somebody did. It was Mr. Swindell," said Grace.

Randall froze. "Nah. That's not possible! We just saw him go into the office. Right? Grace, you saw him go in there. So did Melinda!"

Everyone just stared at Randall. He grasped at straws. "You mean he just died? And we saw him just before that?"

"No . . . after," said Grace.

"What do you mean 'after'?" This was not computing in his doctor's brain.

Grace reignited. "Ground Control to Major Tom! Read my lips: he died at three o'clock this morning. Therefore, we didn't see him down here this morning. We must have seen someone else. Someone who, shit, no one else looked like that. We did all see him, didn't we?"

Both Molly and Grace nodded while Melinda seemed to shrink into herself.

Randall shivered. "Damn, what is going on? What just happened?"

"Nothing I know the answer to," said Molly. "And furthermore, I am not going to dwell on it. It was what it was, and that's all. I'm too old to be surprised by anything and not old enough to explain it. You two can hash on it if you want, but I'm going to get Jimmy on the table. At least I know *he's* here."

They walked off, leaving Randall staring at the wall. *Dang, I think I'm gonna go home now,* he thought to himself. *This is off the scale on the weirdness meter. What just happened? Was it a mass hallucination? Mistaken identity? Whichever, I don't know what box to put it in. Maybe the litter box.*

Randall usually passed off the weird or inexplicable, since this wasn't his first rodeo in that arena. But this one was a ride on the Tilt-A-Whirl off its axis several degrees.

The back door of the department burst open and then slammed closed. What followed was a loud barrage of expletives. Bob Storch, the radiation physicist, had finally made it in from his gig at the U. He lurched his skeletal 6-foot, 7-inch frame through the door. His finger had gotten caught in the big double doors as they closed precipitously. He dropped his briefcase and began shaking his hand as if it had been burned. The commotion brought the group at the console out of their inner reflections on the morning's strange event. Bob composed himself, picked up the briefcase and walked over to the console rather sheepishly.

"Hey, guys. Sorry about the French. Sometimes I'm such a klutz. What's going on?" asked Bob.

"Nothing much," Molly responded.

"Yeah, situation normal," mumbled Randall.

"Well, not completely normal," offered Grace. "Dr. B is trying to replace you. He fixed the water leak . . . at least temporarily."

"Really?" Bob responded with some incredulity in his tone, snapping his chewing gum.

Melinda looked a bit confused. "Yeah, and that was before everything got all weird."

The RTTs exchanged knowing looks with Randall, making an unspoken agreement not to mention the Swindell incident to Storch. He was already off reservation enough.

CHAPTER 5

———

PEARL OF WISDOM

"We are to admit no more causes of natural things than such as are both true and sufficient to explain their appearances."

—Isaac Newton, *The Principia: The Mathematical Principles of Natural Philosophy*

CLEANUP AND RECOVERY

Grace and Molly gave Bob Storch a glowing account of Randall's zip-tie repair. Bob did a quick check of the water leak fix and decided that it looked good enough to last until the day's daily treatment schedule was completed. There was already a serious backup in treatments and grumbling patients. Since replacing the vinyl tubing would take at least two hours, Bob thought it was worth the small risk of a leak to keep treating, but would monitor it closely.

Bob took over the chart checks so Randall could continue patient on-treatment reviews. This task had gotten backed up by the morning's delays, and Randall wanted to get them done before the afternoon consults started to pour in, even if it meant eating his lunch on the run. He was happy to get on with the day and focus on the tasks at hand rather than reflect further on the mystery of Mr. Swindell.

Randall called the first patient to the exam room. He figured he could stream through the reviews. Most of them had been on treatment long enough to avoid the first week "drags." Patients in the first week

55

of treatment took more time because they usually had lots of questions and needed reassurance. After several weeks, the reviews went quickly. Even if the patients were talkers, Randall had a knack for letting them talk while he reviewed the total treatment dose and did his exam, so the reviews usually went fast.

WAFFLE FORTUNES

By 1:00 p.m., Randall caught up with the backlog. He saw and dispatched the reviews fast enough to see each one just as they emerged from treatment. It was well after 1:00 when he finished. He sat on a stool at the console and looked down the hall. Without the hall waiting area filled with patients, the orange waffle pattern wallpaper, put up before his tenure, gave the space an unusual sort of pumpkin colored, Halloweeny ambience. Randall had grown to hate the wallpaper. It was heavily textured with waffle-like indentations. The design was intended to be durable but, over time, repeated hard contact with gurneys and chair backs had rubbed through to the wallboard.

Rather than replace the wallpaper, which building management declared "out of stock," they had attached 3/8" clear Plexiglas in a long strip over the worn areas to "protect the wall from further damage." This made the worn areas even more unsightly, like putting them in a picture frame. A "no spitting on the wall" sign had been added at the entrance, but the many chewing tobacco stains on the wall belied its effectiveness. The VA canteen sold cigarettes and chewing tobacco to the veterans at discount rates. This befuddled Randall, since over half the cancers he treated were borne of long-term tobacco use.

The same waffle wallpaper had been used in the hallway outside the department but had been applied in wide diagonal stripes of alternating orange, brown, green, and yellow. Randall couldn't decide which décor time period this represented. Perhaps the VA was trying to establish a new trend.

The waffle paper had even been used to cover the inside walls of the four elevators just south of the department's entrance. Each elevator sported one of the four colors. Randall was convinced that the wallpaper color of the elevator that first stopped for you each day was an omen for how your day would go: push the call button and await your fate. If it was the green wallpaper elevator, it portended a "good day." If it was the yellow waffle elevator, it suggested "proceed with caution." If the sliding door revealed orange waffles, it would be a "fruity day." But no waffle color was more dreaded than brown, which signaled a "crappy day."

DISCORDANT NOTE

Randall was still hungry. His sandwich bag sat on top of the treatment console. A few sandwich fragments were left inside and a few potato chip crumbs. His coffee was cold. Down the hall, a patient escort delivered a wheelchair patient and brought Randall the hospital chart—the first of his five consults.

Randall was about to get some fresh coffee and take the chart to his office for review when Doris came out into the hallway and waved a pink message slip. Randall hurried down the hall. "What's up, Doris?"

"Dr. B, I didn't want to disturb you while you were doin' reviews. But your wife called. I didn't write much on this here pink sheet. I figured I best tell you myself. "

Now Randall's interest was piqued. "Great. Just what I need. More drama. Fire at will."

Doris leaned in closer to Randall and spoke in hushed tones. "I'm not gonna use her exact words, but I'll give you the rough translation. Firstly, I strongly suspect she's havin' her 'monthly,' and caution is suggested."

Randall nodded. "Makes sense. I got the yellow elevator today."

Doris looked puzzled. "Excuse me?"

Randall waved an arm. "Never mind. It's a tale for another time. Go ahead and give it to me straight up, no chaser."

Doris continued, "Basically, she strongly suggested you not be late comin' home tonight, because, as she put it, it's 'your turn to be the parent and house slave.' Sorry, Dr. B. I'm just the messenger. I told her how busy you were, and that we'd do our best to get you home on time."

Randall rolled his eyes. "How'd she respond to that?"

Doris shook her head. "Not quite sure. After that it was just me and the dial tone."

Randall grimaced. "Lord, have mercy on us poor sinners. I guess I'm going to have to hit 70 mph for a brief spell. Time's a wastin'. Best get to humping. Please try to screen my calls for only the most urgent. You know, fires, earthquakes . . ."

"Gotcha, Boss! How about I take your cup and replenish it with fresh coffee?"

"You read my mind," said Randall. "Here you go. What would I do without you?"

"Crash in a big fireball," shot back Doris as she grabbed his cup and made haste to the communal pot. "Like hogs to the slop, you'd be covered in it. I will be back, forthwith."

Randall sat down at his desk with the new chart and opened it. But his mind was still swimming with incomplete tasks and patient data that needed to be recorded before he lost it. There was just no time for proper documentation. Now this wonderful message from left field. He felt like a baseball outfielder trying to catch a high flyball but getting beaned from behind by an empty beer can. He'd just have to make the Zelda call a side bar and deal with it when he got home.

Randall took several deep breaths and began the chart review. Once he got going, he settled down and put the whole story together. The patient had called the fire department at three in the morning to report his house was on fire. When the fire truck arrived to find him sitting on the couch, reading a magazine with no fire in evidence, they threatened to turn him in to the police. Turns out he had fallen and hit his head, and in his confusion, called for the only help he could think of. The firemen had convinced him to go to the VA ER. Subsequent workup found several malignant tumors in his brain, causing the fire delusion. He needed whole brain radiation, but steroids could tamp down the symptoms, so he could wait several days to start treatment.

Randall went out to the hallway, introduced himself to the man in his wheelchair and began wheeling him to the exam room. He noticed

Melinda sitting on one of the stools next to the console with a disconsolate look on her face. The patient piped up. "Doctor, that girl looks like she lost something in the fire!" His eyes wandered off into the distance.

"Well, we best step up then! What's wrong, Melinda? You look rather morose," asked Randall.

"Morose?"

"You know, upside-down smile," explained Randall.

"Well, Grace just kicked me out of the treatment room because I handed her the wrong block. She told me to take a time out."

Randall locked the wheelchair and walked over to Melinda. "Don't worry about it. She's all bark and no tree. Tell you what. How about you come in the exam room with me until the queen bee grants you privileges again? You can observe on this new consult so you can see what I do."

Melinda brightened up. "Sure. I was kind of wondering what you did in there."

Randall had a new thought. "Even better. I've got five of these today. If you can help usher them in and out of the rooms that would be a big help. You could even do a preliminary review of the charts for me, get vital signs, and do the initial meet and greet. Learn from this one. Do the next one."

Melinda reversed her upside-down smile. "You'd let me do that?"

Randall did an arm wave. "Let you? You're the one helping me. I'm the grateful one here. There are still afternoon treatment reviews to see in between the five consults. Your help will be critical to get through it all. The techs don't need the help. I do. Any clinic this size usually has a nurse helping the doctor. You may have noticed, we don't have a nurse. Welcome to nursing for a day."

Melinda was all in. She wheeled the patient into the exam room and set to work, giving Randall time to do a quick weekly review. Melinda observed carefully and was a quick study. By the second consult, she was already making things run more smoothly. Plus her coming and going improved the scenery by a few points.

After the second consult was completed, Randall prepped Melinda for the weekly review up next. It was fifty-year-old Alonzo McDonald, a huge black man with prostate cancer. The man was in his first week of treatment and was a bit nervous. "Mr. McDonald is rather intimidating, but he's basically a good guy. Don't let him frighten you."

Melinda looked puzzled. "I'm not a baby, you know. I can hold my own."

"Well, it's just that Mr. McDonald used to run a crew of gang bangers that sold drugs on the street. He got caught dealing and spent some time behind bars. He found Jesus on his second forced holiday and has been clean for two years. He allowed as how he may have 'capped' one or two of his competitors, but nothing ever stuck except the drug charges."

Melinda stared at him, speechless.

Randall continued nonchalantly. "He's proud that he never wasted anyone who didn't deserve it. Oh, and he promised he would not shoot me as long as his treatment comes out okay. Still up for a visit with him?"

"Are you serious?" Melinda muttered.

"Deadly. Come in the exam room with us; he won't bite," said Randall, *sotto voce*. "Hopefully."

He lifted his head like a ringmaster. "Mr. McDonald, come on down!" Randall waved him toward the exam room entrance.

The man hauled his massive frame out of the chair and lumbered toward Randall and Melinda. He stood before the two, a head taller than Randall. Melinda came up to the man's shirt pocket but stood her ground, gazing up wide-eyed at Mr. McDonald's bearded face and Afro. The Afro added several more inches to his stature.

Randall smiled. "Ah, Mr. McDonald, Melinda and I were just discussing your case. Is it okay if she comes in the room with us? She's a student in training to be a tech like Grace and Molly."

"It's nice to meet you, Melinda," said Mr. McDonald, reaching out to shake hands with Melinda. Just the movement of his arm created a breeze. He held her small hand delicately in his large paw and gave it a gentle squeeze. It looked for a moment that he might kiss the back of her hand before he let go.

Mr. McDonald hesitated at the door. "I've got just two bits of advice before we go in. First, call me Mr. A, and second, Melinda, you be a tech like Molly, not that other one." Mr. McDonald's voice was surprisingly higher pitched than his body habitus would predict. "Oh, and Doc, you better not be planning a prostate exam on me with her in the room or you're going to be on my *list*."

Randall let out a nervous laugh as he ushered Mr. McDonald into the exam room. "No problem, prostate exam is not needed during treatment since the rectal area gets irritated enough with the radiation. We don't need to stir things up. Besides, the tumor doesn't shrink fast enough over the six weeks of treatment to detect a change. I will have to look at the skin in the treatment area though, for reactions to the radiation. I hope you don't mind dropping trou' in front of Melinda."

"You kiddin' me, Doc? Why would a dude like me mind showing Miss Melinda my 'stuff'? But what's this you say about six weeks? I thought we were done today. Are you aiming to go on my *list*?"

Melinda was surprised by Mr. McDonald's slightly refined manner of speech. He didn't speak loudly, but when he spoke, you listened. He didn't seem to mind wielding power. Randall ushered Mr. McDonald into the exam room and sat him down in the exam chair. Melinda looked rather flushed as she closed the door.

Randall stuttered a bit. "*Err*, Mr. A, we went over that last week when you started. Remember I said there will be thirty treatments over six weeks and five treatments per week? I wrote that down on a piece of paper for you, and you put it in your shirt pocket."

"Yeah, Doc, I've got the paper right here." Mr. McDonald patted his pocket. "I'm just messing with you."

"Good to hear," said Randall, trying not to appear spoofed. "But I already knew that. So, Mr. A, how's your cat?"

Mr. McDonald's eyes welled up with tears. "Damn wife stole my cat and took her to the *Hu*mane Society. By the time I figured it out, they'd already Lutheranized my Pearl. I miss that cat so damn much, I'm . . .

sorry, Doc. Give me a second." Mr. McDonald pulled a linen hanky out of his pocket and dabbed at his eyes. "I swear, if I get my hands on that woman, I'm going to . . ."

"That's terrible. Didn't she do that once before?" asked Randall.

Melinda's head swiveled back and forth between Randall and Mr. McDonald as each spoke.

"Yeah, but that time, I found Pearl before anything bad happened."

Randall patted Mr. McDonald's massive shoulder. "I know how you feel. I had a cat that I lost too. Her name was Myrtle. The next week another cat showed up at my door. She had a big patch of fur missing off the top of her head. I brought her in and cleaned her up. Then she told me that she wanted to adopt me. I couldn't say no. I called her Baldspot. That hair never grew back!"

"Just like you, hey, doc?" Mr. McDonald laughed, pointing to Randall's genetically acquired bald pate.

"Yep, Baldspot is my soulmate," said Randall. "If a new cat doesn't come to your door, maybe you can adopt a Pearl II from the Humane Society. There's lots of cats out there that need a forever home."

What's Up Down There?

Mr. McDonald nodded and sighed, his huge shoulders sagging. "Yeah, maybe I will, Doc. I hope one of them wants to adopt me!" He took a deep, shuddering breath. "Anyways, what's up with my treatment? How am I doing?"

Melinda looked over to Randall. She expected this to be the interesting part. Randall caught her glance and scanned Mr. McDonald's chart studiously. He turned the pages back and forth for a long moment. Mr. McDonald leaned forward in his chair, starting to look concerned.

Randall was getting his payback for Mr. McDonald's little misdirect about the length of treatment. It was amazing how many patients tried to negotiate the length of treatment to be shorter. Then Randall had to explain that could only be done by increasing the daily tumor dose, which increased the risk of long-term normal tissue complications. Shortening the treatment without increasing the daily dose would only sacrifice tumor control. Spreading the treatment out longer made the acute normal tissue reactions, during treatment, much more tolerable, and the reactions usually cleared up within weeks of treatment completion.

This was the point in the explanation that most patients began to glaze over. Randall loved to explain it, but few patients could stay focused on the long version. To those who had the interest to listen further, he described how normal tissues that were rapidly growing, like skin cells and the lining of the bowel, were more prone to be damaged during the radiation. But these sensitive tissues were also able to repair the damage quickly after treatment with a low risk of long-term complications.

It was simple radiation biology and seemed so logical to Randall. He couldn't understand why he had so much trouble explaining it to patients. He got so frustrated that he'd draw diagrams on the exam table paper to bring the message home. The patients would feign understanding and ask to tear the paper off the table and take it home. Randall smiled to himself at this memory. He'd made Mr. McDonald wait long enough.

Finally Randall nodded and broke the silence. "Everything looks good here. We're at 1,000 rads in five treatments, just like we should be. We're on target for 6,000 rads by the end of six weeks. All the calculations look good."

Mr. McDonald relaxed visibly.

Randall continued. "Are you having any problems with your bowel or bladder this week?"

"Not so far." Mr. McDonald shuffled his feet.

"Good. Any skin soreness in your groin area or in the area between your rear cheeks?"

Mr. McDonald blushed and glanced at Melinda. "Nothing yet."

Randall rubbed his hands together. "Great. So much for the tell. Now for the show. Stand up and drop your pants. Good. Now turn around. Excellent. No sign of any skin reactions yet, at least not down here. But please let me know if you get redness or itching. We have some ointments you can use if it gets too bothersome."

Randall glanced over at Melinda. She was looking a bit shocked, wide-eyed, and still.

Randall determined it was best just to continue. "Go ahead and pull up your pants again and don't forget to zip. We don't want you scaring any of the ladies out there when you leave," finished Randall. "Melinda, would you escort Mr. A out, while I finish writing this note?"

A somewhat red-faced Melinda jumped to the door and opened it for Mr. McDonald. He ambled somewhat proudly out of the room and gave Melinda a mini salute with one finger to his eyebrow.

"Thanks to you, young lady, he's not on my list yet. But *he* might be if I don't see you next week." Mr. McDonald walked casually down the hall.

"Sir. Yes, sir," she responded.

When Randall walked out of the room, Melinda was still watching the patient walk away.

"Are they all like that?" asked Melinda.

"Like what?" replied Randall.

"Uh, you know . . ."

"Deceptively smart? No, not all. But never take a veteran for granted until you walk a few inches in his boots. Or was there something else on your mind?" asked Randall.

Melinda stammered, not wanting to go deeper into the topic. "No, Dr. B. You got it right. That was it. You can't tell a book by its cover."

"That's right. You know what they say about a man with big feet." Randall couldn't resist goading her a little.

"*Ummmmm* . . . he has . . . big . . . ," Melinda turned a lovely shade of scarlet.

"Exactly. Big socks. Okay then. Grab the next chart, and let's get cracking."

With Melinda's help, Randall quickly waded through the first four new consults. He caught a few breaks. The brain metastases patient was improved on steroids and could wait to start radiation. It was decided that the spinal cord compression patient could be handled by neurosurgery first, so radiation would come in several weeks. At first, it was thought the lung cancer patient would need radiation to stop the bleeding from his tumor, but thoracic surgery stopped the bleeding after bronchoscopy and planned to take the man to surgery. Another patient thought to have a cord compression by tumor turned out to have a benign vertebral compression fracture that would be managed by orthopedic surgery. All in all, an average day at the office.

Randall kept his eye on the clock with each new consult. The four o'clock meeting was drawing nearer and nearer.

It was already 3:45 as Randall and Melinda were prepping the fifth consult for exam, when Doris interrupted them. "Dr. B, I've got good news and bad news."

Randall almost didn't want to ask. "Okay, I'll take the good news first."

"Mr. Samuels, the new compliance officer, can't make the four o'clock meeting. His secretary called, and he has a family health emergency at home."

Without thinking through his response, Randall yelped. "Yippee! I will get the consults done after all. I mean, that's . . . a bad thing. A really bad thing. I feel really bad for him. I hope it's not too serious. *Um*, what's the bad news?"

"Your wife called again to remind you to be home by 5:30. Sorry, Dr. B."

Randall's shoulders slumped, and Melinda got a strange glint in her eye.

"Dagnabbit!" exclaimed Randall. "So I'm not going to have time to go upstairs and complete the roundup on the documentation for these consults."

Melinda looked worried. "What are you going to do, Dr. B?"

Randall thought for a few moments. "I guess I could come in at 6:00 tomorrow. Then I could get all the paperwork done before clinic starts. Not getting home on time is not an option. There could be lethal consequences."

Melinda offered up a suggestion. "Maybe I could collect some of the documents you need for our charts. I could stay after 5:00 tonight."

Randall looked shocked. Rarely had any VA staff, except maybe

Doris, ever volunteered to stay late except for emergencies. "You would do that?"

"Sure, if you tell me what you need. I think I have some inkling from what you've looked at on the charts. I can't do the exam part but, if you give me a list for each patient, I could be gopher."

Randall almost laughed. "Fantastic! I might live another day. Let's finish this guy's consult and then we can go back to my office for the list making. I've got all my notes in there. Mostly what I need are photocopies of pathology, lab, radiology, and other consult reports, plus admitting H and P's. Oh, and any key summary notes."

"Do the wards have Xerox machines?" asked Melinda.

"Mostly," said Randall. "If not, you'll have to spirit the charts down here to copy the pertinent stuff and then get them back upstairs pronto. It's kind of a stealth operation. Night staffing is limited, so you won't get much scrutiny."

Melinda got up close to Randall and feigned whispering in his ear. "Should we synchronize our watches?"

"Definitely! Always advisable for night ops," said Randall, winking.

CHAPTER 6

———

NO HELP AT HOME

". . . one must still have chaos in oneself to be able to give birth to a dancing star."

—Friedrich Nietzsche

Freeting

Randall scribbled up the document list for Melinda, and she hurried off to the wards. Randall loaded up his backpack for the drive home. He was dreading what he'd find there. He took the elevator outside the department entrance to the first floor. The elevator was wet with snow-melt and lined with dried salt. Exiting at the first floor, he got his first glimpse of the outdoors since morning. It was snowing heavily again, or perhaps still. On his way down the hall to the back entrance, he encountered his friend, Jim Conway, the lead ER physician. He was on his way in to start his evening shift.

The two men stopped walking momentarily. "Hey, Jim, how's things?" greeted Randall. "What's it like out there?"

Jim shook his head in disgust. "It's just ducky, if you like frozen ducks. It was snowing earlier. Now it's freeting. Watch yourself driving home. The roads are like skating rinks."

"Freeting?"

"Sorry, it's a portmanteau word. Use it with my wife. It's a combination of freezing and sleeting," explained Jim.

"Love it," said Randall. "Mind if I use it?"

"Why not? You are going to be walking in it momentarily and you'll find repeating the word in a desultory manner will be quite rewarding. See you, dude. Have a good night." Jim turned, waved, and resumed his trek to the ER, shedding winter layers on the way.

Randall waved back. "See ya. Don't want to be ya this night. Just be alert tonight. Today the whole hospital was going nuts."

"Good to hear," Jim yelled back as he walked away.

Randall continued the long hall hike to the north exit. He walked by the administrative offices, through the Building 70 hallway, and headed out the back door near the post office. The outside walkway was a mess of snow, slush, salt, and ice. He carefully descended the concrete stairs to the parking lot, almost slipping a few times before righting himself using the handrail, also covered with ice.

Randall slip-slided over to the Scirocco and put his backpack down on the ground to fish for his keys in the many pockets of his heavy winter jacket. His thickly gloved fingers fumbled the keys, which promptly dropped and bounced off his boot, landing under the car. The sun was almost down, and the light was in full dusk mode. Plus, the parking lot light was still out.

Stupid daylight savings time!

Randall knelt in the snow, took off his glove and patted around under the car with his bare hand. He was relieved to find the keys quickly. His ungloved hand started to get numb and fumbly. He found purchase for his ascent by grabbing the car handle, but his feet slipped again. He launched the keys into the air, and they skittered across the ice and under the car again.

This time he had to go down to his elbows to fish the keys out from under the car. Anxious to get in the car, he turned the key in the lock and thanked the gods that it wasn't frozen. Randall yanked on the car door handle, but the door didn't budge. The whole door was sealed shut with ice. He got the same result with the passenger door and tailgate.

"Freeting, freeting, freeting!" Randall hollered, remarking to himself what a wonderful and apropos word he had just learned. He kept thinking about the hell that awaited him at home if he was late. He wished there was some remote way to contact his wife. Like some small mobile phone that didn't need to be connected to the wall. The nearest phone was half an arctic circle away back in the hospital!

That's something that needs to be invented! A phone that you can carry in your pocket! Dream on, McDuff.

Randall stood next to the car in a funk, trying to puzzle out what to do. Then he had an inspiration. If only he could get his hands on some alcohol. He thought of the exam room alcohol lamps used to heat mirrors prior to doing indirect laryngoscopy. It prevented exhaled water vapor from fogging up the mirror. *All* he'd have to do would be to hike back to the department, get the alcohol, and pour it in the door seams.

For a brief moment, Randall debated about his backpack, but decided to leave it under the car. It would make the repeat trip easier. Retracing his steps, he found that the back door entrance was locked for the night, and his keycard wouldn't work.

"Freeting lock," intoned Randall.

Randall redirected his path to circle around the building to the east. That required navigating through several snowbanks. He came in through the ER entrance, slogged through the sliding doors and down the hall, stopping at the first-floor elevators where he punched the down button. The elevator doors opened to reveal the dreaded brown wallpaper and a paraplegic vet in a wheelchair repeatedly propelling himself against the back wall of the elevator.

With each impact, he let out a satisfied grunt.

"Hey, man, are you getting off here?" asked Randall.

"*Hunh!* No, I get off on the tenth floor. *Hunh!*" He banged the wall again.

"But this elevator is going down," replied Randall.

"It'll go back up. *Huhn!* Good one!"

"If you don't mind me asking, why are you banging against the wall with your wheelchair?"

The vet stopped his elevator beating and answered. "I don't mind telling you. It's simple. My tenth-floor buddies and I hate this waffle wallpaper, so we like to beat on it whenever we get the chance. We figure if it gets bad enough, they may have to replace it."

"I'm with you there," replied Randall. "Mind if I help?"

Randall started to kick the wall with his snow boot as the elevator car descended to the basement. Juicy, salty water squished out of the wallpaper with every kick.

The wheelchair vet hollered "Hoo yah!"

Randall hollered "Freeting" repeatedly.

"Keep up the good work," said Randall as he exited the elevator.

"Freeting A," shouted the vet.

As Randall unlocked the doors to the department, he could still hear the banging inside the elevator as it rose to the tenth floor. He smiled and made a beeline for the exam room, grabbed the alcohol lamp off the exam table and praised the freeting gods that the lamp was full. He turned and hurried back to the parking lot. His backpack was still sitting under the Scirocco, although now probably soaked and frozen too.

Randall unscrewed the top off the alcohol lamp and removed the wick from the container. In the dim light, he carefully poured the alcohol into the gap between the door and the frame and down into the frozen rubber gasket. After a few blows to the car door with the heel of his hand, he heard a crunching sound as the door broke free. It opened with a firm pull. He carefully replaced the cover on the lamp, stashed it in the car, and grabbed for his backpack. The effort pulled him back out of the vehicle, tumbling like laundry onto the frozen ground.

Freeting A! The dang thing is frozen to the ground! And now ALL of my clothes are wet.

He grabbed the alcohol lamp and tossed the remaining liquid under the backpack. With a yank, the bag broke free and he tossed it in the back seat. His fumbly fingers managed to get the key in the ignition in one try. The trusty Scirocco roared to life, and Randall was off for home. The day seemed like a week, and it wasn't over yet.

Heated seats. That's my next invention! Randall pictured a charcoal burner under the front seat.

Finally Home

It was a white-knuckle drive home on the slippery streets, but Randall made it to the turn off to Creekside Place unscathed. The car almost got bogged down in a plowed mound of snow halfway down the hill, but Randall powered through it. Despite the judicious application of ABS braking to scrub off his speed, the car slid past the driveway. That was just icing on the cake. Now Randall was really pissed and swore like a sailor. He backed up, with the front wheels spinning, and slewed into the driveway. The dash clock was showing 5:29. It might just qualify as "not late." The garage door wouldn't open, so he just abandoned the car in the driveway and stomped to the back door, irate enough to make a noisy and dramatic entrance.

At the last moment, Randall decided to play it safe and reconnoiter at the back door window before possibly jumping from the frying pan into the fire. Scoping out the scene, he saw Kyle and Addie sitting at the kitchen table, drawing on paper with crayons. Zelda was doing dishes quite aggressively. Not a good sign. Her curly red hair created a halo of warning around her head. She was wearing a robe, suggesting she was just waiting for Randall to come home before passing off the evening chores to him and heading for bed. Polluto, the low IQ golden Lab, was asleep in the doorway, as usual. Nothing Randall couldn't handle.

Randall opened the back door, stepped over the dog, and entered the back hall. Addie was the first to spot him and run to him, her strawberry blonde hair flying behind her.

"Daddy, Daddy, you're home!" A very animated Addie reached up to Randall for a hug. "Guess what! Mommy said Charlie is coming for dinner! Daddy, who's Charlie?"

"Oh, he's just an old family fiend," said Randall, neglecting to include the information that Charlie was Zelda's secret code for those wonderful days when she was having her menstrual cycle. Zelda had cyclothymic mood swings during those hormonal floods and claimed she could not be held responsible for anything she did or said during those periods. As a warning to those around her she put a red dot of lipstick on her forehead when Charlie was visiting.

"Hi, sweetie." Randall picked up Addie and kissed her cheek. "Does Mommy have a red dot on her forehead tonight?" he whispered in her ear.

"Yes, Daddy," Addie whispered back.

Knowing for sure that it was "walking on eggshells" time, Randall strategized his remaining greetings. He noted that Zelda was still ignoring his entrance, so he carried Addie over to the table to see what she and Kyle had been working on.

"So, Kyle, what's this creature here?" Randall pointed to a multi-armed, flat-footed behemoth.

"Dat's an octophant, Dad. It's the meanest creature what am," replied Kyle with enthusiasm.

Even though he proclaimed not to be into "little kid" activities like coloring, he still seemed to enjoy it. He often lapsed back into earlier speech patterns when he was happy.

Zelda was still studiously avoiding interacting.

"Impressive," said Randall, tousling Kyle's messy blond hair. "But I thought the liger was the meanest?"

"Not anymore," insisted Kyle.

"And I bet these flower drawings are Addie's, right?"

"Yes, Daddy, they're for you," said Addie proudly.

THROW IN THE TOWEL

While Randall's little discourse with Kyle and Addie was proceeding, Zelda walked over to the trio and threw a dish towel at Randall.

"And this towel is for you too. For the rest of this day, all domestic chores are yours. I will be going out, and you will be staying in. While in, you will make the kids dinner, feed them, bathe them, and put them down for the night. And clean Baldspot's dang toilet! Understood? Did I mention you get dog duty too?"

With that comment, Randall concluded the robe was not preparation for going to bed. It was a prelude for a night out. Who knew with whom, or how, or where? Now Randall was getting steamed.

"*Aww*, come on. I've already had a full day. I'm bushed. Sure. Dog duty. You know me. I prepare for my duty. I walk up and face my duty. Then I say 'Howdy Doody.'" He winked at Kyle.

"Daddy said doodie!" Addie guffawed.

Randall tried to stay neutral. "And where is this 'out' that you're going to?"

Zelda ignored the question. "Oh, and by the way, just so you know, your son had another poop episode today. I don't know what's wrong with your son, but I'm sick of cleaning his pants. He's seven years old, for gob's sake!" screamed Zelda. "You're a doctor. Can't you figure something out?"

Kyle had displayed some behavioral issues in day care when he was four years old. The standout episode was when he stuffed a whole roll of toilet paper deep into the toilet, flushed, and laughed as he watched water overflow onto the floor. Then he ran out of the bathroom yelling that the toilet was overflowing. This got the attention of the teachers and kids. He laughed while they scurried about, not masking very well that he had done it. The day care folks had no trouble finding the perpetrator. Randall had gotten a call from the director stating that Kyle would not be permitted back, and that Kyle needed to see a child psychologist.

No consultation with a child psychologist had ever been set up. This was mostly because of Zelda's firm objection that no one outside the family needed to know their personal business. Randall wasn't keen to pursue it either, because they were soon going to move to Baltimore where Randall was slated to serve his military duty in a Public Health Service Hospital. Randall figured that Kyle would grow out of the problem, but there had been similar issues with Kyle in Baltimore.

Kyle seemed to be slow in developing bowel control. Although potty trained, he sometimes retained his stool until the last minute, then had "accidents" in his pants. Even when he made it to the toilet in time, he had a problem with using toilet paper to clean himself afterward. So he got into the habit of yelling from the bathroom, "Wipe my fanny!"

Zelda had given up on Kyle and deferred the problem to Randall.

"Anything else I need to know?" asked Randall sarcastically.

Zelda shot right back amidships. "Yes. When I get back, it better all be done, and the kitchen better be spotless. Now I'm going upstairs to put on my good clothes. The next sight you see will be my narrow ass headed out that door."

Zelda turned on her heel and stormed loudly up the stairs for emphasis. Randall must have looked rather crestfallen as the kids waited for his response. He said nothing further and decided to eat the meal he was served.

"Don't worry, Daddy, we love you," said Addie. She was a sensitive soul and could read the anger and sadness in the room.

"I know, sweet pea. Daddy loves you guys too. Who's hungry? What do you want Daddy to make for dinner?" asked Randall.

"*Ooo*, can we have macaroni and cheese with wieners?" asked Kyle.

"Yeah, mac and weenies!" yelled Addie.

"Coming up. You guys clean up your crayons and stuff, while I put my work gear away. Then start getting cleaned up for dinner," said Randall.

The kids were eager to comply and ran off to clean up. Randall poured himself a small glass of Riesling to help settle his nerves, and got out the dinner fixings. He took a little sip. While he cooked, Baldspot made an appearance and wove around his legs, practicing her sweetest "feed me!" meow. With that cue, Randall downed the whole glass. "Ah. Good to the last drop!"

Feeling fortified, he turned to the shiny headed feline. "Very cute, fuzzball. I know you don't want me, just some of this butter!"

Despite himself, he dipped a finger in the butter and offered her a little taste. She nabbed the butter, then turned tail and gave him a one-eyed salute. The kids came back, set the table, and eagerly took their seats.

Randall took the pot off the stove and served three plates of squishy orange goo. The wiener slices in the noodles reminded him to address the cat box after dinner. The trio tore into their magic food with gusto. Randall knew it was probably a mistake, but he let Kyle and Addie wash down their mac and weenies with "bug juice." The Kool-Aid cocktail was a blend of four different flavors of the powdered drink mix served on the rocks with little red straws so they could pretend they were having adult mixed drinks. Randall knew the sugar and carb load might keep them both awake, but he didn't mind. Kyle sometimes had nightmares when he went to bed over-sugared; but what the heck, everything was already screwed up, why not go all the way?

Whenever Zelda went off on one of her Charlie toots, Randall knew he'd be awake until whenever she got home. That might be at O'dark hundred if past behavior could be used as a predictor of future performance. With the early morning, he had planned to finish the consults, maybe he would just stay up all night anyway.

Both kids dug in with vigor. Addie took careful, small bites, while Kyle managed to get a cheese smile almost ear to ear. After they polished off the last specks of food, Randall surprised them with ice cream for dessert.

"I like it when you cook, Daddy," giggled Addie.

"Yep, I am a regular Berty Crocker," said Randall.

"Who's that?" asked Kyle.

"Betty's husband," said Randall. "Now stop asking silly questions, and eat your ice cream. Then you two are going upstairs for a bath. We need to clean off all the food that didn't make it inside your little overstuffed bodies."

"But, Daddy, I already let Polluto lick off my hands," Addie protested. "And he cleaned up the floor too."

"And I'm gonna let my ice cream melt before I eat it," said Kyle, sticking out his lower lip.

"Why's that?" asked Randall.

"'Cause I don't want a bath," Kyle grouched back.

"Fine. Take your time. Or drop it for the dog. Then you'll both go to bed without a story." Randall started clearing dishes.

"Kyle! Eat your ice cream," whined Addie. "I already ate mine and I want a story."

"Can you read *Fox in Socks*?" asked Kyle so quietly, Randall could barely hear him.

"Yeah! *Fox in Socks, Fox in Socks*," yelled Addie.

"Sure, but it's a long story. We won't have time if Kyle doesn't hustle," said Randall.

Kyle made his ice cream disappear as if by magic and the two kids brought their empty bowls to the sink. Randall directed the kids to head up to the bathroom, and he drug Polluto to the basement planning to cage him later. Randall hoped Polluto might leave a gift on Zelda's dirty laundry pile. The dog couldn't be left upstairs at night, or he'd chew up the kids' shoes and chase Baldspot.

When Randall came back upstairs, the kids were back downstairs, putzing around in the kitchen. "Hey kids, what do you call it when you get your sucker stuck in your throat?"

Kyle dragged his feet. "I dunno." The finger in his nose muffled his speech.

"Lollygagging! Get upstairs! Mush!" Randall herded them up the stairs like a sheepdog. "Okay, you two, get your clothes off, choose your towels, and I'll get the water running."

Randall tickled them as they ran to the linen closet to argue about who would get the Star Wars towel. He started the bath water and poured in the obnoxious pink Mr. Bubble soap. The kids liked their bathwater very foamy!

While the kids battled over bath towels, Randall went into the master bedroom to lower the shades. He always felt better with the shades down when it got dark outside. Something about the possibility of being seen by unseen "someones" always raised the hairs on his neck. Zelda's clothes were scattered across the floor, and she'd written a lipstick message on the dresser mirror: "Have fun. See you later. Maybe."

Randall shook his head and muttered. "Sleet sneezes! Can't she just give it a rest?"

Randall didn't have the emotional energy to give more of a crap this day. Have fun with the kids he would. Hearing anguished screams, he dashed back to the kids' bathroom. They were fighting over who could hold the bar of Fuzzy Wuzzy bath soap. It had been sitting on the window ledge for three days, and sure enough it had grown the expected hairy soap crystals.

Kyle and Addie decided to take turns holding the soap and climbed into the tub with Addie taking the first turn. They *oohed* and *aahed* about Fuzzy's amazing Afro 'do. Addie accidently dropped the soap bar in the water, and it went all bald. Kyle yelled and splashed water in her face, but she splashed back. Half the splash hit Randall. The water fight was on.

It was wet and wild for a while. Randall felt like a kid again, a very wet one. When the water fight ebbed, Randall soaped up the kids and asked how the day at school had been. They both complained about how boring school was and how unfun it was to come home to a not-happy Mom.

"But dinner was great, Dad," said Addie.

"And the water fight was way cool," said Kyle. "Mom would never let us do it."

Randall nodded. "Yeah, well, this little splash fest will just stay between the three of us, right?"

Both kids made a lip-zipping gesture.

"By the way, you guys, that was some really great crayon art you were doing when I came home," said Randall.

"Yeah," said Kyle. "We're good. We're gonna be artists like Mom. When we came home from school and said we were bored, she got out the paper and crayons. She told us to sit quiet and draw until you got home."

"Neither of you want to be a doctor like me when you grow up? You both want to be artists?" Randall started to fake cry.

"Nah, come on, Dad. Being a doctor is way too hard. Mommy says it makes you too busy to do anything else that you wanna do," said Kyle.

Randall paused, like he got punched in the gut.

Oh geez. That cuts to the quick. I work my fanny off to be a good doctor, and now I'm a bad dad? I wish I could figure this out. I should probably talk to my mom! She would know what to do. Randall scrambled for an answer.

"It does make you busy, but it's a good kind of busy," countered Randall. He prepared to wax poetic on the subject.

Kyle abruptly interrupted. "So why is a liger meaner than my octophant?"

At first derailed by Kyle's non sequitur, Randall hesitated for a beat. *What did he remember about ligers?* There was the joke about ligers and there was the fact that ligers were the biological result of a lion and tiger mating. Randall figured that there must have been some significant family chaperoning at the consummation of that union. Randall chose to tell the joke instead of getting tied up in "hybrid genetics for kids."

"Well, Kyle, the liger is scary because it has the head of a tiger on one end and the head of a lion on the other end, so he can eat you with either end," offered Randall.

"But, Dad, if he has a head on both ends, how does he go to the bathroom?" asked Addie.

"That's what makes him so mean!" said Randall with a loud growl as punctuation.

"Daddy!" yelled Addie. "You're scaring me."

Kyle shrieked with laughter.

"Not anymore, it's story time." Randall pulled the tub drain plug and grabbed towels.

Soon Kyle and Addie were dry and pajama clad. Randall grabbed the *Fox in Socks* book and headed for the master bedroom with the kids in tow. It was their custom to use the queen-sized bed for story time, with all three tucked under the covers with Randall in the middle.

Baldspot hopped onto the bed and settled next to Kyle.

"*Aw*, Daddy. Why doesn't Baldspot ever want to sit with me?" Addie often complained that it was unfair that the cat chose her stinky brother over her.

Randall put his arm around her little shoulders and held the book in his other hand. "More room for us! Now you can help me turn the pages."

Their favorite books had been read so many times that they knew them by heart, so sometimes Randall would liven up the reading with some ad libs. Sometimes he read every other word, or repeated a line, or read a line backward. Seuss's *Fox in Socks* didn't need much livening, because it was rich with tongue twisters involving a rhyming dialogue between Mr. Fox and Mr. Knox, climaxing with the Tweedle Beetle Battle. The first page warns, "Take it slowly – this book is dangerous!"

Randall began reading and read it straight until he got to the Luke Luck section, which he read backward:

"Lakes likes Luck Luke.

Lakes likes duck Luke's.

Lakes licks Luck Luke.

Lakes lick duck Luke's . . ."

At that point Kyle and Addie popped out from underneath the covers and jumped up and down on the bed, yelling at Randall.

"Daddy, read it right! . . . No, no, no, that's not it!"

"It's not?" deadpanned Randall. "It's all the right words."

"But they're backward," said Kyle and Addie in unison.

"Okay, Okay. Don't make a federal case out of it. I'll read it forward, as if that will change much. You think it's wrong? I bet you can't read it yourself!"

"Are you crazy, Dad?" Kyle huffed. "I can read 'hippopotamus' and lots of other big words. My teacher says I'm the best phone a tick reader. She also says I'm a jungle full of drums, whatever that means. Then she gives me harder words. So I can handle it. Now keep reading!" Kyle pointed at the book and flopped back against the bed.

The kids settled back in, and Randall read the words in the correct order, albeit less exciting. He was starting to drift off into Luke's Lake when the jangle of the phone ringing nearly scared the lick out of him.

"What the heck? Who calls this late? Ugh, I hope it's not the hospital!" asked Randall out loud.

Kyle piped up. "Maybe it's Mom calling."

Or somebody found Zelda in a ditch! thought Randall. He sat up to answer the bedside phone. "Hello?" Randall said tentatively.

"Randy, honey, I'm glad I caught you." The quiet voice on the other end was smooth and sweet.

Randall let out a breath. "Oh hi, Mom. Didn't expect to hear from you. Is everything okay?"

"Oh, of course. We're fine. Something just told me to call you. Is everything alright at your house?"

Randall stuttered in surprised. "Y-yeah. We're okay." Addie pulled on his sleeve and pointed at the book. "I'm putting the kids to bed. Can I call you tomorrow?"

"Oh, sure, honey. Just checking in. Dad and I are heading to bed. Something just made me have to call you."

"Okay, Mom. Love you!" He hung up the phone and shook his head in wonder.

"Come on, Dad! Keep reading!" begged Kyle.

Randall's mouth resumed reading about Luke's Duck Lake, while his brain wondered at how well his mom's radar worked.

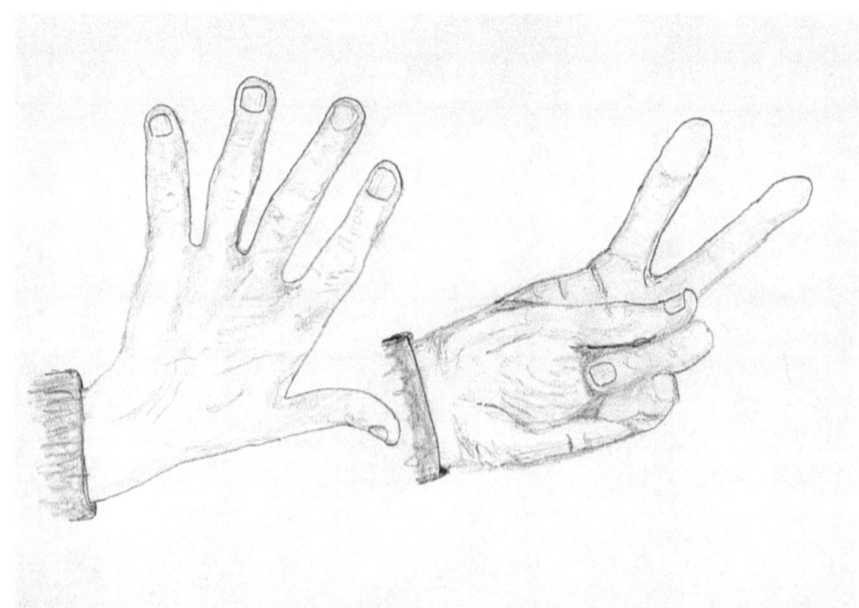

Let me have a show of hands.

CHAPTER 7

———

RUST AND BUGS

"To sleep—to sleep—perchance to dream"

—William Shakespeare, *Hamlet*

FOXY SOCKS

Randall reached the end of Dr. Seuss's *Fox in Socks,* and his eyes slammed shut. He jerked awake minutes later to the sound of choral snoring, the open book still draped on his chest. Kyle and Addie were lying on either side of him, fast asleep. He was tempted just to go back to sleep, but a wiser voice in a remote part of his brain yelled just loud enough to get his attention. Falling asleep on the job could have unwanted consequences. He carefully untangled himself from the two kids and crawled out of bed. Kyle and Addie were sleeping the sleep of the dead. Neither even stirred when Randall carried them to their rooms and tucked them in.

Randall picked up Kyle first and was shocked with how heavy the kid had gotten. He always saw Kyle as a little boy, and here he was, growing without permission! Dodging toys strewn on Kyle's bedroom floor, he laid him carefully on his NASCAR sheets and covered him with his blanket. He wiped a spot of drool off Kyle's cheek.

Randall picked his way back through the landmines without getting injured, and snuck back to the master bedroom. He lifted Addie into his arms. She was a feather by comparison. He padded gently to her room, where Addie had left her small bedside light on. The room was softly lit,

85

creating an aura of quiet coziness. Randall tucked her in bed and brushed an errant shock of hair from her forehead. Randall just stared for a long moment at her angelic face and pitied all the boys she would disappoint when she became a teenager.

Addie's room was neat as a pin compared to Kyle's pigsty. Everything had a place, and Addie made sure it stayed that way. She had at least two-dozen stuffed animals that she carefully displayed on the window seats in her bedroom. Each animal type was grouped together, cats with cats, dogs with dogs, and horses with horses. But center stage was her unicorn unless she was sleeping with it. Randall went to the window seat, picked out the unicorn and put it next to her on the pillow. He kissed Addie's forehead, turned off the light, and quietly left the room.

In the master bedroom, he undressed and got into sweatpants. He noticed that the bedroom shade closest to the door was up, revealing a sparkle of lights in the darkness outside.

Hmmm . . . he thought to himself. *I thought I pulled that dang shade down . . . ?*

In the kitchen, Randall put away the clean dinner dishes and prepared his bag lunch. He pulled some notes together for the next day's early arrival at the VA to finish up the consults he'd left undone. Hopefully, Melinda would have the documents he needed waiting on his desk. So far, the girl was proving surprisingly useful and quite an asset!

Randall was getting a second wind, much to his surprise. He figured the brief post-*Fox in Socks* nap must have helped clear some cobwebs. Randall looked out the backdoor window in the vain hope it would make Zelda's car appear. He resigned himself to the fact that there would be no shuteye until she returned home. Based on past episodes, it could be several hours yet. Nothing to do but wait and fill the time with something semi-productive.

Randall reinspected the kitchen to make sure everything was ship-shape. If not, Zelda would have a bird. No need for an angry avian.

Polluto was snoring and drooling in the middle of the floor. The cat was on her back with all four paws pointing to the heavens. Why couldn't he just do the same? Ignorance truly was bliss.

Randall puzzled what to do until the cows came home. Then he had it. The rusty '73 BMW 2002 that he bought to restore and sell for a profit was sitting in the garage just waiting to be de-rusted. That was always a reliable way to pass the time without wasting time. The old college loans still needed paying off, and that's where the profit would go when the BMW was sold.

The garage was cold, but sanding rust generated body heat, so not a problem. Randall donned his "dirty" gear, put on a "borrowed" surgical mask to avoid inhaling rust dust, and started grinding away at some rear quarter panel body rot. As the sparks flew, it occurred to him how much this avocation was analogous to his day job. Rust occurred when the sheet metal was oxidized by exposure to water and air. Rust was essentially metal cancer. It was his job to stop it and correct the damage.

Randall liked the analogy. When the DNA of a vulnerable body cell was exposed to some oxidative agent or genetic mutation, an aberrant cancer cell was formed. This aberrant cell then could potentially grow unchecked, causing structural damage as it went. Since the aberrant cells originated in the body, the body failed to recognize them as abnormal. As such, the usual checks and balances that thwarted foreign invaders often did not get engaged. The uncontrolled cellular growth could cause disastrous damage to the normal tissues. It was Randall's job to use radiation to reassert control over these renegade cells and allow the body to repair the damage.

Cars were not created with the ability to heal, so Randall had to grind away the rusted metal back to good metal and restore the damage. That meant replacing the lost metal with Bondo, a plastic filler that hardened with a catalyst and could be sanded to blend with the panel surface. Then there was still more sanding, priming, sanding, and painting. Randall was rebuilding the car's body like the body's stem cells or pluripotential cells rebuild the tissues that are destroyed by the cancer. The rust-grinding process was therapeutic. For this remedy he could actually see the enemy.

It wasn't a perfect analogy, but the two processes felt the same to Randall. Perhaps that's how cancer had hooked him. A small imperfection in one part could lead to destruction of the whole. Randall hated imperfection. His obsession with rust-fighting had started in his early college days when the front fenders of his aging '55 Chevy station wagon began rusting out above the headlight bezels. Small bubbles in the paint had advanced rapidly to near self-amputation of the headlights. Not long after he'd repaired the fenders, the front seat had fallen over backward. On closer inspection, the floor panels had literally disappeared from a case of advanced rustitis. The salt-laden roads of the frozen Midwest accelerated the rust process and led to the early demise of many a good car.

Grinding rust sometimes led to a sort of Zen state. Time passed like nothing. Soon the quarter panel was rust free and ready for Bondo. That could wait until another day, so Randall applied a coat of Oxisolve on the bare metal exposed by sanding, before buttoning up the BMW project for the night. The phosphoric acid solution would remove whatever nonvisible rust was left on the quarter panel and leave a protective coating that would prevent rust until the defect could be filled with Bondo and primed. *If only cancer were that easy to manage.*

Randall doffed his dirty duds, hung them in the garage, and went back inside. He stopped to listen for kid sounds, but Mr. Sandman was still working his magic charms. He walked into the kitchen to get a drink of water. The old clock on the kitchen wall read midnight. Zelda still wasn't home, so he decided to fiddle with his guitar to pass the time. He took off his shoes for greater stealth and went into the living room. He got his acoustic guitar out of its case and sat down on the window seat where he liked to play. The seat height was just right for contemplative picking.

Pickin' Fingers

Randall had been working on some songs to play in sing-alongs with Kyle and Addie. He'd found a song about a frog that went bride hunting. The kids loved this one and knew all the verses by heart.

Also he'd been working on one about an old lady. It was a children's rhyme and nonsense song of a type known as a "cumulative." It tells a nonsensical tale of an old woman who begins by swallowing a fly and then swallows progressively larger animals, each to kill the one she previously swallowed. She ultimately swallows a horse and dies, of course.

As Randall was finishing the last verse and the old lady was dying from fatal horse ingestion, he was scared out of his jockeys by a small voice coming from the foot of the stairs. He looked up to see Addie standing there in her PJs holding her "grab." The "grab" was the remnant of a blanket she'd had since babyhood, and she had gradually parted with it piece by piece. Randall figured it would be hers until all that remained was a mere thread.

Randall finished his plucking and looked up at Addie. "Why are you awake, Rosebud?"

"'Cause Mommy isn't home yet, and she promised to give me a kiss when she came home so I could sleep good," said Addie.

"Well, that's why I'm up too. Shall we wait for Mommy together?" asked Randall.

"Yeah. Can we sing some songs while we wait? How about the log song from *Sesame Street*?" she asked.

"Sure, sweetie. Sit right down in the beanbag chair, and we'll do that song. But we dasn't sing too loud or we might wake up Kyle."

Addie's "log song" was another children's cumulative song of a slightly different type. As the verses go on, the hole in the sea bottom acquires a log, the log acquires a bump, the bump acquires a frog, the frog gets a wart, etc. Every time a new characteristic is added, it gets repeated in the chorus, making it a fine test of memory and tongue untwisting. Sung with a good knowledge of physics, the added characteristics could be downsized, asymptotically, to the subatomic level. When the log song was finished, Addie clapped enthusiastically.

"I love it when we get to quarks! More, Daddy. Let's sing the dragon one."

"It's getting late. We should probably get you back upstairs and in your little bed."

"Read me my sleepy time book, please?" pleaded Addie, referencing her second-favorite bedtime story.

"I'm afraid not, Rosebud."

"Just one verse of the dragon song?" Her little puppy eyes could melt an iceberg.

"Okay, but only if you'll go back to bed without any hassle after that."

Randall had just begun to sing the song when the back door slammed, and Zelda came steaming down the hallway. She burst into the living room and gave Randall and Addie the evil eye.

"What the hell are you doing, Randy? And why is she up? Addie should be in bed and you two are down here at 12:30 a.m., playing songs!?" Zelda ranted; her eyes were ringed in red.

"But, Mommy, I couldn't sleep. You said you were gonna kiss me goodnight," whined Addie.

"Randy. Did you feed them junk again? You know what happens when you do that," snapped Zelda.

Before Randall could respond, their attention was drawn to the sight of Kyle walking down the stairs. Baldspot tagged behind him.

"See, now you've got Kyle awake too, and now . . . ," Zelda pointed accusingly at Randall, but she stopped in mid-sentence when she got a good look at Kyle.

Kyle was mincing slowly down the stairs, brushing at his chest with both hands. His breath was shallow and ragged. Instead of stopping at the foot of the stairs, he just continued walking rather aimlessly. Like an automaton, he went into the living room and walked around in circles. Polluto barked and ran around Kyle, enjoying this new game.

BUG OFF

Kyle began to yell and brushed his chest frantically. "Get the bugs off me! Get the bugs off me! They're coming out of the floor!" Kyle stomped his feet on the floor as if he were squishing spiders.

Zelda ran to Kyle and grabbed him firmly by the arms. She tried to make eye contact with no success. She repeated his name loudly, but Kyle paid her no mind.

Zelda shook Kyle, but the brushing and stomping continued. Kyle failed to respond and Zelda became more agitated. Finally she slapped his face, and Kyle came awake like a lit bulb.

Kyle burst out in tears. "*Ow!* Mom, Mom, is it really you? Is this real? Are you real?" screamed Kyle.

"Yes, Kyle, it's Mom. This is real! There's no bugs here. See, there's no bugs here." Zelda stroked his chest and patted his shoulders. "You see, there's no bugs here."

"*Ruff, ruff, ruff!*" barked Polluto, adding to the cacophony. "*Grrr-rrrr . . .*"

Kyle picked up on the "no bugs" litany. "No bugs, no bugs. There are no bugs here . . . but they're in my room! They were coming out of the walls in my room, and there was a hole in my floor, and bad men were trying to pull me into the hole!" Kyle almost choked on the words as they came out.

Zelda went into commandant mode. "Randy! Get upstairs and check Kyle's room. Kyle, it's okay. Daddy's going to check your room and make sure it's okay."

Randall felt action was obligatory and immediately ran up the stairs to check Kyle's room. *As if there would be something up there to check,* he thought.

Polluto clambered up the stairs behind him, nipping at his heels.

What the heck am I doing? I know there are no bugs up here! Or am I going crazy too? Nevertheless, Randall complied with his orders and checked in all the corners of his son's room. Finding nothing amiss, he yelled down the stairs that all the bugs were gone. He came back down and found Kyle crying, cradled in Zelda's arms.

Addie stood in the front hall, holding her stuffed calico kitty, looking at the scene. "What's wrong with Kyle, Daddy? Mommy, what's wrong?" She sniffled and started to sob.

Zelda opened her arms in invitation. "Nothing, honey. Kyle just had a bad dream. Let's do a group hug."

Randall grabbed Addie's little hand and they made a circle around Zelda and Kyle. Randall tried to ignore the smell of cigarettes and whiskey wafting off Zelda. Polluto shoved his wet nose into Kyle's armpit, then licked his face. Baldspot crouched in a far corner, registering the event in his cat notebook. After a few moments, the waterworks settled down.

Encircled by his parents, Kyle's breathing returned to normal. Randall wiped the sweat off his little boy's forehead. Randall knew the world of bad dreams and how vivid they could be. He wished he could take away the hurt, but sometimes being a parent meant coping with feeling helpless.

Zelda broke the silence with a cheery sing-song question. "Who wants some hot chocolate?"

Kyle perked up like nothing had happened. "Me!"

"Me too!" yelped Addie.

"Me, three," echoed Randall.

While they sat at the kitchen table, drinking hot chocolate, Randall and Zelda reassured Addie and Kyle about bad dreams.

Randall started out the discussion. "Nightmares can seem very real, but they can't hurt you. Even adults can have them, especially after a bad day. When you're having one, sometimes you can tell it's just a dream because of the weird stuff that happens. Then just wake yourself up."

Kyle piped up. "Like when I have a pee dream?"

Randall nodded. "Yeah, just like that."

"What's a pee dream?" asked Addie, imagining the letter "P" floating in the sky.

Zelda took over. "If you get a full bladder at night while you're sleeping and your brain doesn't hear the 'go' signal from your bladder, you can get a pee dream. In a pee dream you start looking for a bathroom but can't find one. Or you find one, but there's no toilet. Or the toilet is hanging from chains, and you can't reach it. Or you go in the dream, but feel you still need to pee. Then your brain tells you to wake up and go potty."

Addie stood up on her chair and jumped up and down. "I've had those. And I have never wet my bed. Not like some people I know."

Kyle got up on his chair to protest. "It only happened once, you pee brain, and it was an accident."

"Ha! Well, none is better than one," snarked Addie, and made a Zorro slashing motion with her imaginary sword.

Kyle turned red and was preparing a retort when Randall cut in. "Here comes the judge. Order in the court. You two, cool your jets."

Kyle wasn't quite ready to let things go, so to speak. He demanded Addie say she was sorry. Zelda ordered the two to hug and make up. After some hesitation, they did so, and things returned to semi normal. Soon the chatter turned to more mundane topics, giggling, and goofiness.

The lateness of the hour began to hit Randall and Zelda. They hustled both kids back up to bed after making both go potty first. Randall and Zelda mutually decided they would take a hiatus from earlier hostilities. They did share their concerns about Kyle's "bad dream" and wondered if that's all it was. Randall copped to the mac, weenies, and ice cream dinner as a possible cause of the nightmare, but noted it wasn't the first time such dreams had happened. There had also been some sleepwalking episodes before. They decided that, for now, they would be more careful about Kyle's diet and monitor him for a repeat episode. That would decide whether further action was needed.

They took both kids back to their beds. Addie went right off to sleep, but Kyle was so overtired that he was still jumpy. Zelda's battery life was waning, but she sat down on his bed next to him, rubbed his back, and sang him an old nursery rhyme. Randall kneeled at the foot of the bed and hummed harmony.

Kyle's eyelids finally descended like a flag at evening taps. The little man was soon asleep in the deep. Zelda had flopped forward with her head on the headboard and was already snoozing. Randall helped her get up and walked her to bed. He got another whiff of stale cigarette smoke and old booze. The fragrance made Randall angry again.

He muttered that they'd all be in bed sleeping by now, but for Zelda's little hormone-induced escapist behavior. Randall took some solace in the entertainment provided by wrestling Zelda's clothes off and putting her to bed naked. None of this even roused her, and it only frustrated Randall.

It always amazed Randall how Zelda was a super sleeper. She was able to sleep through alarm clocks, phone calls, thunderstorms, and all manner of mayhem; and she could do it in almost any position. One afternoon, Randall had come home from work and found her sitting at the kitchen table, asleep, with her head propped up on the pulled-out napkin drawer. At a formal dinner party, she greeted Mr. Sandman while eating and slumped face-down on her plate of spaghetti. It had made for interesting makeup. She rarely did sight-seeing as a car passenger, because eyelids are not transparent. Randall had concluded Zelda suffered from a classic case of "carcolepsy."

As a consequence of Zelda's sleeping talents, it was usually Randall who tended to the kids when they issued a late-night wake-up call for an emergency glass of water or had a fresh case of the upchucks. Once asleep, Zelda slept the sleep of the dead, so there was little chance she'd wake up before Randall. This night was no exception.

The upshot was that Randall was stuck with the chore of buttoning up the house for the night, which included putting the dog in his basement kennel and doing the final kid check. According to Mr. Clock, he'd have to sleep fast if he was to get up at 5:30. He reckoned he'd be lucky to get four hours of sleep. *It's already tomorrow, for pity's sake.*

When everything was finally in order, he dragged himself up to the bedroom, escaped from his clothes, and flopped into bed. He was too tired to pay much heed to the naked woman next to him. The mind was willing, but the flesh was unable.

B-17 FLYING FORTRESS-WW II

CHAPTER 8

———

YOU NEED A RESERVATION

"If you are still breathing, you have a second chance."

— Oprah Winfrey

Come Morning

The next morning came too soon. It was still dark when Randall had to get up, and a bitter winter wind shook the house. He stumbled to the bathroom, with barely enough energy to switch on the light. When he looked in the mirror, he wished he'd left the light off. Randall wondered who belonged to the haggard face that stared back at him.

Randall moved as quietly as possible. He didn't want to risk a time-sucking encounter with Zelda. Although it was a low risk that she'd wake up, he didn't want to push his luck. Her hair still smelled of cigarette smoke, maybe with a hint of *au d'cannabis*, from her carousing the night before. The thought made him angry again, but he took some small comfort in that she had come home safely. Things could have been much worse.

Randall snuck into Kyle's room, stepping over a toy Millennium Falcon and a TIE Fighter. A herd of vicious Legos conspired to attack Randall's foot, but he managed to stifle his cry of pain and make it to Kyle's pile of blankets. Among a suspicious number of dirty socks and used tissues, Kyle slept like a puppy, panting and drooling slightly. Compared to his loud and frenetic waking state, Kyle looked so innocent

97

and peaceful. Randall leaned down to kiss Kyle's forehead but decided maybe it wouldn't be very sanitary. He chose instead to take an internal snapshot of the moment and reflect upon it when his patience with Kyle's antics ran short.

Randall negotiated his way out of the room without further attacks from Toyland and crossed the hall to Addie's room. Pictures of kittens and horses adorned the bedroom door. She loved anything fluffy and cute. The path to her bed was lined with stuffed animals, doll clothes, her own discarded dress and undies, and other soft detritus. Among the throngs of stuffed animals surrounding her, Addie seemed tiny in her big bed. She held her bedraggled calico kitty in one arm.

Ever since Addie was a baby, she had periodic asthma attacks, especially if she caught a cold. But the attacks could be set off by dust or pollen, animal dander, or Mars in the wrong declination. When the attacks were bad, she got extremely short of breath and overly anxious. Not being able to breathe set off her "fight or flight" response. There were many nights when Randall sat at her bedside to keep her calm. He read books, made up stories, and sang songs.

If an attack was really bad, he gave her a subcutaneous shot of adrenaline. He hated having to stick her little arm with a needle, but it usually worked when nothing else would. It was always a relief to see her able to take a deep breath again, but the drug left her agitated for several hours afterward. Her hands shook, and restful sleep was a long time coming. He was uncomfortable leaving her side until she fell asleep. Even then he checked her breathing by holding a small mirror up to her nose to be sure it fogged up. Then he'd haul himself off to bed to sleep a few hours before morning, and race to work for another day at the VA circus.

No need to do the mirror check this morning. Addie was snoring with a soft little whistling sound. Randall tip-toed through the stuffed animals and went downstairs. He grabbed his thermos of coffee, a breakfast sandwich, his briefcase, and a warm hat, then headed out. In the garage, the Scirocco grumbled about the cold, but started anyway, not unlike Randall. Most of the Creekside Place inhabitants were not yet stirring as Randall directed the balky car up to 84th Street and the freeway.

The VA was just beginning to come alive when Randall made his way inside. It seemed as if he never left. He felt like he hadn't slept the previous night so, in effect, Monday never really ended. Randall was almost grateful for the busy day ahead. It would keep his mind occupied enough not to dwell on whatever Kyle's bug dream was all about. He thought it might be a night terror, but child psychology skills were not in his toolbox. The double doors at the department's entrance were still closed and locked. It was too early for any of the staff to be in yet. He put down his gear and unlocked the doors.

As Randall entered the department and closed the doors behind him, he recalled how the deceased Swindell had appeared in this very spot the day before. It gave him a chill and the hint of an odor like spoiled milk. It still wasn't making any sense. He decided to put that thought temporarily in the same lockbox as Kyle's bug dream. Kyle might need to see a child psychologist, sooner rather than later. Both problems could be taken out and examined in greater depth when there was more time and energy. This was not that time.

Randall determined just to immerse himself in the present and focus on getting through the day. On his desk were copies of the documents Melinda put together. He busied himself reviewing the data and dictating the five consults. By the time he finished, the staff had arrived and begun the workday.

Melinda popped into his office. "'Morning, Chief. Did I get everything you needed from the stuff I copied? Did you get any sleep last night? You look like you've been 'rode hard and put away wet.'"

Randall stomped his foot and whinnied. "Neigh! Not a wink! I need me some oats! I'm grateful you were here to help—you did a great job. I had everything I needed and just finished the dictations. I'm ready to start the new day. But you are correct in noting that my tank is running a bit low. Nothing a fresh cup of joe can't fix."

Melinda swooped over and grabbed Randall's nearly empty cup. "Coming right up, Dr. B."

While Melinda was fetching, Doris came in and delivered morning greetings and several stacks of paperwork. She plopped them on Randall's desk.

Randall returned the greeting and groaned. "Dang paperwork is like chickweed. Pull it out and next time you look, there's more."

Doris clucked. "Don't you go and try to make me feel sorry about it. Just doin' my job. Why are you here so early? You're no robin, and you don't like worms."

Randall gave his best Jack Nicholson smirk. "I was here paying you back in advance for the stuff you just dumped on me. If you check your Dictaphone recorder, there's five, count them, five new consult dictations on it. And the best news? They are all STAT consults and need to be on the hospital charts by end of day. And I know you can do it, honey."

Doris scoffed. "Saddle up and ride your sad horse outta town, mister!"

"Gladly. I guess I'll be leaving now." Randall got up and feigned preparing to go home.

Doris stammered. "You . . . you . . . can't do . . . Nice try! I got your halter tied up here. Now sit down before I hobble you!"

Randall reversed gears. "Just cranking your chain. I'm not going anywhere until I finish my second cup of coffee. Give me the highlights of today's cockfight."

Doris shook her head. "It's too early to be crankin' any of my appendages. Alright, here's the highlights of your day. There's seven treatment reviews, five follow-ups, and another batch of consults. That makes a total of about two dozen, including what came in yesterday, not figgerin' for anythin' extra that comes today. How many can you handle?"

"How many we got left?" asked Randall.

"About seven, but I think we can get by with three for today. I'll probably be typin' up your five new ones all day anyhow."

"Any meetings I need to know about?" asked Randall.

Doris nodded. "Just the compliance officer at 2:00. Nothing else so far, but the day is young. Never know what other tomfoolery the front office folks might come up with."

Randall screwed up his face. "Sounds doable. You know, Melinda helped me a lot yesterday. I'm thinking I might use her again today to get through this mess."

"How did she help?" asked Doris.

Randall looked up and collated the effort in his mind. "Got patients into the rooms, did preliminary interviews, babysat them when necessary, and provided lots of help with key document copying. She saved you a lot of work."

Melinda came back with Randall's fresh coffee. "Here you go, Chief." She even threw in a little curtsy.

Doris gawked as Melinda served Randall. "If he's a chief, am I an Indian?"

Melinda was quick on the draw. "We all are, Doris. We just exist to serve and protect. From what I've seen so far, you are a master at that very job. He's the only doc we've got, and we have to save his skinny butt, even if it's only from himself."

Doris could not help but laugh out loud. "I can live with that. I think the old chief here would like your assistance again today. Are you game, Pocahontas?"

Melinda squinted as if the sun was in her eyes. "Given my lack of rapport with certain techs out there, I think helping you is feasible. That is, if it's okay with Sitting Bull."

Randall grunted and grimaced like an old Indian chief. "How! Plan seem good to me. Me finish magic bean water and papyrus. Then prepare raid on patients. Now go from my teepee."

When Randall completed the paperwork and signed off on the dictation, he walked through Doris's office on his way to see patients. She handed him a telephone note.

Randall did an eye roll. "Not more distractions!"

"Calm down, Dr. B," soothed Doris. "Your friend Dr. Shepard just now called. He says it's been a while and wondered if you wanted to have a lunch meet up and catch up."

Randall gaped a bit. "Dang, I was just thinking about calling him. Can you call him back for me and tell him I'm busy right now? But I promise to take him up on that offer soon, as long as he pays."

Doris nodded. "I'll make it happen, but a bit more politely than what you just said. Should I set somethin' up?"

Randall shook his head. "Not just now. Tell him I'll call soon. Find out when is a good time to call."

Doris nodded. "Will do."

Randall walked to the hallway, past waiting patients, and headed to the treatment console. On the counter was the rack holding the charts of the reviews and follow-ups that had arrived thus far. Instead of avoiding the waiting patients, he uncharacteristically greeted them as he passed, shook some hands and, at the chart rack, motioned for Melinda to meet with him.

Randall took the first chart from the rack and scanned the contents. He narrated the case in summary as Melinda listened. It was a follow-up visit by a patient who had been treated with radiation for early-stage prostate cancer. A Polaroid headshot on the inside front cover showed an older Native American man.

Melinda had a question. "I've noticed these Polaroids on the charts. I think I know why they're used, but I was wondering how it got started."

Randall liked questions, but today he was reluctant to use up valuable time answering them. Nevertheless, he felt a good answer was fair. He explained that he had begun the routine of taking the Polaroid headshots to beef up their patient ID procedure after an unfortunate incident. And Polaroids were not the sole solution.

The techs had called for "Mr. Jones," who was next up for treatment, but Jones had gone to the men's room. "Mr. Smith" decided he'd waited long enough and responded to the call. The techs failed to notice that "Mr. Smith" was not "Mr. Jones," took him into the treatment room, and gave him "Mr. Jones'" treatment. When "Mr. Jones" came back from the men's room and asked when he was going to be treated, the techs realized their error.

The good news was that both were being treated for prostate cancer, and their treatment fields and dose were quite similar. The bad news was that Randall had to explain the mistake to both patients. That had gone pretty well, but he was royally pissed about the error and went on a rant about proper ID. The techs complained bitterly about having to verify name, birthdate, Social Security number, and photo check before each daily treatment. However, they soon chose acceptance as less distasteful than a repetitious Randall rant.

Felix

By the time Randall finished the monologue, Melinda seemed anxious to proceed. "Well, Dr. B, are we ready to talk about the patient?"

"Ah, yes," said Randall. "Onward and upward. He is Mr. Felix Sternfellow, a Menominee Indian. He lives way up in northern Wisconsin on the Menominee Reservation. To get here, he drives to Iron Mountain, Michigan, where, at 4:00 a.m., along with forty other vets, he catches the VA bus to Milwaukee. Veterans who make that long trip just for a routine follow-up deserve VIP treatment."

Melinda looked amazed. "Wow. I'm not sure I'd go through all that just to see you."

Randall looked hurt. "The heck you say."

"*Ooops*. That didn't come out right," said Melinda. "I meant it would probably be okay to see a VA doctor closer to home. Like at the Iron Mountain VA. And if there's a problem, they could contact you by phone for further instructions."

Randall backpedaled a bit. "You're right. And they do have that option. But oddly enough, some of these guys enjoy the bus ride, and they seem to like coming back just to visit. I'm sure it's not all my charming personality."

Melinda smiled. "I'm sure you're right."

Randall blinked and cleared his throat, then continued. "Mr. Sternfellow completed treatment two years ago. He's been doing well, and his PSA has remained unmeasurable. PSA is a blood test marker for prostate cancer activity. It looks like today's result is still good. We just need to see if he's having any aftereffects from the radiation and any symptoms of new disease. Sometimes the PSA does not pick up a recurrence if a more aggressive form of the cancer grows back."

"I see," said Melinda, taking notes. "Should I go get him? It looks like he may need some help."

Randall nodded. "Sure, you go ahead. I'll meet you in the room."

Mr. Sternfellow, a large bearish man, graying at the temples, sat in a wheelchair by the front doors where he had just been deposited by Ira, the transport clerk. Ira had seen Melinda for the first time earlier in the day and noted the way the generic white uniform didn't look so generic on her. He just stood next to the wheelchair, gawking at her. Melinda waved to Mr. Sternfellow and announced she was coming to get him. Ira took the cue and whisked the wheelchair down the hall to the exam room door.

Somewhat surprised by the sudden action, Melinda took a step back. Ira turned beet red and stammered his explanation. "Here's your customer . . . uh, your patient . . . *hmm* . . . Mrs . . . I mean, Ms . . ."

Melinda knew his job was to deliver patients to the department, not anything further. She just smiled and thanked him for the help. The smile stunned Ira into silence.

Ira nodded wordlessly, then dashed off down the hall.

Melinda approached Mr. Sternfellow and noticed his baseball cap, which had "World War II Veteran" stitched on one side and the profile of a B-17 bomber above the brim.

"Mr. Sternfellow?" asked Melinda.

His slouched body looked tired, and he kept his eyes on her shoes. "Yes, Ma'am. That's me. All day, every day. No one else wanna be me."

Melinda let her smile come through in her voice. "You look perfectly fine to me. Here, I'm going to roll you into the exam room for Dr. B and get some vital signs. Then he'll be in to see you. My name is Melinda. I'm helping him today. I like your hat. Did you fly one of those planes in the war?"

"I flew *in* one," corrected Mr. Sternfellow.

Randall walked into the exam room, overhearing the tail end of the conversation about the B-17 hat. It was new news to him. He reached out to shake the patient's hand. "Hey, there, Mr. Sternfellow. Good to see you. Hope you're doing well."

Mr. Sternfellow shrugged. "Fair to middlin', Doc. Pretty good shape for the shape I'm in. I studied all night for my urine test. Hope I get a good score."

Randall chuckled. "Good one, Mr. Sternfellow. It may shock you, but I've never heard that one before." Melinda was a tick behind the beat but got the joke and laughed as well.

The patient waved an arm. "That's 'cause I just made it up. Doc, Miss Melinda, just call me Felix. Sternfellow is too serious."

Randall nodded agreement. "Okay, Felix. Did I hear correctly that you were on a B-17 crew? How come I never knew that?"

Felix shrugged again. "You never asked."

Randall put the chart down on the exam table. "Well, I'm asking now. We have a few extra minutes for the story. Shoot."

Felix hesitated for a bit. Randall knew vets were not always forthcoming about wartime experiences. So he didn't want to press.

Then something seemed to click, and Felix began. As he went into memory, his language became more accented. "Funny you say 'shoot.' Here's why. My Menominee spirit name is Flying Bear. It was given to me at Elder Ceremony. When I was young boy, I big like a bear and a fast runner. Now still big, but not so fast. My spirit name is how I come to fly in a big bird in Army. That what shaman say, anyhow."

Felix chuckled to himself, apparently lost in memories. Randall and Melinda sat patiently, knowing the full story would come in Menominee time. After a long pause, Felix continued, "I could speak many things, but we not have sweat lodge time. Instead I tell you how I die three times in one day in Germany sky."

Randall and Melinda exchanged surprised glances. Randall thought, *not another Lazarus story!* Melinda didn't know what to think.

Felix looked into the distance, more upright and energized. "Flying Bear was tail gunner on B-17. A corporal. Sit in plastic bubble tail of plane. Keep lookout for German fighter planes. Messerschmitts. Fokkers. They the worst. I call 'em 'mother Fokkers.'"

Melinda was getting excited. "Did your bomber have big guns? Could they shoot down a Fokker?"

Felix nodded. "Tail gunner have two 50-caliber machine guns. Make Swiss cheese of Fokker, but hard to hit. They fly fast. Anyway, we flying on mission 21. Still remember. Mission part of operation Tidal Wave. Over 1,000 B-17s fly that day. We lucky. Many squadrons lose planes and crews on way to target, but we still flying. P51 Mustang fighters fly with us to protect, but we not have enough. Too many Jerry fighters. Then it just us and our guns. Sitting ducks. If not German fighters, it flak so thick you could walk on it in air."

"Wow, I'd be so scared I'd wet my . . ." Randall shook his head. "Could the B-17s maneuver at all to get away from the fighters?"

Felix didn't move his head, just kept his eyes straight forward. "Not with full bomb load. Need to go straight to target and back or run out of fuel and ditch plane in English Channel. Even empty plane handle like birchbark canoe. We take heavy flak on way to hunting ground in Ploiesti. Big oil refinery. Flak made many holes in body and tail, real close to me. I not hit, and plane still fly okay. Get to target. Can see nothing. Big clouds cover everything. Pilot have to turn around to go back to base in England."

"Oh, my goodness," exclaimed Melinda. "You flew all that way and couldn't drop your bombs?"

So you were bombstipated. Randall held back saying that out loud.

Felix held up his arms as if showing the bank of clouds. "Yes, but many B-17s found holes in clouds, dropped bombs and wipe out oil tanks. We fly away and I see black smoke clouds behind us many feet high. Ploiesti soon be ashes."

"Well, at least you got to fly back safely!" offered Melinda.

Felix grunted. "Bear not out of trap yet, Little Dove. Bomb load is 6,000 pounds. Makes plane too heavy to fly back on little fuel. So pilot drop to 3,000 feet, fly over empty farm field and drop bombs. No one to hurt. One bomb drop too soon and blow up big barn. Pilot take plane up higher and almost there. Fokker dive from above. Strafe us with cannon fire. Nearly cut plane in half. Both starboard engines on fire. Wing fuel tank blow up. Whole front of plane on fire and plane drop from sky."

Randall realized he had stopped breathing. "My God! What did you do then?"

"I sit, strapped in tail gunner seat. Think that I soon dead. It is all over. Time to meet Great Spirit. This first time I die."

Melinda furrowed her brow. "But you're still here! The Great Spirit must have sent you back."

"Ways of Great Spirit mysterious, Miss Melinda," said Felix.

Jumping from an Imperfect Airplane

"How did you get out on time?" asked Randall.

"Great Spirit yell in my head. Get big butt out! Spirit help brave who help self. Unbuckle quick like rabbit, squeeze out of tail gun pod like new baby. Fire coming fast from front. Want to run other way, but must go through fire to get out. I think maybe I squeeze out through hole for waist machine gun, but no parachute. Flying Bear can't fit in tail gun pod with chute on. Waist gunner dead on floor covered in blood. His chute full of bullet holes, but I take off him and put on me."

Melinda sucked in a breath. "How did you know it would still work?"

Felix laughed ironically. "Better choice than fire. I barely fit through the hole with chute on but squeeze through. Hang outside plane. Ask Great Spirit help me. Let go into empty air. I fall and pray, then pull ripcord. Chute open and grab body like bird claws. I float down. Give thanks for chute." Felix took a big breath. "But plane fall next to me and explode. Chute catch fire, fall like rock."

"The chute caught fire?" blurted Melinda. "How high up were you?"

Felix laughed at the question. "Not sure, but high enough to die when hit ground. Take long time to fall. Too long. Time to think. Remember life mistakes. Check self. . . shirt burn off. No more worry. All over soon. Forget mistakes. Second time I die that day."

Randall figured that there was another miracle coming but couldn't imagine what it would be. Not many survive a free fall. "So did the Great Spirit reach out and catch you?"

Melinda forgot herself. "Did you live?"

Felix nodded and smiled, gesturing to his chest. "Looks like it." He continued his story. "As I falling, look down, see smoke from barn we bomb. It same farmer's field. I close eyes and wait to hit ground. I not hit ground. I land on back in large haystack. I think, me dead? I open eyes, see sky. I frozen, then legs and arms work. Thank Spirit, lay back and rest. Then I . . ."

There was a pounding on the exam room door. The door flew open, and Grace poked her head in.

"There you are! We've been looking for you. Why are you in here?" shouted Grace.

"Where else should I be?" asked Randall calmly.

She directed her nose at Melinda. "I meant her, wise guy. We need her help."

"Well, you'll have to carry on somehow, because Melinda is helping me now. We're in the middle of an important follow up, so unless it's a fire emergency or a code, don't bother us. Please close the door quietly on your way out." Randall maintained a quiet but commanding voice.

Grace grunted once and did as she was told.

Randall encouraged Felix to continue. "Sorry for the rude interruption. Please finish the story."

Felix went on to explain that after resting, he gingerly rolled himself off the haystack only to encounter a farmer, his wife, and two sons running toward him, wielding shovels and rakes. They began to beat Felix with the farm implements, screaming something in German. He understood not a word but figured they were trying to convey their annoyance with his B-17 disposing 6,000 pounds of bombs on their farmland.

Just before Felix almost faded into unconsciousness from the beating, he heard the sound of an approaching vehicle and different loud voices yelling, "*Halten sie!*"

The voices belonged to German stormtroopers who pulled the farm family off Felix and stopped the beating. They threw Felix in the back of their *Kubelwagen* and hauled him off to prison camp.

Randall interrupted again. "Don't tell me. That's the third time you died that day. And like before, it was another unlikely savior. A German officer. Your Great Spirit surely is mysterious. I'm going to have a chat with him."

Felix again nodded. "As say on your TV, *Cowabunga*."

He shook with a full belly laugh and continued. Turned out prison camp was a plum assignment. The Germans had imprisoned him in an American officer detention center. Since it was a camp strictly for American officers, he received special treatment, which included medical care, good food, and decent beds. They rather unenthusiastically interrogated him for information about deployment of Allied forces.

"They didn't torture you for information?" asked Melinda.

"No, they no torture officers," said Felix.

"But you said you were just a corporal. Why did they think you were an officer?" asked Randall.

Felix explained that American propaganda had led the Germans to believe all crew members on Allied planes were officers. In this way, if captured, they would not be tortured like enlisted men. In addition to that, Felix had further perplexed his German captors by only speaking in the Menominee language. They took it as some kind of code talk and tried unsuccessfully to break the code during his detainment. Two months later, the camp was liberated by the Allies, and Felix was freed, fully recovered from his injuries.

"That's amazing," said Melinda. "If the prison camp had been worse, you could have died four times."

Felix nodded stoically. "Three times enough. I am bear, not cat."

"Felix, I am really surprised. I've known you for two years, and you never told me any of that," said Randall.

"You never have time." Felix winked at Randall. "And Young Dove not with you before."

"So true," said Randall. "Just one more question. I have other Menominee patients who don't speak Menominee. How is it that you are so fluent?"

Felix nodded. "Some people want forget tradition. Not me. I lucky."

Felix further explained that both of his parents spoke Menominee when he was growing up as well as English. Later, he was chosen by the elders to teach Menominee to the schoolchildren on the reservation, so the language would not die. Since the war, that is what he had done. Sadly, of late, the children didn't want to learn the old ways. They wanted to fit into the white world.

Felix lamented that he couldn't find other speakers in the tribe who wanted to teach Menominee when he was gone. "I afraid language die with me. When I die fourth time."

Melinda and Randall found it hard to know what to say next, and Felix seemed to be done talking. For the first time, Randall understood why the left side of Felix's face was scarred. Randall waited several beats and began asking about his present health. Soon the exam was completed, and Randall assured him that the cancer seemed to be gone.

"Your fourth death is far off, my friend. You have graduated to once-a-year follow up. I'm honored that you have told us your story. We will keep it sacred," said Randall.

He helped usher Felix back out into the hallway where they both endured dagger stares from Grace. It had been a long "exam," but one he was glad he had not rushed through. Randall was thankful to the Great Spirit for all he'd learned by just listening.

Sometimes patients had a lot to teach.

Jumping
OVERBOARD.
9-JUMP/OVERBOARD
10/22 RB

CHAPTER 9

COMPLIANCE IS MANDATORY

"All I want is compliance with my wishes, after reasonable discussion."

—Winston Churchill

TOTE THAT BARGE

It was way past noon when Randall and Melinda finished the morning's workload. The long follow-up with Mr. Sternfellow set them somewhat behind, but Randall still wasn't sorry about that. Randall sent Melinda off for lunch and headed to his office to ravage his bag lunch. Walking through Doris's office, he saw that his office door was closed.

Doris rose from her desk and motioned for him to stop. "Sorry, Dr. B, I didn't want to interrupt you, but I thought you were kind of runnin' behind. It's 2:00, and the compliance officer is waiting in your office. Did you forget?"

"Of course, I did. I never remember stuff I don't want to do," Randall whispered, thinking about how he might be able to sneak away. "What's he like?"

"Well, he's got on a nice suit, a floral jungle tie, and his shoes need shinin', but he seems like a nice man. His hair is sort of unusual, but it's neat." She gave him her best motherly look from below furrowed eyebrows. "His name is Winston Samuels. Be nice to him."

"I'm always nice," said Randall.

"Of course you are, Dr. B. Just be extra nice today, okay?"

"I will be compliant, but I'm hungry and haven't had my lunch yet. This meeting stands between me and food. Not a good game plan."

Doris clucked her tongue. "You poor boy. However will you survive without immediate sustenance?"

"Will my sacrifices never end!" said Randall, putting the back of his hand against his forehead like Scarlett O'Hara. "Oh, well, my duty comes first."

Randall heaved a great sigh and headed for his office door.

He found Mr. Samuels sitting in the government-issue gray chair next to his desk. Doris's description was fairly accurate except for just a few details. The man had skin as dark as ebony and his long hair was done up in cornrows. The big man rose from the chair and towered over Randall. He held out a hand that, to Randall, looked like a baseball mitt. At first, Randall was afraid to put his hand in that potential bone crusher, but he manned up and took it.

Mr. Samuels was first to speak. "So good to finally meet you, Dr. Biedermeier. My name is Winston Samuels, but everybody calls me Winnie. Please. You do so as well."

Randall was frozen. *Winnie? As in 'The Pooh?' How am I gonna say that with a straight face?* He found his voice and responded. "My pleasure, Winnie. Everybody calls me Dr. B. Please do so as well."

Randall found himself responding with the same lilting Jamaican accent as Mr. Samuels. He was immediately embarrassed that this might be viewed as mocking, but Mr. Samuels saved the day.

Samuels continued shaking Randall's entire arm. "You know, Dr. B, It's a funny *t'ing*, but whenever I speak to people the first time they like my accent so much they use it too. It must be infectious. *Ha, Ha, Ha.*" The man had a deep and profound laugh. The walls seemed to vibrate.

Randall stuttered a bit. *Is this a tradition I should be aware of? Am I being tested? Am I passing?!* "S . . .s . . .orry, not sure why that happened. Guess I caught the infection too. Didn't mean to offend you."

The handshake continued as Mr. Samuels stared Randall straight in

the eye. Randall blinked first and took in the man's details as they stood
with clasped hands. His suit did little to hide his massive shoulders and
arms. When the shake finally ended, Randall invited him to sit. Randall
rotated his desk chair and sat as well.

The Uncola

Samuels spoke in a deep baritone. His voice and manner reminded Randall of the actor Geoffrey Holder who he'd seen in a number of commercials for the soft drink 7UP. In the commercial, Holder appears in a white suit and large white hat explaining that the Uncola drink is special because it's made from the Uncola nut and it's "simply mahvelous." Here in person though, Randall didn't feel so mahvelous.

"So, Winnie. What can I do for you?" Randall wiped his sweaty palms on his grubby lab coat. Samuels rubbed his hands together and crossed his legs, displaying woven leather sandals, perhaps a new trend in winter footwear.

"Dr. B, I am so honored for us to finally meet! Ha ha ha! I will try to explain my business here. First let me say that I am a Vietnam veteran, and I have talked with many of my veteran friends who have been patients down here. They all tell me what a wonderful job you are doing. Many VA colleagues here say the same t'ing."

Randall blushed a bit. "That's great to hear. I wasn't aware anyone upstairs noticed us."

"Oh, quite to the contrary, sir. We are very aware of this department. We've been reviewing the performance of all our departments and must tell you that this is one of the most efficient. Every department in this hospital should run as efficiently as yours. Ha ha ha!"

Randall began feeling a bit suspicious that the flattery was preparation for something onerous. "*Hmm.* There's an old saying that 'no good deed goes unpunished.'"

Mr. Samuels repeated his deep Uncola laugh. "Ha! So you are growing suspicious that I am a Greek bearing gifts. Let me assure you, I am not Greek. The only gift I have for you is here in my pocket. I know I am interrupting your lunch, so I brought you a bag of Chippie's Banana Chips to tide you over. Here, give them a try. They are a Jamaican snack favorite, and I have been told you favor bah-nah-nahs."

Randall's mouth watered. He took the bag, opened it, and tried one. "These are delicious!"

"Mahvelous!!" replied Samuels. "Ha ha ha! I am so glad you like them. Perhaps you can eat them with your lunch while I explain my business."

"That's a great idea. Where can I buy these Chippie's?"

"Oh, that would be a secret. They would only be available by special arrangement." Mr. Samuels winked.

Randall felt oddly confused and a little scared but tried to hide it. He only nodded. "I get the picture. Go ahead. You talk. I'll eat and listen."

No Good Deed

Samuels explained that the VA had long-range plans to supplement the meager budget it was allotted by Congress. They hoped to make up the deficit by using private medical insurance carriers whenever a veteran had such coverage. Many veterans double-dipped by coming to the VA once a year to a primary care physician for a chronic illness and getting the VA to cover the cost of multiple prescriptions. But for other medical care, these veterans would go to private clinics and hospitals because they distrusted the quality of VA care for procedures and diagnostics. This saved such patients the cost of co-pays when their private insurance won't cover all the cost of expensive meds. The problem with this plan was that the VA had never been designed to charge fees to veterans when there was a gap in coverage, since its budget was determined by inpatient and outpatient visit statistics.

Randall felt like he just stepped off the Tilt-A-Whirl. "This does not sound like anything in my bailiwick," said Randall. Most budgetary talk flew noisily over his head like a flock of three-wattled bellbirds.

Samuels looked at Randall like a grade-school teacher trying to catch young Billy up on a lecture from last month. "Ah, but I think it is. What you do here can easily be broken down into codes that link to specific charges. I have done some research and your national groups, such as the American College of Radiology, have published procedure code criteria that could easily be used for the purpose. The other group, I think you call it ASTRO, has done similar work. We just need to work with you and your staff to determine a method to record this data. So simple!"

Randall's mind was trying to tread water with one leg tied behind his back. "That's where we might have a problem or two. My staff is busier than the little boy who dropped his bubblegum in the chicken coop just keeping up with the daily workload. And the VA won't authorize overtime if we have to extend the treatment day."

Samuels squinted at Randall. "You have a chicken coop?"

Randall chuckled. "I guess you were not a farm boy. Let's say we're busier than a four-way cold tablet trying to go all four ways at once."

"Ah! Now I understand. Again, this is so simple! We are prepared to provide you with an additional clerical staff person to help with this. But your other staff will have to assist as well," said Samuels.

So many details to wrap his mind around! Randall grabbed some paper to start scribbling notes.

Samuels broke into a toothy smile. "I have been assured that a third RTT position may be authorized, and that overtime can be used for your current two RTTs while we are recruiting for the new position. Let me assure you the new position was not related to your chicken coop humor."

Randall laughed. "I didn't think so. Tell me more. This is getting interesting." Randall prepared to take more notes, thinking he'd better get the proposal on record. This gift horse might be a real boon. He figured there would probably be a price to pay for all this goodness so best compose a rebuttal in advance.

Samuels cleared his throat loudly. "Ah, I suspect you're soon going to tell me why you can't do all this, but before you bombard me with those reasons, there's one more area to cover. My staff and I have done an analysis of the coordination of care or, shall I say, the lack of it, especially for oncology care. Patients who need some combination of radiation therapy, chemotherapy, and surgery get boggled by conflicting appointments."

Samuels put his hand on his belly and laughed, as if recalling a joke punchline. "Ha ha ha! Scheduling for diagnostic studies adds to the confusion. Thus we have proposed the creation of a new position. We are calling it 'patient advocate.'" He swished his hand in the air, like defining a rainbow. "The appointee will work with each patient requiring such overlapping care to coordinate their schedules and speak with the necessary leaders on their behalf."

Randall smiled and nodded with delight. "That's something I've been requesting for years, but to no avail."

Samuels grunted loudly. "Where do you think they got the idea? I mention this now to alert you that the new appointee will be reporting to you in the next several days."

Randall's head almost spun off his neck. "What?! The old VA mare never moves that quickly!"

"Ha ha ha! Her name is Elizabeth Angeles. You will be her lead. We are aware that you already hold a weekly conference with Hematology/Oncology and Radiation Oncology departments that you call the HORO conference. She will be part of that conference. We'd like you two to move toward adding Surgical Oncology to the mix."

Randall couldn't resist the opportunity to alliterate. "So if we add Surgical Oncology, it will become the HOROSO conference. We may as well add Radiology, Pathology, and Dietary down the line!" he joked.

To his surprise, Samuels raised his arms in praise. "Ha ha ha! We are distilling the same rum! That is exactly right! But please stop at HOROSO. We don't need a HOROSORAPADI conference if we add Radiology, Pathology and Dietary. That makes it sound like a song from *The Sound of Music*."

Randall looked shocked. *Where had this miracle come from?*

Samuels read Randall's expression well. "Don't act so surprised. Your constant reminders to administration acted like Chinese water torture. They figured if they finally gave you what you've been repeatedly asking them for that you'd finally stop bugging them."

Randall laughed. "Well, sure. I'll stop pestering them about that, but I've got more in the pipeline."

Samuels grimaced. "I figured you did. Go ahead, give it to me."

Randall did as requested. "I'd like to add that ACR and ASTRO have also published criteria for space and equipment based on patient load and complexity of cases treated. The data you're proposing to collect can also be used to that end. I have already collected such information, and would it surprise you to learn that we currently have 50 percent of the recommended space, equipment, and personnel?"

Samuels raised his eyebrows. "I did not know that, sir."

Randall seemed to get six inches taller. "We have 1,500 square feet and one treatment unit to service 500 new cases per year. That translates to forty to fifty patients under treatment per day to be managed by one physician and two RTTs. We have .75 radiation physicists and one full time secretary. The ACR guidelines for our patient load are 3,500 square feet, two treatment units, five RTTs and two MDs. Plus, we need a simulator. I'm just saying," added Randall.

Samuels looked shocked. "My goodness. I did not realize. Let me say again what a fine job you are doing despite a shortage of resources. I cannot help you with all of that, but I can help to the extent I mentioned. It may be a good start toward your goals. Are you willing to work with me on this?" asked Samuels.

"No need to twist my arm! Indeed I am. What's the next step?" asked Randall.

"Mahvelous!" enjoined Samuels followed by his rumbling laugh. "I'll not be twisting arms, sir. Only lemons. I've seen the commercial too. All we need now is to arrange a one-hour meeting with your staff in which I will explain what I've told you. Then we will develop the forms to collect the data. Simple!"

Randall rose from his desk chair and tried to stand as tall as he could. He motioned for Samuels to join him and patted his shoulder as they exited the office to set up the meeting date with Doris. This day was going better than it had started.

Randall gestured toward the secretary's desk. "I believe you have met Doris already. She will do her magic and come up with a date that works the best."

"Oh, Miss Doris had already worked her *maah-gic* on me," said Samuels with a prolonged emphasis on the 'ma' of magic. "Her sweet tea is bewitching."

Doris blushed to carmine and put her hand to her mouth. "I know a good thing when I see it. By the look on Dr. B's face, you two must have had a particularly fine meetin'," giggled Doris.

"We have, we have, and I look forward to our next meeting," said Samuels. After setting the meeting date, Samuels gave Randall a brisk handshake, winked at Doris, and took his leave.

Doris fanned her pink cheeks. "Quite a handsome man, don't you think, Dr. B?"

"I hadn't noticed," deadpanned Randall. "He certainly had some interesting news for us that may be good. I'll tell you more when I can. You can't believe every promise you get, especially from a slick talker like him. Every fox is smiling when he steals eggs from the chicken coop. Anyway, did anything else happen while I was in the meeting?"

"Dr. B, you sound just like my grandpappy when he was dealin' for tobacco. I'll trust you'll share when you can. Well, there's two reviews waitin' and one consult. Other than that, let's see. Oh, we got this from the Chief of Staff's office. I thought it might need a look see right away," said Doris.

"Boy, we never get anything good from that office." Randall grabbed the interoffice brown envelope and unwound the red string tie from the flap. He pulled out a short memo and read it.

"Anything earth shatterin'?" asked Doris.

"To them, maybe. To me, not so much. It says that I have been selected to do building inspections on the grounds along with some other department heads," said Randall.

"Inspections? Here in the hospital? Whatever for?" asked Doris.

Randall shook his head. "The memo says that there are over 100 buildings on the forty-five acres that make up the VA grounds and that many of them have historic designation. Some date back to the 1860s, and the VA administration is required to inspect them periodically to maintain that status. Many are unoccupied."

Doris turned slightly red in the face. "Why have doctors doin' inspections? They don't have enough time to see patients as it is! There are more administrators than they need, and they just sit around creatin' make-work for us to do. Why not engineerin'?"

"Exactly my thoughts, but since the administration may have good plans for us, this may not be a good time to be uncooperative," said Randall.

"Really? Did Mr. Samuels have enough good news from on high to make up for time-wastin' inspections?" asked Doris.

Randall nodded. "Seems likely, if I read Samuels correctly. But there's no free lunch. We may have to play some games to get the payoff. What I've learned, so far, is that you need to have their attention to get what's needed. You can be an aggravating squeaky wheel or a cooperative well-oiled gear. I hate being the former. I don't want to succeed by aggravation. So I guess I am more comfortable with the latter. I think if encounters with us are not onerous and it makes them look good in the process, it's a win-win."

"At last! We might get an ark to save all our animals," rejoiced Doris.

Randall raised a fist in the air. "Find out when I have to be at the orientation, and tell the COS office that I'm a history buff. But good news, I will be clothed."

"Oh, Dr. B, I hope so! You are such a cad. I'm on it, Chief," said Doris. "Notch one for the good guys . . . I think."

CHAPTER 10

———

WHAT'S IN A NAME?

"The world is full of obvious things which nobody, by any chance, ever observes."

—The Hound of the Baskervilles, Arthur Conan Doyle

Old Spice and BO

By the time Mr. Samuels left the department it was 2:45, and there was still half a day's work to do. Somehow it would all get done, but the techs would have to put in for overtime. Grace and Molly complained bitterly to Randall that they would not get out at 4:30 again! The heavy workload was cited repeatedly. Randall just kept quiet and listened. He dreamed of a day he would get out at 4:30 or get overtime. Salaried folks left only when the work was done.

That's why I get the big bucks. How's that song go? You work sixteen hours, and someone owns your soul?

His mind snapped back to the discussion with Samuels. For the first time, Randall had a possible answer to the staffing shortage, but he wouldn't reveal it to the techs . . . not just yet.

After the tech ranting subsided, Randall, Grace, Molly, and Melinda hunkered down around the treatment console to finish up charting for the day. Melinda had found a space near the end of the console to help however she could. With the sudden drop off in external stimuli, every-one's adrenalin had reached a nadir. Randall squinted at the entries on the treatment sheet which seemed to have become rather fuzzy. Molly mumbled to herself and erased an incorrect addition. Grace had finally cleared all the "night before" vodka from her system, and her irritation level had moderated to the point that she almost stopped grumping. Randall looked over at Melinda, and noted that even from a distance, and despite the long day, she still looked clean, fresh, and unwrinkled.

Melinda took advantage of the lull and dared break the silence. "*Uh*, Grace, Molly, thanks for putting up with me today. It's my first week. I still have to get used to how you guys work. I learned a lot. I hope I am more helpful tomorrow than I was today."

Grace waved a hand. "*Aww*, don't worry, kid. You're gonna be fine. You're smart, and you've still got a lot of energy." Grace surprised even herself with the slight hint of support.

"Thanks. I mean it. Both of you were great today," said Melinda with a polite smile.

Randall could not believe what he was hearing. He reconsidered spilling the beans about the nascent offer from Mr. Samuels, and assuage the griping about overtime, but again decided to hold his tongue. Better not to raise false hopes that might later be dashed.

Still, Randall felt he had to say something. "Say, Melinda, you were a big help today. You streamlined getting all the reviews done. Sorry, guys, that I took her away from helping you."

"It's all good," said Molly.

Melinda took this as her cue and decided to change the subject. She smoothed out her uniform skirt on her thighs. "I'm curious, what's the difference between radiation therapy and radiation oncology?"

"Oh, geez, don't get him started on that," said Grace.

Randall caught a faint whiff of fragrance, perked up, and looked up from his page. He was surprised that Melinda was standing right next to him. She had moved like a sylph.

"I'm glad you asked, Melinda. It's a point of some confusion." He thought he recognized Melinda's scent as Opium by Yves Saint Laurent. Zelda used it when she "went out."

"Here we go," said Molly. "We're never going to get out of here tonight. Grace, order us some pizza." As usual, this did not stop Randall from expounding. Plus, he knew it was time for a good bedtime story.

"Now, now, no need to get testy," said Randall. "This won't take but a minute."

"Or fifteen!" added Grace.

Randall was not deterred. "Well, radiation therapy, or radiotherapy, was an early term used when radiation first started to be used for treating cancer. Practitioners of radiation therapy were called radiation therapists or radiotherapists. Since radiation was also being used to take X-ray images of the body, mostly to look at the bones, the term radiation therapy was used so that the treatment use of radiation would not be confused with the diagnostic use. Since you three started your training by learning diagnostic radiology, you know that diagnostic radiology imaging techniques now include more than just X-rays. There's ultrasound and nuclear scanning as well." He stood tall, in his lecturing Plato pose.

"Yeah, that's called nuclear medicine," said Molly.

Randall scoffed. "Except some of the images they get are so vague, it's sort of like trying to find gray geese in the sky on a cloudy day. I call it 'unclear medicine.'" Randall chuckled at his clever turn of phrase. "But it will probably improve with time."

"So where does the term 'radiation oncology' come in?" asked Grace, now somewhat more curious.

"Are you sure you want the whole story? You're the one who wanted to keep this short."

Grace plopped her hands on her ample hips. "It's your fault you've got my interest, mister. Finish the story!"

Randall put his hands up in surrender. "All right! You asked for it! As radiation therapy evolved as a subspecialty, it included more oncology, the study of cancer and its biologic behavior. The radiation equipment for treatment also became more complex, so even more specialized training was needed."

Molly sighed. "There is ALWAYS more training! I think they just like making up new certificates!"

Randall pointed at Molly dramatically. "Right you are! That led to separate board certification for radiation therapists. Most radiation therapists never liked the term 'radiotherapist' because of all the jokes about them being the doctors who fixed radios."

Grace sniggered. "By 'most,' Dr. B means him. He got razzed a lot. Still a tender spot for him."

Randall rolled his eyes, then remembered his father's basement electronics repair shop. "Ha ha. My father was a radio therapist. They always sounded better after his ministrations. ANYWAY, diagnostic radiology technicians also needed more specialized training to assist in the setup and treatment of patients, and they became known officially as radiation therapy technologists or RTTs. They too then had to have separate training and certification."

"Oh, I see," commented Melinda.

"Wait for it. There's more," chimed in Grace, who may have heard a version of the story before.

Randall gestured as if to a large crowd. "Yes, well, there is now a movement afoot to change this naming system."

Molly sighed. "Again? Haven't there been enough changes?"

"Part of the reason is that the doctors who refer patients to us have not really received any teaching in medical school about what we do. They think that because I am called a radiation therapist, I'm just a 'button pusher' who knows how to turn the machine on and off."

Grace knew how this was going to go. "Again, he speaks from experience. Other departments have no idea what we do!"

Randall was on a roll. "Furthermore, they believe that I know little about cancer and that if they send me a consult on a patient, I am going to give that patient radiation automatically just to build up my numbers and get a bigger budget. They think that the real oncologists are the medical oncologists, and that real cancer treatment is done with cancer drugs." His voice went up a notch.

"Even I know that's not true," said Melinda with a tone of disbelief.

Grace scoffed. "Do you, now?"

ASTRO

Randall raised a hand. "You all should know this if you have been awake. In your training, you guys have had more of an introduction to what we do than the average medical student ever gets. We have a national organization, the American Society of Therapeutic Radiology and Oncology, known as ASTRO."

Molly raised her hand as if to speak.

Randall interrupted. "Yes, that would make us ASTROnauts. No, we're not space cadets."

"Dang it! You beat me to it!" Molly joked, snapping her fingers. She gestured for him to continue.

"ASTRO is promoting a change to call the doctors 'radiation oncologists' instead of radiation therapists. The radiation therapy technologists will then be called 'radiation therapists' or RTs, which is what the doctors used to be named. Finally, the departments will be called Radiation Oncology, like this department is named instead of Radiation Therapy." Randall finished with one finger raised for emphasis.

"So will I be promoted to doctor?" asked Grace sarcastically.

"In your dreams," said Randall.

Molly raised her hand. "Do you think ASTRO will get the change pushed through?"

Randall gave a small shrug. "Probably, but it will have some opposition, because it means that new radiation therapists will be required to have several years of additional training beyond two years. It will also mean that many radiation therapy departments will have to become separate departments and break administratively from radiology to become radiation oncology departments. Some radiology chiefs will be miffed, because they will lose income generated by radiation treatment. Others will be glad to rid themselves of constant requests for new million-dollar pieces of equipment."

Grace rolled her eyes. "Welcome to the circus!"

"I never heard this part before," said Molly. "Does that mean techs like me will have to get more training to remain certified?"

Randall shook his head. "Good question. Probably not. They will most likely 'grandfather' you in but require some kind of continuing education. This is the story you'll hear in the news release, but who wants to hear how this name-changing business got started in the first place?"

"Not me," said Grace.

"Come on," came Molly's irritated reply. "Please go on, Dr. B. This is not as boring as usual."

Randall gave them all his Groucho Marx stare but quoted Rodney Dangerfield. "I don't get no respect!"

After a short pause and a giggle from Melinda, Randall continued. "Well, my mentor in residency training, Dr. Juan Angel del Aguilar, is one of the founding fathers of ASTRO. I remember one day in our weekly physics conference he came into the room and interrupted the lecturer. You have to understand that del Aguilar was sort of like a Cuban Napoleon. Whenever he came into a room, he commanded it. He was short of stature but could bully a seven-footer."

Randall puffed his chest and held his hand on his belly. He paced left, then right, then finished the story. "He carried an envelope and a transparency sheet. He gestured to the lecturing physicist to move aside and placed the transparency on the viewer. In accented but otherwise flawless English, he calmly stated that he was going to show us a perfect example of how little respect our specialty received. On the screen we could see that the envelope was addressed: 'Dr. Juan Angel del Aguilar, Radio The Rapist, Pendarvus Cancer Hospital, 1510 Cataract Blvd., Colorado Springs, Colorado.'"

At first, the three techs looked confused, so Randall wrote out the address on a piece of paper.

"Oh, my God," gasped Molly. "Now I get it. Who sent the letter?"

Randall raised a fist. "A damned medical oncologist sent it. That letter launched del Aguilar on a personal vendetta against medical oncologists and he vowed to lead the charge to change the title from radiation therapy to radiation oncology. He's still alive, and I think he will refuse to die until that goal is achieved."

"Now I don't care who you are. That's funny," laughed Grace. "Say, didn't you tell us a story about your old boss before? Something about him standing on a street corner, watching women walk by?"

Randall nodded. "Why, yes. I believe I did, but there's no time to repeat it now. We have to finish closing out these charts, and you guys need to get out of here. You trying for more overtime?"

"*Aww,* can't you just tell the short version?" pleaded Melinda, accenting her request with a ponytail flip. She added puppy eyes to spice up the request.

"Girl, there is no short version," croaked Grace.

"She's right, young lady, hold your water," added Molly.

Grace interrupted. "Actually now that I think of it, I'd like to hear it again, 'cause I forgot how it ends. It will bug me all night trying to remember. Maybe if Dr. B can do the story-lite version."

Randall smiled. "I can try. You stop me if it goes too long."

"Deal," said Grace.

Randall began the story. "Del Aguilar hated that Medical Oncologists would promote new chemotherapy drugs of questionable effectiveness. For example, if a new drug produced less than 50 percent shrinkage of tumor in two out of the ten patients, they still proclaimed it a 'partial response' even though the response never lasted very long. The remaining eight patients might get no response, just side effects of the drug."

Molly clucked her tongue. "That chemotherapy hardly sounds effective. That's a scorched-earth policy! Poison the whole body just to get to a few cancer cells? It's certainly nothing to crow about. At least radiation targets just the tumor, with a whole lot less collateral damage to healthy tissue. Geez. Those guys had some nerve. No wonder del Esquire was ticked off."

Randall laughed. "The name is del Aguilar. He went on to compare treating the same tumor group with radiation. Then there would be a complete tumor response in five of the ten and at least 50 percent shrinkage in three more. Plus, there would be fewer side effects from radiation than chemotherapy and the response would last a significantly longer time. The key word here is 'significant.'"

Molly huffed. "That's EXACTLY why we do what we do. Because radiation is significant. And shows significance!"

Melinda interjected. "Oh, you mean like in statistics. Like where the P-value has to be less than .05 before something is significant?"

Grace looked puzzled. "Pee value? What's pee got to do with statistics? All I know is I don't want it on my scrubs."

Randall laughed again. "Everything. It's all about P. The lower the P value, the more significant is the effect of the treatment."

Grace's eyes widened as she vaguely recalled her long ago statistics class. "Oh, yeah. It's a different P."

Randall was used to ignoring Grace's "gutter-think." "I was at a national meeting once where a medical oncologist was giving a talk about some new drug, quoting paltry responses and bragging about how much promise it had. Del Aquilar went up to a microphone after the talk to comment. He thanked the speaker for his presentation, and then launched into a story of being a young man in Havana, trying to attract pretty young Cuban girls. He described how short and *flaco* he was, and made up for his *feo* face by wearing fancy clothes. He would stand on an empty *plátanos* crate in front of the bodega, leaning against the building, smoking a pipe, trying to look cool. Whenever a pretty *chica* would walk by, he whistled and gave her the okay sign. Perhaps two out of ten girls responded enough to even turn to look at him, but those two would laugh at him and just keep on walking."

Melinda showed a mix of respect and pity. "I'm not sure if he was brave or foolish!"

Randall held up a hand. "But wait, it gets better! When the presenting medical oncologist said, 'Well, that wasn't a significant result, no matter HOW you dress it up!' del Aguilar laughed and concluded by saying that a female glance was a partial response, but it was totally insignificant to his intentions. He deftly compared this to the ineffectiveness of the drug in question: del Aguilar smiled and repeated, 'Chemotherapy is no good no matter how you dress it up.'"

Grace got a look of devilish pleasure. "That was righteous. Stabbed his point in good! That chemo dude was hoisted by his own petard."

Melinda got it. "So it's like, if it's insignificant, why brag about it?"

"You nailed it!" said Randall. "Now let's clear this slate and get out of here. I need to get home to my little fam damily. Evening traffic is going to be a bear with all the FWS coming down."

"Oh, I loathe the fluffy white sh.... oops." Grace lost control of her tongue again. "Be careful when you get home. Not all the bears are in the woods . . ."

Daddy, What Do You Do?

Randall had traveled the familiar route back to his house so many times that he was on autopilot. He was so engrossed in listening to Mike Waters hosting on NPR radio that it was only the tightening of his stomach that alerted him that he was almost home.

He took a few deep breaths as he pulled up the driveway. He saw movement in the upstairs window. Addie was jumping up and down, waving two of her stuffed animals in the window. By the time he came in, she was barreling down the hallway, dragging the stuffed calico kitty by the paw.

"Daddy! Play your guitar right now! We have to finish our singing!!"

"Hello, my little Rosebud! I'm so glad to see you!"

He put down his briefcase and his lunch bag, peeled off his coat, hat, boots, and gloves. Finally, he could hug his daughter. "Yes, we will sing again, I promise. But might not be tonight. I don't know about you, but last night was pretty short and I am super tired. Where's Mom?"

Addie pointed toward the ceiling. "Up in her studio working on a painting. She has to finish it by tomorrow. She has chicken and veggies ready to cook for dinner. She wants Kyle to eat healthy tonight, so he doesn't have another sugar nightmare. Mom told us to color or play in our rooms until you come home."

Randall looked around the kitchen and saw covered bowls of food ready to cook. They were cat and dog safe. "Sounds good. How's Kyle doing today?"

Addie looked up at Randall and whispered. "Mom says he's real antsy, but school was okay. Want to see what I drawed?"

"Sure. I bet you drew a hippopotamus," guessed Randall. "Or, let's see, a unicorn."

Addie laughed. It was a running joke of theirs. "Right on the second guess, Daddy. How did you know?"

"Just lucky, I guess. Hippos are so big you can use up all your crayons to draw them. You wouldn't want to waste your crayons."

Addie chuckled. "Yeah, then you'd have to buy me new ones."

Randall remembered a riddle. "Say, Addie, what's the difference between a hippo and a Zippo?"

Addie put on her irritated face. "I'm just a little kid. How would I know?"

That didn't stop Randall. "One is a big, fat water-dwelling mammal, and the other is a little lighter."

Addie looked even more irritated. "Dad! I don't get it. What's a Zippo?"

"A little lighter," said Randall, knowing he was just making things worse.

Addie stamped her feet and yelled at Randall. "And I still don't know what that is!"

Randall laughed and Addie got angrier. "Sorry, Rosebud, a lighter is a metal thing that's used to light cigarettes. You know, you pop the top off, turn a little thumbwheel, and it makes a flame. Zippo is the company that makes them."

Addie's lights came on. "Oh, yeah! Steve Summers, Mom's friend from high school who gave us Polluto, has one of those. He's always smoking when he comes over."

Randall turned serious. "*Hmm.* Has he been over here a lot?"

Addie thought for a moment. "Maybe every couple of weeks. Usually before you come home from work, he and Mom go up to the balcony outside Mom's studio and smoke. It smells real funny."

Randall grimaced a bit. "Do they now? Good to know. Let's go see what Kyle is drawing."

Randall took Addie's hand, and they walked over to the kitchen table. Polluto was sitting in the corner, gnawing on a remnant of something, hopefully a bone.

Kyle was hard at work, apparently trying to color both sides of his drawing paper at once by rubbing his blue crayon as hard as he could. There were little bits of blue wax ground through the paper and into the newly polished table. Sometimes Kyle got so focused on what he was doing that he completely blocked out the world around him. Randall bit his tongue, composing a comment about ruining the table, but decided to hold off. It was just crayon.

Randall walked over to inspect the drawings. "Hey, Kyle. Nice drawing. Kind of looks like my radiation machine at work."

Kyle pounded the crayon tip into what looked like the treatment couch. "Yep. That's it. I remember it from when you took us to your work at the VA last summer. I'm using it to kill bugs. Die, die, you filthy bug!"

Randall nodded. "Looks quite effective."

Kyle continued to pound. "It works fantastic. My Big Blue Zapper machine makes magic bug rays, like how you use it to kill cancer bugs. I remembered it in my head, and then I drew it." Kyle drew more wavy lines coming out of the machine toward his bug target.

"Daddy," said Kyle, "I know you have to go to work every day. Mommy says you're at work and you don't do enough around here or help take care of us."

Randall was somewhat taken aback. "Mommy says that?"

Kyle nodded. "Well, not all the time, but she says it a lot when you're still at work. But I've got eyes, and I see what you do at home. You mow the lawn, shovel snow, and lots of house stuff. Plus you make us mac and weenies. You read us stories and sing with us. But I don't get it. She thinks you want to be at work and not at home with us. Is that true?"

Randall shook his head. "Of course not, big guy. I'd rather be at home more often. But the work I do is very hard, and it takes a lot of time to do it right. That's why I'm so late sometimes. I take care of a lot of sick people. I can't leave until I'm sure everything is just right for the next day."

Kyle nodded but shrugged. "I know the part about the sick people and the cancer. But I don't get how you do it. I don't get what the big blue zapper thing does."

Randall smiled. He was glad Kyle noticed he wasn't always gone and didn't think he was totally worthless around the house. "Well, my work is kind of complicated to explain."

"But I'm a smart kid, and you're a smart dad. I bet you can explain it to me so I get it," said Kyle.

Randall was having a daddy nirvana moment. His son actually wanted to know about something other than the new *Star Wars* movie!

Addie had just rejoined Kyle at the table to finish working on her drawing, which was indeed a very small and precise attempt at a unicorn. "Yeah, Daddy, I'm smart too," said Addie. "You can 'splain to both of us. What are you 'splaining?"

The X-factor

Randall stood and held out both arms for attention. "Okay, kids. You ready? Daddy is going to try to explain what it is I do at work. I'm going to say what I do, but at first you won't understand some of the words, because they're complicated. Then I'll try to explain the hard words. So here goes. Patients come to me with a very bad disease called cancer. Cancer is one of the words I will explain later. Then I use a special machine that makes just the right kind of X-rays to make the cancers in the patients go away safely. We call it the treatment machine. Now repeat after me: 'Radiation makes cancer go away.'"

Kyle and Addie repeated the phrase. Randall moved his arms like a conductor. "Good. That's perfect! Now I know you probably don't know what X-rays are or what cancer is, so if you're ready, I'll try to explain them to you."

Kyle had an antsy attack. "I know what X-rays are. That's when they take pictures of your bones. I had X-rays that time you thought I breaked my leg."

"That's right! And it was a good thing that your leg bone wasn't broken. Bones take a long time to heal."

"Superman has X-ray vision, Daddy. Are you like Superman?" said Kyle, looking up at his dad like he was starstruck.

Randall was pleased to be reaching the kids at some level. "Well, some of the equipment I use can take X-ray pictures of stuff inside the body. So it does give us some real-life superpowers. Now to understand X-rays, I want you to think about what energy is."

"I have lots of energy when I get up in the morning," offered Addie. "But after school it runs out, and I get tired."

Kyle started jumping up and down. "Not me! I always have energy! Mommy says I should live in the jungle, 'cause I always go, go, GO! I'm an energy machine!"

"And a sound machine!" Randall started drawing on a blank piece of paper. "Exactly. Your body makes energy from the food you eat. The food gets its energy from things that grow in the sun, like plants. Animals get their energy from eating plants. With me so far?"

Both kids seemed to be soaking up the imagery. They had never thought of their food this way.

Randall drew a cartoon sun with wavy light rays coming out and reaching a cartoon earth. "The sun is the source of much of the earth's energy. That energy travels to the earth in the form of what we call radiation. Radiation energy travels in waves. You can see some of it as light, but you can't exactly see the waves of radiation with the naked eye."

Kyle started laughing hysterically. "Dad said NAKED!"

Randall rolled his eyes and continued. "But if you could see them without special equipment, they'd look like the little waves of water you get when you throw a stone into a pond."

"Yeah, I like throwing rocks in a pond and skipping flat ones on the water," said Kyle. "Remember we did that at the park last summer? You took us there!"

Addie's voice squeaked in excitement. "Hey, Daddy, I can see waves in my water glass when you wiggle the table!"

"Yes, that's right! Some of the radiation coming from the sun we can actually see, and that's called 'visible light.' That's sparkling in your glass right now. But some of the radiation has more energy, and our eyes can't see it. You can feel it though. It's got enough energy to make your skin feel hot and turn red." Randall stroked his daughter's pink cheek.

"I got a sunburn last summer. It really hurted," said Addie, touching her shoulder, remembering the pain.

Randall was pleased that they seemed to be on the correct glide path. "Radiation is darn powerful! Some of that radiation is so strong that it can pass right through you. Some of those powerful kinds of radiation are called X-rays. The man who discovered them was a scientist named Wilhelm von Roentgen. We can just call him Bill. At first, he couldn't figure out where the radiation came from, so he called them 'X' rays."

Randall was surprised the kids were still interested. He decided to go with it. Maybe he had some future scientists in his kitchen?

Kyle could barely contain himself. "I've got some X-Men comic books, Dad! I wonder if they knew Mr. Bill!"

Ah, there was the association Randall should have expected.

"The word 'ray' is shorthand for radiation," said Randall.

"Yay! Superman X-rays again!" Kyle bounced like a sunbeam on a mirror. "He has X-ray eyes, and he can see inside things and even blow things up. That's cool!"

Randall put up both hands, palms out. "You're on the right track, Buddy, but I'm far from being Superman. I don't have any special abilities. I just know how to work the treatment machine and how to set it, so it makes the right amount of radiation to kill the cancer. I can't give too much, or it will harm both the patient and the cancer. I can't give too little, or the cancer won't be completely killed. The amount has to be just right."

"Just like *Goldilocks and the Three Bears*!" observed Addie.

Addie's comment surprised and pleased Randall. She was getting this. "Exactly. The Three Bears 'just right' amount."

Kyle had a question. "So you just use one kind of radiation to kill cancer. Did you say there are other kinds of radiation too?"

Randall nodded. "You're right, Kyle. Radiation energy comes in different kinds, like kids in a family. Just one of those kinds is X-rays. And only the most powerful kind of X-rays work to kill cancer. Those are the kinds that my Big MEL treatment machine makes. Other kinds of radiation are less powerful than light and X-rays. For example, a radio station sends us music on the radio using radio wave radiation."

"I don't get it, Daddy," said Addie. "How can stuff you can't see make things happen?"

Randall understood their frustration. It was a difficult concept. "I know it's confusing, Rosebud, so let's do an experiment."

Randall opened the kitchen do-dad drawer and took out two flashlights. First he took the small flashlight and put the light bulb end up his nose. When he turned it on his entire nose turned red.

"*Ew!* Now it's got boogers on it!" said Kyle, but at least he was still interested.

"Wow. Daddy's Rudolph the Red Nosed Reindeer!" shouted Addie.

Randall then put the little light under his chin, but not much changed. Putting the big flashlight under his chin, his cheeks lit up bright red.

"Looks like my sunburn! What's happening?" asked Addie, her face alight with curiosity.

"Glad you asked. The light from this small flashlight was strong enough to shine through my nose, but not through my chin. The big flashlight has a stronger beam of light so it could shine through to my cheeks," said Randall. "X-rays behave like this, but they are so powerful they have enough energy to pass all the way through your body including the bones, if the X-rays are strong enough. Those are the kind my treatment machine makes."

"Wow, like Luke Skywalker's light saber, right, Dad?" asked Kyle.

"Not quite, but very close. If the X-rays are weaker, we don't use them for cancer treatment. But we do use them to take X-ray pictures of your insides. You know how we put film in Mommy's camera? It changes color when it's exposed to light. Remember, light is a form of radiation."

Kyle looked down. "Yeah, I remember how mad she got when I played with those canisters and long plastic stuff in the backyard." Kyle also remembered the paddling he had gotten. Certain memories imprint well.

"Well, X-ray film works a lot like that. We put the film on one side of you and use a picture-taking X-ray machine to send the weak X-rays through your body from the other side of you. The parts of your body where there are bones don't let the X-rays get through, so it makes a white shadow on the film."

Randall drew a crayon sketch to illustrate a body in front of an X-ray machine. Then he made a little skeleton picture that resulted.

"Cool!" the kids said in unison, remembering the X-ray films they had seen when Randall had shown them his department at the hospital.

"But what about the other stuff that isn't bones?" asked Kyle. "Why does it look different?"

This was getting into deeper water already. "That other stuff is what we call the soft tissues. No, not like Kleenex, but like muscles and fat. They let some of the X-rays get through and the film turns gray. The parts where almost all the X-rays get through, like air in the lungs, turn black on the film," said Randall as he shaded in different parts of his stick-figure drawing. "You guys get it now?"

"Kinda," replied Addie.

"Sorta," said Kyle.

"Alright, maybe this will help. To treat the cancer, we use a stronger beam. We aim the X-rays so we don't harm the good parts of the body that don't have disease." Randall twisted the top of the big flashlight to make the beam get narrower. "We make it into a skinny beam, like the flashlight."

"So you light saber the bad stuff away with the powerful X-rays?" said Kyle, now able to draw a parallel.

"Yep! You could put it that way!"

Kyle swung his Magic Marker around, mimicking a light saber battle.

"Take that, cancer! Never win, you will!" Kyle did his best imitation of Yoda's voice. "Give into the dark side, we will not! The force we have!"

Addie looked concerned. "Daddy, how come the good stuff around the cancer isn't killed too? I still don't get what cancer is."

"Darn good question." Randall went to the refrigerator and took out a basket of strawberries. "Okay, see how this strawberry is all red and juicy, but this one has a black mushy spot with white stuff growing on it?"

"Yep," said Kyle.

"The mushy strawberry was healthy yesterday, right? Somehow, since yesterday, it got sick with a disease that makes it feel and taste bad."

"*Ew!*" Addie stuck out her tongue. "Get rid of that one before they ALL go bad!"

"Exactly! Just like that strawberry, some people can be well one day, and they can get a disease that makes them sick the next day. One of the diseases that people can get is sort of like the bad spot on the strawberry, and that's cancer," explained Randall.

He wrote the word "Cancer" on his piece of paper and asked the kids to copy it down and say it.

"Daddy, I'm sorry, but what's cancer? Did you tell us already and I forgot?" asked Addie.

"I said the word, but I didn't explain it yet," said Randall, momentarily at a loss for a way to convey the concept. A little Oompa Loompa man scurried around in his brain for a good explanation tool. After opening several empty drawers and two cluttered closets, the Oompa Loompa finally came to the right filing cabinet.

HOME SCIENCE

Randall slapped his forehead. "Hey, Kyle, run upstairs and get your Junior Science kit."

Kyle ran upstairs, and Polluto chased after him, barking. Kyle brought the kit downstairs. He hadn't touched it since Christmas, but Randall figured now would be a good time to demonstrate the microscope. He set up the scope and took out a tongue depressor from the box. He asked Addie to open her mouth, and he took a gentle scraping from inside her cheek. She gagged a little, but managed to keep it all in.

He spread the scraping on a glass slide, put on a cover slip, and put the slide under the lens. He focused on the mucosal cells of her cheek and had both kids look.

"Those round things you see are called cells, and there are millions of them in your body."

Randall drew a sketch of a cell on his paper. The kids copied what he drew.

"Together, these cells make up everything that's you. Some make up your lungs, your heart, your brain, and everything else. The black spots in the middle are called the nucleus," he explained.

Randall wrote the word "nucleus" on the paper and the kids copied it in on their drawings.

"What's a 'new klee us,' Dad?" asked Kyle.

Randall scrambled to make the explanation simple. "In the nucleus is all the information that tells each cell how to grow. You have a nucleus like this in every cell of your body! The nucleus of a skin cell, for example, tells the cell how to be skin."

"Oh!! It's like the skin cell has a brain. And a 'new klee us' of a butt cell tells it how to be a butt?" Kyle looked immensely proud of himself.

". . . *uh*, yes! Good thing your nose cells don't think they're butt cells. Anyway, sometimes when a cell, like the skin cells, makes more skin cells, there's a mistake in that information and a cell begins to grow out of control. The mistake makes the cell misbehave, and it doesn't follow the rules. Then that crazy cell makes more crazy cells." said Randall.

"Like us when we're bad?" asked Addie.

"Oh, sweetie, you are never bad. Every kid, like every cell, is good. But sometimes the behavior is bad. Bad information in the cell can make bad spots in the strawberry we were talking about. So then someone like me has to come along, like a parent, and make them behave again. If they get out of control, they start hurting the good parts of the body. Those bad cells are called cancer cells."

"Yeah, they need a time out," said Kyle who had some experience in the area.

Nobody noticed that Zelda was standing just out of sight in the kitchen doorway, eavesdropping. She smiled as she witnessed the little science lesson.

Randall expanded on the cancer concept. "If we catch the cancer spot before it gets too big, a surgeon can help. That's a doctor who has been trained to cut the cancer away before it can spread to the rest of the body."

Addie frowned and looked like she was in pain. "Doesn't that hurt, Daddy?"

"Actually, we have amazing medicine that allows that to happen without hurting you. Sometimes though, the cancer spot gets bigger, and it can't be cut away without hurting the body too much."

Kyle seemed to be following this. "Then what do they do? Is the person a goner?"

"Hopefully not! Then doctors like me make the cancer go away using radiation treatment machines. The X-rays change the cancer cells on the inside, so they stop growing out of control and then die. It's a complex process, and we have a lot of calculations to get just right. It's gotta be stronger than sunshine, but not as strong as a light saber."

Addie shook her head. "That's an awful lot of stuff to know. How did you ever learn it all? I'll never be that smart."

Randall almost wanted to cry. "Oh, sweetie. I'm no smarter than you. When I was your age, I didn't even know half of what you already do. It took a long time for me to learn what I needed to know. I'm sure you could learn it even faster."

Kyle looked left out. "How about me? I'm smart too, aren't I? I could do what you do if I wanted to."

Randall put a hand on Kyle's shoulder. "Of course, you could. If you wanted to. That's the key. It's hard work, and you'll never finish it if it's not something you really want to do. You gotta really have a passion for it, you know, like *Star Wars* is for you."

Kyle nodded and then shook his head. "Yeah, I'm not sure I'd love it as much as *Star Wars*."

Addie shrugged. "Me neither. I really like horses."

Kyle laughed. "You love unicorns too, and they don't even exist."

Addie guffawed back, "Yeah, and like *Star Wars* and light sabers are real!"

"They are if I want them to be!" Kyle poked Addie in the ribs.

Addie poked back. "Then unicorns are too."

Randall intervened. "Alright! Enough already. You two, stifle. It's way too soon to decide what you want to do when you grow up. But know this. Both of you are smart enough to do whatever you want when you get there."

Both kids silenced and pouted.

"He started it," said Addie.

"She finished it," said Kyle.

"Are you two done now?" asked Randall. "Can I finish the lesson?"

There was a murmured chorus of "Yes, Dad."

Randall folded his arms. "Good. One final point I want to make is this: I don't do any of this alone. I'm part of a team. We all work together to get each patient's treatment just right. You know, 'Three Bears.'"

Kyle couldn't stifle. "So does that make you Goldilocks, Dad?"

Addie couldn't contain her tongue either. "No, that makes him 'Old-ilocks.'"

Randall laughed in spite of himself. "Good one, guys. Yes, just look at these flowing locks of hair." He stroked both sides of his head. "It's just right and just left. None on top."

All three laughed, and Zelda stifled a giggle from her eavesdropping spot in the doorway.

When things settled down, Randall concluded the lesson. "Alright, let's finish this up. The summary is this. We learned about radiation, X-rays, and cancer. We can kill cancer with X-rays, but you can't give too much X-rays or you damage the cancer cells and the good cells. You can't give too little, or you can't stop the cancer cells from growing. But if you give just the right amount of X-rays, then the misbehaving cancer cells die, and the good cells live. Even though the good cells get hurt a little by the X-rays, they can heal and survive because they are good cells. You see, it pays to be good." Randall was unable to resist throwing in a little parenting lesson.

"Does it work all the time?" asked Addie.

"Not always, but more than half the time, and that's significant." said Randall, remembering del Aguilar. "And it's always worth trying, especially if it means we may save someone."

Zelda took her cue from Randall's last comment and entered the kitchen. She made a loud pronouncement. "Did you guys know your daddy saves people's lives every day?"

Kyle looked up at Zelda and then turned to Randall with stars in his eyes. "He does? Wow!"

Zelda whistled loudly. "Yeah, he's way more important than a dime-a-dozen artist, like me."

"Huh? What dimes?" Kyle looked confused.

Addie was looking at her drawing paper and seemed zoned out of the dialogue. "Mommy, you're an artist! Can you draw a cell 'new klee us' for me?"

Randall decided to keep quiet. He wasn't yet sure what the drift was. Best to let things sort out. Then Zelda seemed to soften her hard stance and went to a kitchen cabinet where she had stashed some drawing pencils. "Sure, sweetie. I can draw a cell picture for you."

Randall relaxed but stayed alert. One could never quite tell whether Zelda was issuing accolades or tickets to the doghouse. Zelda had taken some nursing classes before going to art school, like she had wanted to, thinking that you could actually earn a living as a nurse. She hadn't really liked it and felt it put her in competition with Randall. So she dropped out and went back to art school at Randall's insistence. After all, it was what she loved.

Randall took the opportunity. "Yeah, Zel, why don't you draw the cell? I'm a hack artist. Stick figures are okay for X-ray drawings, but this requires much more of your skill and abilities with details."

Zelda remembered the details of cellular structure. She whipped up a rather impressive diagram of the nucleus, mitochondria, and organelles. For a bit of pizazz, she threw in some coiled DNA. Then she explained the parts to Addie and Kyle.

Addie got excited when she studied the final product. It was a superior depiction. "Now I get it! Momma, you're magic!" Randall could swear Zelda had visibly melted hearing Addie's comment. Addie was so warmhearted; she could melt an iceberg.

After more pointing and explaining, Zelda decided science hour was over. "How about we fuel some of those hungry cells of yours, kids?"

Zelda stood up. Polluto read the cue with his food radar on high alert and started drooling.

Randall knew what was coming next, so he chimed in. "How can I help with dinner?"

He had learned early on never to ask, "What's for dinner?" This led to a lecture on gender inequality, antiquated parental roles, and the indentured bondage of marriage. All Randall knew was that he was hungry and didn't want to wage a battle of the sexes.

"Chop some onions and prepare the cilantro. We are having baked chicken, bulgur wheat, steamed broccoli, and tempeh." Zelda took nutrition very seriously.

"Sounds delicious, doesn't it, kids?" Randall led the charge to rally the troops. Sometimes they needed a lot of encouragement to ride the health-food train, especially after the "Dad night" mac-and-weenie escapades. He did tend to ignore it, though, when the kids slipped some of their broccoli to Polluto under the table.

It had been a long time since they had all cooked together, singing and helping each other. It was a welcome change. The kids seemed to thrive on the cheery mood both parents shared, and even ate most of their broccoli. Zelda surprised them with some organic whole-milk ice cream with carob chips.

When they finished their bowls, Addie asked, "Can we have more ice cream? And finish talking about cells?"

"Yeah, I scream, you scream, we all scream for ice cream," chanted Kyle. "I want X-rays on mine."

"I want Y-rays on mine," said Addie.

"Why not?" Randall was amazed they were still interested.

After ice cream, Zelda excused herself to go upstairs for some "fresh air," a euphemism for smoking on the balcony just off her art studio. Her studio was really just a spare second-floor bedroom she converted into an art studio, complete with drawing boards, easels, and a host of art supplies. The key component was a padlock on the door for when she was "working on a deadline" and didn't want to be disturbed. It was sort of a "woman cave."

Randall wasn't exactly sure what went on when she was encamped there but had his suspicions. He had given up trying to talk her into giving up cigarettes of all types; she just stonewalled him. He lectured her about all the lung cancer he saw, but she was unmoved. He often wondered if she smoked just to spite him and his profession.

Kyle jumped up from his chair and caught his elbow on the table edge. "*OW!!!* Stupid table!" He had forgotten about the injury he still had there. He stomped around for a while, yelling at the walls, the floor, and his sister. He even cursed the table for existing. Randall and Addie just stayed out of his way until the wind from hurricane Kyle died down.

Kyle shook his arm as he settled down. "Dang, that hurt. It got my funny bone, where I scraped my arm last week, but it's not funny."

Addie tried to suppress a giggle, and Kyle stared daggers at her until they all laughed.

Kyle rubbed his elbow and asked Randall to check it for bleeding. The injury raised a question in his mind. "Dad, when I scrape myself bad, do the scraped cells get killed?"

Randall delighted in his son's curiosity. "Yes, they do, but the cells left behind can heal the damage. Each cell follows the instructions that are in its nucleus. Isn't that the elbow road rash you got last week when you fell off your bike?"

"Yeah, it was right here where I whacked my elbow. It was super bloody. And so cool!" Kyle furrowed his brow as he tried to see his elbow. "How does it look?"

Randall shook his head. "Hey, Buddy, there's nothing to see. It's all healed up, and no new damage done."

Kyle stretched and twisted his arm to get a better look. "Hey, where did it go?"

Randall was blessed with another teaching moment. "It healed! The skin cells grew together to heal it up, and then they stopped growing once it was all better."

Kyle's mouth gaped. "That's amazing, Daddy. I didn't even know it was happening!"

Addie had been thinking since the talk about radiation and cancer. "Daddy, can I get cancer? Can I get it from not washing my hands? Or from eating a yucky strawberry?"

"No, sweetie, you don't get it that way. Kids don't usually get cancer, so please don't worry about it. If you're worried, I'll check you every night when I tuck you in." Addie put her arms around Randall's legs and gave him a hug.

Kyle wormed his way between Randall and Addie. "Is there a new klee us for pooping? I bet there is. 'Cuz your body poops! Ha ha ha! Poopy poopy poopy . . ." Kyle nearly fell on the floor laughing.

Randall turned to Addie, who was not sharing the hilarity.

Addie shook her little head in disgust. "Kyle always thinks about poop, but he never wants to go," said Addie, in a very adult tone.

"Kyle, if you'd rather laugh and do poop jokes, that tells me this discussion is over."

"Can you get cancer from eating too much ice cream?" asked Kyle, mostly as a diversionary tactic.

Randall knew Kyle's attention span had run its course. "No, but too much ice cream causes a buildup of alkaline phosphatase in your duodenum, which spreads on down to your hippocampus and, at night while you're sleeping, you blow up all over the walls of your bedroom," said Randall. "Then I have to clean up the mess, and I get really mad."

"Daaaddddy," screamed Addie. "You're scaring me again."

Despite his effort to stifle a laugh, Randall blurted out a loud guffaw that soon spread to both kids. They held their sides, tears of laughter filling their eyes as they slapped the table and the countertop.

Then they heard the studio door upstairs slam shut, followed by rapid thumping footsteps down the stairs. Zelda huffed into the kitchen and assumed her iron maiden pose. She shot them an intense truth-seeking stare. "What's so funny, you guys? What's with all the noise?"

All three conspirators put on their serious faces. "Nothing!" the poop-fest participants responded in unison.

"Daddy told us a funny joke," said Kyle.

"Yeah, it was a funny riddle," said Addie. "About a hippopotamus."

"That's right," said Kyle, looking over at Addie, who was nodding her head slightly. "It was about a hippy dippy hippo."

"I'm sure it was very droll," deadpanned Zelda. "Now guess what happens next?"

"Dad already said it's time to go upstairs and clean up for bed," said Kyle.

Before Zelda could muster a rejoinder, Kyle and Addie both ske-daddled out of the kitchen and up the stairs.

Randall was proud of the kid's ad lib obfuscation. It was his turn to ad lib. He decided this might be a perfect time to tell Zelda about the Swindell story.

"Hey, Zel, you're not going to believe what happened this week. Got a few minutes to chat while the kids get ready for beddy?""

Zelda nodded reluctantly. "Why not? Half the night's wasted anyhow."

Randall shook his head. "My, my. So somber. Perhaps some levity first? What's the difference between a hippo and a Zippo?"

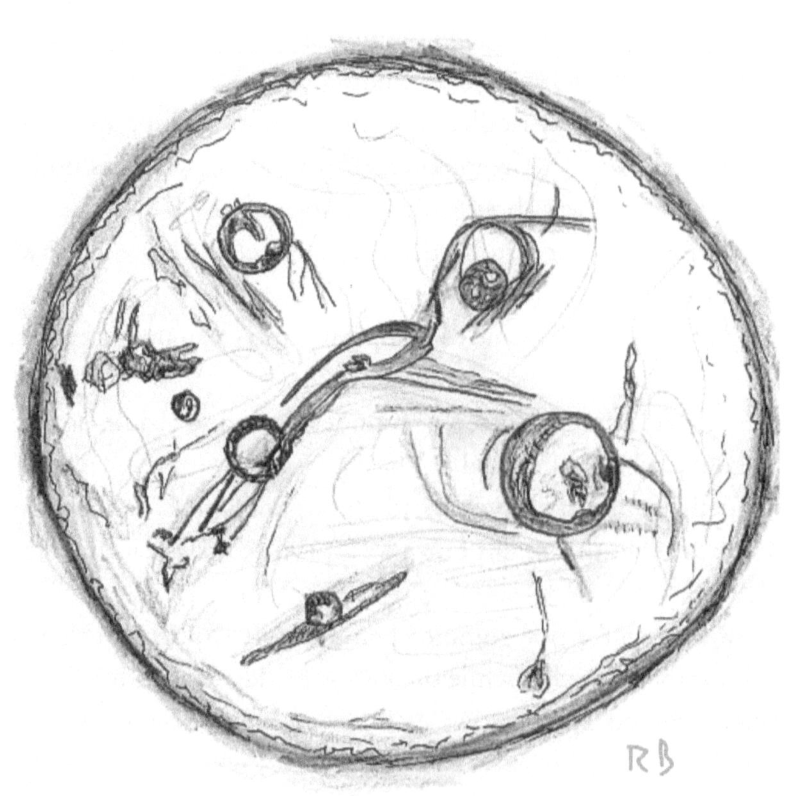

RB

CHAPTER 11

———

UNCLE PHIL MAKES A COMEBACK

"The boundaries which divide Life from Death are, at best, shadowy and vague. Who shall say where one ends and where the other begins?"

— *The Premature Burial,* Edgar Allan Poe

Shade of the Past

Morning came bright and sunny, but exceedingly early. The alarm hadn't gone off yet, but bright light shone through the bedroom window and pried open Randall's eyes. Although the bedroom windows faced south, the morning sun reflecting off the fresh snow that fell overnight was intense. He raised his head off the pillow and shook a fist at the offending light beams. He muttered loudly. "What the heck?!"

The same shade that had recently knocked down the cherub lamp was wide open. Randall was certain he'd lowered all the shades before bed, including the replacement shade. He wanted to ask Zelda if she opened it for some reason, but she was sawing lumber like a chainsaw. The alarm clock showed it was 5:40 a.m. He could have slept another twenty minutes. *That's almost an hour and a half in dog years!* It ticked him off enough to bring him fully awake.

Might as well get up and get an early start. He lumbered out of bed and walked to the window, feeling more like the worm than the bird.

149

He could feel the outside cold leaking into the room through the old leaded glass. At least six inches of new snow covered the ground like vanilla frosting. Cold, wet, slippery vanilla frosting. He sighed and girded his proverbial loins, although medical school Anatomy didn't identify exactly where his loins were located.

The post-snowstorm clear skies had paved the way for arctic cold and the outdoor temperature had fallen to the mid-teens. Randall shivered, pulled down the shade and got ready for work. He tiptoed through his morning routine and kissed the sleeping kids on the forehead before going downstairs. He thought he might need a coffee IV before it would do him any good. Fortunately, taking it by mouth in large quantities woke him up by the time he pulled the Scirocco into the VA's Siberian parking lot. He was right about needing extra time to maneuver through the new snow. His early departure netted an on-time arrival.

Randall hauled his weary frame in the back door of the Radiation Oncology Department. Grace and Molly were at their posts warming up Big MEL. Bob Storch, the medical physicist, lurked around the entry to the treatment room looking like Ichabod Crane in a white smock. Randall could smell Al Kornberg's acrid pipe smoke from down the hall where he was holed up in his office, looking busy doing nothing. A stack of charts were already sitting out on the console for Randall's review. He escaped temporarily to his office.

The respite was short-lived. Melinda soon sauntered into his office as he was shedding his winter gear. Randall breathed her in; she smelled much better than the pipe smoke. And there was the ponytail, the tailored uniform, and the shoes. And those two buttons. Randall forced himself to turn his attention to the proffered chart. He made a correction and Melinda hurried back to the console. He let out a sigh.

Doris tootled into his office with a small stack of paper and a broad smile. "Good Mornin', Dr. B. How are we today?"

"Is that the royal we or the me we?" asked Randall grouchily.

Doris looked a bit offended. "Now, Dr. B, I know you're probably not fully up to snuff yet, but we are runnin' a finely geared department here! Let's repeat together that we are fine, we are happy, and we are gonna have a nice day."

Randall shrugged a bit. "Yes, Mother. We are fine. And that's as much as you'll get from the me me."

"I love when you call me sweet names. I know how much you love your mother," said Doris in her cheery singsong.

Randall snickered. "What do I have on today?"

Doris cocked her head to one side. "Well, besides your lab coat, here's what's on the front burner. You'll be pleased to learn that this morning, there is nothin' besides reviews, follow-ups and only one consult request. The usual caveat still applies. I can't predict what new requests might come from the wards and clinics."

Randall nodded. "That goes without saying."

"But I said it anyhow," said Doris. "You tend to forget that and, when we get an emergency consult, I'm the one who has to listen to you complainin' like a cow that needs milkin'."

Randall shook his head. "I don't complain that much. *Moo.*"

Doris just stared back at him, and Randall blinked first. "As far as meetin's, I did arrange for the compliance officer to meet with you and our staff next Thursday at 8:00 a.m., but there's no meetin's for today. Oh, and the meetin' about buildin' inspections is Friday at the noon Chief's meetin' in the Director's conference room."

"That sounds okay. I hope that's written down somewhere! I think I just may make it through the day, if I can avoid having to explain how radiation treatment units work to our new student, Melinda. See if you can keep her corralled for another day," requested Randall.

"I'll do my best," said Doris.

Randall left his office to start the weekly reviews. When he reached the waiting hall, Ira, the transport clerk, was wheeling a gray-haired veteran down the hall. Randall stepped back to avoid being run over, and a waiting patient grabbed his elbow. "Hey, Doc," blurted Mr. Dithers.

Randall deftly pulled his arm away and juked to the side. "Not now, Mr. D. I'll be seeing you soon. We got your PSA back, and it's fine, so stop worrying. We'll talk more in a second."

"How'd you know what I wanted?" asked Dithers.

Randall put his hand to his forehead. "I am the Great Carnac."

Mullet's Lament

As Ira pushed a wheelchair patient toward a spot behind a parked gurney, he looked up and saw Melinda walking her graceful walk out of the treatment room and up to the treatment console. The ponytail, uniform, and the shoes worked their magic; Ira forgot to stop pushing the wheelchair and rammed it into the back of the gurney. Both patients hollered out in surprise on impact. This drew the attention of all present, including Melinda, but Ira only saw Melinda.

For a moment, Ira just stopped and stared at his feet, wiping sweat from his brow, and smoothing out his upswept mullet. He looked up again. "Uh, Miss Melinda. You're looking well today. I've brought you Mr. Gerald Fitzpatrick for his treatment."

The wheelchair patient rubbed his bruised knee and said, "It's Patrick Fitzgerald, you conehead numbskull."

Ira shrugged as he turned red. "Yeah, what he said. Is there anything else I can do for you, Miss Melinda?"

Melinda just stood in place, smiling enigmatically. "No, I believe you've done quite enough for now."

Ira seemed baffled by the smile. "I, *uh* . . ."

Mr. Dithers was amused by Ira's schoolboy behavior. "Looks like Mr. Ira the transport has got a crush on someone. Go on, you one-trick-pony, speak up like a man. Introduce yourself to the lady."

Somehow emboldened by the derision, Ira complied. "My name is Ira, Miss Melinda. I'm a transport clerk . . . I, uh, guess you could say, I transport patients." Ira pulled out a handkerchief to wipe his brow.

Melinda seemed not to comprehend Ira's true intent. "Yes, I remember you. We've met before. Do you need another patient to take back upstairs?"

"No, Ma'am, I mean, Miss. I, uh . . . you're new here? Are you a resident?" Ira stumbled for something to say.

Molly and Grace appeared and took in the little drama, enjoying Ira's squirming struggle.

Melinda finally got that Ira was introducing himself. "Oh, no, nothing like that! I'm here as part of my Radiation Therapy Technician Program. I hope to be a senior tech someday, but Grace has that job now. I don't think she'll be leaving anytime soon! I'm just glad to get some experience in radiation oncology. It's just so fascinating, don't you think?" She waved her arm, indicating Grace. And sending out a magical mist of Opium perfume.

"Um, sure, Miss. If you like tumors, I guess . . ." Ira still seemed transfixed.

"I think it's amazing what we can do with energy that we can't even see. I don't have any patients for you just now. Well, Grace and Molly are here. I better get back to work." Melinda turned on her dainty heel to join her two colleagues.

Grace scowled at Melinda. "Come on, pipsqueak! We have work to do! Quit chattering with the help!" Grace waddled off to get the next patient.

"I hope you get your dream, Ms. Melinda. Maybe someday, if you'd like to . . ." Ira trailed off as she disappeared into the treatment room with Grace.

Mr. Dithers got up and walked over to where Ira was watching Melinda's departing form. He elbowed Ira in the ribs and whispered to him. "Nice swing in her backyard, eh? Tough luck though, kid. If you want *her* attention, you'll have to make a bigger splash than that, not wilt like yesterday's flower."

Ira whispered back to Mr. Dithers. "Zip it, old man. I will find a way to help her get her dream. Then she'll notice me."

Ira pretended to get a beep on his pager and dashed away from the old man, heading to the elevator. Mr. Dithers cackled a dry laugh.

The rest of the day went smoothly for Randall, as Doris had predicted. Somehow Melinda was so preoccupied with shadowing Grace and Molly that she never got around to pursuing Randall with her usual questions. Randall gathered his take-home items and put on his coat and hat for the trip home.

As he walked out the back door, the cold hit him in the face like a sharp slap. *I can't believe it's dark already. I hope I can see to get my key in the lock.* He completed the long walk back to his car, then had a sudden flash of a thought, like a loud voice had boomed in his head: *Go back!*

Reflexively, Randall responded to the mental shoutout with a shoutout of his own. "For what?"

Another doctor in the parking lot, walking to his car, looked up in surprise when he heard Randall's outburst. He called out to ask if Randall was okay. Randall called back that everything was fine. He stood there in the cold, trying to figure out why he needed to go back inside.

After a few seconds, Randall swatted his forehead. How could he forget? He had promised family members to check three inpatients on the wards and provide progress reports. All three were under treatment and not doing well. Not only did an in-person visit assure the patient that they had not been abandoned, but it made Randall rest easier to keep the families apprised when bad endings were imminent.

Randall especially needed to see Phillip Woodstock, an eighty-eight-year-old man with advanced prostate cancer that had spread to the bones. Randall was distantly related to the man who insisted that Randall call him "Uncle" Phil. Randall wasn't sure what the official familial moniker was for the grandfather of his sister's husband but figured Uncle was as good as any.

Randall repositioned his gear and hiked back to the Radiation Oncology Department. He unlocked the back door and shrugged out of his coat. He put on his white lab coat and was halfway to the elevator when he realized he still had his knit hat on. That would have been a look to foster patient confidence. As he went back to put it on his desk, he tried to puzzle out where his brain had taken a wrong turn.

Randall wrote down the location of each patient on a slip of notepaper and made for the elevator. The first stop was the seventh floor to see Mr. Urmanski. Then he could take the stairs down to see Mr. Krzyzwicz on the fifth floor, and then Uncle Phil in the SICU on the fourth floor.

Ships in the Night

As Randall walked into Mr. Urmanski's hospital room, the patient sat up in bed suddenly and yelled, "Duck, Doc! Hit the deck!"

It seemed such an urgent warning that Randall dropped to the floor without further thought. As he hugged the tile, he asked, "Uh, Mr. Urmanski, why did you yell for me to duck?"

"The ship, the ship coming through the window. Good thing you were quick, Doc. It almost hit you."

"Is it gone now?"

"Yeah, you can get up. It's safe. It was a big one."

Randall got up slowly and dusted off his white lab coat. He picked up the stuff that had flown out of his pockets and walked over to the bedside. Randall was treating Mr. Urmanski for lung cancer that had spread to the brain.

"Mr. U, how are we today? Still having the headaches and seeing weird stuff?"

"Yeah, but both are much better since the treatment started. That's only the third freighter today."

"Good. Perhaps by next week, you can be discharged. Still seeing the roses?"

"Just one rose now, not three, and only when I look to the right."

"Fantastic. I know how you hate flowers." Randall found it was better to go along with the patient's version of reality. Truth was subjective anyhow.

"Doc? Am I gonna make it? I've got to go downtown and buy a Cadillac."

"Sure. We're all going to make it." *No need to specify what we're going to make. Everyone likes a little reassurance.*

"Good, good. That's what I was thinkin'."

Randall approached gently. "Lay your head back on the pillow. I need to examine it."

"Okay." Urmanski was an older man but allowed himself to be cared for like the little boy he was on the inside.

Randall put his hand on Mr. Urmanski's forehead, and then moved it to the top, right side, and left side of his head. He moved his hand back to the forehead and held it there.

"What's up, Doc?"

"Who are you, Bugs Bunny? Just doing a scan."

Urmanski squinted one eye. "What's it show?"

"I'm not done yet. I need you to close your eyes and think about your favorite thing to do. Tell me when you have it."

"Okay, got it."

Randall knew to trust his gut. "Looks like you're walking your dog."

"Yeah, Jim Bob and me. Walking along the lakeshore."

"Good. Now I am getting a good read. Wow, things are looking great. All three tumors are nearly gone, and there's healing all around them. New York City, just like I pictured it."

"Huh?"

Randall spoke in a soothing tone. "It means good, Mr. U. All good. Just keep walking Jim Bob until I'm done."

Randall stood there with his hand on Mr. Urmanski's forehead for a few more minutes until he heard soft snoring. He walked quietly out of the room, checking the window briefly for ships passing in the night.

Hospital hallways at night were a scary place to be. Randall felt like his only protection was the white lab coat, but it wasn't much. Besides being filthy, it had a tear in the side pocket from carrying too much gear and catching the pocket on a doorknob. Stethoscope, notebook, patient notes, emergency color codes, and handbooks took up the rest of the pocket room. Randall felt these devices were like amulets that would ward off the evil that lurked in the hospital's hallways and wards. That and whatever magic he could conjure.

Randall started heading for Mr. Krzyzwicz's room but found his feet heading to the fourth floor instead.

"Uncle" Phil

He headed to "Uncle" Phil's room on 4CS ward. Phil's pain had gotten better, but he had lost his appetite and stopped eating. Randall had gotten Phil admitted that day for supportive care. Phil's wife was too disabled by arthritis to visit him, so she checked on his condition with Randall by phone.

When Randall arrived at the door of the hospital room, he found the hospital chaplain at Phil's bedside. Not sure whether to interrupt, Randall stopped just inside the door. The chaplain looked up as Randall entered.

Randall held up a hand. "Sorry, Chaplain, didn't mean to barge in. I can see you are having a private moment. I'll come back in a few."

The chaplain shook his head. "No, no. You must be Dr. Biedermeier. I'm Chaplain Bill. Come on in and pray with us. Phillip and I were expecting you. We knew you were on the way, and we were just waiting for you."

Randall looked bemused and shook the chaplain's hand awkwardly. "You were both waiting for me?"

The chaplain nodded his head emphatically. "Yes. We were."

"But I didn't tell anyone I was coming up here," said Randall, a bit flustered.

"The message still came through. Now we don't have much time. Please stand by the bedside near Phillip's head. He can't hear well or speak very loudly. We're going to do a final prayer," said the chaplain.

Randall shrugged and shook his head. "Final prayer. I don't do the prayer thing. But I'll listen."

"That's fine. I didn't expect you to know the prayer. Just be present."

Randall did as requested but felt rather silly. He looked down at a shock of white hair hanging over Uncle Phil's forehead. The man's eyes were closed. Randall found it hard to tell whether Uncle Phil was breathing. The chaplain ended the prayer and was silent for several moments. Randall looked down at Uncle Phil's quiet form for about thirty seconds, wondering if he'd breathed his last.

"I think he's gone," said the chaplain.

Randall put his ear down near Uncle Phil's nose to listen for breathing. Hearing none, he stood back up and reached for his stethoscope to listen for breath sounds. Before he could get it to his ears, Phil suddenly opened his eyes and turned his head to look directly at Randall.

Uncle Phil spoke out in a loud and clear voice. "Good, it's you. I knew you'd come. Please tell my wife I love her."

Randall started to respond, but Uncle Phil just closed his eyes and his head lolled to the side. He let out a final, sighing breath.

Randall suddenly felt panic and checked for a pulse and breath sounds. There were none. "Chaplain, did you just see . . . hear . . . ?"

The chaplain put a hand on Randall's shoulder. "Yes, I did. And before you ask, let me just say that I have seen many mysterious things in my time here. I would tell more people, but in my experience, they don't believe me, that is, unless they were with me, like you were tonight. And no, I don't understand it, but pursuit of the answer is why I do this. One day I might figure it out. Your Uncle Phillip has given you an assignment. Now go carry it out. I know I can count on you. I'll inform the ward nurse and the family of Phillip's passing."

Randall thought again of the voice command he heard in the parking lot. "No problem, Chaplain Bill. I will personally pass the message to Uncle Phil's wife."

Chaplain Bill reached into a pocket and drew out a card. "Good. He knew you would carry out his wishes. Here's the details about the funeral arrangements."

Randall walked weak-kneed from the room and leaned up against the hallway wall for a moment. This ranked right up there with the Swindell Lazarus act. Randall realized he was hyperventilating. He thought for a few seconds he might have to breathe into a paper bag, but he settled down after a few deep breaths. With only one more patient to go, he took another deep breath before walking on.

It's a Gas, Gas, Gas

Randall mustered enough energy to go up a floor to 5CS. Joe Krzyzwicz was a middle-aged man with prostate cancer. During treatment he had developed diverticulitis and a perforated sigmoid colon. He needed an emergency colostomy. When Randall got there, it was pretty quiet except for two nurses tending to a malfunctioning IV pump. As Randall approached Mr. Krzyzwicz's cubicle, he could hear the man moaning in pain. Randall pulled the drawn curtain aside and found the man doubled over holding his belly.

The man's wife was at his side, trying vainly to help. "Joe, Joe, what is it? What can I do? Oh, doctor, thank goodness you're here. Can you do something about Joe's pain?"

The comment made Randall feel guilty all over again, because he had missed the signs and symptoms of the bowel perforation for about a week. Randall had attributed the left lower quadrant pain to pelvic bone metastases, which was present in the same area. This delayed the surgery and made it more difficult. Furthermore, Randall felt helpless since this was now a surgical problem.

Randall struggled to think of how he, the "button pusher," could help. He asked the SICU nurses if there were orders for more pain medication. The nurses wrangling the IV pump said there was no such order, and the pain was a new issue. They needed an order from a surgeon to give Joe any narcotics and the on-call surgeon was in the OR with an emergency.

Frustrated, Randall returned to the cubicle and presented the bad news. He said all he could do was to examine him further. Randall asked where the pain was worst. Mr. Krzyzwicz pointed to his right upper quadrant. Randall thought that was odd, since the surgery was in the left lower quadrant, and that area wasn't hurting. Randall asked if the nurses had given him any solid food yet. Mr. Krzyzwicz said he had eaten some oatmeal in the morning, and the pain had started soon after.

Randall checked Joe's abdomen and heard gurgling bowel sounds. That was a sign that perhaps bowel contents were on the move. Randall began abdominal palpation to check for tenderness, but there was none except in the right upper quadrant. Randall pushed deeper to check for rebound tenderness and Joe took in a breath.

"That hurts, Doc!!"

Randall reassured Joe. "That's because I'm poking you so deep." Randall held his hand on Joe's abdomen, which increased the rumbling. The pressure was followed by a mighty blast of flatus from the colostomy. "*Thbthbthb. . . !*" The sound pierced the silence of the SICU.

"Omigod, the pain is gone!" shouted Mr. Krzyzwicz.

"It's a miracle. You're a healing angel, Doctor," cried Mrs. Krzyzwicz.

Responding to the sound of escaping gas, the two nurses appeared at the curtain and asked what was going on. Mrs. Krzyzwicz told the nurses what had just happened and lauded Randall's prowess. The nurses were not impressed, but Randall thought there was no harm in taking credit for the apparent miracle of the gasses.

Go Time

Randall decided that, with pass time over, it was time to blow the pop stand. Randall bade goodbye to the Krzyzwiczs and headed for the elevator. As he stood waiting to see which color waffle paper he'd get as a newly minted miracle worker, a surgery resident he recognized walked by. Spotting Randall, he asked what a radiation oncologist was doing on the wards so late at night.

Randall decided mild obfuscation was in order. "Oh, just working a little magic and a few miracles. But my work here is done. Time to hit the road."

The resident looked dubious. "A likely story! I'm off to dig out an impaction and put a G-tube back where it belongs."

"Better you than me!" said Randall back.

The resident looked back in disgust. "One of these days, I'll get the easy duty."

The elevator dinged and the door slid open, revealing green waffle paper. *Another miracle,* thought Randall.

As the elevator headed down, Randall wondered how the message from Uncle Phil had gotten to him. Tired of idle speculation about weirdness, he dismissed the thought and checked the information about the funeral arrangements that Chaplain Bill had given him. The viewing was from 1:00 to 3:00 p.m. later that week followed by a short service at the Stanislaw Funeral Home on the south side. Randall figured he'd have to take off during lunch to make the visitation. Perhaps another miracle would get him there.

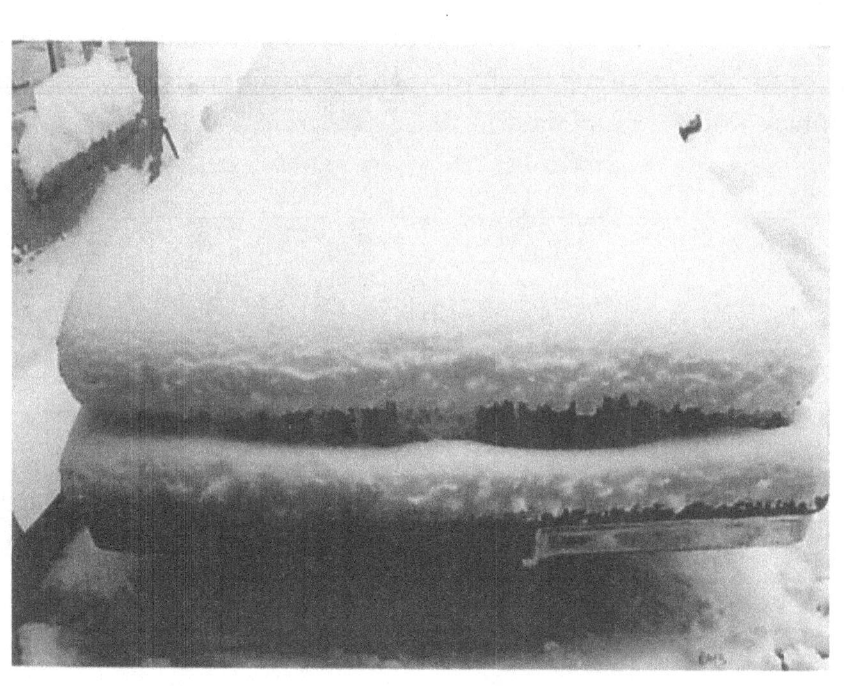

CHAPTER 12

MAHALIA TUNES IN TOKYO

"Whenever a man does a thoroughly stupid thing, it is always from the noblest motives."

— *Picture of Dorian Gray,* Oscar Wilde

To the Office

The next morning, Randall gunned the Scirocco and spun the front tires on the frozen snow covering Creekside Place. He knew he had to get his derriere in gear at work to get through the morning in time to get away to the funeral home during lunch. In preparation, he'd packed a lunch he could eat in the car on the trip there. That meant something that wouldn't fall apart while shifting the four-speed. He'd overcome his tendency to bury PBJ sandwiches in the dashboard while shifting into third gear, but occasionally had to clean crushed banana out of the dash tape deck on the radio. If there ever were an Olympic event involving eating while road rallying, Randall thought he just might be competitive.

Doris Music Time

Randall found a prime spot in the aerobic parking lot. He had surprising pep in his step as he made his way through the entry maze. He eschewed taking the elevator down just one level and always tried to take the stairs. No point in risking the brown elevator to start the day when you only needed to go down one story. He circled around the elevator area to the back-door entrance, let himself in the department, and deposited his traveling gear in his office. As usual, the brisk jog through the cold left him a bit sweaty, and his glasses fogged up after he entered the warm building.

Doris was in her office, typing dictation at about 140 wpm on her Selectric. At the same time, she was softly singing the spiritual "His Eye is on the Sparrow," which Randall recognized from his Mahalia Jackson album. He could not comprehend how Doris could simultaneously sing and type, but he was sure if there were an Olympic event . . .

While donning his lab coat, Randall walked into Doris's office, which was between Randall's office and the department hallway. It also had an outer door leading out to the department's waiting room/hallway. The tiny rectangular space could just barely accommodate Doris's large desk. The desk protruded into the passageway between the two offices, leaving a space only wide enough for one person at a time. Two people had to turn sideways to have enough room to pass each other.

"Hey, Doris, what's up in dictation land, and how's Mahalia today?" asked Randall.

"Oh, my lands, you recognized the song. I didn't think anyone from up around here would know that spiritual. I'm almost done with your consults from yesterday. I'll have them for you to proofread in about thirty shakes of a lamb's tail, but you can start with these." She handed him a folder of papers.

"Thirty shakes?"

"Land's sake, Dr. B. I forgot you don't calculate Southern Style. Three shakes is about a minute, but I need longer than that."

Randall chuckled. "I think I can do this calculation. You need about ten minutes."

"I knew you could do it. Now get to it."

Randall took the folder but paused. "Columbia Record Club."

"Excuse me? What's that now?" said Doris.

"In college, I 'accidentally' joined the Columbia Record Club and the first record they sent me was good old down-home gospel music. I wasn't very worldly at the time and thought 'what the heck do I want with Negro spirituals?' But after I listened to the record, I was amazed by the singer's voice. The sparrow song was just about my favorite one of the lot. Can't quite place the singer's full name, but I remember her first name was Mahalia. Your singing kind of sounds like her."

"Well, glory be," exclaimed Doris. "Who would have thought gospel music would win you over? Don't recall that singer's name from anywhere, but I never had money for records. We was too poor."

"That's a shame. You would have liked her music. It must be strange to find that a sliver of southern culture reached these hinterlands. Every once in a while, a blind pig finds a mushroom," said Randall, laughing.

"Lordy, now I'm really shocked. My Mama used to say the blind pig one all the time."

Bob Storch appeared at the outer doorway to Doris's office holding a twelve-inch vacuum tube. He looked at Randall expectantly.

Randall held back on further pig-based banter. "Good morning, Bob. Did that come out of your toaster? What's up?"

Bob gave a weak smile and muttered something unintelligible. Randall motioned him into his office.

Bob ducked through the doorway. His height-conscious slouch made his voice sound choked. "Doctor B, this is the main power modulator for the orthovoltage unit. I was warming the machine up because we've got a skin cancer patient to start treatment at 9:00. When I dialed it up to 140 KV the unit shut down, so I turned off the breaker and checked inside the power unit. This tube is blown. See the filament pieces inside?"

"Yep. It looks fried. Do we have a spare?"

Bob shook his head. "No spares for this puppy. You know that unit dates back to the fifties. I can order one and it can be drop-shipped, but it won't get here until tomorrow."

"Can we afford it?" asked Randall.

Bob nodded. "I asked Mr. Kornberg. He got all flustered and said he had to check with Radiology. You know, life is tough when he has to make a decision. Thankfully, they said okay because it was for patient treatment. But I need your say so to cancel the patient's treatment for today."

Randall smiled at Bob. "No problem. It's a smallish basal cell, and one day's delay won't hurt anything. Say, if this tube is blown, can I keep it in my office for a paper weight? When I was a kid, my dad repaired busted radios, and I was his designated tube tester. I never tested one this big before."

Bob wasn't sure if Randall was pulling his leg, so he took a chance and guessed serious with a dash of kidding. "*Umm*, sure, this tube won't let any paper escape. Go ahead and keep it, if you want. I've got a whole closet full."

Randall gave Bob a crooked look. "What else you got in that closet, Bob?"

Bob laughed nervously. "Just my Slinky collection. They were hard to play with when I was a kid. We lived in a ranch-style home, and it had only one step: the front porch. One 'ka-zing' is all I got. I forgot to bring them inside one night, and it rained. Rusty Slinkys suck."

Randall wasn't used to any humor coming from Bob's direction and suspected the story might be true, but he decided not to pursue it. "That's a shame, Bob. Our bungalow had lots of stairs. One 'ka-zing' after another. Tell you what, you take care of ordering the new power tube, and Doris will cancel the patient until tomorrow. If I can find my old Slinkys, I'll trade them for the blown tube. Deal?"

Bob's face lit up. "You'd do that? That would be great. I'll get started on it right now." Bob bean-stalked out of Randall's office.

Tuning in Tokyo

As Bob got halfway out of Doris's office, he encountered Grace who was headed into Randall's office. Bob and Grace met chest to face halfway through Doris's office, Bob towering above Grace. Each would have to turn sideways to get past each other through the narrow passage. This was a physics conundrum neither had yet considered. Should they pass from front to front? Back to back? Or back to front, spoon style? In a split second, each had to consider the pros and cons of each one, while appearing nonchalant.

First they tried rotating in unison, but ended up front to back. That didn't seem right. One would be butting the other. Butt to butt was definitely wrong and potentially scandalous. Finally they choreographed the move to front to front and began to shuffle sideways. For some reason they stopped in mid-passage. Grace seemed to be contemplating the fact that she was looking at Bob's shirt pocket, full of pens, pencils, and rulers. Bob was looking straight down at Grace's blouse, seemingly transfixed by her protruding female appendages with plenteous protrusion to observe.

Grace was wearing a new pants suit uniform, the blouse of which had a V-neck that emphasized her décolletage. The blouse was decorated with miniature US flags and looked quite patriotic. What was more, her hair was washed and coifed. She appeared scrubbed, shiny, alert, and clear. Bob detected a faint waft of lavender in the air.

Bob and Grace stood there, face to chest, for what seemed like a hiccup in space time. Randall and Doris watched the motionless ballet, awaiting the next moves. Bob just stared intently at the objectives, chewing and clicking his gum, then slowly placed his open right hand over Grace's left breast. He squeezed it like the bulb of a turkey baster.

Grace responded abruptly as though Bob had just tuned in a powerful radio broadcast. "Robert Storch, what the hell do you think you're doing?" said Grace in a loud growl.

Bob jerked backward, his head hitting the wall behind him. He let go of Grace's breast like it was a hot potato. "Ordering a new vacuum tube?" yelped Bob in a voice an octave above normal.

He tried to escape, but Grace pinned him to the wall with a stiff finger to his solar plexus. She used the finger to pre-punctuate her final outburst. "And I've got a new order for you, Buster. If you ever touch me again, I'll make you a necklace out of your family jewels. They're an easy reach for me." She raised her left hand into a slowly closing fist like a crab.

"Did I just do what I think I did?" croaked Bob. "Omigod, I thought I was just thinking it."

Grace actually had to laugh at the remark. "Well, thinking and doing were never your strong suit, Mister Bobby."

Randall decided it was a perfect time to play referee. He mimicked whistling a play dead and swept his arms in an umpire's "safe" gesture. "Steady on folks. Why don't we all just agree that nothing happened here except a little accident. Sort of like Adam and Eve tempted by the snake and apple in the Garden. Just common human frailty. What's done is done. No harm, no foul. I am sure Doris will agree that nothing untoward happened."

Doris nodded vigorously, stifling a laugh. "Heavens, no. Nothin' to see here, folks!"

Randall made shooing motions. "Now, Bob, run along and make that tube order. Grace, what did you need me for? Come on in my office. My, you are looking nice today. Is that a new uniform?" asked Randall.

Bob was relieved to be pardoned and ran off. Grace glided into Randall's office. She was a bit surprised and more than a little pleased by the effect her transformation had made. She smoothly transitioned into a picture of calm.

Grace's voice usually sounded like a cross between a grunt and a groan, but the dulcet tones that ushered from her mouth this time purred like a well-tuned V-8 engine. "Thanks, Dr. B. No need to dwell on what happened. Bob is odd but harmless. I just needed you to check a calculation on a patient that's up for treatment in about ten minutes."

"Uh, be happy to," said Randall. "Before I do, I want to ask if you're sure you're okay with what Bob did. If you'd like me to take any action regarding his little misadventure with your . . . new uniform, I could have HR do a little intervention with him."

Grace waved a hand like the queen pardoning a commoner for a breach of etiquette. "Nah, he's just a harmless oaf. I can handle him."

Randall detected a hint of a smile under her scowl. "Are you sure?"

"I am," responded Grace with an air of bravado. "Thanks for noticing my new uniform. I suppose you're wondering why the big change.

So you don't get the wrong idea, it's because of my dad. He's been diagnosed with Parkinson's. He's also gotten stone deaf. Up 'til now, he's
been driving me to work every day, but the doctors made him give up
driving. He can barely turn his head to the side anymore and can't hear
horns honking."

Randall made a lame attempt to add levity. "How about geese?"

Grace gave Randall her sucking lemons look. "Are you and Bob secret brothers?"

Randall took umbrage for his "geese" remark. "Sorry. Sometimes I
try to deflect bad news with stupid jokes. I'm sorry to hear about your
father's health problems. He's a cool guy. I chatted with him a few times
when he came in to pick you up when we were working late. Wasn't he
an auto mechanic?"

FIREBIRD

Grace looked away and sighed. "Yeah, he was. He's retired now. From
now on, I'll have to drive myself to work."

Randall was surprised. "You can drive?"

"Oh, yeah," said Grace. "I've even got a car in storage. Bought it
brand new with cash. It's a '68 Firebird. But I hate to drive it to work
because it gets dinged up in the VA lot. Now I'm going to have to."

Randall looked puzzled. "Can't you drive your dad's car? I saw it. It's
just a beat-up Toyota Corolla."

"How do you know that?" asked Grace.

"When I could still park in the Engineering parking lot next to the
East entrance, sometimes he parked next to my car to wait for you after
work. Once, he striped my rear fender while pulling out of the space. I
matched the stripe on my fender to a mark on his front bumper."

This was news to Grace. "You never said anything."

"Nah. It wasn't bad. It rubbed right out," said Randall.

Grace thanked Randall for not mentioning it. "Dad sold the Toyota. It was crapped out anyhow. From now on I'm the family designated
driver. Dad said he'd pay for car insurance on the Firebird, but he made

me promise to clean up my act before he'd let me drive it alone. I think you probably get my drift. Well, this is me cleaned up. Want a ride in the Firebird sometime? It's damn quick. You'd enjoy it."

Four on a Door

Randall wasn't sure where that was going but was spared explaining a noncommittal response to Grace's suggestive question when Molly came huffing into Randall's office. She and Melinda had been trying unsuccessfully to maneuver a hefty gurney patient onto the treatment couch.

"What's the holdup here, Grace? Mr. Gordo is waiting. We need another tugboat to move him. Melinda and I don't have enough horsepower."

Randall jumped at the opportunity for a smooth segue. "Come on, let's all go and give the old heave ho. Grace and I just finished checking a calculation." Randall did a quick visual check, signed off on the chart, and handed it back to Grace.

In the treatment room, Mr. Gordo looked like a beached whale lying on a plank. He'd been just over 400 pounds at weigh-in on the ward. A special lift had to be used even to get a weight. Randall decided they should use a slide board for the transfer to avoid herniating themselves. On a three count, they slid Mr. Gordo to the treatment couch, which groaned and sagged a bit with the weight. They rolled him a bit to his side and extricated the slide board. The treatment couch groaned and creaked again.

After the patient was positioned correctly, the four left the room, triggered the electric motor to close the lead-lined entrance door and gathered around the console. Molly set monitor units and started the treatment. They all waited together for the treatment to end so they could unmount Mr. Gordo from the table.

The mechanical complaints from the treatment couch bothered Randall. "Molly, when you send Mr. Gordo back to the ward, call the charge nurse and tell her to have the team weigh Mr. Gordo again. The weight limit of the treatment couch is 425 pounds. If he's getting close to that or over it, we may not be able to treat him."

Molly nodded. "Okay, Boss. But they won't be happy. The nurse will probably call you to object."

Randall made a raspberry noise with pursed lips. "How is that a change from normal? I would be happy to disavow her of any choice in the matter."

Melinda looked thoughtful. "Could he actually break the couch?"

"You bet, Then we'd be screwed to a wall. We wouldn't be able to treat anyone until it was fixed. It could take weeks to repair. Who knows what we do when a patient weighs above the limit?" Randall loved playing teacher.

Grace was first to respond. "We use the old 'Four on a Door' technique."

Randall was pleased someone remembered. "That we do. Care to explain?"

Grace laughed and began. "Down in storage we have an old metal door that was removed from the block room. Engineering hauls that down here and sets it up on two sawhorses. The treatment couch gets moved to the side and the door setup takes its place. The patient lays on the door and we fiddle with the treatment head position until everything is lined up. It's not perfect, but better than no treatment."

Molly looked shocked. "Sounds pretty primitive, but I've seen worse. Had a guy once who was so big they couldn't get him out of bed, so they brought the whole bed down and we treated him in the bed. They guessed he was over 550 pounds. I've even got a Polaroid."

Even Randall was impressed. "Where did that happen?"

"It was at St. Lucrative when I was in training," said Molly.

The little group laughed at the reference. Randall added a comment. "You know, we operate on a budget about half of that hospital's Rad Onc Department, but I think we do just as well, if not better."

"Yeah, we're the best radiation oncology department on the block," added Melinda.

"The little engine that could," threw in Grace.

"Speaking of that, what do you all think of Grace's new outfit?" asked Randall. Grace turned a light shade of red.

Molly was the first to comment. "I've been meaning to say something about it. Your new outfit is . . . it's amazing, Grace."

Melinda began humming the tune to "Amazing Grace."

Grace acted oblivious to the hymnological reference, but the red shade deepened. Randall and the other techs did their best to stifle laughs. The monitor unit clicking sound stopped. It was time to go back in the room and rotate the patient for the second treatment field.

The three techs headed to the room to set up the new field, and Randall called after them. "I'll hang around near here and help you get Mr. Gordo off the table when he's done. Do you know where Bob is? I've got a quick question for him."

"I think he's still in the workshop," said Molly.

"Thankfully, far away," grumbled Grace.

Dropping Shoes

Randall found Bob making a custom block. "So, Bob, how'd the tube order go?"

Bob hadn't heard Randall enter and jumped like a frightened cat when he realized Randall was standing right behind him.

"Cripes, Dr. B, you scared the bejesus out of me," yelped Bob. "Could you please get some louder shoes? You're always sneaking up on people."

"All the better to monitor the proletariat," said Randall in a mock menacing voice.

"I guess," said Bob. "It seems to be working. Well, the tube is ordered and should be here from GE tomorrow. It has to be shipped from California."

"Good, good. Pony Express is dispatched. Looks like a complicated block you're working on. You always pay such close attention to detail." Randall was trying to soothe the nervous beast.

"Thanks Dr. B. Most people don't notice how hard I work in here shaping these lead blocks. It's a thankless job."

"Well, I thank you, Bob, for your fine work. By the way, do you chew Wrigley's Big Red gum?" asked Randall.

Bob missed a beat. "Huh? Er, yeah, how'd you know?"

Randall shrugged and waved an arm. "Just a wild guess. Just call me a gum guru. By the way, good job on the tube order. Well, gotta run. The girls are gonna need lifting help in a minute or so."

Randall left the workshop. Bob let out a sigh of relief. He was half expecting Randall had come in to talk to him about adjusting Grace's left prepectoral appliance. He couldn't stand the suspense.

Just when Bob was relaxing, Randall did a Detective Columbo move and reappeared at the workshop door. "Oh, Bob, I almost forgot, I meant to thank you for the nice job tightening the upper hinge on the front door to the department this morning. I almost couldn't get the door closed and locked last night. You're the only guy who can reach that hinge without a ladder and I couldn't find ours."

Bob tensed his shoulders again, his breath shallow. When would the other shoe drop? "Yeah, no problem. We'll probably have to replace the hinge though. That's the third time in two weeks I've had to tighten it."

Randall hit his fist on the workshop door, and Bob jumped a bit. "Alright with me. Just clear it with Kornberg first, or he'll have a hissy fit. Well, thanks again and happy chewing, CinnaMan."

Gotcha! thought Randall as he walked back to the hall. He took several steps toward the treatment console but returned to the shop doorway yet again. "Say, Bob, by the way, when you're finished here, meet me in my office. We need to chat in private about something. In about ten minutes? Thirty shakes?"

Bob felt like a schizophrenic elevator. "Sure, Boss. Ten minutes."

Melindus Interruptus

After getting Mr. Gordo off the treatment couch, Randall went back to his office to do some paperwork while he awaited Bob Storch. He found

Melinda was waiting there for him, sitting in the chair next to his desk with her legs not so demurely crossed. Beneath her skirt hem, an ample amount of leg was on display, ending in her dainty shoes. She otherwise looked quite innocent above the supraclavicular area. Her ponytail emphasized her long neck.

Randall prodded himself mentally to remain strictly professional. "Hey, Melinda, what's up?"

Melinda got up from the chair, smoothed down her skirt with both hands, and went to close Randall's office door. She sat down in the chair again and put her hands in her lap. "Dr. B, I have a suggestion and a request."

Randall kept his focus on the paperwork in front of him, but he really didn't see it. "Make it quick. I've got a meeting with Mr. Storch in here in about five minutes." Randall felt moderately aggravated. He was not in a mood for any female manipulation.

Melinda nodded and cleared her throat. Randall stayed focused on his paperwork and began to initial boxes that didn't need initialing.

Melinda's voice was clear and measured. "I'll be brief. Since I've been helping you with follow ups and reviews, it seems that it speeds up the flow. But it doesn't require a Rhodes scholar to do it."

Randall nodded agreement without looking up. "You're right. Weighing the patient and getting the vital signs means I don't have to do it. I'm way overtrained for that duty. Most clinics have a nurse or a medical clerk to do those things, but we don't have one yet."

Melinda shifted in her seat, which raised the hem of her skirt another inch. Randall still didn't look up. "This may be out of place for me to say, but Mr. Kornberg is supposed to be the chief technologist here, right? But from what I see, he hardly does anything except order supplies and keep the exam rooms stocked. Why couldn't he put patients in the exam rooms for you? Pretty soon I'll be too busy helping Molly and Grace to help you. I'll bet the man is bored not having anything else to do. He might like being more involved."

Randall put a hand to his chin and looked up at Melinda. Her face beamed with benevolence. "*Hmm.* That's something to consider. It would take some convincing, but I think we could make that happen, if you'd be willing to help."

Melinda liked that suggestion. "I'd be happy to. What's your idea?"

Randall stroked his chin some more and took off his glasses, checking them for dust specks. "This is just off the top of my head, like my former scalp hair, but you and I both know you were helping me with patients just to get familiar with the process. But Mr. Kornberg doesn't know that. To him it could be part of a new training program for student techs. What if you were to go to him on a really busy morning and ask for his help? You know, as a struggling student just trying to succeed. I'll bet he would be more amenable to pitching in to help you than if I order him to do it. Exactly how that works, I wouldn't know, because I have only been the victim of feminine wiles, not the perpetrator."

Melinda smiled broadly and lit up the room. "I think I get your drift. I will give it my best try."

Randall filled in more details of the plan. "Then if he helps you with one or two patients, thank him, but say that he probably shouldn't do any more patients on your behalf without my permission, since that task isn't in his job description. He doesn't like to come to me unless he has to, so you offer to ask my permission in his stead."

"What if he doesn't want to help me?" asked Melinda with a Mona Lisa smile.

Randall raised both hands. "Now that's a silly question coming from such a smart and influential young lady. I have no doubt you have the means to handle it. Now if that's an adequate response to your suggestion, what's your request?"

Melinda leaned back in her chair and adjusted an errant lock of hair. Somehow the shifting hoisted the skirt hem another half inch and created new stress lines in her blouse architecture. "I've been reading about how Linacs make X-rays, and I just don't follow it. It's so complicated. I know you know it like human anatomy. Could you find some time to explain it to me?"

Randall coughed and cleared his throat. He looked at the wall clock.

Bob Storch was due any minute. "Tell you what. I'll have Doris set aside an hour for us to have a teaching session sometime in the next several days. If you successfully pull off the Kornberg Gambit, I won't cancel that hour."

Melinda arose quickly and looked for a second like she might hug Randall but took a step back. "Deal. Now I'll get out of your hair."

Randall got up to walk her out. "That should be easy. There's not much hair to get out of."

Melinda reached up and patted him on the head. "Yes, but it's so nice and shiny."

She turned on her heel, went past Doris's desk and into the hallway just as Bob was headed in. Bob stopped abruptly when he saw Melinda coming and backpedaled.

Coffee Beaned

Randall was about to return to his paperwork when Bob knocked on his open door to announce himself. "Excuse me, Dr. B, you wanted to see me?"

"Oh, right," said Randall. "Have a seat right here." He pointed to the chair next to his desk.

Bob sat down but was so tall he looked as though he was still standing. He was self-conscious about his height and went into a slouch, even sitting. It didn't hide anything, just made him look more awkward. "I have something to tell you, before you start your business with me."

Randall folded his arms. "Okay, shoot, I'm all ears."

Bob had a few false starts, but finally cut to the chase. "I have been thinking for quite a while about getting out of radiation physics. All the responsibility about keeping the machine running accurately and calculating complex dose distributions is keeping me awake at night. I'm always afraid I might make a mistake that could wind up killing a patient. Plus I hate working for the VA, and I can't stand working around Grace. She does strange things to me."

Randall was a bit stunned but was sympathetic. "Sorry to hear that, but I understand what you mean."

Bob continued. "So whatever is on your mind about anything at all will no longer be relevant, because I'm giving you my four-week notice. I'm also requesting that you not tell anyone in the department for a few weeks. I want to announce it myself when I'm ready." Bob handed Randall an envelope.

"Are you sure?" asked Randall, incredulously. "Is there anything we can do to work things out?"

Bob remained adamant. "No need. I've made up my mind. I'm sorry if this puts you in a bad position, but it's something I have to do. There's a friend of mine who's interested in the job. He doesn't have a PhD yet, but he's well trained and has an MS in radiation physics. You'll have to convince the VA to accept him as only PhD eligible."

Randall resigned himself to the new reality. *What was the old saying about life is change, but it ain't nickels and dimes?* "You have been giving your plans a lot of thought. If you're unhappy here, then I will be the last person to stand in your way. I'll keep it to myself until you say you're ready. If you don't mind me asking, what are your plans?"

Bob smiled for the first time in Randall's memory. "I've purchased a coffee plantation in Costa Rica. My wife and I have traveled to San Jose for the last several years for vacation. We've fallen in love with the place and, when this plantation came up for sale, I was in the right place at the right time. We've put all our savings into it."

Randall was truly taken aback. "Wow! That's no small change. You've taken a leap few of us ever take. I am amazed and fully approve. So no more physics?"

"I figure I'll use a lot of physics keeping the place running," said Bob.

Randall stood to shake Bob's hand. "I'll accept your letter of resignation under one condition."

"What's that?"

Randall slapped Bob on the shoulder. "When you bring in your first crop, send me a postcard and a bag of coffee beans."

In response, Bob slapped Randall's shoulder so hard, Randall thought it might leave a mark. "You've got it." Bob walked out of Randall's office happy. He had finally gotten the Costa Rica news off his chest and did not have to undergo an inquisition about his encounter with Grace. He had always wanted to tune in Tokyo just once before he headed to Central America. And he had done it and gotten away with it. Small triumphs were underrated.

Randall called out to Bob to come back. Bob rolled his eyes. Was he being Columbo'd again? "Yeah, Boss, what is it?"

Randall looked apologetic. "Almost forgot. Can you get me the contact information on your physics friend so I can call him as soon as possible? What's his name?"

Bob quietly sighed in relief. "It's Dan Graham. Here, I've written it down on this card."

Randall took the card. "Thanks. Good luck, Bob. I'm already jealous. You won't be seeing much snow down there."

Bob headed back out to the hallway and called over his shoulder. "I know. I may be crazy, but I'm not stupid."

Lucky bastard, thought Randall. *No snow, no Grace, no VA, no patient worries.*

Randall briefly entertained the thought of asking Bob to take him along. No, that was a pipe dream. At least the list of suspects for who was playing Gummo Marx was shorter. If the gum appearances stopped, perhaps the mystery was solved.

Randall sat down at his desk and scratched his head. *Just when you think things are figured out, they're not. Oh well, roll with the punches. Dan Graham might be a breath of fresh air.*

Randall finished signing off on his reports and brought the papers out to Doris's desk. Doris scheduled a free hour, two weeks hence, to do the Linac tutorial with Melinda. There was just one consult left before he could leave for Uncle Phil's funeral. Randall looked forward to closing out that mystery.

CHAPTER 13

FUNERALS ARE US

"For strange effects and extraordinary combinations, we must go to life itself, which is always far more daring than any effort of the imagination."

— *The Adventures of Sherlock Holmes,* Arthur Conan Doyle

GUM SIGN

On his way out of the department to Uncle Phil's funeral, Randall noted that the Radiation Oncology Department sign was, once again, punctuated by a faded wad of red gum. With no time to stop and check it out, he made a mental note to extract it later.

Randall high-tailed it to the Scirocco and motored off to the Stanislaw Funeral Home. Steadying the steering wheel with his thighs, he opened his bag lunch and managed to eat and drive. He knew drinking and driving was frowned upon, but he was pretty sure eating while driving was legal, as long as you didn't get mustard on your steering wheel. As he gained some distance from the hospital, he felt his abdominal muscles relax, and he took some deep breaths.

By the time Randall found the funeral home, his lunch had disappeared as if by sleight of hand. He parked and walked to the front entrance of the two-story Lannon stone structure. If the architect had intended the building to emanate an aura of "substantial," he had succeeded. The ornately carved mahogany entry door required some heft to open and made Randall feel as though he were entering a well-guarded castle. *I wonder why the dead and access to the dead would need to be so heavily guarded?*

He stepped into the foyer and felt his stomach knot up around his PBJ sandwich and carrots. He hated funerals. The odor of flowers was redolent in the air. The heavy fragrance made him sneeze. *Is it to protect them from flower snatchers? Oops, better stay stoic.* He could hear the sound of people chatting in hushed tones in the large visitation room to his left. He spotted a somewhat kyphotic old woman in a wheelchair who seemed to be the center of attention.

Memory of Funerals Past

Randall flashed back to his Aunt Tilly's funeral when he was thirteen years old. She'd become depressed in her mid-forties and had hung herself from a basement floor joist. He had sat at the funeral, wondering how anyone could self-destruct like that. His father had always said suicide was a permanent solution to a temporary problem. He recalled just sitting in an uncomfortable folding chair staring at Tilly's still form lying in the casket dressed like she had been called back to her Maker on her way to a party. It seemed so odd; she was there but she wasn't.

Randall thought her face looked inhuman and waxy. He realized makeup couldn't make her look alive and the spark of life could not just be painted on.

No one at Tilly's funeral talked about the suicide. It was as if she'd died of natural causes, no discussion about why or if anyone had noticed she had any problems or tried to help. The elephant in the room seemed invisible to all present. Most of all he remembered the cold and empty platitudes. Would they be echoing in this grand room as well?

As soon as Randall passed through the foyer, the wheelchair woman turned her head, and a broad smile crossed her face. She rapidly spun the wheelchair 90 degrees and propelled herself over to Randall before he had taken two steps. She was surprisingly quick and brought the wheelchair to an abrupt halt in front of Randall and held out a hand to him.

Randall took her frail hand in his. "Mrs. Woodstock?"

The woman spoke in a thin, weak voice, albeit with a strong spirit. "Yes. You are Dr. Biedermeier, I presume?"

Randall nodded and squeezed her hand gently as if it were fine China. "I am, Ma'am. Please call me Randall. There's no need for formalities. We're almost family."

Mrs. Woodstock took a deep breath to speak as loudly as possible. "That's right, you're Diane's brother. I'm told you have a message for me."

Randall was tempted to ask how she knew he had a message but decided not to go down that road. "Why, yes, I do have a message. I was at your husband's bedside at the end, and he asked me to give you a message."

She motioned for Randall to lean down and whisper the message in her ear.

Randall leaned down close to her ear, picking up a strong scent of lavender. "Your husband said his last words to me. He asked me to tell you that he loves you. He may be gone from this life, but I'm sure his love is still alive."

Mrs. Woodstock slowly nodded her head. "I knew it. And I'm sure of what you say. He still talks to me."

Randall raised his eyebrows and parted his lips. "You knew it? How's that possible?"

She put a bony finger on Randall's chest for emphasis. "Now hear me and hear me well. There's knowing from learning in your brain, and there's knowing from listening to your heart. This inner knowing is far more important and trustworthy, my dear. All things are possible, as you will learn if you pay attention, young man. Remember this day well."

Randall felt his heart swell.

She looked anxiously back to the visitation room. "Now you must run along and get back to your patients. That's another thing I know. I'd better get back to my family, at least the ones who aren't at my house right now, robbing me of anything of value."

Randall looked surprised again. "Robbing you?"

"That's another thing you'll learn one day. Just because someone is family doesn't mean they won't try to take advantage of you. I'm betting half of them wish I'd join Phil soon so they can take everything. Promise me you'll never betray family." She tapped her finger on Randall's chest again to emphasize the point.

Randall took Mrs. Woodstock's hand again and squeezed it. "I promise. Just call me if you need any help." He reached in his pocket and gave her his card. "Here's my numbers. Any time. Say hello to Uncle Phil for me."

Mrs. Woodstock nodded, her eyes moist, then briskly hove her wheelchair around and motored back to the lion's den. Randall waved a little wave and took his leave, grateful to depart before the service. The message was delivered. His job was done. He'd gotten a powerful message as well. It was kind of a bonus.

During the ride back to work, scenes from the day ran through his mind. Too many things were happening that did not fit in Randall's scientific frame of reference.

Why did everything have to be so complicated? Where the heck had simple gone? Commotion, emotion, fast motion, slow motion, and suntan lotion. He who's lost hesitates. Waste makes haste. Now you're cooking on all cylinders. That's the flaw in that ointment. The lost shall be first. Slow down faster. Smooth is fast. Slow is smooth.

Randall was sure that a wandering brain was a sign of something. Speaking of signs, he was shocked to see the hospital sign appear in his windshield. He had arrived back at work with no conscious awareness of how he had gotten there.

Kornberg's Folly

When Randall returned to the department, Mr. Kornberg was hovering near his office. He anxiously informed Randall that the VA Fire Marshal had come by in Randall's absence and done a spot fire risk assessment.

The Fire Marshal determined the exam room alcohol lamps were a fire code violation and had to be removed. The only alternative was to order glass bead mirror warmers, but they cost $500 each. Three were needed. Mr. Kornberg really had his undies in a bundle because it was way outside their supply budget. Randall suggested that he start a wastebasket fire in the exam room and set off the fire alarm. That should get the attention of the administration and free up some dollars. Mr. Kornberg was aghast and backpedaled a bit, suggesting that he had just thought of a way to do an end run around the problem.

Randall was a bit disappointed. He liked the idea of starting a fire.

"That's what I like about you, Mr. Kornberg. You're quite the innovative problem solver. I think I'll put you in for employee of the month," said Randall sardonically, patting Kornberg on the shoulder.

"You'd do that for me?" Kornberg asked with a bright smile lighting up his face.

"Of course, you're an important part of this operation," said Randall, certain he'd made Mr. Kornberg's day, despite there being no such VA employee of the month award. It might even soften him up for Melinda.

SCREE-AH-YAH
11/12
It was —
BIONIC BUNNY !
BB

CHAPTER 14

P. NESTOR DIAZ

"I have the heart of a small boy. It is in a jar on my desk."

—Stephen King

STRANGE DUDE

Randall grabbed a cup of coffee to bring himself back to the present and reviewed the records he was sent for the next patient. The funeral interlude put him behind schedule by almost an hour, and he loathed to keep patients waiting.

The next consult was P. Nestor Diaz, a fifty-six-year-old man who had been treated with radiation therapy for prostate cancer two years previously at Mt. St. Elsewhere Hospital. Although he was a veteran, he didn't trust the VA, so he had chosen to get his treatment at the private hospital. Afterward, he had an ongoing dispute with the treating doctor about the treatment's $110,000 price tag and reluctantly transferred his follow up care to the VA. Given the standard treatment the patient had received, Randall figured it wouldn't be too difficult of a consult. All he'd have to do is review the case, do an exam, and get Mr. Diaz set up for routine follow-ups.

Randall was about to enter the patient's room when Melinda hurried up to him.

"Uh, Dr. B, before you go in there, I think I should warn you. Mr. Diaz is a bit strange, and he's not alone. He's in there with his mother and a 'friend,'" said Melinda, while holding out a limp wrist.

It took a moment for Randall to connect the dots, but then he nodded his understanding. "Thanks for the heads up. I'll be on my best behavior."

Randall entered the room with his loins girded. Once in the room, Randall quickly took in the scene. Seated to the left was a large Hispanic man with a shaved head. He was dressed in black leather, including biker jackboots. Sitting next to him was a short, thin Caucasian man with a blond crew cut. His neck was tattooed with a Nazi swastika. He too was clad in black leather pants, biker jacket, and black boots. His right hand was holding the larger man's arm. Seated across the room from both men was a tall aristocratic looking Hispanic woman with aquiline features. Her gray hair was drawn back in a tight bun. She wore a long black lace dress and a small black hat. A funereal black lace veil obscured her face.

Randall, making a quick assessment, held out his hand to the large man, who slowly reached for the proffered hand like a stalking cat preparing to pounce on a bird.

"Mr. Diaz, I presume?" asked Randall.

"Just call me Diaz. Everybody does," said Mr. Diaz, nearly crushing Randall's hand.

Randall grimaced and gritted his teeth. "Good to meet you, sir," he squeaked. "Is this your family?"

Diaz gestured with his chin. "This is my friend, Danny, and that is my mother, Maria."

Randall shook hands with both in turn while trying to suss out the dynamic he had just walked into. Mother and friend at a prostate cancer consult? He decided to ease the subtle tension in the room with some benign banter.

"It's nice to meet you all. So, Mr. Diaz, what does the P stand for?"

Diaz stayed stoic. "Nothing. It's just an initial."

Randall seized on the chance for a story. "Yes, I've run into that before. I had a patient once named R. B. Jones. His mother just liked the sound of the two letters. They didn't stand for anything. Problem was, when he was drafted and filled out the forms, he entered R. B. Jones. The Army wouldn't accept that and handed the forms back with instructions to enter his full first and middle names. To make it clearer he changed it to R (Only) B (Only) Jones. The Army clerk looked at it, shook his head, and said he would make it so. When R. B. got his dog tags, they read 'Ronly Bonly Jones.'" Randall laughed nervously at his funny story to prime the pump, but his audience of three remained stone-faced.

Tough crowd. Better stick to my day job. Randall loosened his tie just a bit. A bead of sweat formed on his brow.

MOTHER KNOWS BEST

"The 'P' stands for Paco," said Mrs. Diaz. "He's named after his father. He hates the name, so he never uses it. He thinks it makes him sound like *un niño pequeño*."

Mr. Diaz rose from his chair and screamed loud enough to be heard in the hallway. "Mother! I brought you here to help, not embarrass me!"

Danny grabbed Diaz's arm and tried to pull him back into his chair. "Nestor, calm down," he soothed. "You promised to behave."

Diaz just became more infuriated. "I will not calm down, Danny, I won't! Mother always does this to me. That's why I have never told her the truth."

Diaz turned to face his mother. "Alright! If you must know . . . I'm gay, mother! I'm gay! But it's not my fault. Radiation did this to me. Radiation made me gay!" he bellowed. "It was YOUR idea that I get radiation treatment. Now look at me. It made me bleed from my ass too. Every time I take a dump, I crap blood!"

Now all the waiting patients could clearly hear every word, even through the closed door. Randall was concerned how they would react.

Diaz's mother appeared unmoved as Diaz continued his rage, pounding his fist against his chest with loud thumps. "If that's not bad enough, those bastard doctors charged me a hundred grand for what they did to me. I'm totally broke. What am I going to do now?"

When Diaz finally fell silent to catch his breath, Mrs. Diaz lifted her veil, revealing a pinched face and hooded beady eyes. But she didn't look at Diaz. She just stared straight ahead at the wall. Randall thought she might burn two holes in the wallboard.

The room went silent for a long moment. Finally, Mrs. Diaz raised her arm and pointed a bony finger at Diaz. "You fool. You and I both know the truth. You've always been as gay as a three-dollar bill." She paused while Diaz quietly fumed, then added a final comment, as if for punctuation. "Don't blame the radiation."

Mr. Diaz stood stock still in the middle of the room with clenched fists at his side. He seemed to get even taller, towering menacingly over Randall, Mrs. Diaz, and Danny. Then Diaz abruptly turned to his right and kicked the metal wastebasket that sat on the floor next to his mother's chair. The wastebasket careened off the wall and ricocheted into the exam table. Old used exam gloves and crumpled paper towels flew out of the wastebasket and scattered on the floor. Randall flattened his own self against the door. Danny tried to pick up the mess, but there was no place to put it. The wastebasket was pancaked, as was Danny's confidence. Randall could hear shouts of alarm from the hallway.

Mrs. Diaz was unphased by her son's display. She rose from her chair and pushed Diaz in the chest with the flat of her hand. Her move was so swift that he was forced to back pedal and plop back down in his chair. She stared daggers at her son for a long moment and then reared back and slapped his face. He cowered away, all the steam whistling out of his protest like a train engine pulling into the station.

When Mrs. Diaz spoke again, her voice was as tight as a piano wire. "Look at him, Doctor. He's all bluster and no luster. Just like he's always been. He's never been man enough to admit he's gay, just like his father. He wasn't man enough either. The rotten apple doesn't fall far from the tree."

The room fell silent again. Randall was at a total loss for words. Mrs. Diaz turned on her heel and sat back down in her chair. She pulled her veil back over her face, like the visor of a motorcycle helmet. She was clearly done with the conversation.

Grace opened the door enough to poke her head into the exam room. "Everything okay in here? *Err*, we heard some noise."

Randall looked up at Grace and excused himself to go talk to her. He whispered the signal for a possible security alert, the fear showing in his eyes. Out loud he stated that everything was alright, and that there had just been a little accident. Grace nodded her understanding and left to call the hospital police.

While Randall and Grace conferred, Diaz was feeling quite betrayed. His carefully orchestrated disclosure was falling apart. Self-deception was crumbling. He couldn't understand how his mother had known his secret. Hadn't his cover-ups been convincing? He was stunned by the revelation that his alpha-male father was gay as well. That was probably why the marriage had broken up. How had he missed all the signs?

Diaz felt the steam pressure building up again. He could hold it in no longer. "No, no, no!" he roared, as he rose and stalked toward Randall with his fists raised.

Randall did a small sidestep as Diaz headed for the exam room door and began to pound on it, yelling at the top of his lungs. "Radiation made me gay!"

Mrs. Diaz showed no response to her son's outcry.

RAMPAGING BULL

Diaz stopped banging on the door and yanked it open. He slowly stomped down the hall repeating his "radiation made me gay" mantra in a loud booming voice. All eyes turned to the big man as he stalked down the hall with Randall following behind him like a shepherd vainly trying to corral a lost sheep.

Patients waiting in the hall began to leave their chairs and scatter. Those who remained looked terrified and held their hands over their vital body parts.

Just a few patients were bold enough to challenge Diaz. "Hey, man, what's your problem?" shouted Mr. Dithers.

"Cool it, Buddy, before you hurt somebody!" bellowed Jimmy Burdin from his gurney.

Molly, Grace, and Melinda had been setting up a new patient in the treatment room, with the help of Bob Storch, when they all heard the commotion in the hallway.

"What the heck is all that yelling about?" blurted Grace. "Bob, get out there and check what's going on. Someone may need help."

"Me?" asked Bob meekly.

"Yes, you. Anyone else in here named Bob?" said Grace derisively.

Bob shuffled cautiously out of the room and put his head on a swivel to survey the situation. He saw Randall trying to corral a very large skinhead in leathers. Bob was torn between helping his boss and running for cover. Randall spotted Bob and motioned him to join him. Bob shook his head. Randall used a more emphatic arm gesture to get Bob to move, after which he sidled cautiously over to Randall.

Bob leaned down and whispered in Randall's ear. "That man looks crazy. What the heck do you want me to do? I'm just a physicist. I deal with atoms!"

Randall was rapidly losing patience with Bob's lack of chutzpah. "And I'm just the lead radiation oncologist, and I don't want to get hurt either, but we've got to keep him away from the patients. Just help me keep him contained. I think he's just a big sissy, and we're probably safe. Besides, you're taller than him. Just stay an arm's length clear of him. And no sudden moves. I'll try to talk him down. Grace called the hospital police. We just have to contain him until they come."

Bob nodded his head tentatively. "Okay, Boss."

Danny had come out of the exam room and was walking slowly behind Randall and Bob. Randall stopped to put Diaz's chart down on top of the console to free up both hands.

Despite his outward calm, Randall could feel early panic rising. He had always made such an effort to portray to his patients that radiation was a safe treatment. That was no mean feat because most of them were already skeptical about radiation. Now this ditzy Diaz was proclaiming to the world that radiation could make one gay. Why would his patients believe such a lie? Sometimes the most ludicrous lies are just the ones some people believe.

Randall tried to counter Diaz's blasphemy. He didn't want to yell, and sound demented like Diaz. Two insanes don't make a sane. In a lame effort to tone his voice down, what came out was weak-voiced and barely audible.

"No, no. Listen, Mr. Diaz. Radiation didn't make you gay! It can't do that."

Oh, crap, that sounded wrong! Randall thought. *I shouldn't have said the man's name in front of other patients.* Randall worked hard not to fall into the paranoia pit. If some administrator were to walk in and see Randall playing matador with this bull of a man, who would they judge as the crazy one? *No time for sideways thinking. Focus, man.*

Randall tried speaking again. This time it was a bit choked but came out more clearly. "Listen to me, sir. OUR radiation didn't make you gay! Not here, it wasn't us that treated you!" *No, no, no. . . that didn't sound right either.* Randall wanted to go back and scrub the words from the air.

He stuttered out a revision. "I mean, radiation doesn't make anyone gay, whoever gives it! Not like gay is a bad thing . . ."

Diaz had stopped yelling and was now just staring at Randall with hate in his eyes. The look scared the crap out of Randall. It was the same fear he felt during his recurring nightmare about Viet Nam, even though he'd never been there.

After Randall was nearly drafted in 1969, he still dreamt about being pinned down in a wet foxhole just outside a MASH unit to escape mortar attacks during the Tet Offensive. *Why was this dream memory coming back now?*

Randall stood frozen in the middle of the hallway in a near vaso-vagal shutdown but was startled out of it when the diminutive Danny ran past him. Danny weaved and pivoted in front of Diaz and began to corral him like a sheepdog.

His mind clear again, Randall ducked into Doris's office. He hurriedly directed her to call the hospital police again to send someone ASAP. When he rejoined the bullfight in the hall, Randall found Mr. Kornberg had bravely joined the roundup. Randall, Bob, Al, and Danny formed a loose circle around Diaz. They closed the circle slowly with Diaz standing stock still, his head slumped on his chest. Then Danny broke ranks, launched himself at his friend and gave him a bear cub hug. All the fight seemed to drain out of Diaz.

Shepherding

Danny's voice was slow and calm. "Now, now, dear boy, come this way. Let's be calm." Danny reached up and patted his cheek like a mother comforting her son. "Nestor, Nestor, you're okay. You're safe. You're alright. Let's take a time out."

Slowly Diaz's huge form seemed to further deflate. Danny kept talking as he gently guided Diaz back down the hall. "Let's go on back to the exam room. We can discuss all this further when we get there. Everything's going to be alright."

It was remarkable to Randall how the little mouse man had the power to dampen the volcanic big man. But perhaps Danny and Nestor were yin and yang.

Randall began to collect himself as well and tried to settle down the upset onlookers. "Ah, nothing to see here," said Randall with moderate conviction.

The waiting patients began to return to their seats.

Back in the exam room, Mrs. Diaz still sat, unmoving. She said nothing as Diaz and Danny resumed their seats.

Randall rejoined them in the room and braced himself for another storm between Nestor Diaz's fire and his mother's ice, but there was no clash. The stillness was strangely scarier than the earlier outbursts. Something about Maria Diaz's absence of human engagement sent chills up Randall's spine. Assessing the charged situation, he decided it would be best to give the "family" a time out, by themselves.

When the Diaz clan was seated again, Randall began to inch from the room. "Why don't you three just take ten and discuss things in private? If you'll excuse me, I need to check, *uh*, on some other business. I'll be back shortly, and we can finish things up."

Security in Aisle One!

Randall hustled to Doris's office with all due alacrity and found a hospital security guard being briefed by Doris. The officer was bulky large, with muscles gone part way to fat. He sported a going-gray buzz cut. He was properly intimidating in his dark blue uniform, black ammo belt, holstered .38 caliber revolver, and night stick at his side. His name badge read "Smith."

Randall introduced himself. "Hello, Officer Smith. I'm Dr. Biedermeier. Thanks for coming down."

Smith put a large right thumb under his equipment belt. "Ms. Hicks, here, was just giving me the heads up on your wacko patient. How can I help?"

Randall glanced at Doris and nodded, signaling a "well done." "Well, it was a bit dicey a few minutes ago, but I think we have things under control now. But if you could stand by here until the man leaves, we'd all feel a lot more secure. He was kind of scaring my other patients, not to mention us. He is rather large and was acting threatening. But it looks like you could handle him."

Smith nodded affirmation. "Former Army MP, Doc. I know how to handle the rowdy players. Do you want me to brace him up?"

Randall wasn't quite sure what that meant in MP talk, but it didn't sound like a good idea. "Probably not necessary at this point, Officer Smith, but I would appreciate it if you just standby until I'm done with him."

Officer Smith tapped his boot heels together quietly and nodded. "You got it, sir. How long do you think you'll be?"

Randall pondered. "Probably not more than ten minutes. Will that work?"

Smith made a half salute. "Not a problem, sir. I'll be in the hall just outside Ms. Hicks's office."

Randall smiled a half smile. "Good man. I'll be walking Diaz out through this hall with his mother and friend soon. I want him to see you. You won't have any trouble figuring which one he is. There should be no need for interaction, unless . . ."

Smith gave Randall a sly nod. "I know 'unless' when I see it. Seen it before." Smith took his place in the hall, and Randall weak-kneed into his office for a breather.

Randall flumped against the wall, and he did some deep breathing to settle his heart rate. His inner critic started to taunt him. *What the heck, Randy? You almost froze back there in the hall! Why'd you almost lose it? It was like your old 'Nam willies. You would never survive mortal combat. Enough with this crap, Biedermeier. Buck up, and be professional!*

Randall took a final deep breath, raised his chin, adjusted his tie and walked back into the hall. He crossed his fingers in his pocket and reentered Diaz's exam room, somewhat apprehensively. The room was silent, each person staring off into the distance.

Randall's nose could detect a hint of lightning ozone mixed with failed deodorant. The black leather and lace added an eerie undertone.

Randall cleared his throat loudly and the sound seemed to bring the Diaz threesome out of their trances. Randall cut right to the chase. "So, Mr. Diaz, let's, *uh*, reschedule your consult. I've rather run out of time to finish this properly. I think we can all agree that you have family issues to resolve amongst yourselves. We can, *uh*, do the full consult, *uh*, later."

Diaz and Danny tacitly agreed to the proposal. Mrs. Diaz remained stoic in her black-clad state of perpetual disapproval and said nothing. Under her cold gaze, Randall felt like he was in trouble for not cleaning his room. He was glad to escort the trio out of the exam room and down the hall past Officer Smith, who stood watching, legs apart, hands behind his back. Smith scowled at Diaz as Doris handed him the date of his new consult appointment.

Then Randall asked Officer Smith, as a courtesy, to escort the patient and his entourage back out to the parking lot. Randall also requested, in front of Diaz, that Officer Smith be present in the department when Diaz returned for his rescheduled consult. Diaz was about to protest when Danny elbowed him.

Randall returned to his office to find Grace waiting for him with Diaz's chart.

"Dr. B, you left this chart on the treatment console. Is this guy a new treatment start?" asked Grace.

"What's the name?" asked Randall.

"Let's see, it reads P. N. Diaz."

Randall had to laugh to himself when he heard the name spoken out loud with the two first initials. *How oddly appropriate!*

Grace was still waiting for a reply. "Well, Dr, B?"

"What? Oh, yeah, that's the chart from today's consult," said Randall. "No worries. He's already had treatment elsewhere. We're just going to follow him. I'll take the chart for dictation."

"Was that the guy you called the hospital police about?"

"Yep."

Randall returned to his office to dictate a note on Diaz. It would be a challenge to make a politically correct account of the encounter. After all, Diaz could always read it for himself later if he requested his medical records. So best keep it benign as possible.

Before he could start the dictation, Randall felt like he had to settle his nerves. Calm during the event, but shaky afterward when the adrenaline rush fades away, and your mind plays out possible alternate outcomes. And the second guessing. How close had he come to being punched out? Had he subjected his staff to unnecessary risk? Did he put his patients in danger? He'd felt pretty good during the standoff when he'd been stoked up but getting unstoked was proving to be unsettling. Randall decided cookies and coffee were in order. That proved to be what the doctor ordered.

Randall was finally able to put Diaz in the rearview mirror and complete the dictation. He asked Doris to read it over for political correctness. The rest of the day rolled along smoothly, right up until Randall was visited by the Hospital Security chief. Doris knocked on the open door of Randall's office.

"Chief Ostastralznovich is here to see you, Dr. B," announced Doris. Randall motioned him to come in, guessing it was a follow up on Diaz.

The chief walked in, and Randall rose to greet him. "Hey, Peter, how are you doing?"

As the chief came through the doorway, he seemed to block out all the light from the hallway. He swiped back a cowlick of dark hair. "Only fair until we had to deal with the goofnuts patient you hooked us up with. Then my day improved to middling."

Randall and the chief had enjoyed previous encounters over several years, especially when Vietnam vets with PTSD started acting out in the department. The chief stood well over six feet and made Officer Smith look medium sized. His barrel chest and thigh-sized upper arms made Randall certain it would be unwise to accept an arm-wrestling match with the man. The uniform and equipment completed the Fort Knox impression.

Randall had always had civil interactions with the chief, but he suspected the chief's bite was worse than his bark. It had taken Randall a while to feel comfortable in his presence. This was the guy to take along on a walk down a dark alley.

Randall motioned the chief to sit in the chair next to his desk. "So my spidey senses tell me you're here about today's little circus?"

The chief nodded briskly. "Yep. That Mr. Diaz is quite the number. I thought you'd like to know that Officer Smith followed Diaz and his little coterie out to the parking lot. Diaz proceeded to ram his station wagon into one of our hospital signs while leaving the parking lot. Pretty much totaled his car and got taken to the ER. They patched up a few cuts and bruises. After some astute observation by the docs, he got himself admitted to Psych for observation. Apparently, they detected that the man needed a few screws tightened. Diaz's little blond buddy is hanging out in the family room, if you want to chat. I'm glad you called us. The man has issues."

Randall burst out with a much-needed laugh. "You think? Glad to be of assistance. Sometimes the simple gets complicated, and you just have to bob and weave. You know, float like a bumblebee and sting like a butterfly."

The chief grinned. "You're a regular Ali Muhammed, Doc. Hope we don't have to talk soon."

"Ah, but when we do, I get another story to tell my grandchildren," said Randall.

The chief guffawed. "Better edit the stories for content before you tell them to the under-ten crowd. By the way, I have your request to have someone stand by when Mr. D visits you again. Hopefully, the docs in Psych will have him smoothed out some by then."

"Yes, a consummation devoutly to be wished," said Randall.

The chief looked at the ceiling. "Is that Shakespeare?"

Randall shrugged. "Not sure. But I do know it's some old dead poet guy who wrote stuff. You know, McGillicuddy or Agadaboo."

The chief grinned. "Ah, yes. Those two. In the top ten on the English Literature list. Didn't memorize any of their stuff, but I know yours pretty well. Anyway, all I know is that your department seems to attract a lot of fruits and nuts."

Randall shrugged again. "I try to be a good squirrel. Well, the military makes them and then breaks them. I just try to weld them back together. Just doing my 'Docly Duty.' Hey, wait a minute, we don't get *all* the fruitcakes. What about the guy who blew his brains out in Speech Pathology last week? That had nothing to do with me."

"The reports said he invoked your name just before he yanked the trigger on his S & W," taunted the chief.

"Bollux!" said Randall. "But if you think I am in the danger zone, why not issue me one of those Glock thingies?"

"Nonsense. You have all those X-rays to unleash. Much stronger than a 9mm. And far stealthier. Well, gotta go. See ya, don't wanna be ya."

Randall could not come up with a clever comeback, so he just waved goodbye. He decided it was time to head home to see what adventures awaited him there.

The drive home was automatic. He reviewed the day over and over, while the car seemed to drive itself. When Randall pulled into the driveway, again, he wasn't sure how he'd gotten there. He decided he couldn't leave the car until he left the day behind. He needed to settle his agitation.

MEMORIES OF MOM

Randall leaned the seat back and closed his eyes. He remembered when he had just lost a sectional tennis match in high school. He had dragged his depressed self home, sore and defeated. It took his mother two seconds to figure out he'd lost. She sat him down at the kitchen table and fixed him a Coke with lemon. He mostly stared at the strawberry wallpaper.

As he sat lamenting his loss, Selma had come up behind him, put her arms around his shoulders and asked if he'd played his best. He thought about it for a few seconds and then realized he had given it his all. She didn't need to say more. He figured his mother would ask him the same question today, and he'd have the same answer. The little kid part of him hoped that Zelda might have the same empathy and support for today's sense of inner defeat.

Randall opened his eyes and packed the memory away. He exited the car stage left and strode through the back door. He announced his homecoming to all present. "Honey, I'm home."

He got an immediate Zelda response. "Honey, I'm leaving home. I'm just heading out to Wilson Elementary with Kyle for a PTA meeting. Can you man the poop deck 'til I get home? There's some dinner left over. Addie wanted to wait and eat with you."

It wasn't the response Randall had hoped for, but he thought perhaps Addie could do the job he was after. He shouted his response. "Aye, aye, Captain. I've got the helm."

Kyle said hello to Randall as Zelda pushed their son out the door. She had one more order for Randall on her way out. "Oh, and Randy, Polluto got into the cat box again. I caught him at it, and I can rightly say he had a shit-eating grin on his face. Explains the nasty dog breath! Don't let him kiss you!"

Before Randall could respond, she was out the door, keys rattling. He looked up and Addie was waiting for him in the kitchen with open arms. She gave him her best little-girl hug. "Daddy, you look tired. Can you make us a Coke with lemon? Mom got fresh lemons today."

CHAPTER 15

———

DREAMSCAPE

"Strange things blow through my window on the wings of the night wind..."

—*Ever the Winds of Chance*, Carl Sandburg

Go Fish!

When Zelda and Kyle returned from the PTA meeting, Kyle was unusually quiet and just grunted a greeting to Randall and Addie. They were sitting at the kitchen table, playing Go Fish. Randall was losing badly, and not on purpose. Addie was all puffed up like she'd been named Princess for a Day. Randall asked for aces, but Addie yelled out, "GO FISH!"

Zelda taunted Randall. "Randy, you look like your dog just died. Not easy on the old ego to get shellacked at Go Fish by a five-year-old, eh?"

Randall pulled a card out of the pond, shaking his head again. Another useless card. "Boy howdy! She's ruthless. But if my dog had died, I'd be a happy man. After you left, Polluto chewed the handle off my briefcase. I caught him at it and whacked him on the head with my fist. Damn near broke my hand. Stupid dog just looked up at me and said 'Huh?' in dog speak. Then he ran off like he was daring me to chase him. I tried, but he beat me to the basement stairs and hid behind the furnace. Now, I'm tired, pissed off, AND my hand hurts like a . . ."

203

Zelda made a quieting gesture. "Careful, Randy, the pitchers have big ears."

Addie looked puzzled. "I don't see any ears on our pictures!"

Kyle smirked. "I know what Mom means."

"It's just a figure of speech, Rosebud," Randall said.

Addie was not any clearer on the concept. "Daddy! Mommy says that you're always abuse. And you're being abuse again."

Zelda interrupted. "Honey, I said your dad is obtuse, not abuse. It means that he's confusing." Randall put a hand to his forehead and shook his head. "And don't blame your dad for what I said. I was just warning him not to use any swear words in front of you two."

Addie looked embarrassed. "Well, you could have just said so. Daddy already had a bad day at work. I was trying to cheer him up by playing Go Fish. I can't help it that I keep winning. I'm just that good!"

Zelda laughed. "Well, you did look pretty happy about it when I came in."

A big smile overcame Addie's attempt at pouting. "It was kind of fun to beat Dad."

Kyle slouched down in his chair and stared at the cards. Randall guessed something might be amiss. "So, Kyle, how did the meeting with your teacher go?"

Kyle closed his eyes and made a juicy raspberry sound with his tongue. "Mom says I have to talk to you about it later after *she* talks to you about it."

Randall just groaned and put his head down on the table. "So tired. Why does everybody want to beat me up today?"

Zelda went to Randall and patted his head. "Poor baby. How about I kiss your bald spot and make it all better?"

Randall let out a sigh. "That's sort of working. How about a neck massage? That could make it even better."

Zelda pretended to be extremely put out. "Oh, if I must. Yes, your neck muscles are very tense." As Zelda rubbed and probed, Randall put his head back and began to relax. Zelda took a close look at his face.

"Goodness, Randy, from the large bags under both eyes, it looks like you're packed for a long trip."

Randall shifted and straightened in his chair. "The only trip I want to take is up the stairs and to my bed. You wouldn't believe the day I've had. And the crazy patient."

"Randy, I really don't want to hear any more episodes from the VA Twilight Zone," grumped Zelda. "Especially not in front of the kids. And not with what I have to tell you about school." Kyle looked nervous, like he wanted to escape. "Kyle, how about you and Addie go work on the Lego castle?"

Addie smiled and dashed up the stairs. "Come on, Kyle! It's going to have a big tower for the princess!"

Kyle ran after her and dashed up the stairs, taking two steps at a time. "Yeah, and barracks for my toy soldiers!"

Zelda shook her head. "I don't know if I can handle more of your work stories. It's hard enough to keep our little ship on course, especially with all the strange crap that's been happening.

Addie reappeared at the kitchen door.

"What's up, sweetie? Do you need something?" Zelda was at the edge of her patience.

"Nah. Just wanted to tell you that there's a pile of dog barf on the carpet in Dad's office. It's pretty whiffy. It looks like what's left of a briefcase handle."

Randall's face took on a look of more despair. "Thanks, sweetie. Daddy will clean it up later and then murder the dog. Ignore any howls of pain you hear."

Addie's jaw dropped, and she started to object, but Zelda stifled the objection. "Don't worry, Sweet Pea. Daddy will only murder the dog in his fantasy world. Now go back upstairs."

Randall thanked Zelda for the clarification. "You're right. I don't have the energy to off the dog tonight. But tomorrow is another day. So let me get this straight. Does what you said mean I can't talk about my day anymore?"

Zelda shrugged. "Oh, I suppose if you have to listen to tales from the halls of education, it's only fair I listen to your crypt stories. But if you please, how about just the Cliff Notes version?"

Randall took a deep breath, summarizing his thoughts before speaking. "Okay, here it is. A gay biker in black leather outed to his funeral-clad mother in front of his gay mini buddy in my exam room, claimed radiation made him gay, then went nuts, and caused a ruckus in the department that almost needed the hospital police to quell. And then he crashed his car into the hospital sign upon leaving. That's pretty much it."

"Good. So just a normal day, then," said Zelda.

"Yeah, that's about right. Well, except for the funeral where I met a clairvoyant old lady and back at work we had a fire hazard warning from the VA Fire Marshal. Pretty minor stuff though."

Zelda's curiosity was aroused. "Clairvoyant old lady? Tell me more, please."

Randall related the story of Uncle Phil and his wife. He tried to keep it short, but she wanted every detail. When he was done, Zelda just sat bug-eyed and shook her head. "Randy, what the heck is going on? First, there was that dead patient who came back to say goodbye, and now this. Are you sitting on the edge of a parallel universe or something? Are you having paranormal experiences or just a pair of normal experiences and we just don't understand what's normal?"

Randall looked askance. "Who knows what's normal anymore? I feel like all I can do is observe and record. Maybe at some point it will make sense. But I believe I have to pay attention and not ignore or dismiss it. I need your help with this. I can't handle it on my own."

Zelda reached out, took Randall's hand and squeezed it. It was one of those rare moments where they really connected. To Randall, Zelda was somewhat enigmatic. She was small yet mighty. Her curly red hair paired well with her fiery disposition. Randall thought of Zelda, secretly, as a little fox. He'd never told her that. While some would visualize a foxy lady as a long-legged woman who favored low necklines, his fox was diminutive and lithe. Her freckles and blue eyes gave an initial impression of childlike innocence that belied her mischievous and mercurial nature.

During the momentary connection, Randall reflected on recent events. Lately the household had seemed to settle into a more comfortable routine. Zelda actually seemed to be approaching something closer to happy. Yet Randall still felt a nagging apprehension. His neuropathological antennae sensed something was afoot, but he couldn't quite pin it down. Nothing to do but wait and deal with the present.

Randall and Zelda sat at the table, holding hands for a long moment, not speaking. They stared out the kitchen window at the backyard nightscape. Then a shadowy movement outside caught their attention. Baldspot sensed it too. She stood on hind legs at the window ledge, scanning with keen cat's eyes. She hissed and clawed at the window. Randall and Zelda looked at each other with alarm. Randall rose and turned on the yard lights. A hugely fat raccoon stood frozen in the bright light.

Randall laughed at the sight. "As I suspected. Just old Rocky Raccoon, looking for dessert."

Zelda shivered and let out a breath. "Damn! I thought it was . . ."

Randall broke in. "The bogey man? Yeah, me too. Guess we're both a bit jumpy tonight." Randall changed the subject. "So what's the talk I need to have with Kyle?"

School News

"Oh, that. It's kind of the same old, same old," Zelda sighed. "You know, still having some trouble focusing in class. Short attention span. Doesn't complete his work all the way. Sometimes gets distracted in class and causes interruptions. It's all a little better, but still present."

"Are they still thinking it might be ADHD?" asked Randall.

"Yeah. The teacher said kids sometimes grow out of it. But if it continues much longer—"

Randall broke in. "He might need to see a kid shrink. Maybe take meds?"

"Yeah. What you said."

"What does Kyle understand about all this?"

Zelda started to get watery eyes. "He's confused and worried he might be different from the other kids. You know, a freak and they might start bullying him. I thought maybe you could explain it to him in a way that makes him feel less of a one-off. That he's not the plastic knife in the silverware drawer."

Randall nodded reassuringly. "I think I might be able to do that, but I'd like to wait a few days."

"Whatever for?" asked Zelda.

Randall put a hand on Zelda's shoulder. "Easy. I'm no expert on the subject, and I'd like the chance to do some research, and talk to some people I know before I unload a load of crap on the boy. Besides, I'm in no mental shape to do it today and do it justice. How about for now, I just temporize?"

"Meaning?"

"Tonight, I tell him we've discussed it, it's not a big deal but, when I get more information, we'll have a talk and decide if anything needs doing."

Zelda frowned and thought for a moment. "I suppose that will work for now. Randy, how can you always be so calm and logical? Sometimes you just burn me up!" She punctuated the comment with a knuckle punch to Randall's upper arm.

"Ouch! That hurt!" shouted Randall and when he tried to return the favor, she slipped out of her chair and ran upstairs. Randall steamed after her and finally caught her in the bedroom where they engaged in a tickle fight that led to a pillow fight. When the kids heard the ruckus, they joined in until feathers flew, and Zelda called a halt. The cat stood at the open door, taking note, for future reference, of the odd human behavior. Even Polluto had come out of hiding to check out the action. He snuffled, shook his head, and got out while the getting was good.

What Do Dogs Do?

Before bedtime, Randall asked Kyle to help him clean up the dog barf in his office.

Kyle complained, "Do I have to?"

"No, but I'm asking for your help. Pretty please?"

Kyle sighed loudly. "Oh, alright." They went to the office and moved the desk chair out of the wet zone.

Kyle gagged a bit and squinched his lips toward his nose. "*Ew*, this is gross! That doesn't look like leather anymore. I bet you're pretty mad at Polluto."

Randall started scooping up the gooey globs, more annoyed than angry. "Dogs do what dogs do. When we have them, we should expect to clean up after them."

Kyle laughed and shouted. "Yeah, dogs do dog doo-doo where they shouldn't do."

Randall couldn't help laughing at the comment, even though he knew he shouldn't encourage Kyle's poop talk. "You're right, Buddy. Just like kids do what kids do, but we don't punish them for being kids."

Now Randall had Kyle's attention.

"Are you talking about my school report?" Kyle squeaked and squinted.

"I am. Very clever," said Randall. "What the teacher was talking about today is something a lot of kids your age have trouble with. These days, it's got a fancy name. ADHD. But it's been around forever. When I was a kid, it was part of what they called 'deportment,' which meant how you behaved in class. If a kid was fidgety, bored, or didn't pay attention, the teacher told the parents about the poor deportment and the parents were expected to fix it. And 'fixing' it didn't mean talking about it."

Kyle nodded as he moved Randall's desk chair back to the footwell. "Yeah, lots of kids in class are bored. Some of them fall asleep. I just get jumpy. Sometimes I just look out the window. I can't help it."

Randall nodded. "I had the same problem in school."

"You did? Dad, *um* . . . how did parents 'fix' the kid's deportment when you were in school?"

Randall reflected. "In the deportment department, my mother encouraged, and my dad yelled. One worked, and the other didn't. Which one do you think worked?"

Kyle thought fast. "I bet it was the first one, right?"

"Correct again," said Randall. "So I promise there will be no yelling about this. Only encouragement to do better. I'm going to talk to some friends for advice who know about this stuff. If they think it's a problem that won't go away on its own, then we'll do whatever we need to do. But I promise it won't make you feel bad."

Kyle nodded. "I like that better than yelling. But, Dad, I have to tell you something bad. Please don't be mad."

Randall was feeling most benevolent. "Sure, son, what is it?"

"The whiffy smell isn't coming from the dog barf. It's coming from this pile of dog poo under your desk."

Randall raised his arms in the air. "What?!"

Into the Nightscape

That night, the kids went to bed without much fuss. They had brushed their teeth after only one reminder with minimal shoving and whining. Randall and Zelda put on a rock album as background music for doing the dishes and folding laundry together. Soon they were duetting the familiar lyrics and ad libbing rather unusual harmonies. They danced about, swinging dish towels in time with the music like kitchen matadors.

With the scut work done, Randall and Zelda climbed the stairs to get some shut-eye. As Randall put on his PJs, he recalled how much more readily they could become "cozy" when they were first married. Despite his fatigue, such carnal thoughts began to flood his brain, but they were quickly dashed when he looked over to see Zelda slip under the covers in her long flannel "nothing's happening tonight, Buddy" pajamas.

She uttered her last words of the day as she rolled over on her side. "Randy, mark the calendar—we may just get eight hours of sleep tonight."

Randy checked that all the shades were closed before he eased himself under the covers a few minutes later. Zelda was already emitting soft cat-like snores. The twilight of sleep settled over Randall like a misty fog. Soon Randall was cruising down a smooth and winding road in a

Fathom Blue 1968 Chevy Chevelle. He was approaching a turn near a cliff. He hit the brakes to slow down, but the pedal went to the floor. The Chevelle flew off the road and plummeted into a gulch where it landed with a loud crash, followed by the prolonged hiss of a cat. Randall awoke with a start and realized the crash and cat screech had come from Kyle's bedroom.

Immediately in on-call doctor mode, Randall was awake, alert, and out of bed in a flash. He ran barefooted to his son's room and turned on the lights to find Kyle kneeling in bed, shirtless with bleeding scratch marks on his back. Kyle began pointing at the floor and screaming.

"Jumping Jews for Jesus," exclaimed Randall as he quickly surveyed the room. Baldspot was cowering in the corner. She started hissing with her back arched and tail puffed.

Scene of the Night Crime

Randall had mounted shelves on the wall just weeks before to hold all of Kyle's *Star Wars* models, books, bobbleheads, and other kid paraphernalia. The shelf brackets had magically detached themselves, sending a scattering of shelves and contents about the room. Between screams, Kyle yelled that monster bugs with huge eyes were pouring out of a hole in the floor.

Kyle's eyes were wide open, but he didn't seem fully awake. Randall was no child psychologist, but he knew how many eggs were in a dozen. It had to be another night terror. Randall picked his way through the debris on the floor, sustaining only an evil Lego foot injury, and tried to wake Kyle. Randall could not break through Kyle's fog. Kyle was in total panic mode and just kept yelling. "They're gonna eat me! Kill 'em! Kill 'em!"

Randall tiptoed over the strewn debris to where he thought Kyle's imaginary hole in the floor would be. As if he could see what Kyle saw, Randall kicked and stomped on the bugs. He thrashed with his arms and loudly admonished the bugs to cease and desist. For a few seconds he even thought he could see them squish and die.

Kyle and Randall were now somehow connected in the same alternate reality and Kyle cheered his dad on. "That's it, Dad! Stomp 'em flat! Squish 'em, kill 'em, kick they heads off!"

The din in Kyle's bedroom finally woke Zelda. She staggered out of bed and stumbled to Kyle's bedroom. She stood at the door with a look of incredulity.

She tried to ask what was happening but could not break through the sound barrier. Finally she took a deep breath and bellowed. "Whiskey Tango Foxtrot!? What the hell are you doing, Randy?"

Randall shouted back, like what he was doing ought to be obvious to any casual observer. "What does it look like? I'm stomping bugs!"

"Are you nuts? What is all this stuff doing on the floor? And why is Kyle bleeding?"

"Kyle is in night terror mode! I couldn't wake him, so I had to join him." He lowered his voice and joined her at the door. "Putting a can of whup-ass on the monster heads coming out of this hole seems to be registering in his dreamscape. Try waking him up while I put the hurt on these hole creatures."

Zelda backed away from him. "Randy, you do realize there's no hole and no bugs?"

"Really? That's a relief," responded Randall sarcastically. "How 'bout getting over to Kyle and see if you can wake him? He may be coming out of it if he can see me."

Rousing the Dead Asleep

Zelda nodded understanding and kicked debris out of the way as she approached Kyle. Shoulder shaking didn't work, so she hollered into his face, but he was still in another world. Seeing the blood on the bed-clothes, she pulled Kyle forward and saw the bloody scratch marks on Kyle's back. This made Zelda panic, and she shook Kyle even harder, but he still babbled on about the bugs. Not knowing what else to do, she slapped him sharply on the cheek.

The slap made Kyle go quiet briefly, then suddenly, his body jerked like he'd just received an electric shock. Recognition blossomed on his face. "Mom . . . Mom . . . is it you? Is it you? Are the bugs gone?"

"Yes, big guy, the bugs are gone." Zelda sobbed in relief and held Kyle's face with both hands as Kyle looked about the room, blinking. Randall stopped yelling and stomping. Zelda reached out and enfolded Kyle in a fierce hug, which caused Kyle to emit a monster fart. The incongruity made everyone burst into uproarious laughter.

Randall thought of it as a sudden seismic "mirthquake."

Randall could not help commenting on Kyle's loud eructation. "Did you hear that dog bark?" he asked with his best French accent.

Zelda was still laughing when she replied. "I think the neighbors heard it."

Randall complimented Kyle on his masterpiece. "*Bravo*. That was one powerful passage by the wind section. Bach would be proud. We should sign you up for orchestra."

Zelda continued the accolade. "Wow, son. Great resonance. I can tell you've been working on your embouchure."

Kyle smiled his biggest smile. "That's right, Mom. I'm butt sure! Should I do it again? I think there's another train in the station."

"Not just now, big boy," said Zelda. "Are you back with us? What do you remember about what happened?"

Kyle looked around the room furtively, trying to piece things together. "I was sleeping, an' then I heard a loud crash. Then something hurted my back and I sat up. I saw a hole in the floor and big spidery bugs were comin' out like in a horror movie. They kept coming for me. Are they gone? Really gone?"

Zelda hugged Kyle again, more gently this time. "Yes, honey, they're really gone. Look, Dad is over at the spot where the hole was, and he killed all the spiders that came out. He kicked and stomped them to death."

"Yeah, I think I remember seeing Dad killing them. He protected me, and you saved me too," said Kyle breathlessly. "But how could Dad see them? It was my dream?"

Randall needed a plausible response. "I guess we were tuned in to the same dream station. That's why you don't have to worry about bad dreams. Mom and I will always come and bail you out."

Zelda winked at Randall. "Your dad is right. You know how deep I sleep. Your dream even woke me up. We can't stop the dream from coming back, but we'll always be in the dream to save you." Zelda figured an implanted suggestion couldn't hurt.

Kyle looked a bit dubious. "Are you guys sure about that?"

Zelda nodded. "Cross my fart, and that's no lie."

Randall added, "Scout's on her."

Kyle's face twisted up and formed a question mark. "Oh, alright. I suppose."

Zelda was still puzzled about the scratch marks. "Kyle, how did you get the scratches on your back?"

Kyle looked at the ceiling as if the answer might be written there. "I'm not sure."

Randall looked over at Baldspot still cowering in the corner. "Hey, Buddy, was Baldspot sleeping with you?"

Kyle thought for a second. "Oh yeah, she jumped up on my bed when I was falling asleep and was lying next to my back. I remember because it made me all hot, so I had to take off my shirt."

"I think I get it now," said Randall. "The shelves fell off the wall, the noise freaked out the cat, the cat scratched Kyle's back, and ran into the corner to hide. She's still over there, wondering what happened."

Zelda blew out a breath. "Wow. That's wacky. All that clatter plus a back scratch, and it didn't wake Kyle up all the way?"

"Well, he is your son, and you slept through the shelf crash and the stomping before you even came in here," responded Randall.

ADDIE APPEARS

Addie appeared at Kyle's bedroom door in her pink PJs and bunny slippers. She was holding her stuffed unicorn. Baldspot ran behind Addie, as if taking shelter.

"Loud noises waked me up. I'm scared. Why is everybody in Kyle's room?" asked Addie in a sleepy voice.

Randall picked Addie up and held her.

"I'm sorry about all the racket. It was just an accident. Kyle's shelves fell off the wall and crashed on the floor. That made the big noise. The cat got scared and accidentally scratched Kyle's back," explained Randall.

"You didn't put the shelves up good enough, Daddy," observed Addie.

"You're right. I guess you could say the accident was my fault," admitted Randall, accepting the blame.

Addie didn't let her dad suffer his guilt very long. Her morbid curiosity was aroused. "Are Kyle's scratches bloody? Can I see 'em?"

"Sure, if it's okay with Kyle," said Randall, glad for the redirection of attention.

"No problem," said Kyle. "I got scratched bad and it hurts, but I'm no wimp. Go ahead and look."

"Wow, you're right. It's all bleedy and yucky," said Addie in awe of Kyle's wounds. "Dad, what was all the yelling and pounding on the floor? It made me afraid to come out of my room."

"That was just your dad going nuts as usual," said Zelda.

Randall gave Zelda a look but played along. "Yep, nothing to worry about, sweetie. Situation normal, all . . ."

"Randall! Don't finish that sentence," admonished Zelda.

Randall held up both hands in defense. "Tell you what. I'll take Kyle to the bathroom to clean up his wounds, while you take Addie downstairs to make some hot chocolate. When we're done with the wound dressing, we'll join you down there."

"Will it hurt?" asked Kyle, apprehensively.

Randall ad libbed, "Nah, the hot chocolate won't hurt a bit."

Addie gave Randall her evil eye. "Dad, you're being obtuse again."

Zelda corrected her. "No, he's being obnoxious."

Addie pounded her fist on the bed. "I hate big words. I'm never gonna learn them. Now tell Kyle the truth!"

Randall chuckled and gave forth the gospel. "Yep, Kyle, cleaning up those cat scratches will burn like holy schneikees, but you're a fine figure of a man. You can take it."

"Let's get 'er done!" responded Kyle stoutly.

Later, while the four Biedermeiers sipped hot chocolate, they talked about the night's events. Randall and Zelda didn't want the kids going back to bed still scared about bad dreams. They made it clear that dreams, especially bad ones, can seem very real and very scary, but in the end can't hurt you.

After the hot chocolate was finished, Randall and Zelda conferred at the kitchen sink while they cleaned up the cups and fixings. Zelda whispered to Randall that in the near future, they needed to talk further about the night's events.

"You're right," said Randall. "Kyle may need some kind of evaluation. Right now, I'm not sure what form that will take. Give me some time to cogitate on it. Maybe by morning my superpowers will devise a plan and we can discuss it at breakfast."

"Sounds like a plan," said Zelda. "Let's get those two settled and back in bed. How about you put Kyle down and I do Addie?"

"Deal," said Randall.

BEDTIME REDUX

Zelda took Addie to her room and turned on the lights. Zelda gasped. Both were shocked to see that Addie's room was a mess. Her carefully arranged stuffed animals were strewn about the floor. Her Breyer model horses, usually artfully displayed on shelves, were in complete disarray, scattered all about. One curtain was hanging loose, and the window was partially open, letting in the cold winter air. The room was freezing.

"Mommy!!" shrieked Addie. "What happened to my room?"

Zelda was dumbstruck. Her head goggled around the room in surprise. "Holy sardines in a tin! What in holy, freaking hemlock is going on?"

Addie ran from the room to Kyle's bedroom. "Daddy! Daddy!

Something bad happened in my room. I'm scared." She ran over to Randall who was sitting on Kyle's bed and leapt into his arms.

Zelda followed Addie into Kyle's room. "Randy. You're not going to believe this. It looks like a tornado hit Addie's room. It's freaking me out! Take a look."

All four Biedermeiers crept back to Addie's room. They gawked at the mess in disbelief.

"Dang, Sis, what did you do in here?" asked Kyle.

"I didn't do anything!" exclaimed Addie. "I was in here sleeping until I heard all the noise you and Dad were making. It woke me up, and I came to your room to see what was wrong. My room was fine when I got up."

Randall felt suspicious. "Maybe you were mad about being scared awake and you went back in your room and made the mess."

"Daddy! I did no such thing," rebuffed Addie. "I never went back into my room until now. You know I was with you in Kyle's room the whole time."

Zelda had her suspicions too. "Kyle, did you mess up Addie's rooms before your bad dream? Maybe you sleepwalked in here and messed things up. Then maybe you went back into your room to cover it up by pulling the shelf down. Were you mad at Addie?"

Kyle looked about as if searching for an answer, or even a hidden camera. "Mom, are you kidding? I don't think I did that. The shelf crashed. The cat scratched me. The noise and the scratches woke me up sort of, and then there were bugs coming out of the floor. Dad was yelling at me . . . I don't know!"

Randall held up both hands. "Slow down everybody. Let's stop pointing fingers at each other. What if we're all innocent?"

Zelda shook her head. "Randy, don't even go there. If none of us did this, then who or what did? I don't even want to go there."

Randall grimaced. "I see your point. But we need to consider that something unnatural may have happened. What, I can't guess. But it's not the first time we've been there."

Zelda nodded grimly. "Oh, not again. The lawn mower incident in

Colorado Springs . . . old dead Harold the unfriendly ghost. The shelf crash in Durham."

Randall nodded back. "I can't believe we actually did an exorcism for that one. But nothing happened again after that."

Addie shivered and hugged Randall's leg. "What are you guys talking about? You're scaring me worser."

"Yeah, we should have done that in Colorado Springs," said Zelda. "Randy, we can't just blow this off! Who are we going to call?"

Kyle raised his hand and jumped a bit. "I know, I know. We're gonna call someone who can bust these ghosts in the gut! Or in their butts! Buttgusters!"

Addie was still shaken. "Daddy, Mommy. How can you laugh? Do we really have ghosts?"

Kyle patted Addie's shoulder. "Don't worry, little Sis. I was there and it wasn't that big of a deal. Look, we're still all here and no spooks can scare me."

"Kyle's right," said Zelda. "Nothing we can't deal with in the morning. We all need to get back to bed."

"Exactly," said Randall, trying to sound confident. "No need to start believing in phantoms. We'll figure this out. And nobody is in trouble, so rest easy. Let's do a quick clean-up of both rooms and try to settle down for bedtime. I promise everything will be hunky-dorey from here on, and we'll all get a good night's sleep."

Zelda stayed with Addie in her room, and they soon had the window closed, curtain back in place, and things back in order. The room was still a bit cold, so Zelda crawled under the covers with Addie to calm her down with a bedtime story. Addie requested yet again to hear the tale of Truffula trees as told in Dr. Seuss's book, *The Lorax*.

Randall got the unenviable job of cleaning up the mess in Kyle's bedroom floor well enough for safe passage. He and Kyle stripped the bed, threw the bloody sheets down the laundry chute, and remade the bed. Randall found a broken action figure under the bed and went over to the trashcan to toss it. He noticed one of Kyle's books in the can. It was a kid's book about wild beasts.

Randall removed the book from the trash. "Hey, Kyle, what's this book doing in the trash?"

"I threw it in there. The bugs in my nightmare looked just like the ones in that book," said Kyle with a touch of fear in his voice. "I never want to see the book again."

"Okay, big man, back it goes," said Randall, thinking to himself that he would retrieve it when Kyle was asleep and label it as material evidence. "Want me to read you something—besides that book?"

Kyle handed Randall a thick full-color comic book printed on high-quality paper. "Yeah, how 'bout we read my new *Star Trek* graphic novel together?"

"Where'd you get that?" asked Randall.

"Billy Ichner borrowed it to me," said Kyle.

Randall took the comic from Kyle and looked it over. "Hey, this looks really cool. Let's do it."

Randall lay down on the bed next to Kyle, and Kyle put his head in the crook of Randall's arm. Randall started reading, but mostly describing the pictures as Kyle's eyes drifted closed. When he got to page ten, Kyle was off in La La Land. Randall eased up from the bed, carefully withdrawing his arm from under Kyle's head, pulled up his covers, and tiptoed out of the room.

On his way out, Randall retrieved the Sendak book from the trash can. He went to Addie's room and, as he had expected, Zelda and Addie were both fast asleep with the open Seuss book on the floor. Randall padded down the stairs, put the Sendak book in his briefcase, ascended the stairs, and gratefully sat on the edge of his side of the bed.

He looked across the room. The same shade was up *again*. He was sure he pulled it down before bed. A black rectangle of night leered at him as if it were the opposite end of a telescope. Was there a watching eye outside there just to mock him? Randall grunted, got up, and pulled the shade down. He grumbled that if it happened again, he'd nail the gol' darned shade to the window casing. Then he shuffled back and poured himself into bed. He fell asleep, vowing revenge against whatever was inhabiting his house.

Morning Came Too Early

The next morning, Randall started awake, jumped out of bed, and raced to the bathroom. It was already 6:00 a.m. Time to get up. But he realized he was already up. So time to stay up.

After finishing his toilette, Randall checked the kids, found both still sound asleep, and left them that way. After the night of disrupted sleep, they needed all the sleep they could get. Randall began the Zelda arousal ritual by pulling back the covers. The cool air would work its magic soon enough with bare legs exposed to the chilly room.

The room felt colder than usual. Randall went to the hall and checked the thermostat. It was turned down to 40 degrees and the house was at 55 degrees. "What the flaming flock of geese?!" yelped Randall. "Which kid did this?"

Then he remembered the events of the night before, and he muttered softly. "Rather, what evil force is doing this? Whatever it is, now it's pissing me off!"

Randall reset the thermostat and went back to the bedroom to dress. He was buttoning up his shirt when Zelda grumbled. "Where's my pants? Legs so cold."

Randall pulled the cord on the malevolent shade to let the weak sunlight in. He decided not to relate the news about the thermostat until later. "Good morning!" he announced in a musical tone. "Time to rise and shine."

Zelda pulled up the covers and buried her head under the pillows. "Crap! I hate cheery good mornings. You sounded just like my mother."

Randall responded. "*Hmm.* My very intent. And with good purpose. You are now officially awake."

"Go away and let me sleep!" protested Zelda.

Randall was not sympathetic. "Now don't get your undies in a bundle before you even put them on. Tell you what. You get dressed and wake up the kids, while I rustle up some breakfast. As an incentive, I may have, in my sleep, come up with a plan for Kyle. I can explain it downstairs."

Zelda rose from bed and had a wicked case of bedhead. "Oh, alright! Damn, it's cold in here. Close that window shade. I don't want the neighbors seeing me naked. Get me my robe. Do I need to brush my hair? How do I look?"

Randall gave Zelda a crooked grin. "You'd make my zombie girlfriend jealous, but all the better to wake up kids if you act soon. Here's Mr. Robe."

"I bet you say that to all your dead patients," snorted Zelda.

Later, when a breakfast of Randall's patented blintzes with cottage cheese and jelly had been gulped down by the hungry locusts, Randall and Zelda sat sipping their coffee elixir of life while the kids got ready for school.

Z Interrogation

Zelda was still troubled by Kyle's latest night terror. "Randy, what do you think is going on with Kyle? You're a doctor. You should know what this is. Is he sick? Does he need help?"

She looked exasperated, irritated, and downtrodden, all at once. She was talented that way.

Randall shook his head and took another sip of coffee. "I'm afraid I only have a passing knowledge of child sleep disturbances."

Zelda turned away with a sigh of exasperation. Randall felt powerless and defensive, like a first-year college student in an advanced anatomy and physiology lab. "All my patients are adults with cancer. This issue with Kyle is outside my wheelhouse."

Zelda felt like she might be getting the runaround. "Well, don't you know anybody at that fancy hospital of yours? It's not like you're stuck in the house doing laundry and dishes all day like me!"

Randall forced himself to take a deep breath and shake off the criticism. "You're exactly right. I don't have all the answers here, but I think I know who to call, my old med school friend, Joe Shepard. He's now a child psychologist. If anyone has a clue, it's him." He was relieved to see Zelda soften in response.

Zelda relaxed in her chair and refilled her coffee cup from the carafe. "Sorry, Randy, these night terrors have got me kind of scared. When I saw you dancing around on the floor, stomping and yelling at nothing, I thought at first that you were losing control too. It really freaked me out."

"Hell, I was still half-asleep myself," said Randall. "I guess, in a half-witted way, I wanted to see if, instead of waking him, I could somehow connect with his illusion and take the fear out of it."

Zelda gave a small shudder. "Well, you sure fooled me. But it seems like somehow it worked, because Kyle said he saw you killing the bugs. Weird though, because if it was his dream and he wasn't awake, how could he see you?"

"Yeah, how, indeed?" asked Randall, rhetorically. "That question has been bugging me too. Sorry, bad choice of words. It's been bothering me too."

They ended the discussion, agreeing that Randall would talk to Dr. Shepard and go from there, and they would work together to sort out the problem. Zelda was good with the plan.

Randall was pleased too, because Zelda didn't always like to confront problems or wish to share the responsibility of dealing with them. He thought about how Zelda sometimes seemed to attack him with bared teeth and claws. He was coming to realize that she was scared and defending herself the best way she knew how, just like he was. Parenting was a whole new world for both of them. There was no textbook or repair manual. And Zelda came into the game very young and unprepared. She was only nineteen when they married and Randall was twenty-seven. Kyle had been born in their first year of marriage, and that had really fast-forwarded the process.

Kyle and Addie came down ready to go to school. Randall did a quick check of Kyle's cat scratches, and all looked good.

"How's your back feeling this morning?" asked Randall.

Kyle shrugged. "It's a little sore, but my healing cells are like Superman's."

Randall had another query. "Did Baldspot come back to bed to sleep with you at all last night?"

"Not last night," said Kyle. "I don't care if she ever comes back. I don't think she likes me anyhow. Can I get a cat of my own?"

Randall glanced upward and out. "Well now, that's something to consider."

Kyle saw Randall's eye movement. "That means a definite maybe."

Randall had a tell, and he knew it. "No, that means there's no time to discuss it now. You two need to get along to school."

Randall looked about the room at Baldspot's usual haunts. *Cat AWOL.* "Hey, have you kids seen Baldspot this morning?"

Both kids gave vacant shrugs.

"I didn't see her after she left Kyle's room last night. Maybe she got locked in the hall closet again," suggested Addie. "But I didn't do it. If she is locked in there, it was probably Kyle."

Kyle sputtered, "I did no such thing, even though I'd like to kick her butt for scratching me."

Randall had no time or patience for another scuffle. "Hey, stifle, you guys. I just checked the closet, and she wasn't in there. Could you both take a quick look around the house and see if you can find her? I put out her Meow Mix already, but she hasn't touched it. Usually, she's clawing at my shoes until it's served and then she Hoovers it up in forty-five seconds."

"Alright, Dad," whined Kyle. Kyle went downstairs, and Addie went upstairs, calling Baldspot's name. They were back in five minutes reporting no success.

"No sign of her, Dad," said Addie. "I looked in all the usual spots."

"Me too," said Kyle. "I checked the closets and laundry room. Not a peep out of her."

Randall put his hands on his hips. "Well, I'll be dipped. Where could she have gotten off to? Well she's probably still freaked out from last night. She'll probably turn up by tonight when she gets hungry enough."

Zelda came down from upstairs to drive the kids to school. "Did you all find Baldspot?"

Randall shook his head. "You haven't seen her, have you?"

Zelda shook her head right back. "I wasn't looking, but no sightings on my part. No time to worry about a missing cat now. Let's get going.

You guys get your coats and hats on. We have to scoot to school, or we'll be late."

Randall gave both kids a hug and a kiss. Zelda herded Kyle and Addie toward the back door and paused to hug and kiss Randall. She whispered in his ear that she loved him and then hustled the entourage out the door.

Randall yelled after them. "Hey, everybody, this is going to be a good day. I can tell. Have fun at school."

"We won't," Kyle shouted back.

"Yes, we will," shouted Addie and punched Kyle in the arm.

"That didn't hurt much," cackled Kyle. "You punch like a girl."

The last words Randall heard as he shut the door were Zelda's. "She is a girl, pea brain."

Randall took one more trip to the used coffee depot and, when he came out, found Polluto standing in the hallway with a ripped-up couch pillow in his mouth. It was as if the dog was taunting him. He realized he had forgotten to put Polluto in his cage in the basement overnight. It would be his fault the pillow was ruined. And no time to clean up the mess. He wrestled the pillow out of the dog's mouth after a brief tug of war and corralled him for the trip downstairs. He closed the cage door and looked daggers at the dog. "You must have a death wish, you useless fur bag. If I didn't have to go to work five minutes ago, we'd be having a bit of a *tête-à-tête*."

As Randall headed out the back door, he wondered if the dog had devoured Baldspot for a midnight snack.

CHAPTER 16

PSYCH OUT

"Nature hath found strange fellows in her time."

— *The Merchant of Venice,* William Shakespeare

Randall drove to work with a lead foot, worrying about Kyle, his mind recycling aphorisms. Those little dollops of wisdom kept popping up, but none of them provided much guidance. *Haste makes waste, but he who hesitates is lost. No help there. The early worm gets the bird. Twisted tales. Slow down faster.*

At a stoplight, Randall banged on the steering wheel with the heel of his hand. There was no point chewing this cud to death. He had a working theory and that was better than a theory that didn't work. And a plan. He had a plan. Now, just carry it out.

SHEPARD

Randall arrived at the VA a bit late, and half ran from the parking lot to the building. He decided it was time to call Joe Shepard. He huffed into the clinic and went straight to Doris's office where he asked her to put in a call to Joe Shepard at his private office. He wanted to contact Joe before the Compliance meeting at 8:30. By the time he shed his coat and hat, Doris had the call ready.

"Dr. B, I've got Dr. Shepard for y'all on line 2," announced Doris from Randall's office doorway.

Randall thanked Doris and picked up the phone. "Hello, Joe, long time no talkie," Randall said. "Thanks for calling the other day. I'll take you up on that lunch offer."

"That's great, Randy. How's things at the VA spa?" Joe asked.

"Slightly demented. Like usual. That's kind of why I need to talk with you. You understand crazy. I need to pick your brain," Randall said.

Joe laughed ironically. "Understand? Hardly. Deal with? Perhaps. What's going on?"

Randall was tempted to spill all the details about Kyle's nightmares, but did ask if they could discuss a problem Kyle was having with dreams.

Joe was silent for a moment. "Dreams? Good dreams, bad dreams, or daydreams?"

Randall realized he'd been a bit vague. "Uh, I guess you could call them bad dreams. Terrifying, even."

That clicked Joe to the right channel. "*Hmmm*. The kind with sleep-walking and monsters?"

"The very same," Randall said with a deep exhale.

Joe paused again before responding, "Ah ha, I see. Sounds like Kyle could be having night terrors. They're not uncommon for five- to ten-year-olds. How old is Kyle?"

"He's seven. What exactly are night terrors?" asked Randall, feeling somewhat better since, whatever Kyle had, it had a name. Not a great name, but probably not some rare enigmatic disease with no treatment.

Joe liked to give a studied response to tough questions and paused again before giving his answer. "Well, they can be troublesome, but they're manageable. I don't think you should panic about it. We can discuss the details when we meet. How is Kyle's speech development?"

Randall hesitated a bit. "Not as good as it should be. He still has trouble pronouncing certain words. The 'th' sounds sometimes come out as 'd,' and he runs words together a lot, especially when he's stressed or tired. Addie's only five, and she has less trouble with words. She's a little gem."

"I see," said Joe, noncommittally.

"*Uh*, okay . . . ," muttered Randall. He sensed that "I see" meant "could be bad," because that was the same measured response Randall sometimes gave his patients on sensitive topics. He started having a "what if" party, running worst-case scenarios through his mind: *What if Kyle was developmentally delayed? What if he was destined to become mentally ill? What if he couldn't be trusted at home with his sister? What if he grew up to be a juvenile delinquent? What if he became the teen at the top of the clock tower with the . . . ?*

Joe guessed what Randall's muttering meant. "Randall? Are you still with me?"

"Yeah, sorry. Doris just handed me a note," Randall lied.

"No problem," Joe got the gist. "Just one last thought. Don't let yourself stress too much about it. This is not unusual, and kids are resilient. I'll help get you guys on the right path."

Randall realized he had been holding his breath. "I understand. I guess I knew that, but it's great to hear you say it. I'm fine. We're fine. It's fine. I wasn't worried. I'm as cuke as a coolcumber."

"Sure, you are. Where would you like to meet for lunch?" asked Joe.

Randall tapped a pencil on the desk. "We could meet at Miss Katie's Diner. It's close to your office."

Joe checked with his secretary and was given the go ahead. The lunch date was happening.

Compliance Meeting

Doris appeared at his office door as soon as Randall hung up the phone. She looked impatient. "Dr. B, Winston Samuels is ready to start the compliance meetin'. Everybody from our little department is there already. The group is just waitin' on you. I have to stay and mind the farm. Too many chickens, not enough feed."

Randall glanced at his watch. "Yeah, I figured so. My call ran a little long, but the meeting is just across the hall in the Ortho Room. I'll be right in there."

Doris shook her head. "I'm sorry, but they're not in the Ortho Room. Didn't you see my note on your desk? The meetin' is up on the first floor in the Administrative Conference Room, so they can show slides. The Ortho Room is not equipped for that, and it's too small."

Randall couldn't hide his mini panic. "Oh, dang, I guess I did see the note, but it didn't penetrate to the thinking part of my brain. That conference room is a 'fur piece' from here. It'll take me five minutes just to get there. What room number is it again?"

Doris fast-talked. "It's Room-115C. Down the main first floor corridor, past the second bank of elevators, and then left at the hall to the administrative offices."

"Right, the hallway that goes right past my favorite restroom," said Randall as he headed off in a trot.

Doris watched Randall with a bemused look on her face as he ran for the elevators. "That boy. Sometimes I just don't know. Bless his little heart."

HALVES AND HALF NUTS

Randall made a quick coffee-induced pit stop at the executive restroom and then continued down the hallway to double glass doors. Black lettering on the door read "115 Administrative Offices." Past those doors, Randall thought he had stepped out of the drab VA world and into an expensive attorney's office. He found a filigreed mahogany door with a polished brass plaque that read "Administrative Conference Room." Randall pushed the heavy door open to reveal a large wood-paneled room. A rectangular walnut conference table was the centerpiece surrounded by sixteen black leather reclining chairs. There were ten smaller leather chairs lining the walls. It smelled like old money.

Winston Samuels rose from his chair at the head of the table, reaching his full height and commanding the room. "Oh, thank goodness, Dr. Biedermeier. We thought perhaps you had been waylaid by highwaymen. But then these back hallways are a bit of a maze. Sorry we had to change the venue at the last minute. Please, come, sit down next to me. There's coffee and water at the side table. Help yourself."

"Don't mind if I do," Randall said.

As he poured coffee from a large silver carafe into a fine China cup, he surveyed the room. He was astounded by all the finery. There were portraits of previous Center Directors, historic paintings of the grounds, and shadow box displays of military medals. He wondered what he'd have to do to get similar accouterments in Radiation Oncology. Leather chairs, indeed!

Molly and Grace were already seated at the left side of the table. Bob Storch and Melinda sat at the right side of the table. Randall took a seat next to Samuels.

Randall put a hand on Samuel's arm. "Before you start the meeting, Mr. Samuels, I should tell you that we are a small department and two of our key employees are not present. My secretary, Doris, is downstairs, tending to any phone calls or visitors and my chief technologist, Alan Kornberg, had a conflicting appointment."

Winston leaned back in his chair and exhaled loudly. "That is a shame. Doris will be key to data gathering for this project. She should really be up here. Tell you what. I'll task my secretary, Stephanie, to go down and mind your phones. She'll send Doris up. And please, everybody, please just call me Winston in this meeting."

Randall nodded his agreement. "Understood, Winston. I'd like Doris to be in on this and take minutes for our records." Randall wasn't going to be caught out by "verbal misunderstandings" downstream.

Winston had another question. "This chief technologist you mention. Is it a problem if he's not in this meeting?"

Grace grunted. "Don't worry about him. We'll fill him in."

Randall scowled at Grace. "That's a whole different discussion Winston and I will have to have privately."

Winston pursed his lips and got up to leave the room. "As you wish. I'll go talk to Stephanie. '*Mi soon come.*'"

After Winston left the room, Randall took a sip from his fine China cup and his eyebrows went up. "Holy cow! This is about the best coffee I've had in a while."

Everybody nodded their agreement. "You said it," said Molly.

"Definitely not VA Canteen coffee," added Grace. "Do you believe this place? Now I know where all the budget money goes."

Randall leaned back in his chair. "Yeah, this is the Pentagon's

10,000-dollar toilet seat, right here. But I bet these leather chairs are comfier than those butt cradles."

Bob Storch made an observation. "Those butt cradles are where the joint chiefs do their duty for God and Country."

Melinda guffawed and put a hand to her mouth. "Why, Bob Storch! That was funny. Who knew?"

Molly turned toward the door and held up a hand. "Hush, children, I think I hear Winston coming back."

Winston banged the door open. "No need to all go quiet on me. The tape recorder was on while I was gone." The department crew exchanged worried glances. "Just pulling your chains, ha ha ha! The opulence back in here makes me angry too. 'Specially when our veterans are struggling to get care. But we gonna fix alla dat. So '*Mi deh ya,*' as my father would say, everything is good. Doris will be up here in two shakes."

"Excuse me, Mr. Samuels," said Melinda, "your father would say what now? And what was that you said when you left the room?"

"Oh, I am sorry, little sistern, I's born in Jamaica. And sometimes I lapses into the patois."

"The Pat Who?" asked Randall.

"Patois," said Winston. He spelled out the word phonetically as patwa. "It means the Jamaican language, which comes from old Creole based on English. What the Jamaicans heard the English say became their language. None o' dem could write or spell, so it got funny soundin'. When I leave the room, I say, '*Mi soon come.*' It means 'I'll be back soon.'"

"Yeah, I can see the connection now," said Randall.

Winston seemed pleased Randall was catching on. "The translations seem obvious when you learn them, but people usually just look at me kinda funny like. I try to stop the patois, but it so a part of me. Not let me go. Stephanie hear 'dem so much, she kind of knows 'dem all. So that's 'wicked.'"

"I'm guessing 'wicked' is good," said Randall.

Winston let out his deep Uncola laugh. "*Jah, mon!*"

Bob Storch piped up, "Which means 'You got it, man' or 'jamming,' depending on usage."

Winston's face broke out in a huge smile. "Well! Look like we have a Rasta man up in here! You know the Reggae music?"

Bob answered casually, drawing surprised looks from the group. "Jah, man. I've got all the Bob Marley and the Wailers albums, including when Peter Tosh was still in the group."

"Okay, now. I hope you not just blowin' smoke." said Winston. "Lots of folks claim to know Marley music, because maybe dey hear one of his tunes on the radio. But most of them don't know what Wailers even means."

"That's an easy one," said Bob. "It does not mean that they wail, although they do, but it's after Marley's partner, Bunny Wailer, who helped Marley start the group."

Samuels probed deeper. "'Seh one great,' Bob, what your favorite Marley ditty?"

"Well, that's tough. It's hard to pick just one," said Bob. "It's between 'Stir It Up' and 'One Love.' I think Marley's son David is going to be challenging his dad pretty soon though. I can't wait to hear what he comes up with on his own."

"*Ahh*, yes, Ziggy shakes the stage," said Winston in full basso profundo. "His daddy say Ziggy means 'little spliff.'" Winston began to get embarrassed because of the unusual turn the meeting had taken. He needed to get back into his compliance officer persona.

Doris arrived, a bit out of breath, and entered the conference room.

Winston took this as a serendipitous segue opportunity. "Glory be! The delightful Miss Doris has arrived. Now we can start the meeting. Did you have any trouble finding the conference room?"

"Not a bit," said Doris, "I just followed the signs. My, this is a gorgeous room."

"Coffee is on the side table," said Winston. "Help yourself, and sit where you please. I see you have brought along your own notebook and writing materials. Excellent. Shall we begin?"

Randall got up to refill his coffee. On his way back, he went over to Doris and asked her in a whisper if everything was okay in the department. Doris indicated that it was. He returned to his seat as Winston got up from the table and began his slide show.

Bill 'em, Danno

As Winston began his presentation, the patois seemed to disappear. "This hospital has never had a compliance officer before. I'll try to explain why we have one now, and it is yours truly."

Samuels showed graphic data comparing VA and private hospital workloads and budgets. Bottom line was the VA did twice as much work for half the budget.

Doris swiped her forehead. "*Woosh*. No wonder I'm tuckered out at the end of the day."

"*A mi fi* tell you," said Samuels. "Sorry. I mean that's right. Most VA employees would echo that. And it's not going to get any better with the way the VA allocates budget money. Soon more veterans will be coming into the system."

Randall shook his head morosely. "I figured those grim facts out a while ago. So do you have a fix?"

Winston beamed a smile that lit up the room. "Sure do. It's easy peasy. I have approval all the way up the line that any vet who has private health insurance can be billed for the services we provide."

"Hold your equines," blurted Randall. "To my knowledge most veterans don't have private insurance. That's why they come here."

"*Au contraire*, Dr. B, that's where you're wrong. Recent data shows that an increasing number of veterans are coming here for primary care even though they have a doctor outside the VA. They come to the VA to get free meds because their insurance doesn't cover the complete cost of their many drugs."

"The plot thickens," remarked Doris.

"It also sickens!" blurted Randall. "I see a problem with that. Veterans are not obliged to tell you whether or not they have private insurance. And why would they? You have no other way of finding out."

Winston smiled again and held up a finger. "VA Headquarters was concerned about that too. So they had the Brooklyn VA start asking whenever new veterans signed up for primary care. To their surprise, over 50 percent said they did have private insurance and gave the details of it."

Randall was duly surprised but recovered. "Now that I think about it, it kind of makes sense. Most vets I've dealt with are rule followers by training in the military."

Winston slammed his open palm on the table. "Our thoughts exactly! The only hitch in the plan is that the VA has no computer system for collecting billable data but, with your department's help, we will develop it using the procedure coding system that private hospitals use."

Molly could see where this was going and rolled her eyes. "I don't like it already. I used to work at a private hospital. You're probably going to have us do the coding on all the stuff we do, but why us? We're probably the smallest department in the hospital."

Winston made a calming gesture. "We picked your department exactly because it is small, and you carry out clear cut, easily defined procedures. Plus, yours is one of the best run departments in the hospital."

"Oh, well, I . . . I," stammered Randall. "You mean someone has actually noticed us?"

"Don't be so modest. And don't think that, just because we're administrators, we all have our heads up our derrieres."

"Oh, indeed not," said Randall. "We all know that's a yoga position incompatible with respiratory function."

Samuels bellowed another Uncola laugh, and the rest of the group got an acute case of giggles. When the chittering settled down, Randall suggested refills on everyone's coffee before the discussion continued.

Winston went on to explain that the project would start simply enough with the department collecting data on each procedure using a four-level complexity scale. Forms would be created, and each employee would be responsible for filling them out each day. The completed forms would be turned in to Doris for collation. After he laid all that out, the group looked somewhat depressed. Randall was hoping the proposal wouldn't turn into a long run for a short slide. He was glad he hadn't told the crew about the promise of new RTT positions yet. Better it come straight from the horse's mouth.

Carrots and Bean Sprouts

The Radiation Oncology crew looked at each other with grim faces. Then almost simultaneously, they all turned and stared at Randall, as if expecting him to say what they were all thinking.

Randall was worried his staff might prematurely assume they were about to be taken on a ride down the garden path. "*Umm*, Winston, I believe we're all concerned that this grand idea of yours might be all stick and no carrot."

Grace pushed her coffee cup away, splashing coffee on the table. "Damn straight." She made no attempt to wipe up the spill.

Winston's face took on a look of grave hurt. "Do you take me for a charlatan? I was just getting to the carrot in this salad. It's as awesome as a Marley concert."

"Convince us," said Randall.

Winston put up another slide showing proposed staffing changes for the department. "For your help with this project we've been approved to hire one more RTT and promote whomever you wish to be chief RTT. In addition, while we cannot yet provide an additional secretarial position until the billing program pays off, we can provide Doris with a clerical assistant the equivalent of two days a week. My secretary, Stephanie, will be that person, and Doris will be upgraded to administrative assistant with a 10 percent increase in pay."

The fog of depression lifted. "Land O Goshen!" chirped Doris. "I can get my oil changed."

Molly and Grace looked stupefied that they would finally get some help.

"I can hardly believe it," said Molly.

Grace gave a loud grunt. "Sounds almost too good to be true."

"Oh, I almost forgot," said Winston. "Just a promise at this point, but the chief of staff is fully behind the department creating a new position to assist with running the clinic, either a nurse or a nursing assistant. We will have the funds by next quarter."

Randall's jaw dropped. This was new news. "I don't know what to say, Winston. I am gabberflasted. That's way more carrot than I was expecting. I would have said yes to your project for a bean sprout."

"I was pretty sure about that but, realistically, this is a big project, and I want it to succeed. You people are very good at what you do, but I want to give you the best chance to make me look good as well. Ha ha ha!" Winston pounded the table in laughter. The coffee cups rattled in their saucers.

Winston went on. "If this project works out, we may bring in several million dollars a year to bump up our local budget, and that will easily pay for the new positions. And if it works in your department, I can export it to other departments."

"Well, that makes me feel a lot better about carrots," said Randall.

Winston spread his arms wide. "Is everybody happy? Ha, ha ha!" his voice boomed. "Oh, Dr. B, we need to talk later about the chief RTT designation. There're some VA rules about the position being merit-based. No reason to bore you folks now with the details. As my people say, '*A so di ting set*' or that's the way it is. Do you understand?"

"Yes, it's crystal clear," said Randall. "I like the way your people think. Let me take a quick vote. All in favor of proceeding, raise a hand." All hands went for the ceiling. Grace raised both hands.

"Good, *tek*!" said Winston. "There will be big *tings* ahead for all of us. Stephanie will set up an implementation meeting in the next few weeks. Until then meeting adjourned and 'more life, more strength.'"

Everybody rose to leave and, after saying thank you and goodbye to Winston, Randall and his staff walked back to the department together. On the way back, Randall summarized his understanding of the proposal to make sure they were all on the same page. He asked if his summary fit what they understood.

"I think so," said Molly.

"Yeah," said Grace. "Administrative meetings sure are long-winded, and you guys talk in circles. But I think I got it all. We do some more paperwork, and we get more help. I'm glad I'm just a tech, and Dr. B gets stuck with all the boring stuff. But can we really trust this Winston guy?"

Molly put an arm on Grace's shoulder. "Samuels sounds authentic to me, Gracie."

"That's my read too," said Randall.

Doris was quick to defend both Samuels and Randall. "I think Mr. Samuels knows he can only succeed in his new position if we do. It may be early, but I trust him. You guys should be ashamed for not trustin' Dr. B to look out for us. Dr. B does the 'borin' stuff' in order for all of us to keep our jobs without goin' more nuts. I've heard all your horror stories about how this place sucked like a Hoover before he got here. You should be thankin' him for makin' an effort to improve workin' here."

The group kept walking for a bit while they thought that over. Then Grace shrugged her shoulders and spoke up. "Yeah, I guess you're right, Doris. I'm sure glad I don't have Dr. B's job. It sucks worse than mine."

Doris stepped quickly ahead of the group and turned to face them, holding up her hand like a traffic cop. "So what have you all got to say to Dr. B? All together now . . ."

They weren't all together, but Grace, Molly, Melinda, and Bob all stammered embarrassed versions of thank you.

Doris shook her head. "That wasn't the most enthusiastic gratitude I've ever heard, but it'll do for a starter." Doris then reached up and gave Randall a big hug with a great big thank-you kiss on his cheek.

Randall turned bright red. "Yeah, that's more like it. Any more takers?"

Bob shuddered. "I'm not kissing the boss's anything. Yuck."

Grace looked quizzical. "Might not be so bad."

Molly looked red in the face. "You people are just too much. No more mushy stuff in the main hallway. There's trouble waiting for us back at the salt mines. Let's hop to it."

Melinda nodded her head and agreed. "Mushy stuff should always be done in private. Let's motor."

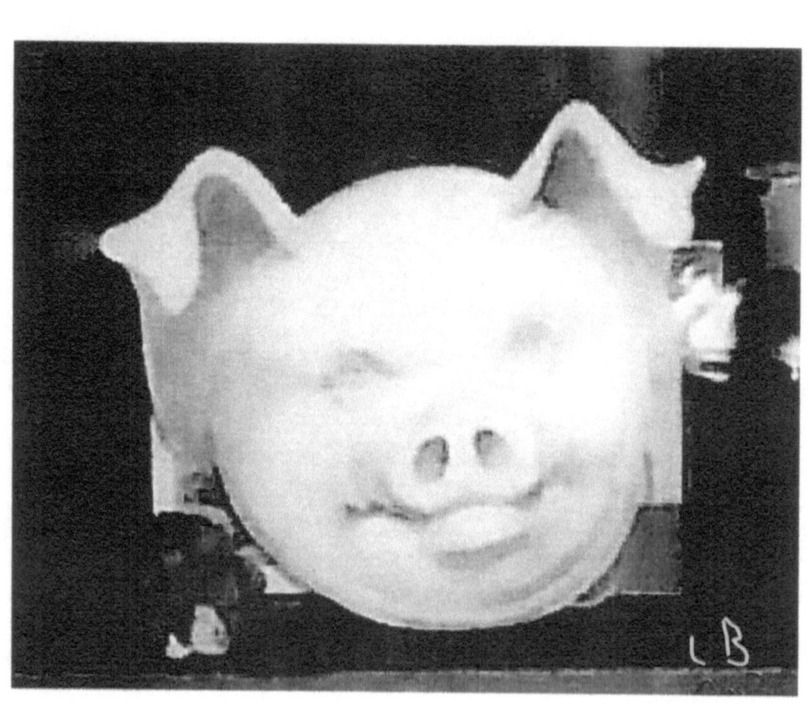

CHAPTER 17

BIG MEL TAKES A LEAK

"Some problems are so complex that you have to be highly intelligent and well informed just to be undecided about them."

— *Why Things Go Wrong or the Peter Principle Revisited,*
Laurence J. Peter

When Randall returned to the department from the Compliance meeting, he was still struck by the contrast between the fancy administrative conference room and his dingy basement department. Maybe he couldn't order any new high-end office equipment, but he could pry the new chewing gum wad off the department sign. He pulled a chair from the waiting area and stood on it to reach the wad. It was still sticky and not even hard yet. It was pretty high up. No one but Bob Storch could reach that high without getting on a chair, but that didn't rule out anyone. There was no time to investigate now. The natives were already restless.

You're on Candid Camera

Randall walked softly over to the Linac treatment console where Grace, Molly, and Melinda were watching a patient under treatment on the CCTV monitor. Their job was to make sure the patient wasn't moving about on the treatment table while the radiation beam was on. An intercom provided two-way communication with the patient. Most patients held very still, knowing that a radiation beam was passing through their body but, with really sick patients, anything could happen. Mostly patient monitoring was like watching paint dry. But as the old saying goes, "familiarity breeds contempt." The same old same old could lull one into inattention. It was a favorite "harping point" of Randall's.

Randall snuck up quietly behind the three techs and watched for a few minutes before he spoke. "How's it going, guys? Is Mr. Bentley holding still?"

All three techs jumped like they'd just been spooked in a Halloween horror house. "Dr. B! Will you ever stop sneaking up on us like that?" barked Grace.

Randall looked innocent enough. "I wasn't sneaking. Just observing."

"Yeah, sure," added Molly.

"No, really," Randall said. "I remembered that Mr. Bentley had a problem with tremors and involuntary movements the other day. We couldn't treat him because of all the fidgeting. I asked the ward team to sedate him before he comes down. Is it working?"

Molly was first to answer. "So far, so good."

Grace nodded her agreement. "Since they gave him some milk of amnesia, he's been steady as a rock."

Melinda laughed at Grace's little joke. She had decided to use more diplomacy.

Randall smiled. "Good deal. If you two don't mind, I'm going to steal Melinda for about an hour. I promised her a primer on radiation and Linac function. According to Doris, I am free for nothing as of now."

Molly smiled broadly. "Why, of course, Professor. We can survive without you stalking around us for an hour. Take all the time you need."

Randall knew he was getting his payback but didn't back down. "Good to hear. Don't bother us unless there's a fire. We'll be in the Ortho Room, peering inside the soul of radiation."

"Be sure that's all you're peering into," grumbled Grace.

RADIATION 101

The Orthovoltage Room housed a low energy X-ray treatment unit used mainly for treating superficial skin cancers. Melinda hadn't really gotten a close look inside the Ortho Room before. At first glance the room seemed scary and medieval. Melinda hesitated at the doorway.

Randall noted her reluctance. "Don't worry. Kind of looks like a torture chamber, but it won't bite you."

Randall explained that the unit was used infrequently and, since the department had no conference room, the room served as a makeshift meeting room. The treatment unit could be moved out of the way as much as possible and a large table moved to the center of the room. The table had been reclaimed from VA discards as well as six unmatched chairs. A 1950's era chalkboard on a wheeled stand and a small desk occupied one corner of the room.

Just above the desk hung several two-inch diameter electrical cables, suspended from the ceiling, leading from the control room next door to the orthovoltage treatment head. Randall further explained that the treatment unit was cooled by circulating oil through the treatment head via two-inch diameter rubber conduits. These conduits were connected to an oil cooling tank in the control room, and also bundled together with the one-inch diameter power supply cables. It was an intimidating array, resembling a rubber octopus emerging from a parallel dimension beyond the wall.

Randall motioned Melinda to take a seat at the table opposite the chalkboard. He'd asked her to bring her assigned *Radiation Physics* text. He went to the board and picked up a piece of chalk.

"So how far have you gotten with your reading?" asked Randall.

Melinda looked a bit disappointed. "I got halfway through reading about the discovery of X-rays and how linear accelerators work. Then I sort of got lost."

Randall was impressed. "The Linac chapter is number six. You mean you got through chapters one to five already on your own?"

Melinda looked down at her hands. "Not really. That all looked like just history, so I started right off with Chapter 6. From the look on your face, I'm guessing that wasn't a good idea?"

"Ed Zachary," said Randall.

"Ed who?"

"Just a friend." Randall wiped chalk dust on his lab coat. "How much did you understand about how Linacs work?"

Melinda's face brightened up a bit. "I got most of it, but it didn't all make sense, because I still didn't get what radiation really is and does."

"Well, you've come to the right guru, my young student," said Randall expansively. "Listen carefully and know the truth."

Randall turned to the chalkboard and began. He went through the discovery of radiation, its nature, and other historic basics. It was heady stuff, but Melinda was absorbing it all until her glass suddenly filled up.

Just about the time Melinda was ready to yell "Uncle," there was a loud banging on the heavy lead door to the Orthovoltage Room. Randall pushed the switch and the door swung open to reveal Molly standing there. She looked exasperated.

Molly's head goggled around the room. Then she spoke. "Sorry to bust in on you two, but we've got a problem. It's not a fire. It's a mini-flood and a short circuit. The Linac is down."

"What! How in the world did that happen?" shouted Randall.

PLUMBING PROBLEM

Molly made a few involuntary gestures before explaining. "Mr. Blevins went on the table for treatment of his prostate cancer with a full bladder, like you asked. We were almost done with his treatment when his bladder let loose. The gantry was below him. The urine ran off the treatment couch, dripped into the treatment head, and shorted something out. Bob is looking at it right now with a sponge and a flashlight."

Randall slapped his forehead. "What next? Of all the . . . let's give Blevins the Fickle Finger of Fate award. Any idea how long it will take to fix?"

Molly did a little stutter step. "Bob thinks it's the low voltage power supply circuit and it might be okay once the wiring is dried out. It didn't blow any high-voltage stuff." Molly looked at the two of them and the busy chalkboard. "Hope I didn't interrupt anything, you know, important."

Randall brushed off Molly's poorly veiled comment. "Melinda, let's go check it out. It's a chance to look inside the treatment head of the Linac as long as you're not repelled by a bit of kidney brew."

Melinda smiled and nodded. She'd just been blessed by the pee gods. "No problems here. I've been wanting to get a good look inside the treatment head--that's where the rubber meets the road."

"You mean that's where the accelerated beam of electrons hits the tungsten target and generate six million volt X-rays," corrected Randall.

"Yeah, that's what I meant!" Melinda quickly gathered her notes and followed Randall out of the room.

Inside View

As Randall, Molly, and Melinda made their way to the Linac Room, Randall couldn't help noticing how much he enjoyed teaching a receptive student. Plus, she was a quick study. The three found Bob Storch bent over the upturned gantry using a hair dryer to complete the drying process. A slightly metallic, fruity odor filled the room.

Randall had to admire Bob's ingenuity. "Hey, Bob, did you actually have that hairdryer in your repair kit? If so, you are one resourceful guy."

"What? I can't hear you with this hair dryer going!" Bob turned off the little air blaster, looking a bit embarrassed.

Melinda couldn't help herself. "Is that your hair dryer? Do you do perms on the side?"

Bob smirked. "Very droll. No, I borrowed it from Grace. Seems she's been packing beauty supplies lately. Don't ask me why. The little blower is drying things up nicely. We should be up and running in about ten minutes."

Randall was pleased that the down time wouldn't be too long. "Good, good. If you don't mind, while you're doing the blow dry, I'm going to point out to Melinda the salient features of Big MEL's treatment head while it's still upside-down."

Bob bowed and gestured to the exposed machinery. "Be my guest."

"Thanks, Bob. And feel free to fill in any details I get wrong or overlook," added Randall.

Bob nodded. "Happy to, Boss."

Randall pointed inside the exposed head assembly. "Going from the inside out, look way down into the center of the beam opening. After the accelerated electrons hit the tungsten target, right there, we get a beam of X-rays coming out that are shaped like a big bullet. We can't use the bullet-shaped beam for treatment, because it's too intense in the center, and too weak at the edges."

Melinda held up her hand to stop Randall. "Let's see if I got this. A bullet-shaped beam would make it really hard to give a uniform dose to the tumor? And it could overdose the normal tissue the beam goes through on the way to the tumor. Sort of like using a bazooka to take out a fly!"

Randall was impressed Melinda had connected the dots. "Indeed, it would! We need to shape the beam to make it uniform. The machine takes several steps to make that happen. The bullet-shaped beam passes through a metal-flattening filter that's the mirror image of the beam. The filter is thicker in the center and thinner at the edges. This flattens the beam out, so we get a uniform dose throughout the beam."

Bob interrupted, "Without a flat beam, I wouldn't even be able to calculate an accurate delivered dose. It would be a wide range of doses."

"Got it," said Melinda. "But how does it make different beam sizes and shapes?"

Bob continued at this point. "If you look a bit further down the path the beam takes, the beam passes through what's called the collimator, just here. It adjusts the size of the beam from 4 x 4 cm up to 40 by 40 cm. The dose will be uniform across the beam, whatever size is set."

Melinda nodded her understanding. "Oh, those are the jaw openings we adjust during set up. I get it."

Randall pointed to large metallic blocks inside the treatment head. "It's basically a set of four lead jaws that can be adjusted in and out independently to shape the beam into any square or rectangular shape. You turn these two red steering-wheel-type devices that circle around the head to adjust the jaws in and out."

Melinda's light bulb lit up. "Yeah, I've watched them do that, but I wasn't sure how it worked. Okay, and these thingies that stick out from the collimator are for holding the lead blocks that we use to make beam shapes that aren't square or rectangular. Those blocks are so heavy. It takes some real muscle to get them mounted without dropping one on the patient."

"The thingies are called accessory mounts," said Bob. "We used to have just a Plexiglas tray mounted where the beam exits. From a pre-made set of blocks of various shapes and sizes, we'd arrange them on the tray, every day, according to a pattern marked on clear X-ray film. The placement was impossible to get exactly the same, each setup. That's why, now, we make the blocks in the shop in the exact shape we need and mount them to Plexiglas trays that can be slid into these linear slots and locked in place."

Melinda whistled. "Geez, I'm glad we don't have to hand build the setup every day anymore. But why do they have to be so heavy?"

Bob took the question. "Well, Big Mel puts out a 6 MeV beam. As I said, the machine can only make a beam shaped like a square or rectangle, so we use the custom block to shield the parts of the beam we don't need."

Melinda put her hand up, looking a bit embarrassed. "Remind me what 6 MeV means again? I'm asking for a friend."

Bob winked. "Tell your friend that we measure radiation in electron volt units. MeV stands for megaelectronvolts, which means one million electron volt units. Big Mel puts out six of these megaelectronvolts. So why do you think we use a 5-cm-thick lead alloy to block out the unwanted part of the beam?"

Lead Pants

Melinda raised her hand like a schoolgirl. "Oh! I know why! Lead is a very dense metal with a high atomic number. Gold and silver are too. High density metals block X-rays better than low density ones, but it still takes a lot of the stuff to block out an X-ray beam as powerful as 6 MeV."

Bob was catching Melinda fever. For once, someone was interested in physics. "Give the girl a brass ring. The amount of gold or silver needed would cost more than the machine, although it would be cool. Lead is both dense and cheap enough for what we need. It takes five centimeters of lead to block out 98 percent of the radiation from a 6 MeV beam. That means the block tray assembly can weigh from ten to forty pounds."

Randall mimed carrying a huge, heavy box.

Melinda laughed. "Of course! That must be why most therapy techs have arms like Popeye the sailorman."

Bob decided the show was over and started to reassemble the blue Plexiglas panels that covered the treatment head. "Okay, guys, time's a-wastin'. We need to clear out. I think we're ready to fire her up for a test run."

Melinda skedaddled out of the room first.

"Looks like Melinda's already fired up," said Bob to Randall, sotto voce, as they walked out of the room.

The lead brick shielded Linac Room door slid closed behind them with a smoothness that belied its weight. Randall took the opportunity to point out to Melinda that the walls of the Linac Room were three feet thick, and consisted of high-density, steel-reinforced concrete plus several inches of steel plate. This amount of shielding prevented them from being exposed to more than the allowable amount of radiation per year for radiation workers.

Bob set the machine parameters for a test run of the Linac and switched on the unit. It ran without a hitch despite the prior pee baptism. He reentered the room and retrieved the ionization chamber he used to measure machine output. The measured output matched the calculated dose, and he gave the go ahead to resume treatment.

Grace bellowed to the anxious patients waiting in the hall that the unit was up again.

"Don't all rush to the front," yelled Grace. "We'll take you in your usual order. And we'll go as fast as we can without screwing up. Just keep your pants on until I tell you to drop them."

Grace loudly cleared her throat. "Uh, Dr. B, I hope you're not planning on taking Melinda back to the Ortho Room to finish your little tea party. Treatments are running about a half hour behind after our un-scheduled potty break. We need your little pupil to help play catch up."

"Of course," said Randall. "Harumph. Melinda, go on and help the girls. We were at a good stopping point anyhow. We'll finish up soon. We're halfway home already."

"Okay, Chief. This is cool stuff," said Melinda with a perky smile and a little hair flip, as she turned to help Grace and Molly.

Randall marveled as he watched her walk away. The hair, the fitted outfit, and the shoes. She was quite a breath of fresh air, and smart too.

IY
RWB

CHAPTER 18

SHRINK THE KID

"My psychiatrist said I was crazy, and I said I wanted a second opinion. He said, 'Okay, you're ugly too.'"

—Rodney Dangerfield

Randall temporarily left the VA at 11:30 the next morning for his lunch date with Joe Shepard. In the car, he thought about the morning's events. Before leaving home, Kyle and Addie both accosted him about the missing cat. After another day of waiting and searching, Baldspot was still MIA. Randall and Zelda were stupefied by this, since the cat could not have gotten out of the house. If she had, she'd be a catsicle by this time since the temperature outside hadn't gone above twenty. All the possible hiding spots inside the house had been searched and, unless she was trapped inside a wall or ceiling, there was no new place to look. Randall didn't want to think about waiting for a foul odor to emerge from some weird place in the house, but Polluto hadn't found a sniff-worthy odor. So the likelihood of a trapped deceased feline seemed remote.

The kids were despondent about the missing cat, and family talk had evolved from wondering if they should conduct a more intensive search to holding an in-absentia funeral service. When they realized they'd looked in all possible feline hiding places, they had held a final goodbye around the kitchen table, each family member paying his or her final respects to the dear departed. By then both kids were begging for not just a replacement for Baldspot, but each wanted their own cat. Randall knew that if nothing changed soon, his resistance would soon be broken down and cat shopping would begin. How could they handle two cats plus a dog? Perhaps plus a cat-eating dog?

PARKING

Randall turned down snow-choked Conover Street and found no open spots in the parking lot of Miss Katie's Diner. The popular lunch go-to had only about ten parking spots, one of which was occupied by a dirty mound of plowed snow. Randall was already late, so he sped out of the lot and looked for street parking. He cruised the streets around the diner like a buzzard circling carrion. Three blocks out and still everything was full up.

At last he spotted a man climbing over the curbside snowbank from the sidewalk to the street and start to clear snow off the windows of his parked car. Randall skidded to a stop just behind the parked car, effectively blocking traffic both ways. He waited impatiently for the man to get in his car and pull out. A car stopped behind him and honked for Randall to get a move on. Randall put an arm out the window to wave the honking car around, but there was no room to pass, and the man just kept honking and giving Randall rude hand signals. Randall huffed and puffed, tapping his fingers on the door frame.

The fellow in the parked car seemed to enjoy the standoff. He just looked around casually and took his time pulling a cigarette out of its pack, lighting it, and tossing the match out the window. After several deep drags, the man waved to Randall and carefully pulled out of the space. Randall deftly maneuvered into the spot, vexing the driver behind him, who sped away, honking and burning rubber.

Randall's heart was racing when he stepped out of the car, and his mind was swirling. *Nice calm beginning to a lunch date. The general public is so gracious. Whatever happened to common courtesy?*

Randall vaulted the roadside snowbank back to the sidewalk. Most of the sidewalks were cleared of snow, but some were still covered with three to four inches. He decided to make up lost time running. The snow cover forced him to run using his special "plotchy" run the three blocks to the diner. A plotchy run is just like regular running but, with each step, the foot is lifted vertically out of the snow and plotched down in the same way several feet ahead. This decreases slippage risk and maximizes traction. The step looked as odd as it felt, but it got him where he was going without butt-flopping. He popped in the front door of the diner, huffing and puffing.

An attractive and finely dressed young hostess approached Randall. Her gold name tag said "Judith." She asked if he had a reservation, and Randall replied that he was meeting someone. Randall's thought process was momentarily diverted by his study of the multiple positive attributes of the hostess.

Randall brushed snow off his coat, caught his breath, and rebooted his brain. "The table is probably reserved under the name of the friend I'm meeting. I'm late. He's probably here already. His name is Shepard, Joe Shepard."

The hostess looked over her reservation list. "Ah, yes, it's under Dr. Shepard's name. I have it here. He comes in here a lot, but he hasn't arrived yet. You confused me when you came in. I thought *you* were Dr. Shepard. You two could be brothers."

Randall pulled off his gloves and pocketed them. "Yeah, we get that a lot. Maybe same father, but different mothers." Randall gave a little nervous laugh.

Judith smiled politely. She was about to take Randall to the table, when Joe Shepard came huffing in the front door, stomping the snow off his shoes. Judith studied the two men, amazed by the resemblance. "Yeah, brothers by another mother," she muttered softly with a little laugh.

At first, Joe looked confused by the comment, but then got the drift. "Oh, the look-alike thing again. It never gets old. Pretty amazing, isn't it? That God would create two odd ducks like us?"

Judith looked from one to the other. "If he turns out to be as good a tipper as you, I will say you're both God's gift."

Randall put a hand to his mouth. "Flattery will get you everywhere. Bless your heart."

Joe echoed Randall. "Yeah, what he said."

Judith asked them to wait a second while she got menus.

"Say, Randall, looks like you got here just before me. Long time, no see." Joe shook Randall's hand. "I would have been in here sooner, but I had a devil of a time parking. Some guy in a gold Scirocco got the parking spot I was eyeing."

Randall tried not to look guilty. "*Err*, yeah, I hear you, parking around here is tough. Same thing happened to me. Good to see you too."

Judith returned. "Right this way, gentlemen. I saved your table by the window, Dr. Shepard."

Joe beamed back at her. "Great, Judith, my generous tipping has not gone unnoticed. You and the food are the main attractions of this place."

Judith had not been immune to the attention provided by her two admirers. She blushed. "Oh, my goodness, I only brought one menu. I'll bring another one right away."

"No bother," said Joe. "I know what I want. Randall here can look over the menu. Give him a minute to decide, but not too long. We're on a short leash."

The hostess pirouetted gracefully and swayed back to the kitchen.

Joe watched Judith walk away. "*Mmm umm mmm.* That young lady has a wonderful swing in her backyard."

Randall was also appreciating the view. "For once, we agree on something. I'd like to play on her jungle gym."

Joe nodded and hummed. He gave Randall a knuckle-punch on the upper arm.

Randall flinched. "Ouch, why do you always do that?"

Joe laughed. "Because I can. Let's call it 'punchuation.' It's so you remember what I say. So, Randall, are you still working in the corner, in the back, in the dark?"

Randall rubbed his arm. "Yeah, you got that right." Randall was surprised that Joe remembered Randall's description of his workplace. "Scintillating scotomata! You've got a good memory for an old man."

"Ooh, good one. I remember that from the list of 'Medical Exclamations' that we made up during lunch back in med school. But give me a break; I'm only six months older than you. Kind of a premature big brother."

Randall nodded. "Premature is right. Just remember, no matter how old we get, I'll always be younger than you." Randall jabbed out with his middle finger knuckle and poked Joe in the arm. "How's that, teach? Did I get it right? So what's good here?"

It was Joe's turn to flinch. "Ouch!"

"What kind of fish is that?" asked Randall, laughing. "Is that a kind of flounder?"

Joe rubbed his arm. "I'm not herring you. You're even more disgusting than I remember."

Randall held up both hands as a sign of peace. "Well, you started it. I'm just playing 'Salmon Says.' Now answer my question. What's good here?"

The Tune of Tuna

"Everything," said Joe, "but I favor the tuna salad. It's like Mom used to make it."

"My mother never made tuna salad," said Randall. "Her specialty was creamed tuna on toast."

"Can't say I've ever had that," said Joe. "Can you make it?"

Randall nodded. "Yep, my mom taught me. It's fairly simple but requires a few tricks only moms know. My dad called it 'shit on a shingle' because it reminded him of what they served in the military. Funny, I don't see a scatological section on the menu. My kids ask for it all the time and they glom it down. Maybe it's because they get to say a naughty word. Now you've gotten me hungry for the tuna salad."

Joe motioned for Judith to send a waitress. She came over and took two orders for the tuna salad special with coffee.

Randall and Joe got down to business while they waited for their meals. "So you said on the phone your son is having some issues?" asked Joe. "Just give me a quick summary."

Randall described the two night terror events, about which he was most concerned. Then he recounted Kyle's slow speech development and strange bowel habits. When their meals came, they both dug in. Joe mulled Randall's story while he chewed and started asking further questions between bites. Randall struggled to answer and eat.

After they'd both cleaned their plates, Joe quizzed Randall further and heard about Kyle's behavioral issues in preschool. Randall also detailed some of Kyle's other mischievous behavior, like the time he had dumped half a bag of cement mix in the front seat of the neighbor's car, because he was mad the neighbor hadn't invited him for dinner. Kyle had denied it repeatedly until Randall had offhandedly asked Kyle how he'd managed to lift such a heavy bag. Before Kyle could think it through, he answered that it was because he was really strong. Big oops moment for Kyle.

Joe laughed. "The kid was strong but not so clever. Randall, it's good to know you can still outwit a five-year-old. Seriously though. I can tell all of this has really got you stressed out. Sure that's all that's going on?"

Randall sighed and shook his head. "Isn't that enough?"

Joe shook his head back. "My shrink senses are tingling at a frequency that tells me other issues are in play."

Randall grimaced. "Damn, you're good. If Kyle's night terrors aren't bad enough, there's been some strange stuff happening at work that I can't sort out." Randall couldn't cover the obvious frustration in his voice.

"Employee behavior or patient oddities?" asked Joe.

Randall looked up and saw Judith looking his way. Their eyes met, and she smiled at him. Randall smiled back.

Joe could tell Randall was distracted. "Earth to Randall. Please copy."

Randall looked back at Joe. "Sorry. I think Judith is hitting on me. Or maybe us."

Joe shook his head. "Don't get excited, big boy. She's just reminding us that the waitress shares tips with her. Now answer the question. Employee or patients?"

"Well, both," said Randall. "But I'd rather not go down that garden path right now. Let's just figure out something for Kyle. I can cope with the other stuff. That's my job."

Joe looked dubious. "You sure about that? You sound a bit adrift in the ocean, like in the sailor's alphabet joke."

"Don't know that one. How does it go?" Randall asked.

"The sailor starts reciting the alphabet. He goes A, B, and then gets lost at C."

Randall chuckled. "Not bad! I'll have to try that on the kids."

Joe fake protested. "The kids? That's perfectly good for adults."

"Not the adults I work with," said Randall.

Joe took the opportunity to throw in a kid's riddle. "Alright, here's one for Kyle and Addie. What did the salmon say when he ran into the concrete wall?"

Randall was stumped but took a shot. "Ouch?"

"Hah. Wrong, but very close, He said 'dam'!"

Randall threw up his hands. "Damn, that was my next guess. Joe, that's enough fish jokes. We should scale back. Anyway, what do you think? Do you think Kyle needs a child psychologist? Could you take this on?"

Why not you?

Joe held up a hand. "Whoa, Nellie! Not so fast there, Speed Racer. First, I have to admit, the kid has some issues, but many kids his age have night terrors. They usually peak around age seven and often just disappear by age nine or ten. No one quite understands why kids get them, but there's some thought that it's a phase of brain development thing. You know, the child hasn't yet learned how to cope with fear or resolve conflict, so it manifests in the dream state."

Randall nodded. "That makes some sense, but Zelda and I can't go without sleep for two more years for that to happen. Isn't there something that can be done now to help Kyle with his anxieties or whatever sets off the terrors?"

Joe looked to the side and grimaced a bit. "Perhaps, but it often requires more than just talking with the child in isolation. Commonly, what happens with children is a reflection of other family tensions or dynamics."

"Oh, that doesn't sound so easy," said Randall, acknowledging internally the many frictions between himself and Zelda.

Joe's tone got very serious. "No, it's not. It sometimes requires meeting with the parents first to gather some basic information about the family dynamic and then meeting with the parents along with the child to see what their interactions are like."

Randall moaned. "It would take Mohammed to drag Zelda to that mountain."

"I get it," said Joe. "Usually, one of the parents doesn't want to be involved; either because they don't want their parenting questioned or they're too afraid they'll be found guilty of bad parenting."

Randall wiped his sweaty palms on his pant legs. "You nailed it."

Joe motioned for calm. "For that reason, I'm going to suggest that you have Kyle see a child psychologist, but that it not be me."

Randall looked crestfallen. "Not you? I don't get it. You're the most qualified guy I know. Why not?"

Joe made writing motions on the tablecloth. "Well, first off. Zelda knows I'm your friend, so she would probably suspect the whole arrangement is a setup against her."

Randall nodded. "*Umm*, good point."

"Secondly, from what you've told me, I strongly suspect Zelda could have a problem opening up in front of a man, especially one who's a doctor."

"Good guess," said Randall.

Joe tapped the table with his fingertip. "*Ah*, but a highly educated guess."

The waitress appeared and asked if they were done with their tuna-fest and queried whether they wanted anything else, such as dessert or more coffee. Joe looked at his watch and told her that they had time enough to top off the fine meal with cherry strudel ala mode and coffee. The waitress nodded and cleared their table.

Randall was surprised that Joe was taking the extra time. "Do we have time?"

Joe nodded affirmatively. "There's always time for a slice of Miss Katie's strudel. Fresh baked. Delicate frosting. Melts in your mouth. And of course, when does coffee taste any better than after a fine sweet meat? I'm sure your ship won't sink in fifteen more minutes. Besides, I want to share some errant thoughts with you."

JOE'S ERRANT THOUGHTS

Randall looked at Joe with squinty eyes. "Errant thoughts?"

Joe nodded with emphasis. "Yes. Let's just say that, for the moment, the science train has left the station. What I say from this point has more the ring of anecdotal data, but it is compelling to me. I can't think of too many others who I would share this with. Are you game?"

Randall grinned. "I do believe I am. Proceed."

Joe continued. "That stuff I just told you about brain development in children may be just a theory of convenience. We doctors want to be able to explain everything that happens to human beings on a scientific basis. Right?"

Randall was attentive. "Right."

"What if some of the observations we make don't fit our current science? There are two choices. Either the non-fitting observation is based on science we don't grasp yet, or we say it is supernatural."

Randall thought for a moment. "Like before we knew the nature of radiation, we explained its effects as magic. Or when we assumed that inherited traits were expressions of God's will."

"Precisely," said Joe. "So we see a child, like Kyle, having a night terror. He's walking, talking, and seeing things not of our well-constructed world. When we try to communicate with him, he's not aware of us unless something very physical is done to break through. Is his brain just malfunctioning? If so, why? Or is it functioning normally for a child, but we don't understand it? It's even more frightening when there is no good explanation. So we fall back on blaming possession by the devil or chemical imbalance, just to name two extremes."

Randall pursed his lips. "That's for sure. It freaks out the kid and the parent. So what's your theory?"

Joe raised a finger. "How about this for something different? When we're born, our brains are unencumbered by any worldly constructs that tell us what the world is. We're *tabula rasa*. The baby's main focus is on survival. It's a helpless little creature that can't survive without its parents. It can only cry, kick, and wave its arms. Can't otherwise communicate. Wouldn't it make sense that evolution might provide the baby with a special neural brain function that permits nonverbal communication with those encoded with the same genes? Namely, parents and siblings."

This was ringing bells for Randall. He was intrigued. "I hear you loud and clear. Keep going."

Joe was getting excited. "Perhaps such special brain functions facilitate communication at a subliminal level between children and parents. And those same brain centers might serve as receptors for other forms of data input that we would not consider natural, like sensing input not of the world as we adults perceive it. Then as we mature and learn to survive on our own, that brain center becomes unnecessary and atrophies. Or perhaps we just no longer acknowledge its messaging as we're inundated by all the external stimuli we receive as we age."

Randall took that in and added his thoughts. "Yeah, then we view those 'other' perceptions as childish and discard them. Like we discard imaginary friends and Santa Claus. But what if some adults keep that special brain function, recognize that it's there and learn to adopt the information it provides? Maybe such people can abide both a 'real' world and a 'child' world? Just for the sake of argument. If such a brain function truly exists. Any idea how this would work? Some neurophysiological bases?"

Joe shook his head. "Only a few fuzzy ideas. I understand neuroanatomy and neurophysiology, but my fuzzy idea requires a better grasp of biochemistry and physics than I currently possess. I thought maybe your radiation physics background could help clear the mist."

Randall scratched his head. "Hmm. That's a big maybe. That's going to be a hard hump to hurdle. What led you to this line of thinking?"

The waitress delivered their strudel and coffee, which both men ignored to avoid a break in the exchange.

Joe looked at the dessert and rubbed his chin. "Well, two things. First, observing kids with night terrors and interviewing them. For them the night terror worlds are very real, and they relate other communicative experiences that are hard to explain. Second, their stories resonate with me, because I had night terrors when I was a kid. To me, they didn't feel abnormal. And I can remember other stuff that seemed real enough at the time, but my parents said I was just imagining things."

Randall cocked his head to the side. "Like what?"

Joe leaned forward and spoke more quietly. "Like trees talking to me or a disembodied voice assuring me I'd be okay and that I would never die. And this was before I ever heard talk of God or religion. And one other really big thing."

Randall raised his eyebrows. "What was that?"

Joe was totally turned on now. "When I was maybe five years old, I begged my dad to build me a tree house in the big apple tree in our backyard. He finally gave in and bought lumber for it. We stacked 2 x 4s and plywood under the tree, then went to work on it. I got to cut wood with a saw, and hammer my first nails. By the following Saturday afternoon, we had the treehouse half done when we ran out of nails. My dad went off to the hardware store for more nails. I was pooped out, so my mother put me down for a nap until my dad came home."

Randall interrupted. "I had an apple tree in my backyard too. My dad cut it down 'cause it always made an apple mess. I always wanted a tree house. Never got one."

Joe gave Randall an odd look. "Thanks for sharing. Anyway, I remember my mom reading me to sleep. The next thing I recall is waking up in pain underneath the tree, lying on top of the pile of 2 x 4s. My chest hurt so bad, I couldn't breathe. I tried yelling for my mother and father to help me, but nothing came out. I just laid there for what was probably minutes but seemed like hours. I thought I was going to die. But then my mother came out of the house, running toward me and yelling. Almost at the same time, my father pulled into the driveway with his truck. He screeched to a halt, leapt out of the cab, yelling my name, and ran to my side."

Randall's mouth gaped. "Did you die?"

"Of course I did, but I was resurrected. That's the miracle. End of story."

Randall shook his head. "Is not. How did you get out there? How did they know to come help you?"

Joe shrugged his shoulders. "That was the mystery. Both my parents swear they heard me calling for help. My mother was in the basement doing laundry. My father was on his way to the hardware store when he heard me calling for him. Without further thought, he did a skidding U-turn and raced home. Later my parents concluded I had been sleep-walking, tried to climb up the ladder to my tree house, and fell off the ladder. The fall woke me up. I couldn't convince them that I had never gotten a word out, but they would have none of it."

"Were you badly hurt?" asked Randall.

Joe rubbed his right chest. "Four fractured ribs and a bruised lung. They called them bucket-handle fractures. Hurt like a mule kicked me. Wind knocked out of me. I'll never forget it, and I know that my yell wasn't made by sound waves. Since then I've always suspected that, at least when we're children, we have special communication and percep-tion abilities. As adults, and especially as doctors, we dismiss and discard explanations that don't fit neatly into our teachings. We get hung up on believing only what we can measure. But I think some adults don't grow out of the ability or lose it. It's always intrigued me. Probably why I went into child psychology."

Randall twirled his spoon and dinged his water glass. "So are you thinking the child brain sends out some kind of vibratory signal like this water glass? And there's a corresponding nonauditory receptor in the adult brain? Plus, it works at a distance?"

Joe nodded. "Not exactly, but pretty close. However the signal originates, I figure it's happening as part of a neuroelectric process that has to go down to a subatomic level. All I know is that's where quantum theory comes in, and that's where I get lost. That's where I could use your help."

Randall rubbed his eyes. "It's not the physics I use every day, but I do know there's some strange phenomena that can happen in quantum land. I've got a few resources I can tap."

Randall and Joe looked down at the table. The ice cream was melted on their uneaten cherry strudel. The coffee had gone cold.

Randall motioned the waitress for more hot coffee. "Don't know about you, but I'm eating my strudel while I can. Believe it or not, I've had some experiences that echo what you said. I could tell you about them, but we don't have the time to do them justice right now. If you add my tales to yours, we can go from an anecdote to a series. If we get a third person to give testimony, we can publish our findings in the *Journal of What's Happening Now*."

Joe agreed and dug into his strudel. "Well, you've got my attention. Can't wait to hear about it. Let's have lunch again next week and continue this pseudoscience." The words came out rather muffled by partially masticated strudel.

"Deal!" garbled Randall, accidentally spitting out a piece of cherry. "Oops. Lost a piece!" Randall popped the stray cherry bit back into his mouth. "Don't sell yourself short, Joe. I'm not so sure our budding theory is 'pseudo' anything. I'll do some quantum diving and buff up on the topic for next week."

Follow-Up Plans

Joe and Randall finished scarfing up their strudel and washed it down with fresh hot coffee. Randall was lost in thought, still trying to absorb Joe's theory of childhood brain function. It was so weird that it made perfect sense to him.

"So, Randall . . . ," said Joe.

"Sorry, I was drifting for a minute there," said Randall, snapping out of his brief reverie.

Joe handed Randall a piece of paper. "Before we depart, let's review. Do not lose hope. Here's what you're going to do. I am somewhat prescient, so I composed this list of five competent child specialists of my acquaintance. Two of them are women. Tell Zelda we met and that I recommended that the two of you choose from the list. Assign the task to her, and I am almost 100 percent sure she will pick one of the women. Empower her with the decision, and she will feel like part of the solution, not part of the problem."

"Joe, I'm not even going to ask how you knew this was coming. You are a gentleman and a scholar. I don't have a problem with Zelda picking a woman, as long as she's good," said Randall.

"I thought not," said Joe. "Sorry you're having this problem, but now you can see why I never married. But enough talk, I've got to run back to the office, and you do too."

Randall snatched the check before Joe could get to it and told Joe it was the least he could do since Joe's good advice was not yielding Joe any billing. Randall rose from his chair as Joe got up to leave. The two shook hands.

"Sometimes it's good to be slow," said Joe. "Remember that advice; it may come in handy. I'm looking forward to your kiddie tale next week when we do lunch. And here I thought you'd be talking mostly about cars and baseball. By the way, you've been a car nut as long as I've known you. What are you driving these days?"

Car Wars

"*Er . . .* a modified VW Scirocco?" said Randall warily.

Joe's eyes narrowed. "Is it gold with a big air dam in front?"

Randall gave Joe a crooked smile and nodded. "Yeah, the air dam is a cosmetic modification. Doesn't make it go faster. Just looks like it could."

"You're a big rat! You're the one who co-opted my parking spot," yelled Joe in mock outrage as he stomped out the door with his fist raised. "Next week I'm getting here first."

Randall yelled back as Joe walked away. "Want a demo ride in the Scirocco?"

Joe yelled back. "Only if you can take a ride in my Corvette without barfing!"

"You have a Vette? Now who's the rat?" yelled Randall, but Joe just kept walking and gave him a little backward wave.

As Randall pulled out of his parking spot, a yellow Corvette streaked past the Scirocco and gave a triple honk. Randall was definitely jealous. Apparently private practice was more lucrative than working at the VA. Randall tried to catch up to the Corvette, but the VW couldn't be pedaled fast enough. He gave up and headed back to the VA.

Luck was on his side when he got back and found a close-in VA parking spot and made it back to the department almost in time for his 1:15 consult.

CHAPTER 19

———

DORIS THE MAGE

"The sun was already declining and each of the trees held a premonition of night."

— *A Passage to India,* E. M. Forster

RUSHIN' ROULETTE

Unencumbered by his backpack and briefcase, Randall made it back to the department, jogging most of the way. He appeared at Doris's office door, breathing heavily.

Doris looked up from her typing. "Hard to run on a full stomach, isn't it?"

Randall groaned. "Yep, I'm chock full of tuna and strudel, not to mention a gallon of coffee."

"I'm surprised you didn't flip your cookies, Dr. B," Doris retorted.

Randall looked a little green. "Me too."

Randall continued through her office to his office and switched his winter coat for his "white" lab coat. He came back out buttoning up. "Doris, you have a gifted, but gratuitous, grasp of the obvious, it's one of the reasons I selected you for this job."

Doris shook her head. "Oh, no, Dr. B, I picked you, the ripest tomato on the vine."

Randall paused and looked out to the crowded hallway while he considered Doris's remark. "Why the heck did you do that, anyhow?"

Doris raised both hands like she was casting a magic spell. "I read the signs. Do you believe in signs, Dr. B?" Her voice sounded like she was doing a Gregorian chant.

Randall backed up a step. "Now you are scaring me a little bit. Just to be clear, I don't believe in magic or astrological signs. I do believe physical signs are important. Like in the diagnosis of disease. Other *physical* signs get my attention too. For example, stop signs. When I see one, I stop . . . usually."

Doris twirled a finger in the air dramatically. "Those aren't the kind of signs I mean. I'm referrin' to hidden signs. The signals not everybody sees, but the sensitive can sense." Doris pointed the waving finger to her chest.

Randall pinched up his face. "You must have had VA Canteen soup for lunch. You're going all supernatural on me."

Doris laughed a mildly evil laugh. "What you don't understand can hurt you. *Bwa-ha-ha.* Posh! It's just good-old, down-home Southern girl intuition. You clearly are not tuned to the same channel."

Randall gave a little shiver. "Is this leading to one of your spiritualist talks again?"

Doris waved a dismissive hand. "There's no hope for those unwillin' to hear the truth."

"Enough already," said Randall. "I get the message. You're dying to tell me something you know, and I ought to, but don't. You are such a gossip. I don't have the time to drag it out of you. The consult is awaitin'. Oddly, I can't wait to figure out whatever your babbling is all about."

Doris shook her head in disgust. "You're not even remotely close. Go do your consult, and try to clear your mind." Doris made shooing motions.

Randall shrugged his "deeply confused" shrug, returned to his office, and set to reviewing the consult's medical records.

Al Steals the Show

Randall was halfway through his chart review when there was a tapping at his door. "Doris, I know your signs are . . ." Randall chopped off the sentence when he turned and saw Al Kornberg standing at the doorway. "Oh, sorry Al, I thought you were Doris."

Al hesitated a beat. "Uh, sorry to bother you, Dr. B, but I need your expert opinion."

Randall felt annoyed by the interruption. "Can it wait? I'm in the middle of a consult, and I'm running behind."

Al looked perplexed and a bit scared. "No, I don't think it can wait. It might be an emergency."

Randall rose from his chair, expecting Al to take him to a distressed patient. "Then let's go. Who's having a problem? Is it Mr. During again?"

Al put up a sweaty hand. "No. Actually, it's me. I think I'm having a heart attack."

"You? My God, what's happening? Are you having chest pain?" asked Randall anxiously.

Al put a hand to his chest. "It's not really pain. My chest feels heavy, like someone is standing on it, and my heart is racing. I feel all sweaty."

Randall took Al by the arm. "Can you walk alright? Let's go to the exam room, and I'll get some vital signs on you."

There was already a patient, probably his consult, waiting in the exam room. Randall apologized to the patient and asked him to go back to the waiting area for a few minutes. Randall led Al to the exam table and laid him down.

Randall tried to remain calm and reassuring. "It could be just a heart rhythm issue. Let's get a blood pressure on you. No need to jump to conclusions."

Randall became concerned when he read a BP of 85/50 and an irregular, rapid pulse of 140 beats per minute. Al was pale and diaphoretic.

"Is it bad, Dr. B?" asked Al in a shaky voice.

Randall tried to be honest without sounding alarming. "Well, your pressure is a bit low, and your pulse is fast. It may just be a rhythm problem, like atrial fibrillation, which can be reversed. We really need to get some other tests to rule out a heart attack, like an EKG and some blood work. Tell you what, I'm going to play it safe and get you up to the ER so we can get you evaluated by the experts."

Al looked about to panic. "Shouldn't we just call a code?"

Randall shook his head and put his hand on Al's shoulder. "No. Trust me, I've got you covered. By the time the code team gets here, we could have you upstairs where all the right equipment is, and there are doctors used to dealing with situations like this. If you call a code, you never know who you're going to get. Could be a bunch of students and nurses. And they'd have to haul all their equipment into this tiny room. It would be a crowd scene. Believe me. I've been there. I'll get a wheelchair and take you up there myself."

Al gulped and nodded. "Okay. If you say so. Let's go."

"It just goes to show, Al. It's just like the sign at the hardware store. 'Summer help. Summer not. Summer sausage.' Better to stick with the wiener you've got." Randall dashed into the hall and let Al ponder that gem.

To the Pros

Out in the hall, Randall spotted Melinda. He sent her to fetch a wheelchair and went back to recheck Al's vital signs. They were stable and his symptoms unchanged. He still looked perplexed.

Melinda looked momentarily confused to see Al on the exam table. "He's the patient?"

Randall moved quickly to position the wheelchair. "Yup. Mr. Kornberg isn't feeling well, and you and I are taking him up to the ER to get checked out. Help me get him into the chair, and you walk ahead. You may need to help clear the way through first floor foot traffic."

"Got it!" said Melinda, as she helped Randall seat Al in the wheelchair.

Randall motioned Melinda ahead, and he wheeled Al briskly down the hall and to the elevator bank. The elevator door opened a fraction of a second after Melinda pushed the button to reveal green wallpaper. Randall decided these were two of the signs, both positive. The trio made it to the ER with all due alacrity, and Randall quickly spotted Jim Conway, the ER chief physician, standing at the ER workstation.

Jim looked a bit surprised to see Randall pushing a man in a wheel-chair. "Hey, Randall! You're in luck today. You just caught me between disasters. What can I do you for?"

Randall introduced Jim to Al Kornberg and Melinda. He followed up with a quick but thorough summary of Al's situation.

Jim listened carefully, nodding his head. "Got it. Sounds like our boy here may be having an MI. We have to at least rule it out. Good you got him here so fast. Gold stars for both of you. We'll take good care of Mr. Kornberg up here. It's right up our alley. You two can scoot back downstairs and tend to your radiation rotisserie. I'll call you when we've got him sorted. What's your extension number?"

Jim had begun wheeling Al away before he finished talking. "It's 2585," shouted Randall after him.

Melinda looked like she had been expecting more. "That was quick."

"It's not what you know," said Randall.

"It's who you know," finished Melinda.

"Right," said Randall. "For Jim, this is just another day at the office. Now let's hustle back to our little salt mine."

Melinda looked around at the seeming chaos and cacophony of the ER. "Wow. This place is intense. To think, everyone here is in such close proximity to the possibility of death. I think I prefer our salt mine to his."

Randall nodded in agreement. "Ditto."

Back to Salt Mining

When Randall and Melinda returned to the department, Grace and Molly greeted them with scolding looks. They were more than mildly perturbed.

"What in blazes was all that hullabaloo with Al Kornberg?" rasped Grace. "Where did you haul him off to? Is something wrong? Why did you steal Melinda?"

"Yeah, what she said," echoed Molly.

Randall held up his hands in surrender. "Slow down. Al wasn't feel-ing well and, to be safe, we took him to the ER. They are checking him out as we squeak." Randall tried to push the calm button. "Probably just a minor case of the 'gobloots' or perhaps an ischemic framistan."

The subterfuge wasn't working. Grace could tell when Randall was obfuscating. "Cut the crap, Dr. B. What really happened?" Grace tried to stare down Melinda for an answer, but she just turned to Randall.

Randall gave up and sighed. "Sorry. I was trying to lighten up the news until we know more. Here's the straight poop. Al is being evaluated to rule out a heart attack. He's got some signs and symptoms that suggest it. So I decided to take no chances and took him to the ER without delay. It could just be a bad heart rhythm thing, but bottom line is he was stable when we got him there. He's in good hands in the ER."

Grace dismissed that *Good Housekeeping* seal of approval message with a vulgar hand wave. "*Bah*, I wouldn't trust those quacks with my dog. If anything bad happens to that man, I'm, I'm, I'm going to . . ." Grace's eyes teared up and she turned an even deeper shade of red. "I'm going up there right now!" She threw down the chart she was holding and hustled down the hallway.

Randall was flummoxed by Grace's unexpected response to the news, but thought it best not to try to stop the runaway train.

Randall shouted out to Grace's departing form. "I'm not sure they'll be allowing visitors yet, but go on up and check. Don't barge into his cubicle if they're in the middle of some test. Al will probably be happy to see a familiar . . ." There was no use continuing. Grace was well out of earshot.

It was Molly's turn to talk to Grace's empty wake. "Sure, girl. You go on up there. Melinda and I will hold down the Alamo, right, Melinda?"

Melinda nodded and then shook her head.

"Who would have thought?" muttered Randall.

"Anyone with eyes and ears," whispered Molly.

"But Al's old enough to be her father," Randall whispered back.

Molly grabbed Randall's arm for emphasis. "Yep, and that's as far as it goes. Don't go leaping to conclusions. When Grace first started here, it was just the two of them. Let's just say they sort of depended on each other."

Randall looked upward and reverse smiled. "*Hmm*. I think I get it. Kind of a codependency of semi-competents?"

Molly nodded. "Ah, you *capiche*."

"Me too," said Melinda.

"Okay, guys, fun's over," said Randall in a loud voice. "Time to get the wagon train rolling, or the Indians will have us circling the wagons. I've got a consult to see and you guys have X-rays to dole out."

"Aye, aye, Captain. And we'll be a-doin' it minus our first mate," said Molly with a hand salute. She called the next patient to come to the radiation chamber.

MR. LEGG

Back in his office, Randall finished his prep for the consult. It was a patient named Armand Legg. He had an early-stage prostate cancer but refused surgery when he learned that surgery could cause loss of bladder control and impotence. At age sixty, he wasn't willing to give up either manly function.

Taking the patient chart and his note-taking clipboard out to the hallway, Randall called for Mr. Legg. It was the same man he'd shooed out of the exam room to make way for Al Kornberg.

"Mr. Legg, I'm Dr. Biedermeier," said Randall. "It's nice to meet you. Sorry about booting you out of the exam room earlier, but we had an unexpected emergency with one of our employees."

Mr. Legg returned Randall's handshake. "Nice to meet you, Dr. Biedermann." He drawled like he was sitting on the front porch in the Kentucky heat. "No problem. What I've got ain't no emergency. Just call me by my nickname, Army. Onliest person what's Mr. Legg is my pappy. *Heh heh.*"

"Okay, Army, then you can just call me Dr. B; everybody does," said Randall, ushering Mr. Legg into the exam room. They both took seats.

Randall liked to open by getting acquainted. "So, Army, what did you do in the Army?"

Mr. Legg shook his head. "That's the thing, Dr. B . . . I weren't in the Army. I was Navy. I was second engineer in the engine room, mostly on destroyers. That's why I got forever grease under my fingernails. And probably in my blood. You got a test for blood grease, Doc?"

"Yeah, we do, it's called a lipid panel," said Randall with a little chuckle.

"You guys got a test for everythin,' right?"

"Almost, but what we need is a serum porcelain level to identify patients who are just crocks," said Randall.

"Not sure what that is, but I'm glad you do," said Mr. Legg. "If you don't mind me saying, Doc, you got a funny name and, well, you kinda look like Groucho Marx."

"I've heard that once or twice," replied Randall. "If you don't mind me saying, you have an unusual name too. Plus, you sort of look like . . ."

Mr. Legg interrupted. "Jimmy Durante. Yeah, I get that a lot, big schnozzola an' all. Pappy was a mean ol' coot. He picked the Armand moniker and the middle name. Some family thang. But he tol' me it was cuz he figured I'd be a pain in his hinder, and he wanted to beat me to the punch."

Randall looked down at the chart. Mr. Legg's middle name was Allan. He concluded Pappy really was a mean one.

"Don't feel too bad about the name," said Randall. "I've seen worse. I had a patient once named Mann White, who was black. His father reckoned that on an alphabetical list by last name his son could pass for white. When I heard that I figured that somewhere out there is a white guy named Mann Black. I keep looking."

Mr. Legg gave a hearty laugh. "That's a good one, Doc. Now, I'll be lookin' too. Say, Doc, that's one old wristwatch you got on. Ain't that a windup one from the second big war?"

Randall raised his wrist. "This one? Yeah, good eye. It was my dad's. Army Air Corp. I'm just using it 'cause my expensive self-wind runs slow. Got to get it fixed."

Mr. Legg got a gleam in his eye. "Well, bring the sucker on in here and I'll fix 'er up for you. Watch making is my hobby. Probably just needs a bit of nose grease to get the gears righteous again."

Randall looked puzzled. "I've heard of elbow grease. But nose grease?"

Mr. Legg reached up and pinched the right side of his large proboscis between thumb and forefinger. Some white goo issued out of the large skin pores. He wiped some of it off his nose with his finger and held out the finger for Randall's inspection. "This here is nose grease. Watchmakers been usin' it for a coon's age to lube watch parts. Comes outta these little holes in your nose skin. Need to slick up a gear? Just give the ol' schnoz a squeeze. Nose grease has got a fancy science name, but I done forgot it. You can probably look it up in one of your thick science books."

Randall found that what he learned from patients was sometimes more entertainment than reading novels. "Well, I'll be dipped in tar. Let me try that." Randall gave his own nose a squeeze and, sure enough, he produced a small sample of white grease. It was, indeed, smooth and slippery. "I'll bring my watch in tomorrow. I wish there was some way to search for all the little facts in the world, like there would be some big encyclopedia that got updated daily with new information. But for now, I'll ask my skin doctor friend."

"I've got my watch toolkit with me upstairs," said Mr. Legg. "I can pop off the watch back and take a look inside 'er. Probably have it ticking like new in the shake of a pigtail."

Randall promised that, after radiation, he'd have Mr. Legg's prostate ticking like new. Mr. Legg was all in for radiation as an alternative to surgery. Randall scheduled him for simulation and treatment.

Jimmy

Later, Randall stood by the treatment console as Jimmy O'Loughlin shuffled out of the treatment room. He was a bit weak from not eating well, and Molly held his elbow in support. Jimmy's wife Sally was waiting for him and took over from Molly. Randall greeted Jimmy and Sally. He asked if Jimmy was eating any better since being put on viscous lidocaine to ease the pain from the temporary radiation irritation.

Jimmy nodded. "That stuff helps me swallow, but it tastes like horse pucky, and it makes my tongue numb. I ate better last night, but I'm still down about fifteen pounds. I feel weak as a kitten. I got kind of dizzy when they got me up off the treatment couch." Jimmy stumbled a bit, and his wife steadied him.

Randall reached out and helped. "Careful. There's a huge mogul in the floor tile right there.'

Jimmy laughed. "Doc, I don't think I could manage the bunny hill right now."

Jimmy had started treatment two weeks earlier for a locally advanced lung cancer, which had eroded into a large airway and ruptured a blood vessel. With no prior symptoms, the fifty-five-year-old suddenly started coughing up blood. The copious amount of blood had scared the stuffing out of him, and he'd gone straight to the ER. A chest X-ray showed a large growth near the root of the right lung. Surgeons deemed him inoperable and sent him to radiation to stop the bleeding.

Randall and Sally sat Jimmy down in a hallway chair. Randall stood and visually assessed the man. "You do look a bit peaked. Is the dizziness going away now?"

Jimmy sat up straighter in the chair and looked around the hallway. "Yeah, I think so. The spinning is getting better. I was feeling stronger this morning when I woke up. Oh, and here's something. The blood stopped coming up three days ago, Doc, so that's good . . . ," Jimmy hesitated, like he had more to say.

Randall gave a Jimmy a little cheer. "Bravo! That's great. It usually takes a week or so for the radiation to kill enough tumor to stop the bleeding and for the body to heal the blood vessel. And I have some good news too. The weekly beam films we take of your chest to verify proper positioning of the treatment area are showing good shrinkage of your tumor. It seems quite sensitive to radiation."

Sally's face lit up. "Honey, you see, that's more good news. There's no reason to feel so down."

Randall sensed there was more going on than Jimmy had admitted to, and he put on his Sherlock Holmes face. "Jimmy . . . , what else is going on?"

Jimmy looked like he had been caught with his hand in the cookie jar.

Sally was having none of it. "Jimmy! Talk to the doctor. How can he help if you clam up?"

Jimmy rolled his eyes. "Oh, alright. If it will make you feel better. It's probably nothing though. It was just kinda strange. I'd rather not discuss it here in the hallway in front of these old Gomers. Is there some place private?"

Randall gestured toward his office. "You're right. There's no privacy in this hallway. All the exam rooms are full. Let's go into my office. You can look at my *Playboy* centerfolds on the wall." Randall made a smirky smile.

Sally gasped and clutched her cross necklace.

Jimmy picked up the cue. "Sal, relax. Can't you tell the doc is pulling your leg? Lighten up."

Jimmy stood up tentatively and didn't wobble. He was able to make the short trip to Randall's office without help.

When everyone was seated, Randall bade Jimmy to begin. "Alright. What's this strange thing that's going on?"

Jimmy took a breath and sat forward in his chair. "This is going to sound nuts, but I had the weirdest dream last night. *Er*, actually, the last two nights."

Sally almost rose from her chair. "Honey, you didn't tell me you had the dream twice!"

Jimmy put up a shielding hand. "I didn't want you to worry any more than you already were."

Randall interrupted. "Go on. Tell me more about the dream."

Jimmy continued. "Both dreams seemed so real that I can't shake them from my mind. I keep seeing the images. Basically, what I saw was the grim reaper, like you see in storybooks. You know, with the black-hooded robe, skeleton face, and the scythe. He's there in front of me. In my face. And he keeps repeating 'It's your time. It's your time.'"

Randall shivered involuntarily and searched his mind for something comforting to say. It wasn't the first time a patient of his had told him of a premonition of death. They were true often enough not to discount them as just anxiety based or psychosomatic. Randall himself had sensed the shadow of death lurking in hospital room corners or hovering around ICU beds. But this was not the time to admit such demons might exist. It was his job to provide comfort and ease. Sometimes that required truth veneered with a bit of confabulation.

Randall kept a calm, relaxed face, despite his contrary inner thoughts. "Having dreams like those is pretty common when you're going through a life-threatening experience like this one. It's only natural that the fears you're living with each day sometimes show up in your dreams."

Sally visibly relaxed a bit. "Really? Well, I suppose so. Like how you keep reliving a car accident afterward."

Randall nodded his agreement. "Just so. It's just the way your mind processes the bad stuff. Obviously, there are no guarantees we can make in this business, but every indicator we have so far is looking good for you, Jimmy. The tumor is shrinking, the bleeding has stopped, and your oral intake is improved. We can add a dietary supplement, and you'll be gaining weight soon. In one week, the radiation fields will be shrinking, and the esophagus will get less radiation. So that should make swallowing easier too. Let's just stick to the program and use our mental light saber to X-out the bad dreams."

Randall wasn't sure he believed that all of what he said would come to pass. It was certainly a shared goal. A target. The desired outcome. But certainly not a guarantee. At least Jimmy and his wife seemed to accept it as enough of a possibility to ease their discomfort.

"You see, Jimmy?" said his wife. "Just what the doctor said. It was just a bad dream. Think positive thoughts, and don't let your mind dwell on the worst."

Jimmy reflected back on the vividness of the dream and wasn't quite ready to buy the ranch but decided not to dwell on it further. He just wanted to get the heck out of the clinic and lay down in his own bed. At least Sally was happy now. "Yeah, you guys are right. Color me a happier guy. Doc, sorry to take up your time with my creepy head stuff. It helped to talk about the dream. I think now I can let it go."

"Good man," said Randall. "I think you've got another beam film due tomorrow, and I'll bet the tumor shows another shrinky-dinky."

Randall walked the O'Loughlins back out of his office and bade them good day as Grace came shuffling down the hall, back from the ER.

Al Update

Randall couldn't fully read Grace's facial expression, but she'd clearly been crying. Her eyes were red. "So, Grace, what's the verdict on Al?"

Grace looked surprised. "Didn't your friend Jim call you?"

"He might have, but I've been with patients. Hey, Doris, did Dr. Conway call?" shouted Randall towards the office.

Doris came out of her office, waving a yellow message slip. Melinda and Molly joined the three in the hallway and asked about Al.

"Dr. Conway just called and asked you to call him back for details on Al's status," said Doris.

"I've got the details," said Grace glumly. "Listen up. Al is stable for now, but they think at least one coronary artery is blocked and that he needs bypass surgery. They've got it set up at a private hospital in town for tomorrow. He could be out for a while and may not be able to come back to work."

"Thank God, he's not ... I mean, he's okay," exclaimed Molly. "Well, not okay, but not ... you know what I mean."

Bob Storch ambled by and asked what the huddle was about.

"Aren't you Mr. Oblivious!" snarked Grace. "Al had a heart attack right here in the department, and you missed it. Where have you been hiding?"

"I've been installing the new vacuum tube in the Orthovoltage Control Room," replied Bob, with more than a hint of disdain. "Doing my job, not like some people around here."

"Easy big boy," snapped Grace as she started to tear up. "Al could have died ... and ...."

"Sorry," said Bob. "Is he going to be alright?"

Randall summarized Al's situation for everyone once again. He suggested that they have a moment of silence to ask their respective gods to watch over and protect Al in the days ahead. Then looking at the gawking patients, he motioned the staff to get back to work. Since chart rounds had been preempted by Al's emergency, Randall suggested they have an early chart rounds the next day. It was agreed.

Randall had Bob hang back for a moment and asked him if he was ready to announce his departure to Costa Rica. Randall put a hand on Bob's arm. "Bob, I was going to tell them at chart rounds today, but . . . ."

Bob looked at the floor. "I guess it's okay, Dr. B."

"Well, how about I announce it at chart rounds tomorrow? I'll bring donuts, and we can all get high on sugar. I'll give you a nice departure speech. Deal?"

Bob nodded. "Deal."

With that, Bob slunk away, and Randall made a note to stop at "Bill's Bag'O Donuts" on the way home and make use of the baker's dozen coupon he had stuffed somewhere in his lab coat.

CHAPTER 20

NIGHT CALL

"I like to leave messages before the beep."

— Steven Wright

MIND GAMES

When Randall got home from work that evening, Al Kornberg's heart attack was still on his mind, as well as Jimmy O'Loughlin's perhaps prescient dreams. Randall was wrung out, pooped, drained, deflated, half-mast, and pureed. Yet he was still upright, taking oxygen and expelling CO_2. Zelda was waiting for him at the door. This was highly unusual, since she was often playing with the kids or working on art up in her studio. She had put on nice clothes, as if going to a job interview.

Zelda did a pose. "Hi, sweetie. Welcome home. Geez, you look like you were shot at and missed, then shit at and hit. Whatever is wrong? Are you sick?"

Randall blew out a breath. "Nah, just another day at the office. You look way better than I feel. What's the occasion?" Zelda was being outwardly charming, but Randall felt something sinister was lurking under that façade.

Zelda preened a bit and looked innocent.

Randall put down his briefcase and swiveled his head. The house was spotless. "Are you going somewhere? Is someone coming over?"

"No, situation normal . . ." Zelda looked ready to pop.

"Come on, Zel, spill! What's going on?"

Zelda started to look like a kid who had just knocked over a lamp. "It's just . . . I don't know . . . are they coming to take the kids?"

"What?" Randall loosened his tie and slipped his feet out of his brown leather shoes. "Who?"

"I don't know, THEM. You know, like, the people who take kids. I'm not making any sense . . . . When you talked to the psychologist . . . does he think we're crazy? Like we messed up the kids somehow? Are we not fit to be parents?"

Randall realized that she had been building this up in her mind all day, much like Randall's "what if" extravaganzas. He reached out and pulled her in for a long hug. She resisted for a bit, then relaxed into him.

When they broke the hug, Randall tried to calm her down. "Zel, stop being so paranoid. You're a great mother for the kids. You do your best, and that's all anyone can do. Joe told me that Kyle's night terrors are quite common, and there are things we can do."

Randall reviewed his lunch with Joe in some detail, and Zelda seemed relieved to hear night terrors were a common stage of neurologic development in kids. He left out the more supernatural speculations he and Joe had discussed.

Zelda looked more relaxed. "So we didn't make Kyle FUBAR?"

Randall shook his head and waved a hand. "Not a bit of it."

Randall showed Zelda the paper Joe had given him with the information about the two child specialists, an LPC and an LCSW. "These are two women who Joe recommended for Kyle to see. He said they both work with kids and that he knows they have plenty of experience. Here, you decide which one seems like the one for us, and make the appointment. We'll both go in with Kyle."

Zelda went into one of her self-deprecation fits again. "Randy, none of these letters after the names mean anything to me. It's like going to one of your hospital office parties. Everyone has a name tag with alphabet soup after the name. It's supposed to show how important and educated they are, but it just looks like alphabet vomit to me!"

Randall recalled his own name badge, which read "Randall Bieder-meier, MD, FACR." "Yeah, I feel you! My name badge even intimidates me. It's not about the letters though. It just means they went through the necessary maze to be able to do what they do. The real choice is whether we hit it off with the one you pick, letters or no letters."

Zelda was still not convinced. "Oh, Randy, I don't know. What would I even say? I don't understand kids. How would they even know my kid? Crap, I barely understand my own kids."

"Well, the way Joe explained it to me, a child specialist has training on how kids develop and how they communicate. The specialist would be focused on supporting the child and helping the family understand his or her behaviors. Usually, the behaviors are just clues that help us to see what the child is trying to express. The specialist would teach Kyle the skills to get what he wants, and also help us recognize his needs bet-ter. Our kids are not on an island alone. We're on the island with them."

Zelda looked a bit more comfortable with the idea. "That does sound better than the judgy Freudian shrink I had pictured in my mind. I feel way better that it can be a woman we choose. I suppose I can start with the one on 84th Avenue, since it's close to our house. The card says she has late office hours." Zelda seemed to be getting a bit of her confi-dence back.

Randall gave Zelda's hand a squeeze. "Shall we call her together?"

Zelda nodded, and they walked into Randall's study. She picked up the handset of the old rotary phone Randall liked to keep in there. It seemed to take forever for each number to click by. Zelda smoothed out the front of her outfit while the phone rang, as if stepping into a role of competent mother. When the receptionist answered, Zelda spoke clearly and calmly, asked intelligent questions, and made arrangements for their first visit. Randall was amazed at the change; he hadn't seen this side of Zelda in a long time.

The receptionist told Zelda that the therapist was in the office and had ten minutes before the next patient. She said Zelda could talk with her about what to expect on the first visit. Zelda looked surprised and agreed.

After a round of questions and answers, Zelda said goodbye and hung up. "We will meet with Ms. Chelsea Andretti next week Wednesday at 4:00. You can be home by then, right, Randy?"

Randall nodded emphatically, making a mental note to change his calendar. The phone call had transformed Zelda and charged her with enthusiasm.

Whatever magic spell had overtaken Zelda, it lasted through dinner, bath time for kiddos, and story time in front of a nice fire in the living room fireplace. Zelda made chicken enchiladas and fresh broccoli with cheese sauce. The dinner was so good, the kids forgot they hated broccoli. Infused with a surfeit of food and stories, Kyle and Addie were both soon ready for bed. Both wanted to pray for their disappeared cat and said quiet vocal prayers wishing for a replacement, or maybe two. It wasn't long before both sprouts were far away in dreamland in their respective beds. But just before dropping off to sleep, Addie had reached for a nonexistent cat to hug, and whimpered softly in her sleep.

Randall and Zelda crept downstairs to relax in front of the waning fire. Randall sat in "Rex the Wonder Chair," sipping a nice glass of Schlink Haus Riesling. Zelda chugged her wine glass empty and laid down on the carpet in front of the glowing embers.

Randall's eyelids fluttered downward. "That was a great dinner, Zel. I think you've found the secret to a pleasant parental night's sleep. Stuff the kids with food and stories."

It took Zelda a few seconds to respond. "Man, I'm stuffed like a Thanksgiving turkey. My eyelids feel like they weigh five pounds. Get me some toothpicks from the kitchen to prop them open. I'll never make it upstairs. You could pull off my clothes and make me your sex slave right now. I wouldn't be able to resist."

Randall almost choked on his sip of wine. "Dingleberries! If I had the energy, I'd really do you up just so. But not to worry. I don't think Jumping Jack Flash has any jump left. It's to bed we must hasten, for morning will soon come us to chasten."

"Oh, Deuteronomist dinosaurs," barked Zelda. "What a relief! My maidenhead is safe for the night. I agree we must hasten, and I bet I can hasten faster than you."

Despite her apparent terminal lethargy, Zelda popped up and beat a hasty retreat up the stairs. "Last one up the stairs gets to do the dog duty, lock the doors and check the kids!"

Randall moaned. "Once more, the loafing lucky loser."

Randall completed his assigned tasks and prepped for bed. He found Zelda fast asleep with her covers at half-mast. He enjoyed the view for a long moment and wondered if her previous offer might still be valid. Instead, he used his imagination and settled for a kiss on her forehead, a quick peek under her nightgown, and reluctantly pulled up the covers.

When his head hit the pillow, Randall's conscious mind quickly unraveled its hold on reality. His subconscious wandered, unfettered. He started counting monitor units and briefly found he could see individual X-rays traveling simultaneously as waves and particles. He told himself to wake up and write this discovery down if he wanted scientific fame and fortune. But he was too far gone, too mired in a deep state of entropy.

Ringing in the Night

At first Randall thought the harsh ringing was the alarm clock alerting him to the start of a new day, but when he squinted at the bedside clock, it was only 2:10 a.m. Had he set the damn alarm wrong? As he came out of his dream fog, he realized it was the bedside phone ringing. *Who the hell could it be at this hour?* Grabbing for the receiver, it slipped out of his hand. It fell to the floor with a soft thump. He knelt down on the floor, flailing around in the dark, trying to find the receiver. He found it in his shoe, found his ear, and joined the two.

Randall's throat was full of sinus drainage, and he rasped a hoarse greeting. "Hello, Hello?" At first there was no response, but he thought he could hear some sniffling and choking. "Hello, is anyone there?"

"Is this . . . is this Dr. Biedermeier?" asked a woman's shaky voice. The caller was clearly in the midst of crying.

"Yes, this is Dr. B, who is this?"

"This is Sally O'Loughlin. My Jimmy is dead! He got up to go to the bathroom. When he didn't come back, I went in there and I found him just sitting on the toilet. He wasn't breathing. I tried to wake him up, but . . . oh, doctor, what do I do?" She dissolved into tears again.

"Mrs. O'Loughlin? Sally? Take a deep breath. Yes, breathe. Calm down so I can hear what you have to say . . . are you still there?" Randall asked several times before she started talking again.

"I'm sorry to call so late, but . . . after we talked today . . . in the clinic, you gave Jimmy your home phone number. I found the paper in his shirt pocket when I was trying to wake him. I thought it would be okay to call you. I can't believe he's gone. Just like that! And on the toilet. How could that happen?" She started choking and sniffling again.

"I am so sorry, Sally." Randall soothed her as best he could. "Sometimes things happen and there's no obvious rhyme or reason." Randall thought that sounded pretty lame.

He didn't have a clue what to say but he just kept talking while Mrs. O'Loughlin cried. He wasn't exactly sure what he was saying, except he felt moved to fill the space with words. After a few minutes, Sally settled down enough to be more coherent.

"Thanks for listening and talking, I needed to hear someone's voice!" Sally cleared her throat. "I just have no idea what to do next."

"That's okay, it's not like we get a lot of practice before we have to deal with, *er*, this kind of thing," sympathized Randall. He wasn't sure what to do either. *Call the police? The coroner? A plumber?*

Zelda sat up in bed suddenly and grabbed Randall's arm. "Randy, who the heck are you talking to? It's after 2:00 in the morning. Is that your secret girlfriend?"

Randall cupped his hand over the phone's receiver, whispering to Zelda. "It's the wife of a patient! This is serious!"

"Sure, it is, Randy. Give me the phone, I'll fill her in on a few things," snapped Zelda, pulling the phone out of Randall's hand.

"No, no, give me the phone back! It really is a patient's wife. He just died on the toilet in their bathroom, and she's freaking out," exclaimed Randall, trying to wrench the phone back. "Don't make it worse."

Zelda kept a firm grip on the phone and put it to her ear. "Who is this?" Zelda growled into the phone. Randall could barely hear the voice on the other end. "Sally? Your Jimmy died tonight? . . . In the bathroom? . . . On the john? . . . Oh, geez, I'm so sorry. I didn't mean to sound so . . . harsh."

"I told you so, now give me the phone back," said Randall sternly.

"No, Randy, I got this," said Zelda, pushing him away. "Sally needs a woman to talk to now."

Randall relented, and Zelda began listening to Sally tell her tale again. Soon Zelda was overcome with compassion as she imagined losing Randall so suddenly.

Zelda listened intently. "Jimmy had a bad dream about the grim reaper. Wow. That must have been creepy. What? Randy gave you our home phone number? He never does that."

Randall sat on the edge of the bed, totally amazed as the two women commiserated. He motioned to Zelda that he needed to pee, and she motioned him to go ahead because the girls were having a chat, and he wasn't needed. When Randall came back to the bedroom, Zelda was still on the phone with Sally, mostly listening and saying, "*uh huh*." When he sat down on the edge of the bed again, Zelda handed the phone back to him.

"Here's the phone back. We're done," said Zelda. "She wants you to tell her who to call to deal with Jimmy's body and so forth. I don't have a clue. Poor lady. If you ever croak on the john in the middle of the night, Randy, I'll kill you! Now I have to pee."

"Mrs. O'Loughlin, Sally, are you still there?" asked Randall. "Good. Did you and Zelda have a good talk? *Uh huh*. You're going to meet for lunch next week? That's, *uh*, that's good. Yeah. Okay, do you have a piece of paper and something to write with?"

Randall explained who to call to pick up the body and then discussed notifying the family, planning funeral arrangements, and pulling together any legal papers.

She said that Jimmy was very thorough and had everything put together on his desk. When Randall rang off, Sally still sounded upset but in control.

Zelda sat down on the bed next to Randall and gave him a hug and a kiss. "You are one sweetie puss," said Zelda and stroked his bald pate.

"Me? What'd I do?" said Randall, looking mystified.

"You know."

Addie appeared at the bedroom door. "Mommy, Daddy, something waked me up, and now I'm scared. Can you come tuck me in?"

WHAT ABOUT BOB?

The next morning, Randall remembered to buy donuts for chart rounds. Before the chart review began, Randall indicated that the donuts were to mark some special news that Bob had to convey. The group was stunned to an awkward silence by the news, and Bob looked around expecting someone to say something.

Randall grabbed into his bag of tricks. "I'm sure we'll all want to wish Bob well in his new venture. No doubt the world of coffee beans will be much improved by his involvement. Let's take a few moments to go around the table and express our good wishes to Bob. Doris, would you like to start?" Randall figured that Doris, being well suffused with Southern hospitality, would be the best icebreaker.

Doris quickly found her voice. "I'm sure I speak for everyone here. We're really gon' to miss you, Bob. You do so much 'round here. Can't imagine how we all will do without you. Makes me jealous though, 'cause you get to follow your dream. I see the signs. I'm still waitin' for mine to show me the way. And the signs show me that Bob will do just fine down in Costa Rica. Godspeed, Bob."

Doris rose and put an arm on Bob's shoulder and kissed his cheek. Bob turned a brighter shade of pale and managed to sink lower in his chair. Doris smiled and pointed to Grace who was next in line.

Grace mumbled and stumbled for a bit, then croaked out a weak congratulations and good luck. Molly was a bit more effusive and quickly passed the talking stick to Melinda.

Melinda gave Bob a huge beaming smile. "Oh, Bob. That is so exciting. I almost wish I could go with you. Do you have family going with you?"

Eyes widened. Few at the table ever even thought of Bob as possibly being married or having a family. Or even a dog. Curiosity was rampant.

Bob sat up straight and smiled. "Yeah. My wife, Jean, is really excited about going down there. We and the two boys have been down there for vacation the last three years, and we all love Costa Rica. And we all speak Spanish now. Last year we found this plantation for sale. Couldn't pass it up. Life is short. Gotta live your dream. We're bringing Poncho too."

"Poncho?" asked Grace.

Bob nodded. "Our chocolate Lab. Lazy pooch loves Costa Rican coffee. Only thing that makes him get jazzed up enough to retrieve sticks. We'll be driving down through Mexico. He'll be good protection."

Randall rubbed his chin. "How old are the kids?"

"Let's see. Jake is ten and Little Bob is turning eight next month," said Bob.

Molly couldn't contain herself. "Little Bob?"

"Yeah, it's kind of like calling a fat kid Tiny. He's already 5' 11". If he keeps growing like he is, I'll be looking up at him soon. Jake is built more like his mom. He'll probably top out at six feet."

When all the questions were finally answered, the group set to devouring jelly filleds and glazeds. There was even some hugging and laughing. In two weeks, Bob Storch would be polishing his Spanish. Time to start the search for a new radiation physicist and stock up on zip ties. He tried to remember the name of Bob's friend. Then it came to him. Dan Graham. Like the cracker.

Story Pressure

After chart rounds, regular business resumed, and Randall sat at his desk, thinking about his lunch with Joe Shepard. He wasn't sure he could wait another week to finish their discussion about quantum theory and the workings of the human brain. The story he wanted, no, needed, to tell Joe was burning a hole in his brain. He slammed the chart he was reviewing down on his desk and dialed Joe's office number.

Joe's receptionist, Melanie, answered. Randall identified himself and asked if Joe was in the office.

Melanie was polite but firm. "I'm sorry, Doctor. He's with a patient. Can I help you with something?"

Randall paused for a moment, thinking. "Joe and I had plans to have lunch in about a week, but some . . . new issues have arisen, and I was wondering if we could make it sooner."

"I understand," said Melanie. "I'll check the schedule."

Randall could hear her paging through the appointment book. "Sorry, he's booked up at least a week around lunchtime."

Randall threw his pen at the wall. "Darn. I've got a problem that can't wait."

"Doctor, could you hold for a second while I take another call?"

Randall was getting frustrated but tried to remain civil. "Sure, no problem."

After a short wait she came back on the line. "Dr. Biedermeier, how about lunch with Dr. Shepard today?"

Randall frowned. "Today?"

Melanie's voice became less formal. "The call I just took was his 11:30 cancelling. He doesn't have another patient until 2:30. Is that enough time?"

"Plenty," said Randall cheerily. "Probably more time than I can get away with."

"In that case, I'll make the reservation. I'm sure he'll want to join you. All his wife packed for his lunch today was a PBJ sandwich and a pickle. Plus, he's with Mrs. Schwartzenheimer and her little Butchy now. They usually drive him batty, and he'll be pleased to talk to a sentient human being to settle his nerves."

Randall couldn't tell if she was joking. He almost felt guilty for feeling irritated. "I'm not sure I'm the right one to settle anyone's nerves, but I'll do my best."

Melanie laughed loudly. "Please don't let on that I mentioned Mrs. Schwartzenheimer and son. I'll set up the lunch at Miss Katie's Diner for noon sharp. Assume it's a go, unless I call you back."

Randall was astounded things had worked out so well. The stars were aligning. "Thanks for your help. You remind me of my secretary, Doris. I'm sure Joe couldn't survive two days without you."

"You pegged it just right," Melanie responded. "Now give me your call back number so I can call you if there's a problem."

Randall slapped his forehead. "Oh, yeah. My number." Randall did as bid, hung up, and rose from his chair to give himself a high-five.

Then Randall panicked momentarily. He hadn't checked *his* schedule. He hustled into Doris's office. "Doris! Please tell me I can go out for lunch today. Is there something I don't know about?"

Doris looked at Randall smugly. "Oh, lots and lots of somethings. But saints be praised, you have nothin' pressin' from 11:30 to 2:00. Where are you going to be? And who is she?"

Randall looked sheepish. "Just over at Miss Katie's Diner. And it's not a she. It's my friend, Joe Shepard, MD. Yes, again."

Doris just looked up and smiled. "You should be golden if you take your beeper."

Randall patted his coat pocket. "Check. Have beeper."

Doris pursed her lips. "Got live batteries in it? Remember last time?"

Randall nodded. "Better page me to make sure it's working."

The beeper chirped, and Randall was given a hall pass. He made it out of the VA without a hassle, and was seated at a window table with Joe at the stroke of noon. They checked the menu and ordered.

"So what was so all-fired urgent that we had to meet again today?" asked Joe. "All Melanie could tell me was that some new issue had arisen. What's the issue?"

Randall hunched down and leaned forward. He looked left and right like a CIA agent checking for surveillance. "It's in regard to the story you told me about when you fell out of your tree house."

"Yeah. What about it?" asked Joe, looking slightly worried.

Randall was almost whispering now. "Well, as I may have mentioned, I have one remarkably like it. I thought I could wait a week to tell it to you, but it's been looping in my brain like those song bugs. I think the only way to stop it is to tell it to you."

Joe frowned deeply. "I thought you were going to do some physics research first."

Randall realigned his silverware with the plate. "I am. I will. But I think you need to hear this first. Well, at least I need to tell you."

The food arrived. Randall was momentarily distracted by the rather sumptuous waitress. He watched as she walked away.

Joe chuckled. "I see you're not so distraught that you can't make anatomic evaluations."

Randall blushed slightly. "You have to stop and see the roses."

Joe nodded. "Indeed, you do. How about we eat with all due alacrity and save story time for coffee and strudel? Can you hold fire until then?"

Randall nodded and shook his head. "Not sure. But I'll try."

LAWNMOWER INCIDENT

While Randall ate tuna salad, his hot-to-tell story ran in his head like a sports replay with full audio and video and some parts in slow-motion. He wanted to get the details right so he could give Joe a succinct summary. Their time together would be short. Randall felt his mind zoom to the past.

Randall and Zelda had lived in Colorado Springs for three years during his residency training. The three-bedroom ranch was the first house they had owned. Before that, it had been one-bedroom apartments. Addie was about ten months old. That Saturday morning, Zelda had driven off with Kyle to go shopping in their underpowered 1965 blue-and-white Volkswagen Microbus. Driving it made her feel like a hippie. All the rusted-out hulk lacked was a peace symbol spray painted on the nose. If there was a crosswind, the flat side of the lightweight bus acted like a sail and the bus started to yaw. To avoid being blown off the road, it had to be tacked like a sailboat.

Randall had mowing to do. He put Addie down for a nap in her crib, which was set up next to his desk in his spare bedroom office. Zelda worked nights as a banquet waitress at the Broadmoor Hotel, so Randall would be the PIC (parent in charge) while she was at work. If

Addie got fussy, he could just reach over and pat her little tummy or rub her back. A heavy four-drawer file cabinet sat up against the wall just inches from the doorway. The door opened inward, and the knob was on the side near the file cabinet.

He and Zelda had been on edge in the preceding weeks because of some strange happenings in the house. They turned off lights at night, but somehow the lights were back on in the morning. The thermostat would be turned down at bedtime but turned up the next morning. They heard strange sounds at night with no clue to their origin. The sounds were the traditional "bumps in the night." They heard creaks, groans, tapping, rattling, and faint voices. Kyle was only two years old and was ruled out as the perp, since he was too small to reach the thermostat. One night, a frightened Kyle slept between his parents in their double bed and the disturbances were even worse than usual. So they'd ruled out Kyle as the source of mischief.

Then they really got spooked when a neighbor described the behavior of the house's previous owner, Harold Schmidt. The man had lived in the house for over twenty years and was fanatical about its upkeep. He painted the house every year, and the yard was always meticulously neat. Poor old Harold had gotten cancer and died at home just weeks before Randall and Zelda bought the place. Zelda was convinced Harold was an unfriendly ghost, hated kids, and wanted them all out of "his" tidy house. Randall gave Zelda's idea short shrift and told her she was being overly superstitious. But he couldn't deny the chills he felt whenever another "event" happened. He just never admitted it to Zelda. Best to be the strong husband and family protector.

Before Zelda had driven off with Kyle, she had reminded Randall to check on Addie before he went out to mow. "We're gonna be gone a long time, Randy, so don't forget you have a daughter! If anything happens to her, your ass is grass."

Randall had followed the two out to the car, holding Addie.

Randall brushed off her snarky remark. "Don't worry. I'll keep a close watch on her. Ghosts don't come out during the day."

Zelda opened the passenger door and strapped Kyle in his car seat.

She walked around to the driver's side and gave Randall a fisheye stare. "Look. I know what you think about my Harold the Unfriendly Ghost idea, but humor me. If he doesn't exist, watching Addie won't cramp your style. But if I'm right . . ."

Randall grabbed Addie's little hand and waved it goodbye to Zelda and Kyle. "I got it. Old Glue Eyes is on the job."

Addie uttered a soft bye-bye to go with the wave as Zelda pulled out of the driveway. Randall took Addie back inside to put her down to nap. Addie was a good little napper. He was pretty sure Addie would sleep long enough for him to finish the mowing job. He cleaned up some dishes in the kitchen and cleared toy clutter off the living room floor before heading outside. Just to be sure, he peeked in at Addie, who was making sniffly snoring sounds in her crib. He walked up closer just to look at Addie's little face. Randall thought she was the cutest little bug ever.

While she slept, Addie clutched her white blanket with the sateen bunting and had it scrunched up into a ball. Certain she was safely asleep, Randall left the room and almost closed the door. He decided to leave it open a few inches to let in some light. Addie sometimes got scared if she woke up to total darkness.

Randall went outside to get the mower started. The day was getting hot, and kids were playing ball in the field across the street. Randall watched for a second, wishing he could do that instead of mowing. A yank on the starter cord, and Randall set grass to flying. Then as he was on the fourth pass across the lawn, above the noise of the mower and with ear protection on, he thought he "heard" a scream for help. He stopped and abruptly shut down the mower.

He almost shouted, "What the heck?" He tore off the ear protectors and listened hard, thinking that perhaps one of the children playing in the field had fallen or gotten hit by a baseball. But all the children looked fine.

Hearing nothing further and seeing nothing amiss, Randall felt foolish and overly jumpy. He could hear his father's voice harping at him. "A job half done is hardly begun. So do the other half." Randall had become a "get-er-done" sort of guy, so he restarted the mower and continued the job. He had no sooner begun mowing again when he "heard" the same cry for help. This time it seemed more urgent.

Randall shut the mower down and shouted to the neighborhood and beyond. "Sorry, Dad, gotta go!"

Without having a concrete reason to believe his next thought, he became certain the distress call was coming from Addie. As soon as he thought it, he knew it was true. He bolted into the house, through the living room, and stumbled over the coffee table. He picked himself up and limped to Addie's room; the door was closed tightly.

Randall shouted to the house. "I thought I left that open!"

He could turn the doorknob and the catch released, but the door wouldn't budge. He put his shoulder into the door, and it moved a few inches. Through the narrow opening, he could see the heavy file cabinet was now several inches in front of the door, completely blocking it. Pushing with all his strength, Randall finally got the file cabinet moved back enough for him to enter the room. He slithered through the narrow gap, turned on the light, and ran to Addie's crib.

At first Addie looked to be fine, just rolled over on her side. But when Randall rolled her onto her back, he saw that the sateen bunting of her blanket had somehow torn loose and was wound tightly around her neck. Addie's face was a cyanotic blue. Randall untangled the bunting from her neck and Addie suddenly came awake, gasping for air. Soon the gasping was replaced by full-throated crying.

Randall released the breath he didn't realize he'd been holding. He picked Addie up and held her to his chest, rubbing her back.

"You're okay, sweetie. Daddy's got you now. You're okay. You're okay. Thank God, you're okay." His eyes filled with tears. "How could this have happened?" he yelled at the universe.

Randall carried Addie to the kitchen and gave her a drink of juice. She had finally stopped crying. "Let's not tell Mommy this happened, okay, sweetie?" Randall requested of Addie, as if she could rat him out.

Addie was just finishing her juice when Randall heard car tires screeching to a stop in the driveway and car doors slamming. Zelda and Kyle came barreling in the front door and burst into the kitchen.

Zelda spied Randall holding Addie. "Thank God, she's okay! Give her to me! Let me hold her!"

Randall, shocked and dazed, handed Addie to Zelda, who clutched her in a tight hug. "My baby, my baby. *Shhh*, it's okay, You're okay. Randy, what happened?"

Kyle stood looking at the three, bewildered. "Was Addie hurted?"

Randall was stunned. How had Zelda and Kyle known to come back? They were supposed to be gone for hours. There would be no secrets about this little mishap. "No, Kyle, Addie's okay. We just had a little scare."

Kyle now just looked scared and came up to pat Addie on the back. "Hey, little Sis. I heard you call me for help. I'm glad you're safe."

Randall looked puzzled. "Zelda. Why are you guys here? You just left the house. You haven't had enough time to shop. Why did you come back so soon?"

Zelda wiped tears from her eyes and shook her head. "Randy, I don't honestly know. I got about halfway to town, and Kyle began to scream that someone was hurting Addie. He just kept yelling that we had to go home and save her. Then I started to feel this awful sense of dread too. Something just clicked in my head, and I knew I had to turn around and come home. I even ran some red lights. Holy Hopscotching Hottentots, Randy! What the heck just happened?"

Randall led them all to the living room and they huddled together on the couch just recombobulating. When things were settled down a bit, eyes wiped and noses blown, Randall recounted what had happened. When he was done, Zelda sat there wide-eyed, almost in shock.

They could deduce no rational explanation for the strange confluence of events. All they knew for sure was that something had happened to Addie and that, somehow, she had called for help. The important thing, they decided, was that Addie was okay, and their little family was still intact. At that moment, they realized that they, themselves, were the most precious entities. That was the good news.

The bad news was all the unanswered questions. What had caused the bunting to unravel and encircle Addie's neck? How had the file cabinet moved? How did Addie speechlessly cry for help at a distance? They had no answers that fit their understanding of reality. Zelda had applied a semi-scientific name to it. She had called it "Phantom Talk." Randall thought that was as good a name as any. He knew only one thing for sure. He was, sooner or later, going to figure out their little Biedermeier mystery. As a scientist, he strongly believed that everything under the sun could be explained. But sometimes we just don't yet have the knowledge to carry that out.

The Ranjoe Show

Randall's replay newsreel was flipping random numbers on his virtual screen when the waitress appeared at their table, offering a coffee warm-up. Randall was still rather in driftless territory. Joe knuckled Randall on the shoulder to reboot his computer.

"Earth to Randy. Please acknowledge," said Joe. "I'm full of noodles and strudels. I want my story."

Randall started a bit. "Sorry, man. I was just running the memory on rewind and fast forward to refresh the details. I'm ready to give you the Cliff Notes version now."

Joe checked his watch. "Well, we've got thirty minutes left. Hit me."

Randall's abstracted version took about ten minutes. During the story, Joe was quite attentive, and once shooed the waitress away to avoid interruption. When Randall finished, Joe just sat back in his chair and looked around the room as if, somewhere, there was a sign posted with the answers.

After a long moment, Joe just uttered a somewhat nonsensical exclamation. "Holy Hypnagogic Happenstances!"

Randall nodded. "Yeah, what you said."

Joe went on. "Now I see why you were so zoned in on telling me about your little lawnmower incident. Toro be praised. One more story like that, and we can publish. I can't believe how closely your experience parallels mine. It sure gets me thinking that there's more here than meets the eye."

Randall nodded. "Here, here! I'm not one to invoke the supernatural or holy interventions when something doesn't fit our version of the real world. I'm almost certain there's an ability within the human brain that we don't understand that permits communication beyond our known five senses. I almost want to use the label ESP, but what if it's not extra-sensory, but a well-developed sense we all have but don't realize?"

Joe nodded his agreement. "Yes. But such an explanation would be politically incorrect in both the secular and nonsecular world, not to mention the scientific one. Mind if I ask a personal question?"

Randall nodded his agreement and wondered how it could get more personal.

"Are you and Zelda religious? I mean, are you regular churchgoers?" asked Joe, searching Randall's eyes.

Randall shook his head. "Not really. I was raised Lutheran but couldn't handle all the guilt. I believe in a creative force, but I'm open to many ways to characterize it. Zelda is more into New Age stuff. She grooves on Khalil Gibran. His stuff is very pithy, and I got lost trying to read his books. She also likes Edgar Cayce, the American clairvoyant who claimed to channel from his higher self. She spouts quotes from the *Bhagavad Gita*, prays to the Peruvian six directions and does smudging with burning sage."

Joe raised his eyebrows. "So you could say her dogma got run over by her karma. She sounds a bit eclectic?"

Randall nodded. "Oh, did I mention Yoga meditation?"

"*Namaste!*" quipped Joe.

"True enough," said Randall. "But if your interest is piqued in, say, an eyes-wide-open stroll down this path together on the QT, what can it hurt? The problem with science discovery is that each of us goes down our own little rabbit hole often unaware of other rabbit holes. With what you know about brain function, and what I know or can find out about biophysics, maybe we can get a peek at an explanation that's not just confabulation."

Joe pondered a bit. "*Hmm.* That makes sense. We might even need to add a few other rabbits to our brain trust."

Randall smiled broadly and pushed his chair back to relieve table pressure on his burgeoning belly. "I've got a few ideas, but they aren't ready for prime time yet. I still want to have a confab with my physics contacts and bone up more on quantum physics and how it might interplay with biologic function. Especially in the brain. Then we should meet again and set up more time."

Joe was floating down the same creek. "In the meantime, there's some brain function studies that are using new imaging techniques that I've been meaning to buff up on. When we meet again, I'll try to have that unraveled. Let's have our lunch meeting next week as planned for updates, then figure out when to have a longer meetup. Let's both think about who else might be resources we can tap."

It was agreed and they went forth. Then Randall remembered the Gibran quote that Zelda had taped to the wall above her easel in her art workshop: "Yesterday is but today's memory, and tomorrow is today's dream."

RB

CHAPTER 21

THE LATEST POOP

"To me, every hour of every day and night is an unspeakably perfect miracle."

— *Leaves of Grass,* Walt Whitman

It's My Potty

The next weekend, Randall was "enjoying" one of their patented Biedermeier "bedlam breakfasts." Zelda was cooking bacon while on the phone with the elderly next-door neighbor, Fred Bush. The kids were making a racket, and she couldn't quite understand Fred's Parkinsonian voice. She did make out that Fred was having some kind of issue with their dog, Polluto. Once more, she rued the day her old high school buddy and ne'er-do-well, Steve Summers, had "gifted" them with Polluto, then a lovable brown fuzzy puppy. But Polluto had "grow'd like Topsy," hit ninety pounds, and wasn't looking back. His size and his bratty behavior now ranged between "not that lovable anymore" and "that dog has to go!"

Zelda asked Fred to hold the phone a second, put her hand over the mouthpiece and yelled. "Kids, quiet down, I'm trying to talk on the phone! Kyle, if you have to go potty, please go to the bathroom. Randy, would you please pay attention to what's going on around you and get Kyle on the john!"

"But I don't have to go," whined Kyle, who had crept under the table to hide.

In addition to the usual tune-out technique Randall used when chaos surrounded him, his mind had been rather obsessively dwelling on what he was now calling, mostly to himself, the "Uncle Phil Episode." He had been reluctant to talk about it with Zelda, since she had usually been a bit too ready to invoke the occult as an explanation for the unknown or unusual. He was pretty sure that would be the result again if he shared the episode with her. Once on a roll into the twilight zone, she was unstoppable. No one was safe in the path of the redheaded "woo woo" freight train.

"Randy, for Pete's sake, would you wake up and smell the odor of dead roses coming from *your* son's southernmost orifice?! Please transport him forthwith to the potty zimmer!" Zelda's face had turned a vibrant red.

"Yes, Mother," said Randall sarcastically, but slithered out of his kitchen chair to transport Kyle upstairs.

She pointed her finger in Randall's face, close enough to poke his nose. "And no more lip from *you*, either!"

Randall hauled Kyle out from under the table and was struck by the foul odor. He remembered when he was a kid and did the same thing. He'd go hide behind the couch and be really quiet. Then his mother, Selma, would call out and ask him if he had to go potty. He'd always answer no, so she'd haul him to the bathroom and make him sit until he produced results. While he sat, trying to loosen his load, she'd read from A. A. Milne's *Winnie the Pooh*. As a kid, Randall thought the book was written just for that purpose. When Randall finally released his prize, after much reading and coaxing, Selma always repeated the key line from the book where Christopher Robin tells Pooh, "You're braver than you believe, and stronger than you seem, and smarter than you think." The quote had stuck in his mind and gotten him through some rough times.

Randall pulled Kyle to the bathroom, hoping to catch him before he actually released his cargo. "Whooee, boy, you are certainly fartogenous! Somethin' crawled upside you and died," gasped Randall. "Let's get you to the toxic waste dump."

"But I don't have to go number two," complained Kyle.

"Oh, yes you do, and you are number one at number two, when it comes to fragrance."

Randall was fairly adept at kid waste management, having spent quite a few nights after work caring for the kids while Zelda worked the night shift at various restaurants. Randall put Kyle on the toilet and prepared for the wait. For reasons that were not clear to Randall, Kyle simply sat on the toilet and held back as long as he could. He or Zelda had to sit on the side of the bathtub and try to distract him until he finally let go.

"Dad, I don't want to just sit here," moaned Kyle. "Tell me a story."

"No, you're not getting off until you go number two. Here, read this comic. I'm going to read this magazine." Randall picked up one of his well-worn car magazines from the shelf next to the toilet.

Kyle flipped through the pages of his comic and tossed it aside. "I already read this one," he whined.

"No more talk. Do your job. Here's a different comic." Randall's butt was already sore from sitting on the narrow side of the tub.

Randall had already read his car magazine from cover to cover. As Kyle procrastinated giving forth, Randall's mind drifted off. He reflected on the pure luck they'd had even finding the Creekside house, not to mention finally having a job that paid enough to afford it. During college and medical school, he'd survived mostly on partial scholarships and loans. After marriage and kids, Zelda had to work night shift waitressing jobs to make ends meet. They often passed like ships in the night. Randall came home from the hospital just as she was leaving to hostess an evening banquet. At night, Randall played Mr. Mom, including, but not limited to, dinner, bath, bedtime story, and sleepy time.

Priming the Pump

Kyle kept fidgeting on the toilet and suddenly threw his comic in the bathtub, interrupting Randall's brief reflection. "This comic is boring too. I've read it 651 times. I want a different one!"

There was a small amount of water left in the tub. In moments, the old comic book was a soggy disaster. Randall rolled his eyes. "Smooth move, Ex-Lax. You don't have to worry about reading that comic again. Get over it. You're not leaving this room until you produce a large brown torpedo."

Kyle pounded the window ledge with his fist and tried to wriggle off the seat.

Randall stymied the move.

"But I can't go!" Kyle protested.

Randall grabbed Kyle's shoulders and pushed him back in the pilot's seat. "It's not 'can't,' buster. It's 'won't.' You just have to loosen up and open the bomb bay door."

Kyle looked puzzled. "Bombay door? What's that?"

Randall explained the concept, then had an idea. "Say, remember the Battleship game?"

"Yeah," said Kyle. "I always sink your battleship with my sub's torpedoes."

Randall put up a hand. "That game is all luck and no skill. You're just a lucky ducky. How about you play destroyer, and my submarine is in the toilet water. You drop a depth charge and, *BOOM*, my sub blows up and splashes water all over your hinder."

Kyle laughed at the image but remained steadfastly obstinate. "No. I need you to tell me a story. Your stories relax me enough to go. I want to hear the story about how we found this house."

Randall was flummoxed. How in the world had Kyle known what Randall had just been thinking? Was Kyle a mind reader?

Randall stammered a bit. "But *umm*, I've told you that story 262 times. You want to hear it again?"

"Yeah. Make it 263. I promise that will work. And I know you can talk a lot, Dad, 'cuz you always do, especially when you tell stories."

"Oh, alright," said Randall. "If you promise to do your number two doo-doo that you do so well."

At that moment, Kyle looked pathetically small on the porcelain throne. "I promise."

Randall looked at the ceiling in remembrance. "Remember when we lived in Durham, North Carolina?"

Kyle's face lit up. "Yeah, in the L-shaped house; the one with the chicken coop and the tree house!"

"That's the one. Well, do you remember when Mom drove you and Addie to Grandpa Red's house here in Milwaukee to look for a new house for us?"

Kyle nodded. "I was pretty young, but I remember the drive. It was far and took a long time. I didn't like it in Grandpa's house. It smelled funny, and we had to be quiet. Mom looked for a house every day but couldn't find one. She was real grumpy all the time!"

Randall recalled the prickly mood Zelda had been in quite well. "Yeah, I remember. Sorry you had to go through that. Well, I had plane tickets to fly to Milwaukee over the weekend and look at what she found, but when I called, Mom said there was no reason to come because everything she looked at was no good."

"But she didn't see *this* house, right?" asked Kyle.

Randall nodded. "That's right. So I called her the night before I was supposed to fly to Milwaukee. She said not to bother coming. I told her that I already had a nonrefundable plane ticket, so I might as well come anyhow. We could just drive around neighborhoods to figure out where we wanted to locate. I figured more houses might show up for sale over the weekend."

Kyle passed some gas, and it echoed in the bowl.

Randall's eyes widened. "That's either a thunderstorm or a train coming down the track."

Kyle laughed. "Or a depth charge!"

Randall grimaced. "Oh, crap! I'm about to die."

Kyle giggled, then segued back to the house story. "Dad, I remember you said you had a dream about finding this house, plus you missed me and Addie. And Mom too."

Randall smiled and knuckle-rubbed Kyle's head. "That's right, big boy. I really did miss you guys. And the dream was really strange. It was so vivid. I pictured an English Tudor house with four bedrooms and an attached garage. I told Mom about it. She said I was just making up a story as an excuse to come to Milwaukee. She got real huffy with me on the phone and said there were no Tudors for sale, or she would have seen one."

Kyle brightened up a bit. "I get dreams like that too. They seem so real. And sometimes, after I have one of 'em, something happens just like what I saw in the dream. It's real spooky."

Randall remembered Kyle saying that before, but he had dismissed it as a kid fantasy. Maybe that had been a mistake. "That is spooky. Tell me about one of your dreams."

Kyle thought for a moment. "Remember when I kept begging you for a Mongoose BMX bike?"

"Sure do. You finally wore me down," said Randall.

Kyle lowered his voice to almost a whisper. "The night before you took me to the Big Foot Bike Shop, I had a dream that we were going there to buy the blue one with white stripes. The next day, it happened just like in the dream."

"For real, little dude?" asked Randall.

"For real, Dad dude," affirmed Kyle.

"Wow. You never told me."

Kyle shook his head. "I figured you wouldn't believe me."

Randall nodded. "You're right. I probably wouldn't have then. But now I think I do. I think you inherited the dream thing from me. You're a chip off the old block."

Kyle looked puzzled. "What's that mean?"

"The apple doesn't fall far from the tree."

Kyle shook his head. "Is it chips or apples?!"

"It means you are a small version of me."

Kyle looked rather proud. "That's cool, but I'm keeping my hair!"

Randall reminded Kyle why they were both uncomfortably perched on porcelain. "Great. Now if you want to be more like me, please unload your load. Holding it will make you go bald. Believe me; I know."

Kyle looked to his left with squinted eyes. "I think it's getting close. If you finish the house story, I think it will loosen up my butt."

Randall was pretty sure he was being manipulated but agreed to continue. "My plane from Durham landed in Milwaukee at 10:30 that

Saturday morning. Mom was supposed to pick me up at Mitchell Field at 11:00, but I stood at the arrivals curb until 11:45 before she showed up. She came in fast in her dad's green Ford station wagon and screeched to a halt in front of where I was standing."

Kyle interrupted. "She burned rubber, right? The tires left marks on the pavement."

Randall nodded. "You bet. She killed the engine, and steam came out from under the hood. The engine kept knock-knock-knocking and then wheezed as it died. Mom just sat there at the wheel, staring out the windshield. Finally I tapped on the passenger window, but she just ignored it. After I rattled the door handle, she reached over and unlocked the door. I opened the door, but she didn't look at me or say hello."

Kyle began to chuckle. "Ha, ha. This is my favorite part. Do the voices of what you both said. You know, where you talk like you and her."

"Why?" asked Randall.

"It's funnier when you do her voice," said Kyle.

"Okay, if you insist. I loaded my bags in the back of the car and got buckled in the passenger seat. Then I said to her: 'Not having a good day, are we?'"

Kyle laughed and tooted.

"Then Mom turned to look at me with her dragon lady face. I had to stop myself from laughing, it looked so ridiculous. She just glared for a few beats before lambasting me. 'All because of you coming here, I wasted a bunch of time, trying to find someone to watch our stupid kids while you and I cruise around looking at houses for sale that don't exist. So I left late and got stuck in traffic coming here.'"

Kyle laughed at Randall's falsetto version of Zelda's voice.

The falsetto bothered Randall's vocal cords. He coughed and cleared his throat.

Kyle broke in. "Mom was really steamed, right? What did you say?"

"I told her our kids were NOT stupid, but she shouted back that we were stupid for having them. By this time, I was down to one good neuron, and I told Mom to just settle herself and drive. I asked her why her parents couldn't watch the kids, and she said they had refused. They told her they were done raising kids and were not babysitters. I thought that was pretty lame and told her so. Not my best choice. She clammed up again."

Kyle started squirming on the toilet. "Don't stop doing Mom's voice. Get to the part where you guys drive to the house."

Randall cleared his throat again. "I suggested calmly that she pull the car to the curb so I could take over driving. I told her she was really too upset to drive safely. I told her to put all her worries to rest. Our job was simple. Just find a place to live. Once we got back on the road, she relaxed a bit and said, 'Oh, alright. But there's nothing out there to find. I looked. I really did. I know you think I didn't.'"

Kyle remembered this part of the story and told it. "You told Mom your house radar was working, and you told her about your dream. She laughed at you and said, 'Dream on, buster!'" Kyle did a pretty good falsetto.

Randall laughed and nodded. "That's right. Good memory. Before we could start looking at houses I had to stop at the hospital and pick up some papers. Real close to the hospital, I saw the street sign for Rockway Place. My radar told me to turn down Rockway, so I pulled a hard right and went down the unfamiliar road."

Kyle squeaked out the next line. "'Randy, what are you doing?! See, this just proves that your brain is full of feathers!'"

Randall chuckled at Kyle's rendition of Zelda's response. "You got that right. I told her to relax, we were just exploring. The road curved down next to Hidden Creek and then became Creekside Place."

"And there was the lady pounding a 'for sale' sign in the front yard of your dream house," chimed in Kyle.

"Right. As we got to Creekside, Mom pointed to a nice-looking two-story Tudor house at the end of Creekside. She yelled out: 'Stop the car!' I skidded to a stop and looked. Right there in front of us was the house from my dream. Mom read the sign out loud: 'For Sale, Jess Wright Realty 414-123-4567.'"

Kyle laughed again at Randall's rendition of Zelda's dialogue. "Yeah, and you guys liked it because the house had two doors."

Randall burst out laughing, and Kyle looked puzzled.

"Close, Buddy. It was the kind of house called an English Tudor." Randall spelled out aloud the word 'Tudor.'

"Oh, now I get it. I thought it didn't make sense, 'cause our house has three doors," said Kyle.

"Mom and I liked the neighborhood right away. The other houses were older but in great shape. There was a park across the street and a bunch of kids were playing baseball. It seemed perfect for you and Addie," continued Randall.

"And it was just like the house you saw in your dream, right, Dad?" blurted Kyle.

"Yeah! It was crazy. I yelled out to Mom that the house was exactly like the one I had seen in my dream back in Durham. The trees, the yard, the style were all the same. It was the whole enchilada," said Randall.

"With sauce, right, Dad?"

Randall patted Kyle on the shoulder. "You bet. Then Mom got really excited too and said we should go talk to the sign lady in the yard. She was in charge of selling the house and asked us if we were interested in looking inside."

"And you told her you didn't want to just look. You said you were going to buy it," said Kyle.

"The lady thought I was nuts. So did Mom. She started to tell the lady we couldn't afford it and we'd have to see inside before we could decide. But I just kept saying that we would buy it, because the price would be right and we'd love the inside," said Randall.

"But the sales lady said you could only see it if you had an appointment. And you went to ring the doorbell anyhow," continued Kyle.

"Yeah, I usually don't do stuff like that, but the lady who owned the house was already at the door when I got there. I apologized for interrupting her and said I was going to buy the house. She asked me if maybe I'd like to see the inside first. By then Mom and the sales lady were at the door too. Mom started apologizing for me acting so weird, but the lady asked us to come inside and look around."

Kyle started bearing down, but only squeezed out the next part of the story. "And you liked the house inside, especially my bedroom, right?" asked Kyle. "Then you and Mom buyed the house, and now it belongs to us. And now we're living happily ever after."

"Are we ever," said Randall.

Randall knew story time was finally over when Kyle commenced grunting and straining, his face turning scarlet. After three significant splashes in the water, Kyle regained normal facial coloring and made a pronouncement. "That's a good poop story, Dad. Your submarine is dead meat."

THE HOUSE-CAPADES

Even though Kyle had finally done his duty, he refused to be dethroned until Randall finished the house story. "But you haven't done the part about the mystery door."

Randall groaned. "You have to hear that part too?" He stood up and rubbed his numb hiney.

"Yeah. And there might be some more depth charges that need to come out. I might not be done," whined Kyle.

Randall shook his head and thought the house story should be re-named the never-ending story. "Sure thing, bud. What else have I got to do? When we toured the inside of the house with the realtor, ev-erything seemed perfect for us. Four bedrooms, three bathrooms, a full basement, and a den for my office."

Kyle got excited and accidentally slid off the toilet seat. He left a skid mark behind. "Don't forget the spooky bedroom and attic!" he yelled.

Randall stood Kyle up and cleaned Kyle's backside and the toilet seat. "Come on, man. You're hinder isn't wiped yet. You just made a mess. Now hop back on and finish up if there's really any more in there."

Kyle held his nose. "Wow, I'm pretty stinky. I'm sorry for sliding off, Dad. I got too excited. The attic is my favorite part. I'll stay put on the pot."

Randall started stretching his legs. "Alright. I don't want to do that again. So just as Mom and I walk into the master bedroom, one of the window shades rolls up all by itself, pops out of its holder, and falls to the floor. Mom must have jumped a foot off the ground. The realtor said she would get the shade fixed and redirected us to a large walk-in closet."

"But it wasn't just a closet, was it?" blurted Kyle.

"No. Inside the closet was another door with a latch and padlock," said Randall. mysteriously. "The latch had been added later. It obviously was not part of the original house. I asked the realtor where the door led, and she said it was the entrance to the attic. That surprised me because, looking from the outside, there didn't seem to be room for an attic."

Kyle rushed the story ahead. "And the lady couldn't open the lock for you, right?"

Randall nodded. "Right. I asked her why not, and she said the key was 'lost.' I asked her why the lock was there in the first place. She hemmed and hawed something about a family tragedy and that private things had to be stored up there. She said we'd have to wait to see the attic until a locksmith came to get the lock opened and the stored items removed."

"Spooky! What did you and Mom think then?" asked Kyle, as he teetered on the toilet.

Randall shrugged. "We didn't say much at the time. Just nodded our understanding. But later, Mom got all freaked out, and her imagination ran wild. She suspected everything from deformed children locked in the attic to a dead body mortared in a wall. She said, 'That's probably why they weren't quite ready to show the house.'"

Randall delivered the last sentence in his Zelda falsetto, and Kyle nearly slid off the seat again, laughing. When he stopped laughing, the long awaited second round of depth charges splashed in the water.

"Dad, I just blew up the German U-boat," Kyle announced proudly. "Now you can wipe my fanny."

Randall shook his head and made a Bronx cheer. "You can wipe it yourself, Buster Brown. You're seven years old. All seven-year-olds can do it."

Kyle shook his head firmly. "I don't know how. I can't see back there. You and Mom do it better. When I do it, I get all messy."

"Boy, you've got all your excuses lined up like ducks. Nice try, but we're still bowling for dollars. I'll show you like my dad showed me. He's a veteran, and they had very precise methodology." said Randall.

Randall recalled very clearly how his father had grown tired of Randall's sloppy messes, taken him aside, and relayed the wisdom of the wipe. It was a most important father/son lesson.

Randall began the lesson. "First, you don't wad the toilet paper up before you wipe. Pull four squares off the roll, no more, no less. Then you fold the squares until they make one square and hold it in your hand like this. Then reach back and wipe front to back. Try to keep the paper centered on your rear-end hole as you wipe, and bring it out and look at it. Here, you try it."

Kyle took the folded-up paper and wiped. He brought it out and checked his work.

"It's in the center!" Kyle blurted in surprise.

"Drop the dirty paper in the toilet but drop it on the side so you can see your depth charge. Then repeat with new paper until it's clean."

After two more wipes, the paper came back white.

"I did it, Dad! I wiped my fanny. Look, Dad, it's a big bomb," Kyle remarked somewhat in awe of his handiwork.

"You're darn tootin', sharpshooter. That sub didn't stand a chance."

"Dad, why do I have to look at my poop afterward?"

"Good question. I'm glad you're asking a doctor. It's to make sure you're staying healthy. Check to be sure there's no blood or funny stuff in it. Get used to how it looks so you can tell if it's too hard or too soft. It's like a special doctor spy tool to check the inner workings of your body. If it looks weird, come get Mom or me to check it. Now get your pants up and flush."

Kyle finished up and ran out of the bathroom, yelling for Zelda. "Mom, Mom, guess what? I pooped and wiped by myself," yelled Kyle.

Randall thought, *Sure. All by yourself.*

Zelda was already coming up the stairs. Kyle ran to her and gave her a big hug.

"Way to go, big boy," she said as she hoisted him in the air. Randall joined them on the stairs.

"You would not believe the magnitude of Kyle's revolutionary movement. He is the Lord and Master of Monumental Grunt," said Randall.

"I guess I did have to go Number Two, Mom," said Kyle.

Zelda put him over her shoulder and playfully spanked his fanny, sending Kyle into squeals of laughter. "You can't fool your mom."

FRED SAID

The next day, Randall was reading the Sunday paper. Zelda served up his hot oatmeal. "Randy, did you talk to Fred about the dog yet?"

Randall looked up from the paper. "What? Fred? Dog?"

Zelda looked at him like he was wearing a dunce hat. "Don't you remember? He called yesterday just before you took Kyle upstairs for his big poop-fest."

Randall shook his head. "Perhaps the fumes wiped out that memory. What did he want?"

Zelda buttered Addie's toast. "He's got some issue with our sorry excuse for a dog. It was so noisy while I was on the phone, I couldn't quite make out what he wanted. You know how soft he talks. I told him you'd come over and talk to him."

"Why me?" Randall figured Fred wasn't going to give out a "dog-of-the-year award."

"Well, he asked for you," said Zelda with a quirky smile.

Addie screwed up her little face and asked, "Mom, what's a poop-fest?"

Randall was first to respond. "Your mom gets to answer that one, if I have to sing the Polluto apologia in B flat."

At the word "poop," Kyle had become interested in the dialogue and raised his hand.

"Ooh, ooh, I know that one. That's when people do the Winnie-the-Poop dance at parties."

"You are correct," said Zelda with a cheery wave of her hand. "It comes right after the chicken dance."

"Nicely done," chortled Randall. "I'll head over to Fred's after breakfast."

At that encouragement, Kyle started to recite his favorite singsong poem. "In days of old, when knights were bold, and toilets not invented, they laid their load upon the road and walked off quite contented."

"Zel, I hope you're happy," said Randall with mock parental derision. "You've got Kyle started down the brown brick road again."

"Kyle, stifle the potty talk, and finish your oatmeal!" Zelda pointed a deadly index finger at Kyle's nose.

"I don't like the oatmeal. It has lumps in it," whined Kyle.

"Those are raisins. You like raisins," said Zelda with a big smile.

Kyle just pouted.

"I know a song too," said Addie in a demure little voice. "Can I sing it?"

"You can't sing," said Kyle. "You squeak. Just like a little mouse."

"Mom, Kyle called me a mouse!"

Randall waved an arm in distraction. "Okay, kids, let's give Addie a chance. What would you like to sing?"

"Itsy bitsy spider," said Addie in her loudest and most authoritative voice.

"Alright. Ladies and germs," said Zelda using her circus ringmaster voice. "Before us this morning and for our musical delight is little Miss Rosebud herself. Everybody put their hands together for Addie Biedermeier!"

There was a burst of applause from the audience around the breakfast table.

Addie climbed up on her chair and gave a stellar rendition of the song with all the appropriate hand gestures. Her performance was followed by more clapping, cheers and hurrahs.

When breakfast was finished and the kitchen cleaned up, Randall turned to leave.

"Not so fast, buckaroo. Where are we headed?" asked Zelda.

"*We* are headed next door to do our Fred Bush duty as you commanded, Frau Kommandant," said Randall with a click of his heels and a Nazi salute.

"Ah, yes. Better you than me. It's a dangerous mission."

"If I am not back in two hours, send search and rescue," Randall replied with resolve. "By the way, where is the furred wonder? Did you tie him up outside this morning?"

"Yep, he's tied to the big tree in the front yard. He kept pulling out the stake that you screwed in the ground," Zelda said.

"Uh, oh. Then I think I can guess what Fred is on about. Wish me luck."

Fred Red Alert

Fred Bush had lived on Creekside Place since 1928. He knew the history of each house. He was the self-appointed "watch-dog" of the neighborhood and surveilled what everybody's dog did, especially if the doing was done on his lawn. Fred was a bit eccentric, but Randall enjoyed talking with him.

Randall knocked on Fred's back door and Fred was there in a second, as if he had been watching out the window.

"Oh, Randall, it's you." Fred opened the door, gesturing for Randall to come in. "Thanks for coming over. My sciatica is really bothering me today, and I'm having trouble with the stairs. Come on in. Flossie, bring Randall some of the lemonade you made."

Fred was tall and imposing with a tuft of gray hair surviving on his otherwise bald pate. He'd long since lost what must have been significant muscle mass and moved slowly, dragging his left foot a bit. Soon Randall and Fred were seated comfortably in the living room, sipping lemonade and eating peanuts from a small bowl. A picture window afforded a sweeping view of the large front yard.

Fred eased into the conversation. "So is the neighborhood still to your liking after four years? Still pleased with the house?"

Randall nodded his head. "No big issues yet. The house is fine. I think we're really settling in and are pretty happy here. The neighborhood is great."

"Is the job at the VA going okay?" asked Fred.

"Yeah, I'd give it an okay. Good people to work with, but the VA can get weird sometimes," said Randall.

"That's life, Randall, no matter what you do. Don't take it too seriously." Fred seemed to enjoy his role as the wise neighbor.

History of the House

"Tell me, Fred, do you know when my house was built?" asked Randall. He was hoping perhaps Fred could shed some light on the yet unsolved latched attic door mystery. By the time he and Zelda had done their final house inspection, the attic door lock had been removed. The door led to stairs that went to an unfinished attic that, by then, was completely empty of things. There was still a lingering strange energy though. Both Randall and Zelda still shivered when they went up there.

Fred popped a peanut in his mouth and took a sip of lemonade. "To the best of my reckoning your house was built in 1929. It was the second house to go up on this street. Mine was the first. The first owner was a doctor. I think a surgeon. Had a bunch of kids; five or six, if I recall." Fred reminded Randall of Marlin Perkins narrating the activities of a herd of zebras on *Wild Kingdom*. "After the kids grew up and left home, though, things kind of went bad for the Doc and his wife."

Flossie's birdy voice floated in from the kitchen. "Now, Fred, you don't need to go into that."

Fred waved a hand at Flossie. "Confound it, woman, can't a man carry on a private conversation in his own house?" Flossie just grimaced and held her tongue.

"Go into what?" asked Randall.

"Now, see what you've done," moaned Fred to Flossie. "I was going to skip over that part, but now his curiosity is up and, if I don't tell him, he'll hear it some other way and think we're prudes."

Flossie shook her head and continued peeling potatoes.

Fred began the story. "Well, it seems the Doc's wife got depressed after the kids grew up and left home. Empty nest, I think they call it. She and the Doc weren't getting on too well neither. But she liked to sit in her rocker and look out that bedroom window in the front and watch the kids playing in the park. I'd go out walkin' and see her up there, staring out the window. The kids called her the witch lady of the ghost house. They'd dare each other to stare at her without blinking."

Randall was alarmed. "Ghost house? Why ever did they call it that?"

Flossie couldn't hold back any longer. "You're not going to tell Randall that fairy tale, are you?"

Fred cleared his throat. "Well, someone in the neighborhood will eventually. Might as well be me. Least I tell it straight. But I can stop here if Randall wants me to."

Randall shook his head. "No, no. Don't worry about me. I've lived in some hinky places before. Not much surprises me anymore. Better to have it in the light than keep it in the dark!"

Fred cleared his throat again and had a coughing spell. When it settled, he continued, "One day, the missus took too many sleeping pills. The Doc came home and found her lying dead in bed in the master bedroom. For some reason, he didn't call the authorities right away. When he did call, the police jailed him on suspicion of manslaughter." Fred stared out the window as his voice trailed off.

Randall was wide-eyed. He'd expected some supernatural poppycock, but not a death in his bedroom. Zelda would go ballistic. "The doctor's wife offed herself in the house? What happened to the doctor?"

Flossie came into the living room and offered more lemonade, but stayed. "Fred, don't you go exaggerating again."

"*Hmmph*, woman. I'm telling it straight," countered Fred. "The police, they claimed that the doctor could have prevented the suicide attempt or resuscitated his wife. I'm not real clear on the legal part of it, but he went off to jail for a bit, and all his belongings were kept up in the attic in storage until he was released. He had to sell the house, and the new owners agreed to let him keep his personal stuff there. They installed a special lock on the attic door to secure his belongings. But there's nothing to worry about. The house isn't haunted or anything. Nothing else unusual has ever happened there, that I know of."

"That's reassuring," said Randall with a slight catch in his voice.

"Yup. And that's all I have to say about that." Fred took a sip of lemonade and crunched a piece of ice, punctuating the end of the story.

"I hate to change the subject, but you did ask me over here to discuss my dog," said Randall.

"*Ahem*," said Fred, clearing his throat, "Yep, your dog, Polluto. An appropriate name, I must say. Please, come over to the window with me and look out at my lawn."

Randall saw what looked like a miniature golf course laid out on Fred's lawn. There were small red and green flags scattered about.

"Now the green flags mark where Mr. Milburn's dog has left his calling card on my lawn. The red flags mark where Polluto has left his mark of distinction," said Fred.

"How do you know which is which?" asked Randall.

"Well, I see most of them in live action," said Fred, "but I don't see them all. So to be certain, I've measured the diameter of each dog's product with my calipers. Polluto's are 1.4 cm and Milburn's terrier only makes them 8 mm. That's how I tell."

Randall's jaw went slack. He was tempted to ask why, if Fred had already bent down to measure each dropping with a caliper, he didn't just scoop the poop up and dispose of it. But he thought better of that notion.

"That's pretty high precision for the subject," offered Randall.

Flossie, who had returned to the kitchen, overheard the exchange and called out. "He's a retired engineer, Randall, he measures everything. He can tell you the diameter of the macaroni he had for dinner last night."

Fred ignored the comment as if he had not heard it. He waved off Flossie, and winked at Randall. "The macaroni measured 0.5 centimeters."

Randall now had no doubts about Fred's accuracy. "So do you want the flags back after I do the Polluto poop pick-up?"

"Yes, just put them on the shelf in my garage," said Fred. "The flags, that is. And mind you, you are not to pick up any of the green-flagged doggie doo. That's Milburn's job. He'll be over later."

Randall could tell the business part of the visit was done. Flossie offered them some homemade lemon tarts. While munching these de-lectables, Fred and Flossie regaled Randall with another thirty minutes' worth of neighborhood history. Randall learned about the Bush's Victory Garden during World War II, Flossie's membership in the DAR, and the day Fred accidentally knocked down part of the wall at McDonald's with his Olds. Fred's foot had hit the gas pedal instead of the brake. There was no Happy Meal that day. He blamed it on his sciatica, which had caused him to lose the position sense in his right foot.

When Mr. Milburn rang the front doorbell to get his flag instructional, Randall took the opportunity to take his leave. He did his flag duty and made his way back home with plastic bags rich with the day's harvest. "Damn dog," he muttered. "Polluto may have just acquired a shorter life span."

Randall was still steaming about Polluto when he came back in the house, just as Zelda and Kyle were headed out the back door.

Mosey Over the Lawn

"How'd it go with Fred?" asked Zelda.

"No major problem, but I've got a couple of interesting stories to tell you," he replied.

"Well, save them for later. I've got to run. See you in an hour or so," said Zelda.

"Addie said she was really tired, so I put her down for a nap. We haven't done that in a long time, but she knows her body. Please check in on her."

"Where are you guys going?" asked Randall.

Zelda huffed. "Don't you remember? I'm taking Kyle clothes shopping. His pants are now floods. They only go down to his ankles. He needs to look good for this week. Can't believe he's so tall already. He's probably eating the dog's food between meals.".

Randall had to admit that had slipped his mind. "Oh, yeah, I did forget. Better you than me. Anyway, I still have to mow the lawn today. I wasn't planning on spending as much time dealing with Fred as I did.

But I did learn some really cool suff. Fill you in later. We also need to talk about the dog. He's becoming a real problem."

Zelda frowned and rolled her eyes. "Well, don't forget about our date on Wednesday, Randy. It's important!"

"What date?" asked Randall, obviously not on the same wavelength.

Zelda adopted her "I don't believe it" posture. "Our appointment with Chelsea Andretti, the 'kid shrink,' you doofus. Did you forget already? I'm not gonna do this kid thing all by myself!"

"Of course not," said Randall. "I thought you meant our date to spend the night together doing a mutual study of practical anatomy."

Zelda laughed out loud. "You're confusing imagination and reality again, Randy."

"Can't blame a guy for trying," offered Randall weakly. "Don't worry, the appointment with Ms. Andretti is embedded in my cortical matter." Randall pointed to his kidney area.

"It better be, or I'll embed something where the sun don't shine." Zelda spun on her heel and headed out the door with Kyle.

Kyle had wisely decided to keep quiet during the exchange. He wasn't sure he understood completely what was said anyway.

Randall gave a sigh of relief and went upstairs to check on Addie before he went out to mow the lawn. He found her sleeping peacefully and hugging her threadbare "grab," the remnant of the blanket she'd had since babyhood. The sight gave him a blast of déjà vu about the lawn-mower incident in Colorado Springs.

The incident kept playing in his head while he mowed. He had to remind himself that Addie wasn't a baby anymore. Randall finished mowing and shut down the mower. He took off his ear protectors and, without thinking about it, turned up his hearing to listen for sounds of distress. All he heard was the wind and the burble of Hidden Creek. Unable to shake an odd feeling of dread, he headed inside to check on Addie. He found Addie at the kitchen table, spooning ice cream out of the container.

Addie looked up from her ice cream. "Hi, Daddy, have some ice cream with me. It'll cool you down from your hot work."

Randall felt a sudden rush of delight. His "all is well" chime went off. "*Wheeoie!* Hot work, indeed. Let's eat it quick before Mom and Kyle get home, or we'll have to share."

CHAPTER 22

DOG GONE

"If there are no dogs in Heaven, then when I die, I want to go where they went."

— Will Rogers

Hair Today

Although the Colorado Springs lawnmower incident wasn't a taboo topic in the Biedermeier household, Randall and Zelda didn't discuss it much in the four years since it happened. They had accepted that the episode was inexplicable and decided not to dwell on it. There hadn't been any further Swindell-type incidents at the hospital for several weeks and the intensity of that strangeness began to fade a bit in Randall's consciousness. It wasn't as real for Zelda. She had not witnessed Swindell's mystical comeback.

Yet Randall had to admit that, for whatever reason, he felt a nagging apprehension like something similar was looming on the event horizon. His concern just didn't seem reasonable since things at home seemed to be improving. *No sense worrying about stuff you can't control,* Randall told himself. *We have more "here and now" issues to deal with.*

He mentally reviewed everyone's status, trying to ground himself in the present.

Kyle would see the child counselor soon. That was a big step. Zelda had fully equipped her art studio and was doing a lot of art projects. With Randall's encouragement, she had applied to the Milwaukee

Institute of Art and Design in Graphic Arts. She'd finally overcome the negative mindset about art that her father, Red, had drilled into her. His usual mantra went something like: "There are thousands of good artists out there at least as good as you. But most of them won't make a decent living painting pretty pictures to hang on the wall."

Randall was hoping she could rewrite her inner story to know that art was valuable and needed in this world. Her artistic talent was a gift and needed to be expressed.

Then there was the dog—the big, dumb, pooping machine with a penchant for escaping from the house or yard and running away. After Randall told Zelda about his meeting with Fred Bush, they had decided Polluto had to go. The "for and against" balance sheet was pretty lopsided on the "against" side. The time had come to act. After discussing it with Zelda, they gathered the kids for the difficult discussion. Kyle and Addie moaned and groaned when they were told that Polluto was *canis non grata.*

Randall reviewed the arguments. "Polluto will be happier somewhere where he can run to his heart's content, like on a farm or at least somewhere outside the city. You know how hard it is to keep him in the house. Every time we try to leave, he breaks out of the house and runs around the neighborhood playing 'catch me if you can.'"

Kyle piled on. "Yeah, he runs off into the park and lets you get about two feet from him, then he runs off again."

Randall agreed. "Most annoying. The other day it took me half an hour to round him up before we could all go out to dinner. He doesn't listen to commands, and he never obeys."

Addie teared up, as if finally accepting the idea. "Yeah, and he chewed up my unicorn, Sparkle. That was not nice."

Randall could have added that he had nearly broken his hand when he whacked Polluto on the head to get his attention. The stupid dog was not phased, but Randall's hand had been. And there was his ruined briefcase handle.

Zelda piped up. "And he always does his duty on Mr. Bush's lawn. Did you guys see the little flags he uses to mark to spots for collection?"

Addie looked slightly green. "And remember how Polluto pooped in my room too? I didn't see it until I stepped in it. It was so gross!!"

By the time the discussion ended, they all wondered why they'd kept him this long. Addie had the answer. "Because we all love him. But he's so stupid."

Randall nodded. "And it's because we love him that we need to make sure he goes to a good home. He can't help being one teacup short of a set."

Kyle got a strange look on his face. "Mom, Dad, you wouldn't farm us out if we acted stupid all the time, would you?"

Randall and Zelda just looked at each other for a long moment. Randall scratched his head and looked puzzled. Then Zelda smiled.

Kyle repeated. "Would you?!"

Randall broke the silence. "Of course not. Dog rules don't apply to kids."

Zelda added her two cents. "But there are exceptions. I don't recall what they are. I'd have to look them up in Doctor Spock's book. Nothing that comes to mind . . . oh, except maybe toilet roll flushing and dumping concrete mix in neighbors' cars."

Kyle went slightly pale but tried a segue out of harm's way. "If Polluto goes, can we get another cat to replace Baldspot?"

Addie responded with a jolt of excitement. "Yeah! If a new cat replaces Baldspot, we could get a second cat to replace Polluto!"

Kyle kicked into high gear as well. "Great idea. One cat could be mine, and one could be yours!"

Zelda rose from her chair and held up both hands in a defensive gesture. "Slow down, you're going too fast. I didn't say getting rid of the dog equals upgrading to two cats. Neither one of you took care of either Baldspot or Polluto. Dad and I are not going to take care of a new cat by ourselves, let alone two!"

Randall crossed his arms over his chest and agreed. "Here, here. Enough said."

Addie came quickly with her defense. "But Kyle and I will take care of the cats, won't we, Kyle?"

Kyle nodded vigorously. "Sis is right. We'll take good care of them."

Randall shook his head vigorously. "There will be no 'them.' We can maybe stick with one cat and see how the 'taking care of' part goes. *Er*, that is, if your mother agrees."

Zelda looked at the ceiling and squinted. No answer up there. She was feeling slightly "kidipulated," but could see no immediate harm in the compromise. "Well, I suppose we could give that a try. To be fair, we could all share in kitty care, but understand this: if you two show any sign of shirking your duty, the cat goes to the pound. Got it?"

Kyle frowned. "Does that mean we have to clean the litter box too? And scoop up urped hairballs?"

Randall slapped the table top for emphasis. "Indeedy do. But we'll rotate the doodie duty. Isn't that right, *Mamacita*?"

"*Sí, amigo*," said Zelda. "And we'll all work together to take care of Felix or whatever we name it, won't we? Right kids?"

Kyle and Addie responded in somber unison. "Yes, Mom."

"Who gets to name the cat?" asked Addie.

Randall shrugged. "Kind of depends on the cat. We can discuss that after we pick the right furball."

"*Aww*, Dad! Not the democracy thing again," whined Kyle.

Randall slapped the table with the palm of his hand. "One more complaint and we go back to the 'parentocracy' rule."

Addie grimaced. "I don't know that big word, but I bet it means you pick the name."

"Bingo!" said Randall. "Hey, that's not a bad cat name."

Polluto Out

With the kids and parents singing from the same hymnal, the wheels were set in motion for the dog/cat transition. They placed a newspaper ad offering the big golden Lab for free to a good home, preferably in the country where he could run around ad lib. The same day the ad appeared, a farm-dwelling couple with five kids under ten years old called and said they would like Polluto. The next day, the entire family arrived at the Biedermeier's house in a beat-up Chevy Impala to pick up Polluto. It was a case of love at first sight. They loved the dog, and the dog loved them. Polluto piled on top of the five kids in the back seat of the car. As the car backed down the driveway, the back seat became a cartoon swirl of bodies. It reminded Randall of a panel from a Beetle Bailey cartoon where Sarge and Beetle fight each other in a swirl of motion. Randall and Zelda congratulated themselves on a job well done as they watched the dusty Chevy pull out of the driveway, fan belt screeching and kids laughing.

Cat In

The next day, the Biedermeiers went to a pet store. They bought cat food, cat bowls, a little brown cat bed, and a cat carrier. Then they motored to the pound on Wisconsin Avenue and were overwhelmed by the choices. They tried on cat after cat, imagining how it would fit in their life and house. After a laborious filtering process, the choice came down to a two-year-old male tabby, and a one-year-old black female with a white star on her forehead. After much debate, the final vote was for the black female with the white star.

After completing the paperwork, the black cat, mewling fitfully, was brought out in the carrier they'd bought. After they put the carrier in the car, Randall made the executive decision to let the cat out, so it could roam around the inside of their VW Microbus. There was nothing the cat could do to the inside of the van that hadn't already been done. As soon as the cat was let free from the carrier, she was quiet and began her exploratory sniffing about.

As they were driving home, Addie asked if they could name the cat Blackie. Zelda recoiled at the idea of her little girl calling that name out in the neighborhood.

Kyle stuck his tongue out at Addie. "That's a stupid name. She should have something cooler, like a superhero. Like Deathray. Or Clawful!"

Randall knew this argument needed a diversionary action. "I'd like to name the cat Schrödinger," he said emphatically.

Addie was deeply offended. "*Daadd!* That's a stupid name!"

Randall defended his choice. "It is not. It has great historical significance. It means that the cat can be both here and not here at the same time. Perfect for cat behavior."

"That's surely a humdinger of a name, Randy," said Zelda. "But you're not serious, are you?"

"I am very serious. If you're all good the rest of the day, and stop pestering me about it, I'll tell you the story of Schrödinger's cat as a bedtime story. I guarantee you'll love the name after you hear the story," said Randall. "If you still don't like it, you guys can pick a name."

On the ride home from the pound, the cat jumped onto Kyle's lap where she curled up and started to purr. Kyle, somewhat befuddled, began stroking the cat's head, and soon the cat was fast asleep, emitting little snorting kitty snores.

"Why doesn't the cat like me?" asked Addie in a thin little voice. "I want her in my lap."

"Sweetie, I'm sure the cat likes you too, and she'll sleep with you when we get home," soothed Zelda.

"She'd better," said Addie.

After they'd driven for a few more minutes, Randall said quietly to Zelda that he had read how some cats have an instinct for seeking out humans who need comforting. If a nursing home adopts a cat to be its "house cat," the cat will sleep with the patient who is the most ill.

"Randy, don't be so morbid," snarled Zelda.

"Mommy, what's morbid?" asked Addie.

"Your father."

When the family got home, Kyle carried the cat, sans carrier, into the house and put her down on the floor. She wandered around familiarizing herself with the new surroundings. She took in smells in every nook and cranny of the house and rubbed up against any protruding edge or corner, marking the territory with her scent. She, no doubt, smelled Baldspot's scent and endeavored to replace it with hers.

While the cat claimed her property, Zelda had the kids set up the cat's water dish and food bowl. The little furball was underfoot as soon as the can opener whirred to open a new can of Purina Tuna Feast.

Bad Dog News

With the cat settled in, Randall checked the answering machine. The red light blinked like impending doom. He pushed the button.

He heard a sniffling sound as the recorded message began. "Hello. This is Mrs. Watkins. We picked up your dog Polluto the other day. I'm real sorry to have to tell you this, but Polluto was out in our field yesterday, chasing a squirrel. He ran across the road in front of a big semi and, well, he was hit hard. He didn't make it. We're all pretty broke up about it. Give me a call if you have any questions."

All four of the Biedermeiers listened to the message. There was no way to gloss over the tragic outcome of the dog exchange.

"Dad, does that mean Polluto is dead?" screeched Addie.

"Ah, yeah, I'm afraid so," stuttered Randall.

Kyle howled. "We killed Polluto by giving him away! It's all our fault. No, Dad, it's your fault 'cause you said he had to go."

"Now, kids, that's not fair," admonished Zelda. "We all made the decision. Don't blame Dad or yourselves. Sometimes bad things just happen. It was an accident. Accidents happen and usually they're nobody's fault."

Randall hung his head. "But it is really sad that Polluto was killed. You know I didn't like the darn dog that much, but I did love him. I sort of feel like crying right now. Let's gather around the table and pay our respects to Polluto."

Zelda's eyes started flooding with tears. "Dad's right. Addie, Kyle, take my hand, and let's sit down."

Both kids watered up and started to whimper when they looked at Zelda's face. Randall wiped at his cheeks.

When everybody was settled around the table, Zelda took over as mistress of ceremony. "Okay, guys, we're going to go around the table, starting with me and say something to Polluto as a last goodbye. If he's still on his way to doggie heaven, he'll be able to hear you."

Addie broke in. "Is that really true?"

Randall confirmed the veracity of Zelda's basic principle of doggie afterlife. "Mom is correct. You can look it up in the Book of Canine, Verses 1–3."

Zelda began. "Polluto, you were a big dumb dog, but you were lovable, and you always made me laugh when I wasn't mad at you. You always wanted to run, and when you died you were doing what you loved. I'll bet you are running in doggie heaven right now. Keep on running, big dumb dog."

Zelda squeezed Addie's little hand to signal it was her turn. "I don't know what to say, Mommy," Addie whispered.

"Rosebud," said Zelda, "did you know that after dogs, cats, and people die they hang around for several days to see everyone who loved them? If you talk to them, they can hear you and they'll give you a sign like a lick on the hand, or a puff of breath in the face. Just talk to Polluto like he's right here at the table, bumping into your leg, looking for food on the floor."

"Daddy, is that true?" asked Addie.

"You bet your taco," said Randall. "I've seen it happen. Go ahead and tell Polluto what you're thinking."

Addie took a breath and began. "Okay. Polluto, we had a dog once before. My daddy told me about him, but I was too little to remember him. Now I'm older, and I'll remember you forever and forever. I wish I could see you once more, but I guess that would be pretty scary to see. That truck probably hurted you real bad, and I don't want to see that. So I am blowing you a kiss right now. Please blow one back. Goodbye, good dog."

She held her hand to her mouth, then blew the kiss toward the sky. "Okay, Kyle, you go now."

"That was nice, Addie," said Randall. "Kyle, are you ready, or do you want me to go?"

Kyle's head drooped. "I'm too sad to say anything, Dad. I'll talk to him when I go to bed and I'm alone."

"Good plan, partner," said Randall. "Then I'll say my piece. Polluto, in your short life, you gave me lots of memories that I'll talk about many years from now. Maybe I'll even write them in a book. You were kind of good looking, strong and you were fun to pet when you'd hold still. You were fun to play with and could catch Frisbees with the elite. I won't forget nearly breaking my hand on your head or picking up after you. You were a great runner. I hope you catch that squirrel."

With that said, Randall lurched his head forward and felt the back of his head with his right hand. He brought his hand forward and showed it covered with saliva.

"Daddy, what happened? Are you okay?" asked a startled Addie.

"Well, I'll be dipped," said Randall. "Damn dog licked the back of my head. Will you look at all the drool on my hand?"

"*Ooh*, I just felt hot breath on my face," said Zelda, starting suddenly.

"Me too," yelled Kyle.

"Guys, I'm scared again," blurted Addie.

"Don't be afraid, it's just Polluto saying goodbye back," said Kyle.

The family sat around the table in somber silence for a few moments. Then Randall decided it was time to end the navel exploration.

Randall decided on a ploy to change the subject. "Who wants to go out for hamburgers at Big Boy restaurant while the cat explores the house?"

"Me!" said Kyle, jumping up from his chair with both hands raised.

"Me too!" said Addie, excitedly. "After dinner, can you tell us the story of the humdinger cat?"

"*Um*, that's Schrödinger's cat," said Randall. "Well, I've decided that, because you've done such a good job picking out the new cat, and because of Polluto's bad ending, you get to pick the new cat's name." Randall had decided that the story of a cat in a box with a 50 percent chance of being dead or alive was not the most appropriate story to tell at this particular juncture. He said a silent prayer to Baldspot, wherever she was.

"The force is with us," intoned Kyle.

"Yes. I vote for Blackie," said Addie.

Kyle rolled his eyes. "I have an idea for this superhero cat. We are going to call her my name—I choose Wondercat!" boasted Kyle, his arms up like he was flying.

Zelda smiled. "That's a great name, Kyle! That fits her powers and it's fun to say."

Addie frowned, then gave in. "Okay, fine. It is a good name."

Kyle smiled. "Heck, yes, it is! Besides, she likes me more."

Addie furrowed her brow. "No she doesn't. We can call her Wondercat, if you can make her a red cape. Well, as long as I get to name the next one!"

"Okay, kids," Randall rushed in to head off another battle. "Let's go eat."

The Biedermeier family happily focused their attention on Wondercat after returning from Big Boy restaurant, full of burgers and fries. They followed the cat around as she continued checking out the old cat and dog smells, wandering into every crook and nanny. That night, the little black kitty snuggled into Kyle's bed, kneading bread dough and purring loudly. Kyle fell asleep to whiffling cat snores. Kyle's smile lasted all night.

CHAPTER 23

STEELY MEL

"If someone says that he can think or talk about quantum physics without becoming dizzy, that shows only that he has not understood anything whatever about it."

— *Worlds Hidden in Plain Sight,* Murray Gell-Mann

MORNING WAS BROKEN

Monday morning came without a warning. Melinda was at the back door of the department when Randall staggered in hauling his gear. Randall was grateful for her presence. She was serving as a blocking guard between Randall and several patients who'd been lying in wait to pepper him with questions as soon as he walked through the door. He didn't yet have the energy to deal with them.

"Are you ready for Part II of Linacs 101? We still on for 10:00?" asked Melinda brightly before Randall could even say hello.

"Dang, you remembered," he responded dully.

"How could I forget? Pardon me, but you look awful. Are you sick?" asked Melinda.

"Don't worry, I feel worse than I look," moaned Randall. "Major headache. No sleep last night. Addie had an asthma attack. Probably brought on by our former dog dying. Man, I hope she's not allergic to our new cat! I had to give her an adrenaline shot at 4:00 a.m. and sit up with her until she stopped wheezing."

"Oh, no, that's awful; is she okay?" Melinda's concern wrinkled her face into pretty little crinkles.

"She is now, but I'm not. She gets so anxious when she's short of breath that I have to sit with her and tell stories or read books until she calms down. The adrenaline cranks the anxiety up several notches, and then it's just tincture of time."

"Tincture of time?"

"That means you just have to wait it out," Randall clarified.

Melinda looked at Randall wryly. "What was your dog formerly? A cat?"

It was non sequitur city for Randall. "What?"

"You said your former dog died. I'm just making a joke to lighten the mood. Badly, it seems."

Randall finally computed the reference. "We gave away our golden Lab, Polluto, to a family in the country because he was always running in the city streets, and we feared he'd soon be roadkill. Ironically, two days after adoption, he off and runs onto a busy highway in the country and gets turned into a doggie pancake by an eighteen-wheeler. The kids were devastated by the news. Me, not so much. Not a dog lover. But then again, the kids also went into deep lamentations when the iguana they habitually neglected died last year."

Melinda laughed heartily. "Such high drama. Some days I'm glad I'm single."

Randall grunted under his load. "Someday you may also meet 'the guy' and have a family of your own. Then you won't be laughing. I've got to unload this gear in my office. Come on along."

"Let me carry those physics books," offered Melinda.

Randall looked relieved by the offer. "Great. Here they are. My cramp has a cramp. If we get the quantum physics right, maybe someday the book will carry itself!"

The two of them clamored into Randall's office where he dumped his stuff on the floor and collapsed in his office chair.

"We can put the Linac talk off if you're too tired," suggested Melinda.

Randall waved an arm. "I'll be okay in a few minutes. Just need a fresh cuppa Joe to rev me up. The department coffee should do the trick. It melts plastic spoons."

Melinda came to the rescue again. "I'll get it for you. I'll be right back. Do you want it in your doctor's urine specimen cup?"

"Yeah, that's the ticket. And I take it with the special white powder."

While Melinda left with his cup to get coffee, Randall organized his gear and put on his white coat. A stray lyric of music he'd listened to in the car had gone viral in his aural nerve center, and he started to sing out loud about life being a minestrone.

Melinda overheard the lyrics as she strolled in with his coffee, and sang the response about death being cold lasagna.

"What? You know the song?" blurted Randall.

"Sure. It's by the English band 10CC. People say they are the British version of Steely Dan," said Melinda matter-of-factly.

"I never quite thought of it that way. But you could be right. They do have a lot in common. Not quite like Queen, but heavily multi-tracked. And no Freddie Mercury-type lead singer," expanded Randall between sips of coffee.

"But they have great voices and wonderful harmonies," observed Melinda.

"Indeed," said Randall with gusto. "That's what I love too. *Umm.* I do believe this coffee is opening some neural pathways. Well, I've got a consult to see, so I better get cracking so I can be ready for us at 10:00."

Elisa

Randall finished explaining the treatment simulation process, then escorted the new patient out of the exam room to Doris's office to set up the appointment.

Doris looked up at Randall. "Good. You've finally emerged. There's a young lady named . . ." She looked down at a piece of paper. "Elizabeth Angeles, I think. Anyway, she's waitin' to see you. She's sittin' out in a hallway chair. She seems quite anxious and said she doesn't have much time."

Doris had given Randall a sly wink as she said, "young lady" and pointed to the hallway. "She didn't state her business, but she said you'd be expectin' her."

Doris looked mighty curious, but Randall gave no hint of surprise. "Ah, yes. I saw her sitting out there. I thought she was a family member of one of our patients. If she doesn't have much time, I wonder if she's terminal? She's so young . . . anyway, don't bother getting up. You go ahead and give Mr. Augustine, here, a sim appointment. I'll show her to my office."

Doris had already risen from her chair and looked disappointed not to be involved. "She's a cute one, she is."

Randall raised an eyebrow. "Oh, I hadn't noticed."

Randall went out into the hall and spotted the "young lady" sitting with her legs crossed, revealing a moderate expanse of nicely sculpted lower thigh. She was so small in stature, that Randall had almost mistaken her earlier for a young teen.

As Randall approached, she stood up, and Randall could now account for that initial mistaken impression. She stood little more than five feet tall but, though short, could not be mistaken for a prepubescent teen. She had all the mature female bits in all the right places. Her face was cherubic and framed nicely by shiny black hair worn in a straight pageboy cut. Pouty red lips were overshadowed by deep, glistening eyes that seemed to change color with each slight movement.

Randall reached out a hand in greeting. "You must be Elizabeth Angeles. I've been expecting you to stop by. I'm Randall Biedermeier. Nice to meet you."

"And you, Doctor," said Ms. Angeles. "Mr. Samuels has told me quite a bit about you. It's an honor, sir." When she looked up, her eyes seemed aglow.

"Oh, fiddlesticks," replied Randall. "I'm sure Winston told you enough about me to know 'sir' is an inappropriate appellation in my regard. It's just Dr. B around here."

She batted her eyelashes. "Well, yes, he did. But I thought it would be polite to at least start with 'sir.' And my name is actually Elisabet—it's an old family name. My friends call me Elisa. My enemies call me often to complain."

Randall laughed. "Well, then we already have something in common." He waved a hand toward his office. "Let us retreat to my retreat and chat a bit. I'll introduce you to my secretary and right-hand lady, Doris, whose inquisitiveness about you has already piqued her Southern curiosity to the breaking point. I rather enjoy tickling her fancy. Perhaps you could just ad lib a bit with me as we pass through her gate."

Elisa seemed to get the drift. She smiled and nodded. The two ambled into Doris's office just as Mr. Augustine was leaving.

Randall began to laugh unexpectedly as soon as they got to Doris's doorway. "Now that's a good one. Then what did you say?"

Elisa chortled a bit and stopped walking. She tugged on Randall's sleeve. "Then I said, that's no excuse for flying pants."

They both laughed heartily. Doris looked dumbstruck. Randall turned to Doris and introduced Elisa. "Doris, I'd like you to meet Elizabet Angeles. This is Doris Hicks, mother hen of this ship, the USS *Radiation.*"

Doris momentarily overcame her confusion and the two shook hands. "A pleasure, Ms. Angeles." Doris emphasized the 'h' sound of Spanish pronunciation of the 'g,' and managed a wan smile.

Elisa smiled back. "Likewise, Doris. Just call me Elisa. And before anyone asks, I am not one of the Lost Angels." She chuckled to herself. "Dr. B tells me you run the place."

Doris stuttered a bit. "Well, *er*, if he says so. What brings you to our humble adobe?"

Elisa surveyed Doris for a long moment. "Well, it's because Dr. B is going to be my . . . what's the correct term for it again? Oh, I remember now. He's going to be my lead."

Randall nodded. "That's the correct VA term. That's why the nameplate on my door reads, 'Randall Biedermeier, Lead Physician.' When I first got here, I thought it meant lead, like in the heavy metal, 'cause everybody around here was always yelling at me to get the lead out. Doris and I came here from the South where everything is slower. But then later they told me the meaning was like in: to lead the way. Then I started moving faster."

Doris interrupted. "No, you didn't. I swear, you are still as pokey as a possum!"

Now Doris and Elisa were both laughing while Randall kept his best story-telling poker face. "Well, you've got me there. Sorry, Doris, we were pulling your leg a bit before. I didn't want Elisa to get the idea we were a bunch of stuffed shirts down here."

Doris was swift with her repartee. "No risk there."

Randall continued undaunted. "Seriously, folks. Elisa was hired to fill a new position, called 'patient advocate,' created by good ol' Winnie Samuels. This little lady is going to make sure that all our cancer patients get to where they're supposed to be without any hitches. That part of her job will be mostly appointment coordination, but she'll also advocate for all of our patients' previously unmet needs."

Doris seemed impressed. "Wow, do we ever need a boatload of that." Doris walked over to Randall and poked a finger into his chest. "And I hope that's the last time you ever refer to this young lady as 'little.' We're the same size! And like me, though we be small, we be mighty!"

Doris backed Randall up to the wall, but gave her fake anger away by smiling broadly.

Elisa joined Doris with another chest finger poke. "Yeah, what she said. Don't forget Napoleon. I can give that Frenchie a run for his money."

Randall giggled. "I bet you can, especially with Doris as an ally. Now quit with the poking; that tickles."

With the introductions over, Randall led Elisa into his office and closed the door. He opened it again twenty seconds later to find Doris standing there. "And no eavesdropping." He closed it again.

Elisa had to laugh again. "You're one tough customer, Dr. B. I may have to wear body armor."

Randall looked aghast. "Heavens no. Don't do that. I have so little light in my life. But on to business. Let's discuss your background a bit, and then I'll review your duties. A lot of it will just be a repeat of what Mr. Samuels has told you already, but I need to go over the concept of developing a multidisciplinary weekly tumor conference. You and I are going to raise that child and nurture its development."

Elisa began to look more serious. "Where should I start my story?"

Randall raised both hands. "From wherever you think. Don't be surprised if I ask questions along the way. The most important thing today is just to get acquainted. The tumor conference details can always come later."

The exchange was interrupted by a sharp knock on the office door after which Doris poked her head in. "Dr. B? I hope you haven't forgotten Melinda. It's 10:10 and she's been waiting since 10:00."

Randall turned in his chair and waved a hand. "Of course, I haven't forgotten. Elisa and I were just finishing up."

Doris didn't budge. "Of course, you didn't forget. Perhaps just some minor time slippage?"

Randall rose from his chair. "Excuse me, Elisa. Duty calls. Go with Doris, and she'll set up some time later today to go over, in more detail, what we discussed. That sound okay?"

Elisa rose quickly from her chair as Doris hurried her out of the office after dumping some patient charts on Randall's desk. "No problem, Dr. B. I'll distill my life story down to size and do some research on joint tumor conferences to prepare. It was great to meet you. You are not at all what I expected."

Doris got in a final dig. "No one expects the Spanish Inquisition." Then Doris shooed Elisa out of the office and reminded Randall that it was already 10:15. "Melinda is waiting for you impatiently out in the hall."

Randall had already forgotten. "I remember," he blurted. "I'm going now."

Randall hustled out to the hall with his empty coffee cup and apologized to Melinda for being behind schedule. "Sorry about that. Had an unexpected visitor."

Melinda huffed a bit. "Yeah, I noticed. She looks about fifteen years old. Who is the little waif?"

Randall stretched and sighed. "Ah! She is the new patient care coordinator or 'patient advocate' in VA speak. She's just starting. I'm sort of her supervisor."

Melinda's face clouded over. "Good luck to her with that. What's her name?"

"Elisa Angeles," replied Randall.

"Hope she's got some moxie," said Melinda. "She looks like a featherweight."

"All kinds of moxie," observed Randall. "I don't think the VA knows what kind of battle they're in for. Could be a case of Elisa and Goliath. She fights way higher than her weight class."

Melinda rolled her eyes. "Want a java refill before we start?

Randall nodded. "We 'might swell' do that. Then shall we hie to the fore?"

"We shall," confirmed Melinda.

Before going into the Ortho Room, Randall checked in with Doris, and she reminded him that he needed to call Mr. Samuels.

"Why do I need to call him?" asked a confused Randall.

Doris put on her administrative assistant hat. "You need to let him know that Al Kornberg is taking a medical retirement after his bypass surgery, and that Bob Storch is leaving. I think he can talk to HR about both positions and grease the skids. I'll bet he can get us a replacement RTT for Al without losing the new RTT position he promised. Plus, he can probably set up an HR interview for the physicist friend of Bob's who's looking for a job."

"Did I tell you to remind me of all that?" asked Randall.

"Of course, you did," said Doris with a big smile. "You're the boss with all the big ideas, the rooster of the roost."

"Of course, I am," agreed Randall. "Why don't you call him and have him meet me down here in my office after I finish with Melinda?"

"Your wish is my command," said Doris demurely. "Now get off to your lecture or whatever it is you do in there."

Melinda looked back and forth from Randall to Doris during the exchange, like she was watching a tennis match at the US Open.

Randall looked insulted to the bone. "Doris! Well, I never!" said

Randall dramatically. He walked across the hall, followed by a bemused Melinda, and pushed the metal plate door opener with his elbow.

Doris called after them. "Be good, you two. Don't do anything I wouldn't do."

Randall paused at the doorway and looked back at Doris. She was smirking and waving her forefinger. "You're such a strict taskmaster," Randall called back as the heavy door swung shut.

Melinda took a seat at the makeshift table and laid out her physics books and notepad. Randall went to the board and prepared to wield his chalk.

The Making of X-rays

Randall cleared his throat and collected his thoughts. "We left off on our X-ray quest in 1895, when our friend Wilhelm von Roentgen had started testing the Crookes tube. He was working on a variant tube designed by the physicist Philipp von Lenard. In Lenard's tube the glass at the anode end had been replaced by a thin piece of aluminum to permit the cathode rays to exit the tube and interact with a dense metal instead of glass. He placed a piece of cardboard over the anode end to protect the aluminum and to prevent any light from exiting the anode."

Melinda was already lost at the bakery. "I should know this but remind me about cathode and anode again."

Randall sketched the tube on the chalkboard. "Anode is the positively charged end and cathode is negatively charged. The electrons go from − to +. Got it?"

Melinda drew on her notepad. "Got it."

Randall continued. "Roentgen planned on putting another piece of cardboard in place next. He had painted it with a fluorescent mixture containing barium platinocyanide. No need to remember that name except to understand that exposure to light would make the barium compound glow. Roentgen reasoned that if some *invisible* form of radiation was being emitted after the negatively charged electrons hit the positively charged aluminum target atoms, it might make the fluorescent material glow without being exposed to visible light."

"Sounds like something you'd do," remarked Melinda.

Randall shook his head. "Roentgen was a genius. Way ahead of his time. I'm sure I'm not that smart, but I can dream."

Melinda nodded her head. She understood it and was fascinated. "This is getting good. What did he do next?"

Tell Me Again

Randall held up a hand. "From here on, we're headed into deeper waters. Before I dive into more details, I am going to follow the advice I got from a speakers' coach. Before my first oral presentation of a scientific paper, I was at a loss about how to present gobs of data and stay within the ten-minute limit. Plus, I had to make the main points understandable and memorable. So a speaker's coach, who knew nothing about my subject matter, was hired to critique my presentation. She listened to my talk and, afterward, she said that it was obvious I knew what I was talking about, but that it wasn't clear enough for the nonexpert."

"That would be me, Dr. B!" Melinda seemed a bit more relaxed.

Randall wrote a one, two, three list on the board. "It was me too! The coach told me to redo the talk according to the following outline: 1. Tell them what you're going to tell them, 2. Tell them what you want to tell them, and 3. Tell them what you just told them."

Melinda looked like she didn't approve of the advice. "Good grief, how does that leave enough time to tell them what you need to?"

Randall raised a forefinger. "Yes, but the key to the approach is that, in the end, you've told them your conclusions three times, and that's what they will remember. They can read the full paper for the details."

Melinda prepared to write in her notebook. "Oh. I get it. I have the feeling that you're going to tell me what you're going to tell me, right now. Shoot."

Randall nodded affirmatively. "In brutal summary, we are going to learn how bombarding atoms of gasses and solids with high-speed electrons, which are negatively charged subatomic particles, can produce emissions of scattered electrons and various forms of radiation energy, including X-rays. The basic principle of how the X-rays are generated is mostly the same today as it was back in 1895. But over the past century, we have figured out numerous tweaks to make much higher energy X-ray beams."

"Like the ones we need for cancer treatment," said Melinda.

"Oh, you're good," said Randall. "Now just before we go deeper into the Crookes tube and get to the telling part about making X-rays, we just have to touch on a few more basic concepts."

For the next half hour, Randall explained atomic and subatomic structure, the electromagnetic spectrum, and the development of high energy treatment units suitable for cancer treatment. Melinda took it all in and wrote copious notes.

Having completed the background of the development of high energy X-ray cancer treatment devices, Randall finished off with the function of linear accelerators like Big MEL. "That brings us to Linacs. Look at the figure on page 56 of your book. Think of Linacs as a better way to kick electrons in the pants to get the high energy we need for treatment. The Linac uses a metal accelerator tube, usually made of copper, with a vacuum inside it. At the cathode end, there's a hot filament to boil off electrons to be accelerated to the tungsten anode target."

Melinda studied the diagram for a long moment. "Okay, I see that. But it looks like there's a bunch of other stuff involved."

"Yes," said Randall. "Two things have been added to the mix. First, there is a radiofrequency, or RF generator, that sends an RF wave down the tube; and second, there's a microwave generator called a magnetron that shoots microwaves down the tube. These, combined with a pulsing of negative charges, push the electron down the tube like a surfer on a surfboard at ever increasing speed."

"And the electron shrieks 'Hang Ten' as it rides the wave," said Melinda with a hand wave. "Yippee ki yay!"

"Exactly," exclaimed Randall. "Now for the twist. We need the X-rays to emerge at a right angle from the tube so they can be directed downward through the filtering and collimating system at the patient lying on the table. So the electron beam passes through a series of magnets that bend them down before hitting the target. Then voila, we have 6 MeV X-rays to use as we see fit."

"So, like, the basic process was already there for making X-rays for seventy-five years," said Melinda. "But it took developing the Magnetron and RF stuff and the pulsating electric field to get more horsepower."

"Well, simply put, that's it," agreed Randall. "That's all for today. Next session we'll go into more detail about using the Linac and maintaining it. But for now, you seem to have all the concepts. Good job."

"This is funner than I imagined, and less complicated than I thought," she said, fluttering her lashes. "How can I ever thank you, Dr. B?"

Randall remained stoic. "Respect the machine, 'cause if you don't, it can bite your posterior attachments. Besides that, be a good tech, and don't kill anybody."

Meeting with Mr. Samuels

When Randall and Melinda walked out of the Ortho Room, Mr. Samuels was waiting in Randall's office. Randall informed Samuels of the situation with Bob Storch and Al Kornberg. He also noted that he'd met Elisa Angeles, his initial impression had been favorable, and he'd be meeting with her later to talk in more detail.

Samuels nodded. "Good, good. Glad to hear you liked the young lady. I think she will do well."

Randall leaned forward in his chair. "So what can we do about Storch and Kornberg?"

"I hear you, Dr. B," intoned Samuels. "Like I say to you before, I need the project to succeed. To succeed you need all hands on deck and some extras too. I will get right on this, and we'll get you shipshape. But please, do not say anything 'bout it 'til I have a firm say-so from those idiots in HR."

Randall made a zipping motion across his lips and thanked the man profusely. "I am beginning to see some sunshine on my little patch of beach," enthused Randall. "I feel like we should toast with one of those drinks with the umbrella in it."

"I am totaling my tees, but have one for me, when you get home," laughed Samuels. "Now I must take my leave. There are more fish to fry."

As Randall ushered Samuels out of his office, Doris got Randall's attention.

"Excuse me, Dr. B, but you also asked me to remind you about doing something to wish Bob a successful venture in Costa Rica, and welcoming Dan Graham into the fold. I know you've introduced Dan around since he started this week, but we usually do more than that with new employees."

Randall looked a bit flustered. "We do?"

Doris gave him the evil eye.

Randall took a step back and cleared his throat. "Harumph! Of course we do! I was just kidding."

Doris nodded with a devilish smile.

"Did I have any good ideas?" asked Randall.

"Well, you might have mentioned cake and coffee in the afternoon and a department outing," said Doris.

"Right. I think I remember that. Donuts and coffee after chart rounds this week. The outing was where again?" asked Randall.

"You thought we could all go to a Bucks game, because Bob is a big fan and especially loves Kareem Abdul Jabbar. And Dan said he loves basketball, too, but he's from the Chicago area and rather favors the Bulls."

"Anathema!" scoffed Randall. "We'll have to cure him of that. I don't recall him mentioning that to me."

Doris put her hands on her hips. "Well, Dan dropped by last week, but you were busy in the Ortho room with Melinda and had ordered me not to disturb you two unless there was a fire. Remember?"

"Sure." Randall paused. "But you should have interrupted me anyhow. I could have given him the department nickel tour."

"Sorry, Boss. Just followin' orders." Doris straightened her stance. "I did the tour for you and introduced Dan all around. I gave him the five-dollar tour. It's much longer, and includes a bunch more butterin' up. Don't worry. He hadn't planned to do anythin' more than take a peek at the department. He had just finished droppin' off a passel of papers at HR."

Randall looked curious. "I did an interview with him up in HR a few weeks ago, but we didn't get much time to talk after that. Seemed like a really nice guy. I guess you could say he's the exact opposite of Bob Storch in almost every way. Seemed pretty smart and well-spoken to me. Nice smile, great mustache, and plenty of hair. What was your take?"

Doris thought for a moment. "I agree with all of that. I especially found him quite amusin' and he had a wit as quick as a fox at the chicken coop. Maybe quicker than you."

Randall made a sour face. "Quicker than me?!"

"Alright, Dr. B. Don't get excited. We can't all be quick all the time. I'm sure he has some slow times too. I did learn he's married, two kids, several cats, likes to bicycle, hike and loves baseball. And you probably learned from his résumé that he was in electronics before he ventured into Physics and that he has a passion for Quantum Theory, whatever that is." She made air quotes that framed her eye roll.

Randall frowned. "Hmm. Yeah, Quantum Theory. That's good. I may remember some of that career stuff. I'll bet he's a Cubs fan."

Doris shook her head. "He's not! He said the Cubs are too pathetic, so he roots for the Brewers. He already offered to take the department to a summer Brewers game at County Stadium and have a picnic in the park by the VA duck pond before the game."

Randall gave a fist pump. "I like him better already. Now, what about the Bucks game? How are we going to pull that off on short notice?"

Doris smiled proudly. "I assume you mean the royal 'we.' The Bucks are playing the Lakers Friday night, and I know a guy who can get us a ticket package for 30 percent off. I checked with the crew, and they're all free that night."

"Boy, I have some great ideas," said Randall. "You set it up, and I'll treat."

"Deal," said Doris, and the two exchanged high-fives.

Randall refilled his cup from the department caffeine stores after his meeting with Samuels. After a brief stop at the treatment console to confer about a setup, he walked back to his office and stopped at Doris's desk. "What choice items remain on the menu today? Any special entrees?"

Doris cocked her head toward Randall and gave him a twisty smile. "No, but there's an inviting sweetmeat in your office."

Randall's face brightened. "You mean dessert? As in a patient brought in delectable baked goods?"

Doris shook her head sadly. "Close. But no banana split. I'm sure you remember that it is exactly now that you have your follow-up meetin' with Ms. Elisabet Angeles."

Randall nodded. "I knew that. Gosh sakes, look at the time. Where does it go?"

Doris chuckled. "Yeah, but before you go in, you'd better primp first. You do want to make a good impression."

Randall snorted. "Hah, five hours of primping wouldn't make any difference with this physiognomy."

Doris snorted back. "Well, you've got me there."

Tired of waiting, Elisa Angeles walked out of Randall's office near the end of the verbal dueling match between Randall and Doris. Clearly, she had heard the whole exchange and was smiling broadly. "Hey, guys. Sorry, I was a bit early. Hope I'm not interrupting anything. By the way, what's a physiognomy?"

Doris was faster on the draw than Randall. "His mirror-crackin' mug."

Randall threw up both hands in defeat. "Wounded to the core. Cut to the quick. Mother, you told me there'd be days like this. Doris, that's one!"

Doris looked puzzled. "One what?"

Randall waved a finger at Doris. "For me to know, and you to find out." He turned to Elisa and motioned her into his office. "Come on in, but because of Doris, I haven't had time to primp," he said, stroking his bald pate with his right hand. "So you'll just have to take me as I am, with a less than optimal scalp shine."

Elisa chuckled. "That's okay. I have my Oakleys, just in case. Doris, I'll holler if I sense personal danger."

Doris winked. "I got your six, honey."

Randall asked if Elisa wanted anything to drink. "I'd kill for some coffee. I spilled my hot coffee in my car this morning."

"I hate when that happens," said Randall. "Let's both go get some, and I'll give you the nickel tour of the department before we sit and talk."

After dispensing their brown elixir, Randall made the rounds with Elisa and introduced her to the staff, explaining what she would be doing for the department. The techs were pleased with the idea because they were often the victims of scheduling conflicts. The two returned to Randall's office and sat.

"Wow," said Elisa. "Your department is pretty small for all the patients you have to treat."

Randall made a face. "Yeah, that's something we're working on fixing, but it's a slow go. On the other hand, it's much easier to keep an eye on things. There's no place for gold brickers to hide. But enough about my problems. Tell me about yourself."

Elisa paused and looked up for a moment as if gathering her thoughts. Randall was struck by how smooth and flawless her skin was. She wore a billowy cream-colored blouse and a dark-brown skirt with a small slit at the knee. A loosely knotted multicolored silk scarf adorned her neck.

Elisa cleared her throat. "My father was originally from Puerto Rico and immigrated to the US before World War II. He volunteered for the Navy and was shipped to the Philippines where he met my mother. After the war, he brought her back to the states and they married. My dad stayed in the Navy and was transferred to Great Lakes Naval Station. Ten years later a surprise package arrived. Me. Not long after, I had a sweet little brother, Carlito. We lost him to cancer when he was seven." Elisa's face clouded over, and her eyes became watery.

"So sorry to hear that," said Randall, handing Elisa a tissue. "I can imagine how horrible that was for you and your family." Randall cleared his throat and let the moment settle. "So, did your father remain stationed at Great Lakes?"

Elisa started to become cloudy again. "No, when he was in the South Pacific, his ship was attacked by Japanese kamikazes. He was injured by shrapnel after a bomb explosion. They got most of metal out, but several fragments were lodged near his spine and were too risky to be removed. Twenty years later, one of the fragments migrated and injured his spinal cord. It made him paraplegic."

Randall shook his head in sympathy. "Wow, that's rotten luck. How did you manage?"

"My mom and I did our best to help him, but we couldn't give him the care he really needed. The VAs in Chicago were . . . were . . . not the best for his type of needs. He was medically discharged and accepted to Hobbes VA for care on the spinal cord injury unit. It was a really hard decision for all of us. Mom couldn't afford to leave her rent-controlled apartment in Chicago. She has no family in the US and doesn't speak English very well, but she has a strong connection with the Filipino community in Chicago. I promised to move to Milwaukee to be closer to Dad. I bring Mom up to see him once a month. He's a full-time patient here up on the tenth floor."

Randall was doubly amazed, and just nodded. "Right. I've had several patients from the spinal cord injury unit. They do a good job up there."

Elisa's hair swung when she nodded. "Yes. That's one of the reasons I wanted to work here. You know, so I could keep an eye on him. After my brother died, I decided I wanted to be a nurse. Before my dad got bad, he helped me through school, but now he just lives on a pension and VA benefits. My first nursing job was at Hines VA in Chicago, where I was able to work toward a bachelor's degree. I've always been interested in ways to make the system work better after my experience there. So many things get lost in the cracks. So many people get forgotten."

Randall had to agree. "They sure do. So did you transfer here then?" He was impressed by the depth of her experience and concern.

"Yes. I got a job here, working the night shift in the ICU. I must have done something right. Mr. Samuels had me come to his office a few weeks ago, and he offered me this position." She held out her arms, looking like a flower drawing in sunlight. "I couldn't say no!"

Randall let out a loud breath. "That's quite a story. You and your family have been pushing the rock uphill for a long time. Sounds like you've made it to the top. Perhaps it's time to just hold the rock steady and look around at the view."

Elisa laughed. "How right you are. I bet you have a rock pushing story too."

"I sure do, but this is not the place or time. Maybe later, some day, when we have time to commiserate about lost causes over ice cream bars and coffee in the VA canteen. Perhaps I'll invite St. Jude to join us. For right now, the focus is on you."

"Deal," said Elisa. "That being the case, and before you strain yourself trying to restrain yourself from asking, I'm five-foot one inch. I inherited my height from my mother and my moxie from my dad. Not that my mother doesn't have moxie as well. Both held their own in any battle."

"Glad you cleared that up," said Randall. "You may have prevented an inguinal hernia. I have no doubt that you can hold your own as well. And you will need to in order to make headway on our little project. You'll have to butt heads with some pretty tough customers who will be resistant to anything that looks like change. The VA culture gravitates to maintain the status quo. Only calm seas are tolerated here. Rocking boats are anathema."

"Are there any roadblocks in particular I should be aware of?" asked Elisa.

"Does the pope wear funny hats?" quipped Randall. "Sorry. If you're Catholic, I've got another one about bears."

"No worries," said Elisa. "I am Catholic, but non-prosecutorial."

Randall explained who the players were in Hematology Oncology and Surgical Oncology. They would be the first two departments to co-ordinate with. Randall would set up meetings with both departments to introduce Elisa and discuss logistics. He described similar meetings to be had with Laboratory, Surgical Pathology, and Radiology.

Elisa indicated her understanding as he went. "Can't understand the players without a scorecard, right?"

"Exactly," said Randall. "Once we get all that done, we'll ease into setting up the weekly multidisciplinary tumor conference. I'm pretty sure we can get buy-in from all the stakeholders if we can arrange one key factor."

"What's that?" asked Elisa.

Randall made a grand gesture. "Coffee and donuts. Without that, no one will come. It's amazing how much suffering doctors and staff will endure for coffee and donuts."

Elisa slapped her thigh. "I bake great blueberry muffins. I'll bet I can get the VA canteen to bring a large coffee urn and cups."

Randall looked a bit sideways at Elisa. "And we'll need to beg and bargain for a conference room. I hope you don't feel overwhelmed. It's going to be a lot of work."

"Dr. B, I have no allergy to any letter in the ABCs and that includes W," enthused Elisa.

"That's the *spiritus convictus*!" announced Randall, pumping a fist in the air. "We shall overcome."

There was a knock on the office door, and Doris popped her head in. "What's all the yellin' in here? Is everyone okay?"

Randall was not surprised. He knew the interview had run over by ten minutes. "As O and K as can B. We could not be more O and K. Doris, contrary to what you're likely going to say next, I did not forget that my follow-up appointments started ten minutes ago. But having completed this meeting with great satisfaction, I now have the zest to dispatch them with all due alacrity."

Doris just looked at Randall, slightly bemused. "Alacrity? Dang. I'll have to look that up in my *Funk and Wagnalls*."

Randall rose and motioned for Elisa to go with Doris. "And my good Doris, if you please, kindly make happen another one-hour meeting with Miss Angeles in three or four days' time. Now I must haste to the next task at hand."

Randall zoomed out of the room. Doris and Elisa looked at each other, shrugged, and smiled.

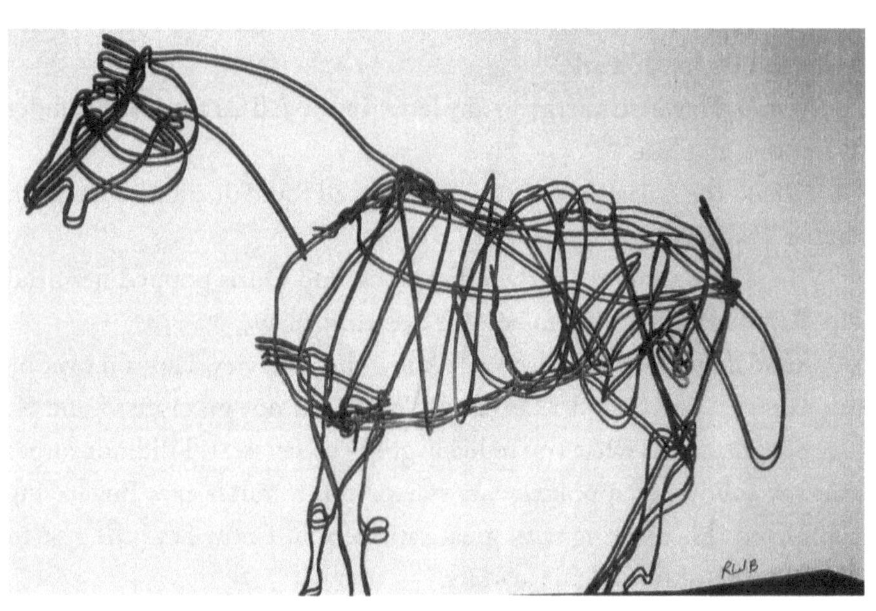
RWB

CHAPTER 24

———

HONEY, I SHRUNK THE KID

"Adults are just outdated children."

— Dr. Seuss

What Meow?

Doris and Randall were both extremely impressed with Elisa's ingenuity. They felt confident that she could solve many of the department's logistic patient-scheduling issues. They began to discuss tasks to assign her.

Then from down the hallway, coming from the direction of the Linac room, there arose a commotion that drew their attention. Both wandered down the hall in search of the sound's origin. It sounded like a cat meowing and a female voice yelling. "Come on down, kitty. Come here. I won't hurt you."

When Randall and Doris got to the block room entry door, they found Molly on a stepladder, reaching toward the ceiling where she had removed a ceiling panel. Melinda and Grace were steadying the ladder. Standing at the edge of the opening and mewling was a dark-brown and caramel-colored tabby cat that looked a bit worse for wear. The cat was tentative and scared.

Randall took in the situation. "Is that cat a veteran?"

"Dr. B! Get serious," chastised Grace. "Sure. I asked him for his social security number, but all I got was '3, 9 yeowl.'"

"How in tarnation did that poor little thing get up there?" asked Doris.

"He didn't say," barked Grace.

Molly turned her head and looked down at Randall and Doris. "It's no use. I can't get it to come down from the ceiling. Any ideas?"

Randall smacked his forehead. "I've got a tuna salad sandwich in my lunch. Maybe we can lure it out with that. Plus, I know cat speak. I should be able to tuna whisper him down."

"Didn't know you were multilingual," said Melinda.

"Sure am. My tongue is ambidextrous," said Randall. "Be back in a sec with Charlie the tuna."

The tuna lure worked perfectly, and soon the cat had devoured Randall's lunch and was rubbing Randall's ankle with his cheek. The cat wanted to make sure to remember the guy who fed him.

"I still can't cipher out how that poor little puddin' got in here," said Doris.

Randall, who now had the cat in his lap, corrected Doris. "Well, shut the front door! He's a she. Looks like she's been cared for. She's a bit dirty and skinny. I suspect she's a stray and not feral. Hasn't eaten in a while. Either came in through the front entrance or found her way into the air vent system and wound up in the ceiling."

Randall looked down the hallway and saw Bob Guardino waiting for an elevator. Randall could tell it was him, because the man always let his beard grow out and his hair go long for his role in the early spring VA Revolutionary War reenactment.

"Hey, Doris. Go to the elevators and get rifleman Guardino to come over here, would you?" asked Randall.

"Sure, Boss," said Doris and she went to hail the planner from Engineering before the elevator came down and he got away.

Guardino approached the gathering with his usual aplomb, but he came to an abrupt halt when he saw the cat in Randall's lap. "Starting a petting zoo, Doc?"

"Yep, and you're next," said Randall. "This little furry gal came out of the ceiling in the block room. Any ideas how she got up there?"

"Easy peasy," said Guardino. "The main air duct exhaust exits above the rear entrance door just down the main hallway from here. Critters get in there all the time and wander around the ducts. They can show up anywhere. Employees find them then call us and we, *er,* 'take care of them.'"

Doris raised an eyebrow. "Please define that."

Guardino clarified. "We toss 'em back outside."

Grace looked horrified. "In the dead of winter?"

"Not our problem, bleeding heart," said Guardino.

Melinda huffed. "Well, you could call the Humane Society."

Guardino harrumphed. "Not my job, sweetie. If you guys want, I could take the cat off your hands right now, and then we're done with this discussion."

"And just throw her outside again?" sputtered Randall. "She would probably just get back in again, maybe die in your precious air ducts and stink up the place for days. Then I could tell your chief who to thank for the odor."

Guardino bristled. "Well, you got a better idea?"

"Yeah!" blurted Randall. "She's now my cat. I'm taking her home with me."

"Problem solved!" said Guardino. "See, I told you. Not my problem." He turned and walked away. As he was leaving the department, he wished everyone a fine day. "Next time we find a possum, Biedermeier, I'll bring it down here."

Melinda looked at Randall in surprise. "How are you going to get the cat home?"

Randall realized he may not have thought this decision through. "*Hmm.* I don't have a cat carrier in my briefcase, but maybe I can stuff her in my backpack for the drive home."

"Good luck with that," said Melinda. "Poor thing would be squished and terrified! Tell you what. I have a cat and a carrier at my apartment. I don't live far from here. I get off at 4:30 and I could bring the carrier back here for you to borrow. You'll probably be here until at least 6:00, I would guess."

Randall nodded. "That would be great. I'd really appreciate that. This cat thing is not as much of a whim as it looks."

"Why's that?" asked Grace.

"We just lost our cat, Baldspot, and then our dog, Polluto, got run over. We replaced Baldspot with Wondercat, but the kids have been lobbying for a second cat because they both want a pet of their own. I've been procrastinating getting one. Now this one drops out of the sky, so to speak."

"Sorry about your cat passin'," said Doris. "Was she sick long?"

"Not exactly," said Randall and then recounted the Baldspot disappearing act.

"Wow, that's as strange as this cat coming out of the ceiling," said Molly.

"Yeah, the universe just gave you a replacement for the cat it took from you," said Melinda.

Randall nodded. "I guess that's true. It does kind of make sense in a nonsensical way."

Melinda gave Randall a big smile. "I'll bet your kids will be speechless when you come home with this furball."

Randall smiled his full voltage smile back at Melinda. "Can't say they're ever speechless, but they'll surely be surprised. That they will. That they will. Another chance for me to attain super-dad status."

On the way home, Randall wondered how Zelda would react. She could freak out or accept it as a gift from the universe. Randall hoped Zelda would see it as an alignment of the stars resulting from her meditations.

The cat delivery plan worked exactly as predicted and "the cat who dropped from the sky" was accepted with open arms. The new cat went immediately to Addie and adopted her. Addie, ever the tender heart, welcomed the little floof into the fold. Because the cat's coloring reminded Addie of a Milky Way candy bar, that became the cat's "official" name.

Peace and happiness had returned to the valley. Everyone slept restfully that night, both kids hugging their respective cats. Everyone, that is, except for Randall who slept fitfully knowing that the next day would bring the first visit with the child psychologist. Plus he'd have to hustle through his day to leave in time for the appointment. There would be hell to pay if he was late.

The following day at work was business as usual, patient-wise. But as the time for Kyle's appointment with Chelsea Andretti drew near, Randall's anxiety ramped up.

At home, Zelda was getting squirrelly. Ironically, Kyle was a mellow fellow. Perhaps having a cat of his own had settled him some. Zelda was hypervigilant about Kyle's behavior and nitpicked even his mildest transgressions. Instead of getting angry, Kyle was thriving on the negative attention. If Kyle got a rise out of Zelda by pushing one of her buttons, he would just keep firing for effect. Randall was mostly spared from witnessing the mental combat. He only saw them at the end of the day, when they were both exasperated with each other and frankly, too tired to fight anymore.

Addie, tired of witnessing the toxic interaction, just got quieter. She knew when a storm was brewing and sought shelter in the safe harbor of her room in the magical world of her stuffed animals. She would be spared going along for Kyle's "shrink" visit. At Zelda's request, Mrs. Bush had agreed to watch Addie until they returned from Ms. Andretti's office.

Zelda had arranged for Kyle to come home from school at noon so she could prep him for the appointment. That morning before school, she gave him a supervised bath, scrubbing Kyle's head with a bit more vigor than usual. She dressed him in one of his nicest outfits, usually reserved for holidays and visits to Grandma's house.

"Mom! I hate these dumb khaki pants! What kind of word is that, anyway? Khaki? Sounds like when good ol' Baldspot had a hairball. She'd go all humpback and yack on the oriental carpet. *Khaaaaaaaak . . .*" Kyle mimed the cat upchucking on the floor. "I miss that."

Zelda's breath was sharp and shallow. "Now, Kyle, Wondercat will start yacking soon enough. I promise. Plus, you get to clean up after her. Let's focus. We need to get you spiffed up. I want you to look nice for the meeting with Ms. Andretti. We need to show the lady that you are a decent kid, and that I'm a good mom. She's going to help fix you."

"What? Mom, what are you talking about? Fix me? Like how

we fixed the dog?" Kyle covered his crotch with his hand and looked scared.

Zelda shook her head. "Pish-posh. Not that kind of fixed. I mean she can help you not have bad dreams and night terrors. And help you not be angry so much."

Kyle looked genuinely confused and hurt. "Mom, do you mean I'm a problem child?"

Zelda glossed over his question. "Now remember. Don't play on the playground today, Kyle. Don't run on the field. No, actually, just don't go on the field. Just . . . just don't be you, just for today? And don't put ketchup on your lunch. This shirt has to stay white. We'll put on this clip tie right before we leave this afternoon."

Kyle crumpled, looking very young and very small.

Randall had overheard this exchange as he passed through the kitchen to grab a banana and refill his coffee. Zelda looked to be at wit's end, so Randall took Kyle by the shoulder and tried to explain the situation again. "Kyle, no, you are not a problem. We talked about the night terrors and how you can feel safe. We're also concerned about the hard time you've had going number two. Sometimes it's hard figuring out how to be a seven-year-old kid. And Mom and I need help figuring out how to help you. It's our first time being parents, just like it's your first time being a kid. We figured it would be good for ALL of us to get some support and guidance from an expert. So it's not just about you. It's about all three of us together. Ms. Andretti is the expert who can help us all."

Randall squeezed Kyle's shoulder, and Kyle looked relieved. Zelda acted a bit sheepish but kept herself busy brushing invisible fuzz off Kyle's shirt.

At Chelsea's Office

That afternoon, Randall rushed home early to make it to the meeting. Kyle stood motionless in the living room, as if afraid to wrinkle his outfit. His shirt was still white, and his khaki "yacki" pants had just a small grass stain.

Zelda huffed at Randall, "Took you long enough!" and she stomped upstairs to dress.

Randall and Kyle waited impatiently for Zelda to get ready to leave.

The tension in the house was uncomfortably palpable. What felt like hours later, Zelda emerged in a cloud of perfume and hairspray, dressed in one of her job interview outfits. When she finally trundled down the stairs, she yelled at Randall and Kyle to get a move on.

Randall thought it wise to remain silent. He shrugged and followed her to the car, prodding Kyle along in front of him.

Zelda acted as though Randall and Kyle were the cause of their belated departure. "Randy, we've got to hustle. Let's not waste time. Get in the car pronto, and motivate your German buggy. We don't want to make a bad first impression with the kid shrink."

Randall was miffed. "*Yas, Massa.* At your service. Tighten your seatbelts."

He put the Scirocco in reverse and did his best *Rockford Files* zippy backup impression out the driveway, notched first gear, and laid front wheel drive rubber up Creekside Place. His passengers were rocked forward and then backward by the laws of physics.

Zelda scowled at Randall, but Kyle yelled out "Yippee Ki Yay!"

She continued to glare at Randall as he raced in and out of traffic to their destination, but Randall ignored her disdain. It was one of his superpowers.

Randall quickly found an empty spot in the office parking lot, slotted into it with a rear wheel drift, and threshold braked to a halt. Zelda was left looking at her shoes. She sat back upright and fixed him with a dagger stare. "Randy, was that teenage display necessary?"

Randall pointed at the dash clock. "We've got two minutes to get inside, 'Ms. Slow Boat to China.' Last one inside does dishes tonight."

The three piled out like clowns from a mini-car and appeared at the receptionist desk out of breath at the stroke of four o'clock. Randall brought up the rear sort of accidentally on purpose.

The receptionist's nametag read Susan Gnami.

"Miss Gnami," said Zelda, pronouncing the name with a long A sound, "I'm Zelda Biedermeier. My husband and I have a four o'clock appointment with Chelsea Andretti to meet with our son Kyle."

The receptionist checked her appointment book. "Yes, I have your appointment right here, Mrs. Beetlemeyer."

Zelda laughed. "We both have names that are hard to pronounce. It's Bee-der- mayer, like in Oscar Mayer wieners. Did I get your name right?"

"Almost," said the receptionist. "It's Gnami, like in Vietnam, with a short A. Just call me Sue, and we're good." Sue confirmed their information and pointed them to seats in the waiting room. "Ms. Andretti is running a bit late."

Zelda's eyes got wide. The receptionist remained calm and soothing. "It could be a few minutes. There are some toys in the corner if Kyle would like to play while you wait."

Kyle wandered over to the play area. He found some *Star Wars* figures and spaceship models. He was fully engrossed in seconds. As Randall watched him play Darth Vader, he noticed that Kyle looked rather "sheveled" compared to his usual untucked appearance after school. Zelda had indeed spiffed him up considerably. Zelda, herself, looked wound pretty tight, close to "blow a gasket" time.

Randall wisely kept his mouth shut yet again. He had learned silence was his best policy when she had devolved to this "wound tight" state of mind. He just reached out and took her hand in his. At first the hand was rigid and cold, but soon it went limp, and she relaxed a bit in the chair.

"Oh, Randy, I'm scared," Zelda whispered. "What if Kyle is on the suicide road? What if this is how it starts?!"

Randall put his arm around her shoulder. "I know how you feel. My mouth is dry as desert air. In a part of my brain, I'm afraid she'll wind up telling us we've FUBARed our son. But in my heart, I know we've done the best we could do with the limited training they provide parents. It's like the reverse of school. You get the test first and then you get the course material to study."

A single tear rolled down Zelda's cheek. "Yeah, and the textbook they give you is written in Hebrew, has random pages missing and has redacted sections."

Randall had to chuckle at that. "Yeah, and there's food stains on the table of contents. And a coffee stain on the summary!"

Zelda guffawed loud enough for the receptionist to glance over at them with a quizzical look that said: "Who are these crazy people?"

Whatever endorphin was released by laughter, it had worked its magic. Both Randall and Zelda felt their anxiety melt away. They looked over at Kyle who was totally engrossed in his imaginary space world.

Zelda was suddenly moved to believe that there was nothing wrong with Kyle. He was just an ordinary boy. "Randy, do you remember when you could just get lost in your childhood fantasies and forget the world? I do and I wish I could turn it on as easily as Kyle does."

Randall recalled how he could play for hours with toy cars made out of wood and convince himself they were real cars. Or he could listen to 78 RPM recordings of *Peter and the Wolf* narrated by Sterling Holloway and cry for the poor lost duck.

"Yeah, it would be great to just push a button and get on that magic carpet ride. When I was that age, I always wanted to be more grown up so I could do all the cool things that adults do. Nowadays, I wish I could go back, but know what I know now. I guess that's why they say youth is wasted on the young."

Zelda nodded and sighed. Before she could reply, her attention was diverted as the office door swung open. A red eyed, red-haired teenage girl walked out of the office followed by a blonde middle-aged woman with a clipboard. The older woman put one hand on the girl's shoulder as they walked to the receptionist's desk. The receptionist gave the girl an appointment card, and the blonde woman whispered something into the teen's ear. The two hugged and the teen went to find her mother in the waiting room.

The blonde woman turned to Zelda, who flinched involuntarily. The blonde lady, dressed in a comfortable-looking long green skirt and matching paisley top, smiled broadly as she approached Randall and

Zelda at a leisurely pace. Clearly unphased by Zelda's blast shields, she offered a handshake and a disarming smile.

"You must be Zelda Biedermeier. So glad to meet you! I hope you found the office without any trouble? I'm Chelsea Andretti."

Zelda's anxiety faded a bit, and her shoulders relaxed as she nodded and took the proffered hand. The beginning of a smile formed on her face.

Ms. Andretti then turned her attention to Randall. "And Randall Biedermeier? A pleasure. I appreciate that you both made time to come in with Kyle today. It's so much more helpful for me to see the family dynamic up front."

She made easy eye contact with Randall. He was beginning to feel comfortable with the woman. She was easy on the eyes too. He had been picturing a pinched-up crone with a bun.

Zelda's tongue became untied. "I like your skirt. I've got one just like that. I like them long for when I don't have time to shave my legs." She blushed a little.

Randall couldn't believe what he'd just heard. The comment sounded rather embarrassing, but Ms. Andretti didn't bat an eye. "Or when you cut your leg shaving. That's what I always do. See my cut?" With that, she pulled up her skirt and displayed a Band-Aid on her calf.

The two women laughed while Randall goggled at the brief flash of flesh. He relaxed a bit further. He figured any shrink who could disarm Zelda so quickly might actually have a chance of breaking through the shield wall.

Ms. Andretti turned to the play area and spotted Kyle. He was still lost in space. "And that must be Kyle over there. He is a handsome young man. Looks like he's quite engrossed."

"Yep, Kyle is quite the *Star Wars* fan. He can do that for hours," said Randall.

"That's a good sign," said Ms. Andretti. "I'll go over and introduce myself."

She walked over to Kyle and crouched down next to him. "I bet your name is Kyle. My name is Chelsea Andretti, but you can call me

Chelsea. How about we build a landing dock for your TIE fighter?" She picked up some blocks and started to build.

Kyle watched her construction attempt for a minute then stopped her. "It doesn't go like that. Here, let me show you." Kyle sketched out how he wanted it and they set to work. It didn't take long for them to finish the block landing dock.

Randall and Zelda looked on in wonder.

"Now that's how to break the ice with a kid," Randall said to Zelda in hushed tones. "I think I already like this woman."

Zelda punched Randall's arm and whispered back. "Jinkies! You just like her legs."

Randall nodded. "They'll do."

Chelsea stood up to admire the block dock assembly. "Say, Kyle. I need to talk with your mom and dad in my office for a bit. Why don't you come along? You can bring along some of these toys in a basket and play while we talk. I may have some questions for you too. Is that okay with you?"

"Okay, Chelsea," said Kyle. He eagerly grabbed a basket and filled it with matchbox cars.

Chelsea gestured toward her office door. "Mr. and Mrs. Biedermeier. Shall we?"

Zelda looked confused. "All of us? I thought you were just going to, I don't know, fix him." She tilted her head toward Kyle.

Chelsea chuckled. "That's a pretty common conclusion for parents when they first meet me. I don't work alone. We're all part of the team, and we figure stuff out together. Come on back."

The three followed Chelsea into her office. Zelda kept glancing at Randall with a look on her face he could not interpret, mouthing something he could not understand.

Chelsea's office looked like a living room. There were comfy chairs, a hanging plant, a low coffee table and boxes full of toys. The adults sat down while Kyle gasped and went to explore the new toys.

Chelsea handed Zelda and Randall a clipboard with some papers. "Mrs. Biedermeier, we talked briefly about your concerns on the phone, but now I need to get a broader and more in-depth view of Kyle's home-life. This is the basic intake packet that everyone fills out. I know it looks like a lot, but we have plenty of time. I'll explain what each form is and why we ask."

Zelda looked confused. "Don't you want to hear about the night terrors and bowel problems first?"

"Certainly. We'll cover that soon," said Chelsea. "But this is our starting point."

Zelda still looked a bit dazed. She nudged Randall rather forcefully with her elbow and pointed to the top of the first paper, which read "Chelsea Andretti, Licensed Clinical Social Worker." Randall responded to her with a Gallic shrug, in the universal "I don't understand what you mean, lady, throw me a bone" gesture.

Zelda finally spoke up. "*Um*, Ms. Andretti? It says here you're a social worker? *Um*, like from Child Protective Services? I thought you were a child therapist." Zelda looked around the office, as if searching for cameras or waiting for men in uniform to burst in to take her son away.

Chelsea fielded this with calm, as if this were standard fare for parents new to the process. "I understand your confusion, Zelda. May I call you Zelda?"

Zelda nodded. "Sure. No need for formality. We're all friends here, right, Chelsea?" Her voice squeaked through her anxiety-stricken larynx.

Randall gave an eye roll but held his tongue.

Chelsea gave Zelda a reassuring smile and tried to explain further. "No problem. I get that a lot. People often don't understand the way we get titled. I am a clinical social worker. I know that people often associate the word 'social worker' with 'people who take away kids.' But that's just one of the many roles a social worker may have. As a licensed clinical social worker, or LCSW, I earned my bachelor's and master's degrees in social work. Social work as a field focuses on working to empower people, create equality, and promote social justice."

Zelda still looked a bit confused. "Social justice? Are we going on a protest or something? If we are, I'd like to protest the menial wages of mothers!"

Randall was still biting his tongue, but the remark was a sign that Zelda had thawed out enough to joke with Chelsea.

Chelsea laughed heartily. "That would be a well-attended protest! Actually, social justice happens on all scales, from big political gestures to the stuff that happens right at home. I've been interested in how to support that in the family, so I had extra training and certification in working specifically with children and families in a therapeutic setting, like this one." Chelsea had an ease about her. Randall figured she had repeated this introduction more than a few times.

Zelda continued to vet Chelsea. "So you're saying you have to have a license from the State to do your version of family therapy, just like a doctor? Like Randy?"

Randall figured Zelda had thrown that in to remind Chelsea that he was a doctor, but he restrained his desire to poke her in the ribs—whatever it took to calm the herd and prevent a stampede.

Chelsea's confidence was not deterred. "Exactly, Zelda. To become licensed, I had to work under clinical supervision for 3,500 hours and take a State exam to prove that I know my stuff. Well, one never knows everything, right? I know kids and families, in general, and you are much more of an expert on your own kids. So we make a team, right?"

Randall was pleased when Zelda nodded and smiled. It meant that she was finally on board and buying the whole package. Zelda turned to Randall and put a hand on his leg as if to say, "I'm ready to rock and roll."

Chelsea went over the forms with them, which covered general family information, medical history, the rights to (and limits of) confidentiality, family history, and the presentation of their concerns about Kyle. While Randall and Zelda filled out the forms, Chelsea settled on the floor next to Kyle. He was making an elaborate scene with blocks and matchbox cars on the coffee table. After a while, Kyle was telling Chelsea a story about the cars, while Chelsea asked questions. It didn't seem like they were doing anything special, just playing.

Zelda leaned over to Randall, whispering in his ear. "What is she doing? I can play with Kyle. We don't need to pay a bunch of money for someone else to play with our kid!"

Randall put a hand on Zelda's arm. "Come on, Zel, we agreed to give this process a chance. Let's just ride out this session and see where the road takes us. It'll be Randy and Zel's marvelous adventure."

Zelda pulled a face and then nodded her assent. Then she started filling out the forms with zeal. The forms took about fifteen minutes to complete, during which time Chelsea left Zelda and Randall alone and played with Kyle. Kyle was all in with the deal and babbled away with Chelsea, basically free associating.

When Zelda announced they had finished the forms, Chelsea gave Kyle some paper and markers. "Kyle, I imagine you are pretty good at drawing. Would you please draw a house, a tree, and a person?" Kyle jumped into the activity with gusto, and Chelsea arose to sit with Zelda and Randall.

Zelda started to get up to instruct Kyle on his drawing, but Chelsea redirected her back to the seat. "It's okay, Zelda, this is just one method I use to learn about Kyle's perceptions of the world. It's not about making a perfect drawing; it's about seeing life through his eyes."

Chelsea reviewed forms with them, hitting the main points, and asking clarifying questions. She also had questions about Randall and Zelda's childhoods, how they met, what their early relationship was like, and generally what life was like at home.

Finally, Chelsea turned to Zelda. "We've got some time left. Let's use the time to focus on home life. I'd like to start with this question. What's a typical day at home like for you, Zelda? Tell me about your daughter too. Any pets at home?"

Zelda nodded but acted like the question was a bit odd. "Yes, we have Addie, who's five. And we have two cats and a dog. Well, we HAD a dog. We had to let him go. Can't say I miss him so much, but the kids do."

Kyle, who had been drawing quietly, piped up. "Yeah, Chelsea, he's DEAD. Mom and Dad made him go away, and now he's dead. It's their fault."

Zelda looked like she had been punched in the stomach. "Polluto needed more activity than we could give him, so we gave him to a family on a farm. He ran into the road and . . ."

Chelsea held up a hand. "It's alright, Zelda. Kyle knows it's not really your fault."

Zelda turned red. "How can you know that?"

Chelsea held up both hands this time. "You're right, Zelda. It's just an educated guess, but the chances are excellent I'm right. Most kids love their parents and . . ."

Zelda interrupted. Chelsea had lit the fuse and knew enough to back away from the explosion. "If Kyle loves me, why does he take everything out on me?! He is such a handful. He's always getting into trouble, talking back to me, picking on his sister! I didn't sign up for this! I wasn't ready to be a parent yet! I feel like I was just barely done with childhood, ready to start my life and become an artist! Suddenly I had a kid, a house, and I'm being dragged all over the country, following my husband's big-shot doctor career! And to top it off, my kid is messing around at school, smearing poop on the walls, breaking stuff, and yelling at me all the time. I swear, that kid just doesn't like me."

Zelda looked surprised at her outburst. It had erupted like a long-dormant volcano.

Chelsea glanced briefly at Kyle, who seemed nonplussed and absorbed in building block garages for the cars. Randall could still see the tension in his shoulders though. Randall remained "mum's the word."

Chelsea paused a beat and then attempted to extinguish the flames. "Zelda, I hear your frustration. Being a parent is tough. There is no training manual, no 'how to' class before you are in the weeds, 24/7. Sounds like parenthood came early for you. With challenging behaviors to deal with, the stuff that's going wrong takes center stage. From my perspective though, there's a lot of stuff going right."

Zelda's shame spiral reversed, and she snapped her eyes up to meet Chelsea's. "Huh?"

"Your son is fed, dressed, and bathed on a daily basis, right?"

Zelda nodded, sniffling.

Chelsea continued. "Think about it. Kyle goes to school. He gets to play outside. He lives in a nice home. He has two adults who love him. Do you realize how many kids don't even have those basics covered?

You two are already on the right track! I can see how much you love your kids. From what you've written and shared so far, you also stay home with them, make sure they are safe, make time to play, sing, and draw. I can see how well-loved Kyle is."

Zelda looked soulfully at Chelsea. "Then why is he so angry and mean to me?"

Chelsea didn't miss a beat. "Kids express their pain or anger through harsh words sometimes. The harsh words have the impact and power to express the power of the kid's feelings. If you listen to the emotion behind the words, however, rather than the common meaning, you'll understand how powerful it feels to Kyle to be inside his own anger. If it's this hard to be around him, it's ten times harder to BE him. As for Kyle saving his worst stuff for you, congratulations!"

Zelda pulled another face. "'Scuse me? I should be happy about this?"

Chelsea raised both arms and beamed a smile. "Actually, yes. If your child shares his worst with you, you have a good strong attachment! It may seem counterintuitive to adults, but kids share their toughest behaviors and feelings with the people they feel closest to. If he didn't feel safe and secure with you, he would be afraid to show his real feelings for fear of losing you."

"He must feel very attached then." Zelda scoffed. "I don't feel so lucky though."

Chelsea laughed. "It's a mixed honor, isn't it! The toughest part for many parents is the sense of feeling alone in the struggle."

Randall began to relax. Chelsea had found the chink in Zelda's armor and was getting through to her.

Zelda sat up straighter in her chair. "That's for sure! I admit, I don't talk to anyone. I'm afraid they'll think I'm an inadequate mother. And Randall is never around! And when he is around, he lets them stay up too late, then feeds them disgusting mac and cheese. I look like the bad guy, because I make them eat healthy and go to bed on schedule!"

Chelsea smiled, continuing to rebuild Zelda's damaged ego. "I bet it feels like you're all alone. And with two kids, you feel completely outnumbered! The time when Randall is home just doesn't feel like enough."

Zelda poked Randall in the ribs. "Correction. I've got three kids."

Randall squawked like one of the Three Stooges. "Hey, I resemble that!"

Zelda squawked back. "Good. I'm glad you admit that you're just a big kid." Zelda teared up a bit and paused. No one spoke. Then she continued in a soft voice. "To be fair, Randy does try to be home as much as he can. And he takes care of the kids when he gets home, so I can have time to be alone. And he sings them silly songs while he picks on his guitar. He's no Andres Segovia. I'm just glad he doesn't tell them about the gory stories from work."

Chelsea got up and walked over to Zelda. She bent down close to her face. "Zelda, you juggle so much. And you care for your family. Maybe it's time to reach out and connect with other parents, or even someone just to support you. Sounds like you deserve it!"

Zelda nodded slowly, as if considering she may not be the worst parent ever.

Chelsea put a hand on Zelda's shoulder. "And I know how much you love Kyle. I know he heard your frustration with his behaviors, and it's good for him to know that you see that he is also doing the best he knows how. He is not a 'problem' to be fixed, right? He's a child to be loved and understood!"

Zelda looked pained. "Of course! I love Kyle with all my heart! I just lose my temper sometimes." Kyle stayed quiet, playing with his toys, but Randall saw his little shoulders soften.

"It might be a good time to go and draw with him. Just remember to let *him* draw *his* picture, and *you* draw *yours*. While you're doing that, I have a few more questions for Randy."

Zelda eagerly scooted down to the floor and hugged her son. Kyle handed her a piece of paper and kept working on his own creation.

Chelsea turned her attention to Randall. "Randy, it sounds like you have a pretty intense job. What's that like?"

At first, Randall just sat with his elbows on his knees, wringing his hands. He didn't quite know what to say. Randall surprised himself (and Zelda) by sharing the stress of dealing with large patient loads. On top of that, he felt he was barely ahead of the learning curve in figuring out the rapidly growing field of radiation oncology, running a strapped department in a government hospital, and having to make decisions about millions of dollars of equipment and staffing.

He finally decided to damn the torpedoes. "I try hard to be a good doctor, supervisor, teacher, and mentor, and I feel like I'm constantly running at top speed ahead of a tidal wave!" The words just came tumbling out, sounding almost like a prepared speech. "And I'm trying to be a good husband and dad too. When I'm at work, I feel bad that I'm not with Zelda and the kids. When I'm home, I'm worried that I'm missing something at work, or that I messed up a dosage, or that the compliance officer is going to find a reason to shut down my department!" He reached the end of his breath. He took in a huge drink of air.

Zelda looked up at Randall with some softness. Randall hadn't shared a lot of the nitty gritty with her; often there just wasn't time!

Chelsea nodded and urged him to continue. "That's a lot to carry, Randall. You have a lot of responsibility. It sounds like a job you could do twenty-four hours a day and never really get it done."

Randall nodded vigorously. "That's the truth! And when I come home, I feel like I never get the 'dad and husband' job right either. It's like I'm always doing something wrong." Randall's voice got quieter. "Zelda just seems so angry all the time, and I feel bad that, so far, she hasn't had the life she wanted."

"You feel like you can't win for losing," Chelsea mirrored.

"Right! We had a lot of fun in the beginning; we both love music and playing around. We love the kids, and we try to create a good home for them. But by the end of the day, we are both just stretched too thin, and our relationship bears the burden." His shoulders sagged. "And the hardest part is not when we fight. We try so hard not to fight or yell in front of the kids. The hardest part is when there is this unspoken tension between us. The deafening silence of disappointment and resentment." He felt like his chest might implode.

The room stayed quiet for a full minute as the words swirled around and slowly settled to the ground.

Kyle grabbed a block and started pounding on his drawing. "It's your fault!! Why can't you just behave? Why do you always have to be a bad kid?! Go away so they can just have the perfect one!" He yelled at his drawing, pounding the little spot that was a person, overshadowed by a huge house.

Chelsea seemed unphased as she went to Kyle and lowered onto a pint-sized chair. She pointed to the drawing. "This person looks so small."

"He's so small, and everything he does is wrong!" Kyle emphasized his words with the pounding of the block.

Chelsea's voice was low and calm. "He feels so small and weak, and he wants to feel big and powerful. He wants to do the right thing."

The block pounding became less destructive. His voice got small. "He's so stupid. Nobody notices the good stuff. They only see the bad kid."

Chelsea matched his tone. "He wants someone to see him. He uses noise to be noticed."

Kyle's voice turned sad, mixed with sarcasm. "Yeah! But they only like HER. She's perfect. She's an angel. They yell, and sometimes Mom throws things. Sometimes Mom says she wishes she didn't have us. And then they get REALLY mad, but they don't say nothing."

The pause was deathly silent.

"It gets so quiet in the house," Chelsea intoned, welcoming more sharing.

Kyle snuck a look at Chelsea, finally connecting. His voice was just a whisper. "When it's quiet, I don't know what's gonna happen. It hurts my tummy. It hurts Addie too. She hides in her room. I know it; I see her scared eyes. I have to do something! If they are mad at me, they aren't mad at each other anymore. Maybe then Mommy will stay." Kyle looked like he had just released a national secret.

A tear ran down Zelda's face. Randall felt devoid of energy for a response. Kyle hesitantly went to Zelda and hugged her. Chelsea took in the push-pull dynamic of the scene and then glanced at the old clock on the wall. Despite the richness of the moment, it was time to schedule a rematch.

Chelsea rose easily from the tiny chair and addressed the silent trio.

"I'm sorry to interrupt the flow here, but our time is up. There has already been some amazing sharing. You all want the same things: to be noticed, loved, and appreciated. Let's pause here and let this all settle."

Chelsea walked over to Kyle and patted him on the shoulder. "You need to take this little guy home and put some time aside to talk about what happened here today. Come on out with me, and I'll have Sue set you up with another appointment."

Zelda gasped and looked up in surprise. "You mean we're not done with this Spanish Inquisition?"

Chelsea laughed. "What do you mean? I haven't even gotten to the hot pokers and the rack yet. If you don't come back, I won't have a chance to use all my specialized equipment."

Zelda stared at Chelsea even harder.

Randall laughed with a sudden outburst of air. "Zel, she's joking. She doesn't use torture devices. Right, Chelsea? . . . Right?"

Chelsea just smiled broadly, displaying even, bright-white teeth. "Of course, not," she said with a Count Dracula voice. "Only for the really recalcitrant cases. Even then there is no blood or bruising. At least not visible."

Kyle picked up on the shift in mood. "*Ooo*, but I like blood. Can we see blood next time?"

Chelsea tousled Kyle's hair. "Well, maybe. Just for you. Now let's get a move on. I've got another patient, and you've got places to go and stuff to do too."

Kyle smiled back at Chelsea. "Alright. If you promise."

Zelda, Randall, and Kyle walked hand in hand to the reception desk. Chelsea guided a wide-eyed Zelda by the elbow. Connections had been made. Circuits had been activated. Lift off was still forthcoming. The parents made an appointment for the following week, and Sue gave Kyle a large lollipop.

Randall deflated and shuffled his foot, looking jealous, "Hey, what about me?"

Sue just laughed and gave him one too.

Zelda shook her head and muttered, "Kids!"

CHAPTER 25

———

SNOW DAY AT HOME

"Wherever you go, there you are."

— *Sukiyaki*, Andrew James Pritchard

SNOW DRIFTS

The evening after the Andretti session, the Biedermeiers were rather quiet while processing the flotsam and jetsam that had floated to the surface. Randall felt grateful that the following day was fairly routine and busy enough to consume his full attention. On his way home from work though, Randall had plenty of time to think about the first meeting with Chelsea Andretti. It had started to snow lightly, the roads were slick, and traffic had slowed to a crawl. Several fender benders on the freeway blocked lanes, so he exited the freeway and used side streets, which flowed only slightly better. Still, no point in getting stranded on a snowy freeway, he reckoned.

While he navigated the balky traffic, Randall had ample time to reflect on what might be behind Kyle's night terrors and quirks. Kyle's DNA certainly played a role, but Randall considered other factors. When Kyle was born during Randall's first year of marriage, Randall had been just a lowly intern at St. Joseph Hospital in Denver. He and Zelda lived in a one-bedroom efficiency apartment attached to the hospital. It was a tiny space, and Randall's schedule was erratic.

During his second month on duty, Randall was on night call from 8:00 p.m. to 8:00 a.m. For any and all problems arising during those hours, he was the first doctor called, no matter what service the patient was on. From nasogastric tubes to pulled IV lines, the calls were continuous. With no sleeping during night call duty, he had to sleep during the day.

Daytime sleeping was nearly impossible, because Kyle cried every hour on the hour, with colic pain, full diaper, hunger, or just no obvious reason. While Randall tried to sleep, Zelda often got fed up with the racket and "put Kyle down for a nap." Then she'd run off somewhere to get away, and Randall woke to the tune of a wailing kid.

Kyle's shrill cries broke through any sleep attempt, so Randall dragged himself out of bed and tried to cypher out what was wrong. After eliminating food and diaper, sometimes holding or rocking him managed to get him back to sleep. Often the crying started anew if Randall tried to put him back into his bassinet. Sometimes Kyle went back to sleep if Randall brought Kyle into bed with him. Then they'd both get a brief nap before Kyle's colic woke him.

Colicky bowel pain caused never-ending, repetitive, high-pitched squeals that pierced the marrow. Even the neighbors couldn't stand it, and they'd call, offering to put the kid out of his misery. The only cure for the colic was for Randall to manually expel hardened stool from Kyle's little rectum. Sometimes, even that didn't work and, with Zelda still AWOL, Randall was so desperate for sleep that he'd put Kyle in the dry bathtub, with blankets and pillows for bedding, and close the bathroom door to partially muffle the crying. It was either that or go nuts from sleep deprivation. Being at home was no better than being at the hospital on night call.

Zelda would ultimately return from wherever she'd run off to and castigate Randall for putting Kyle in the bathtub, but she never accepted any responsibility for the situation or say why she was gone so long just to buy a half-gallon of milk. Or why she came back all red-eyed and spacey. Randall simply replied that the bathtub was much better than infanticide.

Several times Randall returned home after finishing his hospital shift to find Kyle wailing away in his crib and Zelda ignoring him. She said she couldn't get him to stop his bawling and he'd just have to "cry it out."

Once Randall tried to comfort Kyle and found his face bruised with dried blood in his ear canal. Zelda claimed Kyle had bumped his head on the side of his crib. Randall doubted that was true but held his tongue for fear of instigating additional rash behavior. After all, Zelda was only nineteen years old and away from home for the first time with a new husband and a new baby. Not much time to adjust to major life changes. No point in pushing her any harder. Give her some slack to adjust.

Well, crap, Randall thought, *I had to adjust to all those things too, plus it wasn't a walk in the park being a newly minted doctor on my own for the first time.* The memory made him angry in retrospect. *What made Zelda a special case requiring kid glove treatment?* Perhaps he had been too easy on her. He pounded the steering wheel and fumed for a few minutes as he was stuck behind a car that could not make it up an icy hill. *Why did all the bucks stop at his desk?*

Randall thought it odd that the only time he could think clearly about this personal stuff was when he was stuck in traffic. So why be mad at the traffic? Enjoy the brief respite from patients and family. They all just wanted a part of him. Randall tried to remember when he had a life of his own and didn't have to answer to six different masters. He couldn't think of such a time, but the thought brought him back to the present day. Kyle had come a long way since those days, and so had his parents.

Kyle had been a bit testy since the visit to Ms. Andretti, and Randall couldn't understand why. Kyle seemed to be angry more often if things didn't go his way. Even when things were seemingly going well, he did silly aggravating things just to get attention, even if it was negative attention. Zelda was hemming and hawing about talking to a therapist just for herself. However, Randall was coming to the conclusion that it would be good for him to talk to someone he could bounce things off of without repercussions. Venting to the car was helpful, but the Scirocco gave no feedback. Then Randall had a worrisome thought. *What if someone at work found out about him going to a psychotherapist?* It might be construed as though he was headed around the bend, and his clinical acumen might be questioned. But he might make that turn anyhow if he couldn't unburden

some of the stress. He also really wished he could talk rationally to someone about the irrational stuff that had been happening. *Reanimated patients and telepathy couldn't be real, could they?*

Randall thought of Joe Shepard again. He recalled that the year before Joe had taken a leave of absence from his practice for six months
and, when Randall had asked him about it at one of their lunches, Joe
told Randall that he'd taken the time off to get his "bearings straight."

Randall had not pursued it further, deciding that it might be a sensitive subject, and Joe would elaborate if he wished to disclose more.
Joe did not offer more detail and inferred that it was a long story for
discussion at a future time. Perhaps now was that future time. Randall
thought there would be no harm in setting up another lunch date with
Joe. After all, it would make sense for Randall to give Joe follow up on
his referral of Kyle to Chelsea Andretti. And they had theories to explore about noncorporeal communication. He made a mental note to
set up another lunch with Joe.

The stuck car impeding Randall's forward progress finally got traction, and traffic started to move. It was like the roadway had gotten a
much-needed Fleet enema. Randall concluded that it was time for him to
get a mental enema regardless of what anybody else did or thought about it.

In addition to talking to Joe, he resolved to call one of the therapists
that Ms. Andretti recommended and set up an appointment. He would
try to piece things together into some kind of sense. He wanted to call
Ms. Andretti anyhow and ask about Kyle's recent behavior. Perhaps the
initial session triggered something in Kyle as it had in himself. Suddenly
Randall was receiving a distress call from his southern region alerting
him that all the coffee he had consumed at work to stay alert was avidly
seeking an exit. In response, he provided significant additional positive
input to the accelerator.

To Grandmother's House

With enthusiastic goosing of the go-pedal, Randall was soon trail-braking
into a sliding turn onto Creekside Place and pursuing a wobbling path

down the slippery hill leading to the house at a speed not advisable for the conditions. Rather than panic, Randall applied small corrective steering wheel inputs to keep the Scirocco straight. He used the momentum to execute a 90-degree power slide neatly into the driveway, applying just a touch of throttle to use the front wheels to pull the car through the turn. He was proud of his car control skills, but reckoned it might be a one-off lucky event. The snow had tapered off to a light dusting powder. He pulled the car into the garage, and he was just getting out of the car as Zelda came out the back door and ran up to him shouting. At first, he thought she was going to give him grief for his reckless driving.

"Randy! I can't find Kyle anywhere in the house!" Zelda's hair looked to Randall like it caught fire. "He and I had a little incident, and I sent him to his room. When I called for him to come down for dinner, he didn't come. I checked all over the house, and I couldn't find him. He's just gone!"

"The hell you say!" Randall dropped his briefcase in the slushy mess in the garage and quickly retrieved it. He felt suddenly hollow inside: scooped out. "Okay, let's get in the house and both look again. He may be hiding."

Randall and Zelda hightailed it into the house. Addie was standing at the back door, waiting.

"Where's Kyle?" she asked plaintively. "I've been looking all over the house for him!"

Randall put his hand on Addie's shoulder. "Mommy is going to go upstairs and look on the second floor and in the attic. I'm going to look on this floor. Addie, you help me look."

Zelda ran up the stairs, calling Kyle's name, and began searching the second floor and attic.

Randall started checking the first-floor closets and cabinets, under furniture and behind drapes. He and Addie both called out Kyle's name as they searched.

In the midst of searching, Randall's bladder issued another urgent alarm that it was past due for discharging its overload. There was no ignoring it this time. He told Addie to keep searching for Kyle while he went to the pink powder room. Instead of just unzipping, Randall pulled his pants down, took a seat, and let go of what seemed like an endless stream. He found himself suddenly so relaxed that he leaned back against the toilet tank and shut his eyes to think.

As his eyes closed, he had a vivid image of perhaps himself walking outdoors in a blinding snowstorm with red lights blinking at him and a feeling of mortal panic. He couldn't piece together what he was seeing. He opened his eyes with a shudder, and the urgency of looking for Kyle overtook him again. *What the heck am I seeing?* He thought it was probably just an afterimage from driving home in the snow. He pulled his pants back up, flushed, and rejoined Addie in the house search.

"Kyle, it's Daddy!" shouted Randall as he walked through the house. "Don't be afraid to come out if you're hiding. You're not in trouble. Addie, go and stand by the back door in case Kyle is outside and comes back in."

"Okay, Daddy." Addie sounded scared and small.

Randall had finished searching the first floor and was headed down to the basement when the image of walking outside in the snow reverberated in his head again. He could feel the rumbling of passing semis in his bones.

"Holy hopping hip boots!" exclaimed Randall out loud. "Kyle is outside walking in the snow along a street. The red lights I'm seeing are car taillights."

Randall thought that, if Kyle had left the house, he may have left some telltale footprints in the snow. Randall ran back up the basement stairs, went to the junk drawer and grabbed a flashlight, then hurried outside. After a few minutes, he found a trail of size five footprints going down the side of the driveway. Inspecting them closely, he guessed they might be about 20 minutes old since they were beginning to accumulate the white powdery snow. He followed the footprints out into the street where he lost them in tire tracks, then picked them up again in the field across from the house. From there, they led back to the street, heading out of the subdivision where they became obscured once more by tire tracks.

Randall looked back at the house where Zelda was standing outside the backdoor shaking her head. She gestured with both arms extended, palms up. Randall gestured back that he'd found tracks leading away from the house and yelled to call the police.

Randall shivered in the cold wind and scurried back to the house. When he got inside, Zelda was already on the phone giving a description of Kyle and his pertinent information. She thanked the police dispatcher and hung up.

"What'd they say?" asked Randall.

"The dispatcher said that all patrol cars in the vicinity have been alerted to look for a male child matching Kyle's age and description. She said that if he was walking, he couldn't have gotten too far, given the weather," said Zelda nervously. "She said that there wouldn't be too many kids out walking at this hour, so Kyle should be easy to spot if he sticks to main roads. She said to call back if we could think of anything to help them spot Kyle, like what he might be wearing. Oh, Randy, I'm so worried! This is all my fault!"

"I should go out and drive around too. Maybe I can spot him," said Randall. "Where the heck would he go? What was he thinking?"

"Randy, the dispatcher said that we shouldn't go out looking, and that we should stay by the phone," said Zelda. "Please don't go out looking. Stay here with us."

"Yeah, Daddy, I'm scared. Don't leave now," pleaded Addie.

"Sure, sweetie, I'll stay. Come over here, and give me a big hug," said Randall. He hauled her up and they both squeezed each other like getting toothpaste out of a nearly empty tube.

Addie started to cry. "I hope Kyle hasn't got hurted. Maybe a car slided on the road and ran into him."

Randall stroked her hair. "Don't you worry. Kyle probably took his light saber, and he'll slice anything in half that threatens him."

"Yeah, I bet he took it with him," said Addie, wiggling out of Randall's arms. "I'll go check his room and see if it's gone."

"Good idea, Rosebud, go check out his room, and see if he took anything else," said Randall.

Addie ran off and up the stairs. Wondercat skittered out of her way, went off in the corner and hissed. Milky Way had wandered into the kitchen and followed Addie up the stairs.

"So, Zel, what exactly happened between you and Kyle before he disappeared?" Randall tried to retain a calm, non-accusatory voice.

Zelda wrung her hands and looked around the kitchen. "He was coloring on the kitchen table while I was preparing dinner. He asked what I was making, and he wasn't pleased with the menu. He said he didn't like fish sticks or Brussels sprouts and wouldn't eat them. He wanted macaroni and cheese with wieners. Can you imagine that combination? It's gross. When I told him that he'd eat what was put in front of him, he stormed off and said that he'd eat somewhere else. I picked up his drawings from the table and there were crayon marks all over the table. The marks were clearly deliberate, not accidental. When he got upstairs, he shouted down the stairs that Grandma always gave him good food, so why couldn't I? Then he slammed his door. That's the last I saw of him. Then about ten minutes later, I called him down for dinner, but he didn't come. Only Addie came down. We both started looking for him, and then you came home."

"Wow," said Randall. "That was a pretty extreme reaction on his part. It sounds like he went into a rage."

"And it's probably my fault for being so strict with him," moaned Zelda. "If only I'd been less abrupt and parental like my mother. I always hated that. Now I'm doing it to my son."

"It's not all on you," soothed Randall. "Something has been brewing in the kid for a while. Perhaps it's finally coming to the surface. Maybe the session with the shrink has loosened up some of his pent-up anger."

"But what's he angry about?" said Zelda wearily. "Is it me? Am I doing something wrong? I try my best, but my mother was a lousy role model. And they don't teach motherhood in school."

Randall took Zelda's hand and hugged her. She started to cry. "I just want my little boy back!" she sobbed.

Wondercat had started meowing for dinner and nosing around Randall's ankle, but when she heard Addie's thumping footsteps coming back down the stairs, she ran to the corner again with nails skittering across the linoleum. Addie burst into the room, and Wondercat arched her back and hissed again. Milky Way sauntered into the room close behind Addie, looking like Queen of the Prom.

"Daddy, Mommy, Kyle's magic light saber is gone," exclaimed Addie. "I looked all over his room and his heavy winter pants are gone. You know, the ones he wears to school? And his new snow boots are gone too. The purple hat that you knitted for him, Mommy, that's gone too. His pillowcase is off his pillow. And that walking stick we carved from a branch we found when we hiked in the Kepple Moron Woods. That's gone too. Oh, and a bunch of his toys are gone."

Randall looked confused. "I think you mean Kettle Moraine woods."

"Yeah, that's the one," agreed Addie. "Daddy, aren't these good clues?"

"Yes, they are wonderful clues," said Randall. "You are a great detective."

"Like Shylock Combs?" asked Addie.

"Exactly!" said Zelda. "I'm going to call that police dispatcher right now and give her this new information. It may help them to spot Kyle."

Re-Call the Cops

Zelda had to wait for five rings before she got an answer. A male dispatcher answered this time, and Zelda was a bit flummoxed not to get the woman she had talked to. After a few minutes of stumbling around verbally, Zelda explained the previous call.

"Oh, you must have been talking to Tracy," said the male dispatcher. "She just got a call-in from one of our patrol cars. One of our officers picked up a boy walking along the I-94 freeway about two miles from your house. Here, I'll give you to Tracy. She can fill you in on the details."

Zelda looked like she was about to crumble.

"Hello, Mrs. Biedermeier?" said Tracy.

"Yes, yes, that's me," said Zelda. "Did they find my Kyle?"

"It's very likely," said Tracy. "All the boy would tell the officer was that he was going to his grandma's house for supper. He wouldn't give his name, but he said he's seven years old. When the officer asked him why he was walking to his grandma's on the freeway, he said that was the way his dad went when he drove there. Any idea what he might be wearing?"

"Well," said Zelda, "we think he has on a purple knit cap and brown snow pants. He might be carrying a *Star Wars* toy light saber, a walking stick, and maybe a pillowcase with toys in it."

"Then we have your boy," said Tracy. "That's the exact description the officer gave us. He said Kyle had a pillowcase stuffed with toys tied to the end of the walking stick. He was carrying it slung over his shoulder. The light saber was stuffed in his pants. He pulled it out to defend himself when the officer got out of the patrol car and approached him. It took a fair bit of convincing before he put the light saber away. A candy bar seemed to do the trick. Let me radio the patrol car and tell the officer where to deliver Kyle."

"Randy, they found Kyle!" shouted Zelda with her hand over the mouthpiece of the phone. "He was walking east on the freeway to your mom's house."

"Crooked Christ on a jumping frog!" exclaimed Randall. "Just like in the old movie on TV that Kyle and I watched the other day; the kid in the story ran away from home carrying his valuables in a sack tied to the end of a stick. Kyle is a sponge. He absorbs everything he sees. He's the quicker picker upper."

"And about as smart," said Zelda. She took her hand off the mouthpiece as Tracy came back on the phone and told Zelda the patrol car was on the way and would have Kyle back home in about ten minutes. Zelda thanked Tracy profusely and apologized for Kyle causing any trouble.

"Not to worry, Ma'am, that's our job," said Tracy. "You are not the only mother I've had with a runaway little boy this week. It happens more often than you'd think, especially for boys about his age when magical thinking and reality seem to be in a tug of war. I've got one at home just like that, but he's only threatened to run off."

Zelda sighed loudly. "You must be a better mom than me."

Tracy didn't accept that. "Nonsense! It's not hard for me to imagine what you've been through tonight. So do me and Kyle a favor, and don't beat yourself up over it. Just make sure you find out what he was angry about and try to fix it."

Tracy's no-nonsense approach seemed to ease the tension and guilt a bit.

"How'd you know he was angry?" asked Zelda.

"Haven't you noticed? I am clairvoyant," said Tracy. "You take good care now and be sure to offer Officer Pembroke some coffee when he gets there. His shift doesn't end until 2:00 a.m., and it's cold in those patrol cars. Bye now and good luck."

Zelda hung up the phone and let out a huge sigh of relief. "Thank God, they found him, Randy. He's safe. A cop will have him here in about ten minutes. What a nice lady. Randy, I need a hug," said Zelda, melting into his arms. The two hugged for a long minute until Addie got rather jealous.

"Me too, me too," screamed Addie, sending Wondercat scampering again. "I helped find him!"

"You sure did. Come on, Rosebud, squeeze in the middle," said Randall. "Let's make a sandwich. You can be the baloney, and we can be the bread."

"I don't wanna be baloney," said Addie with mock disgust. "I wanna be the hamburger and you guys be the buns."

"Works for me," said Randall, pulling Addie in between the two of them. "Your mom has great buns. Now everybody squeeze until the ketchup squirts out."

"*Eww*," grunted Addie, "that's gross, Daddy."

"Yep, I've got 144 of them."

"Randy, that's so not funny, it's hilarious," said Zelda, laughing despite herself. Milky Way wove herself around their legs and purred loudly. Randall broke up the love fest and put Addie down.

"Addie, honey," said Randall, "Milky Way is hungry. Would you feed her while Mommy and I talk for a few minutes?"

"Sure, Daddy, I'll put out food for Wondercat too. And give both cats fresh water."

"Good thinking, Little Miss Holmes," said Randall, taking Zelda's hand and leading her to the kitchen table where they both sat down on the creaky chairs.

"Zel, let's get our signals straight before the policeman gets here with Kyle. If you're as angry about Kyle's behavior as I am, I know part of you probably wants to shake him silly after the cop leaves and ask him how he could do something this stupid. But the other part of you just wants to be glad he's safe and alive. I say we forget about questioning and punishment and go with how glad we are he's back. I think the best medicine for this little drama is unconditional love. I hope you agree."

"Oh, Randy, that's exactly what I feel too. I am so angry, but I don't think any good would be served by being mad at him. We've got to make him feel that it's okay to tell us what he's angry about, so he doesn't have to resort to such drastic measures to get our attention. He just wants to be noticed and feel that he matters. That's something we all want. He's just a little boy and he doesn't know how to get those things yet. Lord knows, I'm supposed to be an adult, and I don't know how most of the time."

"Fantastic!" Randall gave Zelda a big kiss on the forehead. "Then we're agreed. We don't have much time before they get here. Let's clean up this mess, and make some fresh coffee for the cop."

Zelda rushed around to clean up the kitchen while Randall made coffee. Soon car lights lit up the driveway and the patrol car pulled to a stop at the back door. The red strobes on the patrol car roof were flashing until the car engine was shut off. Zelda rushed to open the back door and ran out to the car. A very large police officer in full regalia emerged from the car and strode up to Zelda. Randall and Addie joined her in the driveway. The garage yard light reflected off the shiny brim of the policeman's peaked cap.

"I gather you are the Biedermeiers?" The officer reached out to shake Randall's hand. He then took Zelda's hand and gave it a squeeze. He put his large hand on Addie's little shoulder. "I'm Sergeant Pembroke. And what's your name?"

"I'm Addie. Have you always been so big? Do you have my brother?" She looked up into his face, which seemed miles away.

"It's nice to meet you, Addie. Aren't you the cutest little pea pod?" said the officer.

"I am not a pea pod. Mommy says I am a rosebud," said Addie sternly.

"I'm sorry, rosebud was going to be my second guess," said Officer Pembroke. "Well, I can tell you are worried about your big brother. I believe I have your missing puzzle piece in the passenger seat. Let me go release him from 'custody.'"

PRODIGAL SON

The policeman went back to the car and opened the passenger door. He took Kyle's hand, helped him out of the car, and gathered up Kyle's belongings. He continued to hold Kyle's hand as the two walked back to Kyle's anxious parents and sister. Zelda leapt forward before the two made it all the way and bent down to wrap her arms around Kyle.

"Kyle, Kyle, my baby boy! I am so sorry I made you mad enough to leave home. I'm so glad you're safe!" Zelda's face was awash with tears.

"I'm sorry too, Mom," said Kyle evenly, but still held the officer's hand. "But I wasn't scared. I had it all planned out, and I wasn't lost. I saw the way to Grandma's house in my dream last night. It was as clear as day. When we drive to Grandma's I pay attention to how we get there. If the policeman hadn't stopped me, I woulda made it."

Sergeant Pembroke interrupted. "Not likely, sonny boy. You were still miles away from Shorewood, and it was getting bitter cold with more snow on the way. You must have been mighty mad about something. What was it set you off?"

Kyle sucked on his lower lip and grunted. "I don't know."

"Mrs. Biedermeier, I've got kids at home too," said Sergeant Pembroke. "I can translate for you, if you don't know already. It means he knows what he's mad about, but he's not talking about it with me around to hear it. Isn't that right, Kyle?"

Kyle's shoulders sagged and he murmured almost inaudibly. "I guess so."

"Ma'am, I think that's my cue to leave Kyle with you and your husband. Kyle, now you be honest with your parents, and tell them what was bothering you. I can't guarantee you won't get some kind of punishment, but this is no time for secrets. You hear me, boy?"

Kyle looked about sheepishly, but still clung to Sergeant Pembroke's hand as if he didn't want to face the music. "Yes, sir," said Kyle meekly.

"Don't worry, everything's going to be alright," said Zelda. "We'll talk about this later. Let's go inside where it's warm."

The group started to move inside to warm up. Kyle still had a death grip on Officer Pembroke's hand, so Zelda took Kyle's other hand and the three walked into the house together. Addie took Randall's hand as they followed the group in through the back door. Officer Pembroke was a big man and the five made quite a crowd in the small hallway.

Officer Pembroke stomped the snow off his boots on the backdoor mat and was first with a solution to the crowding. "Kyle, I'm going to give you back to your mom. She'll get you out of those wet clothes. You're back home and safe now." He took Kyle's hand and passed it over to Zelda.

"Okay," muttered Kyle. He reluctantly let go, and Zelda led Kyle upstairs. Addie ran ahead, carrying Kyle's light saber.

Randall took a breath as he tried to figure out the next appropriate step. "Officer, thanks so much for finding Kyle. We were worried sick. I'll bet you're cold too. I just brewed some fresh coffee. Would you like a cup before you go?"

"That would be a godsend," said Officer Pembroke. "It's been a wild night, and I'm already wiped out with six hours to go on my shift. I was just leaving the scene of a multi-car accident after the ambulances had taken away the victims, and tow trucks cleared away the wrecked cars, when I got the call about a runaway kid. The freeway was tied up for hours, and the traffic really bogged me down."

Randall looked horrified. He thought, *It would have been so easy for Kyle to get in the middle of that, if he'd made it that far.* "Yeah, I almost got caught up in that same freeway traffic jam on the way home from work. Seems like everybody forgot how to drive in the snow today. If I hadn't gotten off the freeway, I could have been in a pileup!"

"You got that right," said Officer Pembroke, taking the proffered cup of coffee and sipping it with satisfaction. "Ah, that's good stuff.

Yeah, as I was about to say, I was just pulling back on the freeway after the accident cleanup when I got the dispatcher call about a missing boy. I just barely noticed a shadow in the breakdown lane next to the freeway. I would have driven on by, but there was this red flash that lit up a small figure momentarily, so I slowed down and turned on my search light. Then I spotted a midget wearing a purple knit hat and carrying something over his shoulder. I pulled off into the emergency lane, got out of the car, and walked up to the little guy."

Kyle reappeared in the hallway with a *Star Wars* blanket around his shoulders and wearing his fuzzy slippers. Zelda followed close behind.

"I'm not a little guy, I'm a kid!" interrupted Kyle. "I wanted to say goodbye before you left. Mom said it was okay."

"Yes, I did," echoed Zelda.

The officer turned to Kyle. "Kyle, you're right. You're a kid and a smart one at that. Your light saber saved you. But why wouldn't you tell me your name when I first talked to you?"

"My mom told me never to talk to strangers," said Kyle. "But then I remembered my dad said it was okay to talk to policemen, 'cause they can help you sometimes. And I was cold, and I figured your car was warm."

"Well, good news, you're home now and . . . ," Officer Pembroke paused as a call came over his shoulder communicator, alerting him to another freeway accident. He pushed the button, and said "Roger that, ten minutes out." He turned to Randall and Zelda. "Oops, sorry folks, my master calls. I've got to tend to this. Here's your cup back."

"No, no," said Zelda. "Keep the cup. We've got plenty of cups. Here, I'll pour you a refill."

"This is one interesting cup," said Pembroke. "There's a bunch of penguins all over it in different poses. What the heck are they doing?"

"*Err*, this is embarrassing," said Randall. "One could say they are all making whoopee."

"I love it," said Pembroke. "This makes my evening. Can't wait to show it to the crew at the station. But right now, I'm out of here. I'll show myself out. Kyle, take good care of your parents and your little sister. Promise?"

"I promise," said Kyle as Officer Pembroke headed out the back door and the doors slammed behind him. The patrol car started with a throaty V-8 roar, the red lights flashing as it backed down the driveway. The siren began to wail as the car headed up Creekside Place.

"Well, I guess that we are the talk of the neighborhood tonight," observed Zelda. "What a nice man, but I'm glad it's over."

"Me too," said Kyle. "Mommy, I'm hungry. Can I have something to eat?"

"Sure thing," said Zelda. "What are you hungry for? Before you answer, it's okay to request wienies with macaroni and cheese."

"Really? That's cool," said Kyle with amazement. "I'm really cold. Can I take a hot bath while you make it?"

"Exactly what I was thinking," said Zelda. "Let's go upstairs and get you in the tub and then put on your jammies. I bet Dad and Addie would be happy to cook up your special order while we do that."

Randall thought it best to let Zelda and Kyle have some time alone and stay out of the interaction for the time being. He agreed to cook up his kid specialty and encouraged them to head right upstairs without further ado.

"Okay, Addie, let's hustle and cook up some grub," said Randall. "Can you get out the box of Krap's Mac and Cheese while I get the wieners ready?"

"Daddy! It's Kraft! I'm on it," replied Addie and headed for the cupboard. "Daddy, how are you right now? When Kyle went missing, it felt like half my heart emptied out. When he was founded, it filled back up."

"Only half your heart?" asked Randall.

"You and Mom were still here so that part stayed filled up," said Addie with a little choke in her voice. She began to tear up, so Randall went over and picked her up again. The two shared another big hug and Randall kissed her neck. Addie put her lips on Randall's neck and gave him a raspberry. After that they both got the giggles that seemed to release the tension of the past several hours. Randall put Addie back down and they set to work with Addie humming "Old McDonald." Randall chimed in with all the appropriate animal sounds.

Randall got water boiling in a pot and dumped in the noodles from the Kraft package. He had a momentary mental panic attack as he imagined what could have happened if Addie had been the one to take the hike in the snow. The image made his stomach flip-flop. It was totally illogical, but he looked over to verify that Addie was still in the kitchen. He found with relief that she was at the counter, standing on her little stool, struggling to cut the wieners out of their plastic package. She cut carefully with a paring knife, her tongue sticking out with the effort. Randall wanted to say something like "be careful" or "don't bite your tongue," but left her to it.

Randall looked back to his stirring, and soon Addie delivered the wieners cut up into coin-sized slices. When the noodles were done, he added the cheese mix and wiener slices. Addie put out a plate, silverware, and a paper napkin. When Randall was in the final stages of stirring the cholesterol progenitors, Addie walked over and hugged Randall's leg. He looked down.

"Daddy," she said in her "teeny tiny" voice. "Please don't worry. I would never run away from home. That would be way too scary."

"Good to know, sweetie. Good to know." He patted her head, while wondering if she'd read his mind. "Well, this glop is ready for consumption. Would you go upstairs and inform the troops that this delicacy is now poised to begin its journey through Kyle's alimentary system?"

"If that means dinner is ready, I'll go tell Mom and Kyle," said Addie.

"Affirmative!" said Randall.

"Daddy! Does that mean yes?" screeched Addie.

"Yes, indeedy," replied Randall as Addie trundled up the stairs with Milky Way close at her heels. For a little girl, she made quite a clomping noise going up the stairs. After she got to the top of the stairs, Randall could clearly hear Addie calling to Kyle that his dinner was ready. He remarked to himself that it was quite a contrast to her teeny tiny voice. Within minutes, Zelda, Kyle, and Addie came thundering down the stairs like a herd of pachyderms and buzzed into the kitchen, closely trailed by the two cats likely imagining that treats might be in store for them as well. Kyle looked warm, fresh, and clean in his PJs, robe, and slippers.

Zelda looked at the food. "Kyle, it looks like Daddy has whipped up your request, but I must say, it looks really gross."

"Yeah, it looks fantastic, doesn't it," said Kyle enthusiastically. "Is it all for me?"

"Yep, each piece of macaroni has your name written on it, and the wienies have your initials branded on them," said Randall. "Addie will be your server. Let me show you to your table."

Randall pulled the chair out for Kyle and sat him down, placing a napkin in his lap. "Sir, would you like to see our wine selection? We have Welch's Grape, a fine purple vintage, and Golden Guernsey Bovine Ambrosia, expiration date in two days. Which would you prefer to stimulate your gustatory receptors and cleanse your palate?"

"Daddy, can't you talk normal?" chided Addie.

"*Hmm*, not to worry, young lady," said Kyle, "I'll have the Welch's and perhaps have the ambrosia after I dine."

"Of course, sir," said Randall and poured him his requested beverage as Addie brought him his plate of mac and weenies. Kyle felt like a king with all the special treatment and started to engulf his food and drink like a macrophage absorbing cellular debris.

As Kyle was downing his dinner, Addie piped up, "When do I get something to eat? I'm hungry too."

"Geez," said Zelda. "In all the commotion I forgot about our dinner. Mommy and Daddy haven't had dinner yet either."

"Thanks for reminding me," said Randall. "I thought the gnawing sensation in the pit of my stomach was a duodenal ulcer brewing. Remind me what you cooked."

"It was Mrs. Fish's Paul sticks, tater tots, and Brussels sprouts, hot about two hours ago," said Zelda. "Now it's a bit more eclectic. I'll try to reheat it. There's not much else left in the house, and it's too late to go out now, especially in this storm."

"*Eww*, Mommy," said Addie. "Do I have to eat that?"

"If Kyle is willing to share his mac and cheese, would you like that?" asked Zelda.

"Yes, but only if Kyle won't get upset," said Addie.

"No sweat, Sis, you can have what's left in the pot, as long as I can have ice cream for dessert," offered Kyle. "But then Addie gets ice cream too."

"It's like making a deal with the devil," said Randall. "It's okay with me, but if Mom and I have to eat reheated fish sticks then we get ice cream too."

"Goody, goody gumdrops," screeched Addie as she got herself a plate and served herself the rest of the mac and weenies.

"We do have ice cream, don't we?" asked Randall apprehensively.

"Oh, ye of little faith," said Zelda. "I may not be the best homemaker, but keeping enough ice cream around is the second commandment of shopping. Thou shalt always buy ice cream to please the masses."

The reheated food wasn't as bad as Zelda and Randall thought it would be. It was just half as bad. Soon there was only the sound of silverware clinking and scraping on plates as all the gustatory delectables were consumed. Subsequently, there were eructation and contented sighs as chairs were pushed away from the table to make room for bulging bellies.

"So Kyle, are you feeling better?" asked Randall.

"That was great, Dad. Now I'm really stuffed," said Kyle as he failed to stifle a prodigious yawn.

"Looks like all the food has gone to your eyelids," said Zelda. "I think we should go back upstairs, have you brush your teeth, and get you to bed."

"Don't you and Dad want to yell at me first?" asked Kyle cautiously.

"Not tonight, young laddie," said Randall. "We will talk about this little escapade when everybody has gotten some rest, and we have had some time to think things through. For now we don't want you to worry about it. There won't be any yelling. We're just going to figure some things out so that we can talk to each other before you get so upset that you feel you have to do something as drastic as run away from home."

"Yeah, Kyle, I was really worried," said Addie. "I'm glad you're home. I would be scared to sleep upstairs without you in your room with your light saber."

"Addie's right," said Zelda. "You're an important part of this family, and your happiness is important to all of us."

Snow Night

Kyle looked relieved. "Mommy, look out the window! The snow is really coming down now. If it keeps snowing like this, we might not have school tomorrow."

Kyle and Addie jumped out of their chairs and ran to the window. Randall wondered about the sudden tack change. Perhaps Kyle was using the snow as an excuse to divert from the topic at hand.

Randall joined Kyle and Addie at the window. "Holy cow!" When he saw how much snow had fallen, he rejected the idea that Kyle was using diversionary psychology. "Look at the outdoor picnic table. There's at least a foot of snow piled up on it already. You guys may be right about school, but one thing's for sure; your ol' Dad won't get a snow day. They'll expect me to be there even if I have to go by dogsled."

"What say we worry about that in the morning?" said Zelda. "Let's get you two up to bed."

"Can we have a story?" asked Kyle.

"Yeah, one of Daddy's made-up stories," added Addie.

"Kids, it's already late," countered Zelda.

"But we're both so wound up that we won't be able to go to sleep, right, Addie?" said Kyle.

"Yeah, I'm as tight as a twisty rubber band," said Addie.

"*Hmm*, I feel like I'm hearing the playback of something I've said in the past. Well, if it's okay with your dad . . ." offered Zelda.

"Come on, kids," said Randall. "Last one up the stairs is a strangulated hernia. Oh, look at them go. I better call my surgeon."

"Randy, you're such a goof," said Zelda, punching him in the arm for emphasis. "Get your derrière up there. Can I come up and listen?"

"Sure, now all I have to do is make something up in the time it takes to ascend the stairs. Hey, there's an idea. I think I'll use my ass end to ascend instead of my legs. That will buy me some time to get creative."

"How about telling a McGillicuddy and Agadaboo story? That always works. Just don't make it too scary," offered Zelda.

"That's a great idea. I'll do the one where they ask for spaghetti."

The McGillicuddy and Agadaboo stories were a continuing series of tales purportedly from Randall's childhood in which the two characters lived in the coal bin in the basement of Randall's childhood house. They only appeared when Randall was alone in the basement, and they threatened to live in his bedroom closet unless he brought them food. They had diverse appetites, which required Randall to go to extraordinary lengths to convince his mother to make the food they requested. Randall tried to avoid going into the basement for this reason, but his mother would send him downstairs to shovel coal into the furnace or fetch preserves or vegetables from the cold storage bin. Because of this, he couldn't always avoid going down in the basement by himself. Every time he did so, he was terrified that McGillicuddy and Agadaboo would appear.

McGillicuddy looked kind of like a leprechaun but wore lederhosen and an Alpine brimmed hat with a luminescent yellow feather in it. He had yellow teeth to match, spoke in a hoarse whisper, and was very sarcastic. Agadaboo looked remarkably like the tar baby from Uncle Remus's tale about Brer Rabbit and the briar patch. He wore red shorts and a white smock that contrasted starkly with his black and shiny skin. He never spoke out loud, but you could always hear what he said inside your head. It had kind of a slurpy sound. They were both incessantly hungry.

Even though Randall's father had a workshop in the basement, McGillicuddy and Agadaboo never appeared when he was downstairs. They claimed it was because of the loud polka music he played and the stinky cigar smoke. Sometimes they told Randall that they might come upstairs and scare his mother if he didn't bring them pickled herring or kosher dill pickles. This time they wanted spaghetti with meatballs in marinara sauce. It took Randall some subtle hints and suggestions to get his mother to cook spaghetti. In addition, he had to walk up to the corner butcher shop and buy meat for the meatballs.

Randall's mother made him take along his cocker spaniel, Waffles, since the dog needed a walk. Halfway to the butcher shop, he and Waffles encountered a man walking a little fuzzy dog. The two dogs were busy smelling rear ends when Randall asked the man what kind of dog he had. The man said it was a little Shih Tzu. Randall told the man that Waffles could be annoying as well.

Then after Randall bought the food supplies and got two quarters in change, the quarters fell through the hole in his pocket and into his shoe. When he got home, his mother asked for the change and Randall found only a holy pocket. His mother accused Randall of using the money to buy a Three Musketeers bar. She wouldn't believe him until she performed a mandatory chocolate cheek check on Randall and found no evidence of candy chicanery.

He explained about the hole in his pocket and his mother told him that money often does that to pockets. A light bulb appeared above Randall's head, and he took off his shoe on the holy pocket side. Sure enough, there were the quarters nestled in the bottom of his Buster Browns right along with Tige who lived there too.

Randall's mother was pleased that Randall had not lied after all, and she cooked up the supplies into a nice spaghetti dinner. The really hard part was for Randall to figure a way to sneak two servings downstairs without his mother noticing it. He went outside briefly after he'd eaten two helpings, saying that he needed to pass some gas. Soon he came back inside and told his mother that two hobos had come down the driveway and were asking for food. Since the train tracks were near the house, and hobos often frequented the neighborhood, offering to do chores for food, this seemed a plausible story. Randall's mother was known to be friendly to hobos.

Randall told his mother that the two hobos would sweep out the garage for a meal. She served up two helpings of spaghetti on plastic plates with plastic sporks and sent Randall out to feed the "hobos." Randall, instead, snuck downstairs and gave the plates to McGillicuddy and Agadaboo, then hustled outside and swept out the garage. When he finished, he went back downstairs and collected the plastic ware. By that time, McGillicuddy and Agadaboo had finished their portions and were asking for chocolate cake. Randall didn't know what to do, because there was no chocolate cake in the house.

Randall's eyelids had drooped closed somewhere around the hobo portion of the story, but he had continued talking without realizing that Kyle and Addie were dead to the world. He was approaching that condition rapidly as well until he heard Zelda's voice come from out of the mists.

"So what happened next?" asked Zelda. "How did Randall finagle getting chocolate cake?"

Randall's eyelids rolled up and flapped like window shades. "What? Oh, yeah. *Er*, to be continued," whispered Randall regaining consciousness. "*Hmm*, I think it's high time for a certain big girl to crawl into her widdle bed with her exhausted widdle boyfriend."

"Okay, Daddy, but would you please tuck me in bed?" said Zelda in her little girl voice. "And bring some chocolate cake when you come home from work tomorrow."

"Sure thing. Don't forget to brush your teeth."

Later, when Randall came to bed, Zelda was still awake. He got under the covers, and they got into the spoon position together, the one that they used when all was well. As he was slowly sinking into a sea of alpha waves, Randall came briefly alert.

"Zel, I've got to tell you something," Randall said softly. "Are you still awake?"

"Just barely," moaned Zelda.

"There are two things I want to say. First, I've decided to see a shrink on my own. It's mostly because of all the wacky stuff that's been happening, like the Swindell incident and the telepathic message from Uncle Phil. It goes back, too, to the lawn mower episode with Addie. I've got to talk to somebody who can make some sense out of it all. It's driving me bonkers. And I just need better ways to deal with the stress at work."

"And here at home too. I know it hasn't been easy," interrupted Zelda.

"Yeah, I was getting to that. It may help me deal with Kyle's issues," continued Randall.

"And me. Don't forget about me. I haven't exactly been a picnic lunch," said Zelda, with guilt in her voice.

"To be honest, yes, but I want you to stop being so hard on yourself," said Randall.

"It's just leftovers that were drilled into me when I was a kid. My dad was so . . ." she stammered and started to feel tears welling up.

"I understand. A little bad parenting goes a long way. Anyway, the second thing I want to say is that I know you probably still feel responsible for Kyle's little freeway escapade. But you shouldn't. Something like this has been brewing for a while like pus in a pimple. It was bound to pop with the right squeeze. What's important is you handled the crisis brilliantly, and I'm really proud of you. I don't think any mother could have done it better. I can guarantee you that Kyle is going to come out of this just fine. And you too. Now no back talk. Understand?"

"Thanks, Randy, I needed that. I love you. I hope you know that."

"I do. I've always known. And you know that I love you too."

"Enough chatter. Get your ass to sleep."

"Yes, Mother."

Snow Help

By morning, the snow had stopped, and the temperature dropped. The sun was shining brightly, giving the impression of warmth but not the reality. Randall was up at 6:30 and looked out the living room window to assess the snow conditions. To his dismay, he could see about fifteen inches of snow and drift in the driveway. He turned on the radio for the local news, learned that the schools were closed, and that many happy children would be enjoying a snow day. Randall was not one of them. And before he could even attempt to get to the VA, he'd have to do just a bit of shoveling. To his surprise, when he went into the kitchen for coffee, Zelda, Kyle, and Addie were up already and scarfing down cereal.

"Hey, how come you guys are up?" asked Randall.

"We're going to help you shovel the driveway," announced Addie with an air of pride.

"Yeah, it's our reward to you for having to eat mushy fish sticks last night," said Zelda.

"And it's to say thank you for telling us a great story before bed. Please finish telling it tonight. I want to find out what happened after the dill pickles," said Kyle.

"*Hmm*, quite a bit happened after the pickles," said Randall. "You guys must have drifted off to La La Land earlier than I thought. I guess I told part of the story with my eyes closed."

"Randy, I sleep next to you," said Zelda. "Sometimes you tell stories in your sleep."

"Are they any good?"

"Yes. I've recorded a few, and I'm saving them for when I might need them."

Randall shuddered about what she might need them for, finished his coffee, and went out to the garage for shovels. He wished he'd popped for the snow blower he'd seen at Nitz Hardware. He admonished himself for being such a cheapskate. Now he was paying anyhow, just in a different way. Soon the rest of the crew was out helping. Zelda and Kyle were actually moving quite a bit of snow. Addie was trying her best, but she might as well have been using a soup spoon for all the snow she was getting shoveled. The snow was way too deep for her to lift high enough.

By 7:30 they had made it about two thirds of the way down the driveway, so Randall went inside to call the department to let them know he might be about twenty minutes late. Fortunately, Doris had made it in and told Randall not to rush because Grace and Molly were also stuck in snow, and most of the outpatients had called in to say they'd be late. Also the VA plows were just getting the parking lot cleared.

Back at Creekside Place, the city snowplow had left a huge bank of snow at the end of the driveway that slowed down the driveway clearing progress but, by 8:00, they'd cleared enough to get the car out to the street. Randall went back inside for a coffee refill followed by his trio of elf helpers. They struggled out of their snow gear and had very pink faces. Randall gave them all hugs and kisses for their help and loaded his work gear in the car.

"Randy, be sure to call when you get to work," said Zelda, standing at the open back door. "The driving could be treacherous out there. Be careful."

"I will," he said, blowing Zelda a kiss. "Get those kids warmed up and have some fun today. Build a snowman or a snow fort later. It's supposed to warm up to the low thirties and it should be good packing."

Randall backed down the driveway and tested the road. It was pretty slippery; he wasn't sure he could make it up the Creekside hill without a running start. He maneuvered the Scirocco in the street so he could back the car up the driveway. Once backed up as far as the garage, he gunned the engine and got a forward running start down the driveway. The car launched out onto the street and, using his momentum to scoot right, he shot the car up Rockway, which was not as steep as Creekside. Despite losing traction briefly on the steepest part of Rockway, he kept the car going forward and made it up to 84th Street. From there the roads were clear enough to make it to work by 8:30.

It was a surprisingly slow day in the department, mostly due to the snowstorm. Many of the outpatients scheduled for the day, for consultation or follow-up, could not make it in, and the bus carrying patients from Iron Mountain VA in the Upper Peninsula of Michigan was canceled. As a result, only a few inpatients showed up for follow-up, and there was one consultation to see. The weekly reviews had already been done for the week, and there were only a few minor problems with the patients under treatment. Randall was so exhausted from the stresses of the previous day and the aerobic shoveling workout that he dozed off in the afternoon while dictating the consultation report. Just before he phased out, he dictated a description of Agadaboo in the middle of a review of dosimetry calculations.

Doris heard the sound of a patient chart falling apart on the floor and came in to find Randall asleep with his head on a pile of papers on his desk. She gently shook his shoulder, and he bolted upright. She couldn't stop her squealing laughter at the backward imprint of a Xeroxed lab report on his forehead. Doris cleaned the print from his forehead with an alcohol swab. She pronounced that she had cured him of mycosis fungoides and sent him home.

Snow Fort

When Randall rolled into the garage, he closed his eyes with fatigue while still seated in the car and drifted off a bit. The mini nap didn't last long as he was aroused by a fist knocking on the driver's side window. It was Zelda, who'd come out to the garage to waylay him.

"Oh, no, not again!" exclaimed Randall, opening the car door and getting drowsily out of the car.

"No, everything is okay," said Zelda. "I just wanted to catch you before you got inside. The kids have something they want to show you before it gets too dark."

Kyle and Addie bounded out the back door like dogs welcoming their master home. The kids looked so excited that Randall thought they might pee themselves.

"Daddy, come to the front yard and see what we made today," announced Kyle in a loud, proud voice. "I was the contractor, and Mom and Addie were subcontractors."

"Yeah, I subcontracted a lot," crowed Addie.

"Alright then," said Randall, waking up a bit more. "Lead on, McDuff."

The kids led Randall down a carefully shoveled path, past the front door and posed like Barker's Beauties on *The Price is Right*. They gestured to the large snow fort that they had erected in the front yard just in front of the living room windows. The fort was at least eight feet wide by three feet deep by three feet high. It had an igloo-like roof with a front entry opening big enough for an adult to crawl inside on hands and knees.

"Holy jumping caterpillar tractors!" yelled Randall. "That is the best snow fort I have ever laid eyes on. I can't believe you guys did all that. It's more than I accomplished today. Can I go inside the fort?"

"Darn tootin," said Kyle. "I'll lead the way."

After a bit of scuffling about, all four Biedermeiers were able to squeeze inside the fort. It was actually pretty warm inside.

"Hey, how about you and Addie sleep in the fort tonight?" suggested Randall.

"No way," said Addie and she scrambled back outside.

"Just kidding," said Randall. He followed Addie out of the fort entrance and lay down in the snow to show her how to make a snow angel.

"Hey, I want to make one," said Kyle, emerging from the fort. By the time Zelda squeezed her way out, all three were making snow angels. Zelda joined in and said she was going to make a snow devil with horns.

"Hey, you guys wait here," said Randall, getting up out of the snow. "I've got just the thing to finish off the fort."

Randall went to the garage and came back with a small American flag. He struck a dramatic pose in front of the snowy edifice and stuck the flag on the roof.

"I now officially dub this structure Fort Biedermeier. Henceforth, we will defend our hallowed kingdom. Klingons beware. Let us all give the Biedermeier salute."

All four Biedermeiers put the thumb of their right hand on their noses, wiggled their fingers and did a juicy raspberry with their tongue and lips.

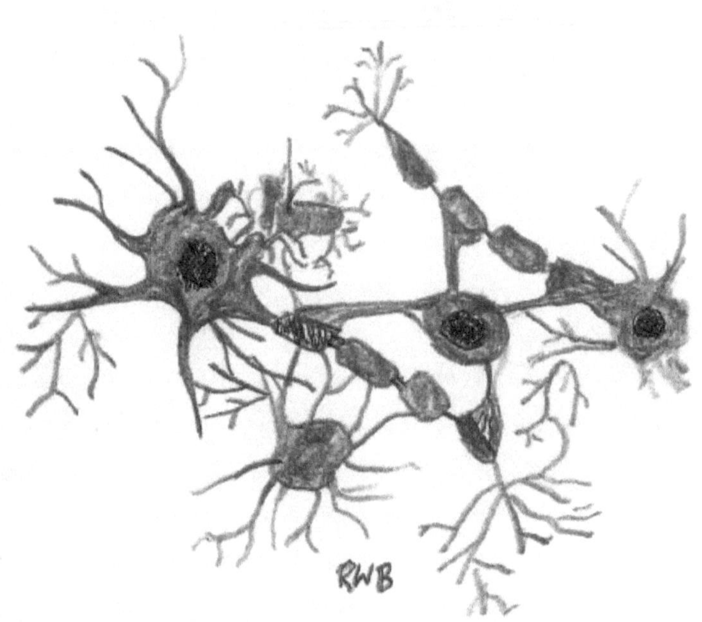

CHAPTER 26

———

QUANTA

"Lead from the back, and let others believe they are in front."

— Nelson Mandela

ACCORDION TO HOYLE

Randall had arranged a longer meeting with Joe Shepard to follow up on their discussion about what they were calling "quantum entangled communication," reluctant to invoke the term ESP. They considered that too narrow and nonspecific for an ability that might be as natural as hearing. It would be their shorthand for nonverbal communication at a distance, until they could assign a more scientifically appropriate nomenclature. They disdained using traditional scientific terms, like telepathy or telekinesis.

Joe had invited two of his colleagues to the meeting: an adult psychiatrist and a clinical psychologist who was also a high-level Freemason. They had discussed adding a cleric but couldn't decide which denomination. Neither Randall nor Joe were avid churchgoers, so there were few choices among their contacts. Randall's assignment was to bring a physicist with a good background in atomic and subatomic theory. Dan Graham was at the top of that list.

Since Dan's arrival he had impressed Randall with his capabilities in Radiation Physics. He was every bit as knowledgeable as Bob Storch despite not yet having his PhD. Even with just a master's degree, he had so far outshone Storch in many ways. One of those ways was his easy personality. At his department welcoming party, he had distinguished himself as personable with a good sense of humor. The staff had taken to him very readily.

A few days later, when Randall had a break between patients, he padded quietly into Dan's office. Dan was so engrossed in his work that he didn't notice Randall walk up behind him.

"Hey, Dan," said Randall, quietly. Dan nearly jumped out of his seat.

"Holy Mary!" exclaimed Dan. "Could you make some noise when you come in? Nearly had a code brown. Buy some squeaky shoes. I'll pay half."

"Oh, how you exaggerate," said Randall. "I figured you'd welcome a break from the tedium. Here, I brought you fresh coffee." Randall handed Dan a cup.

"Now that you mention it, I could use a breather. Tedium is the order of the day when you do QA measurements for the quarterly report on the Linac." Dan accepted the proffered coffee. "Oh, and it's in your doctor's urine specimen cup. That's your favorite cup, so you must want something."

"Dan, Dan, how could you think so little of me?" asked Randall with a grand arm wave. "Why can't I just be concerned about your well-being? Now that I mention it, how are you doing today? You do look a bit tired."

"Well, your friendly visits are usually tied to a special favor you want to wheedle out of me, but I'll give you the benefit of the doubt this once. In fact, it's no wonder I look a bit peaked today. I am a bit sleep deprived. Had a honey of a weird dream last night."

"Oh, really! Do tell," said Randall, sitting down on a large equipment box next to Dan's desk. "I have weird dreams all the time. You know, the really vivid ones. Tell me about yours."

"It was vivid alright," said Dan, with a deep sigh. "I invented a new type of accordion. It looked just like a regular piano accordion, but it had a synthesizer that made the sound. You could make it sound like ten different instruments from a flute to a tuba, depending which button you pushed. When you'd squeeze the accordion in and out, each note played produced vocalized preprogrammed words with the sound of the selected instrument. You could program two, three, or four-word phrases, depending on whether you wanted a polka, a waltz, or a mazurka."

"That is odd," observed Randall. "I'm trying to imagine how that would work."

"Okay, let's say you select three words for a 3/4-time waltz and an instrument. Go ahead and choose."

"Okay, how about the 'You Don't Say' waltz in trumpet mode?" asked Randall.

"That's a good choice," said Dan, with a crooked smile. "To be clear, with each note played on the keyboard, my accordion vocalizes the words 'you don't say' with a voice that sounds like a trumpet. So with each note the three words repeat to form whatever melody you choose. Try it."

Randall knit his eyebrows for a moment as he thought of a waltz and began to sing *you don't say* to the tune of "Waltzing Matilda" while trying to make his voice sound like a trumpet.

Dan narrowed his eyes, trying not to wince. "Not bad. It's almost listenable."

"Seems like it could be done with today's technology," said Randall. "Synthesizers can make just about any sound. All it would take would be to embed some electronics in an old Lawrence Welk special. Then the world would be your oyster. You better take out a patent soon before the idea is co-opted. Have you got a name for the beast?"

"Yeah, I was thinking of calling it 'Voccetone' and importing it from Italy." Dan held an invisible accordion in his hands.

"I think I can say that. Vo Che Tony? Does that sound right?" said Randall.

"Yeah, that's right. Like *soto voce* but with two C's." Dan pushed some desk supplies over to make space for paper and wrote out the word in his very precise, small script.

Randall reached into his invisible wallet. "I'd buy one. Make it expensive to give it an aura of exclusivity."

Dan smiled. "A decent professional accordion costs up to $8,000, so I was thinking $4,995 would seem like a bargain."

"Sounds like you've done your homework," said Randall.

"Always," said Dan. "Now what's really on your mind?" He looked at Randall with penetrating, slitted eyes.

Quantum Cookery

"Coises, foiled again." Randall sat back and slipped off his shoes. It signaled Randall's quest would not be brief. "Actually, I wanted to pick your brain about quantum theory."

"Nice smooth segue. Fortunately, you've picked one of my favorite subjects for brain picking." Dan folded his hands, professorially. "What is it you're looking for?"

"Well," said Randall, sounding a bit pained. "Quantum theory wasn't really my focus when I did radiation physics in training, but lately I've been doing more reading about it in connection with some other matters. Frankly, I've found some of the concepts kind of 'out there' compared to the classical Newtonian physics I learned. I'm hoping you can explain the basics to me like I was ten years old."

"So an explanation that's close to your actual emotional age?" Dan grinned crookedly.

"You've got it," said Randall. "If you don't have the time now, that's cool. We could do it when it's more convenient. I suspect it might take some little time for me to absorb the new data."

"Not the ten-year-old version," said Dan. "Besides, I'm in no rush to finish this QA report. You never read them anyhow."

"I do so read them," countered Randall. "Well, at least the conclusions on the last page."

"Tell you what," said Dan. "You refill my urine specimen cup with coffee, and by the time you get back, I'll have the conclusions concluded and we can wax quantum. How's that?"

"Deal," said Randall and set off on his errand. When Randall returned, they settled in and began the tutorial.

Dan rolled up his sleeves. "First thing to get straight is that classical physics is different than quantum physics."

"I gather," said Randall.

"Put as simply as possible, classical or Newtonian physics, also known as the "standard model," describes what happens at the macro level." Dan picked up a signed Brewer's baseball from the corner of his desk. "For example, gravity causes the apple to fall from a tree." He dropped the ball with a satisfying clunk. "For every action there is an equal and opposite reaction. All that stuff. It's what happens to complex matter like planets, people, and plants."

"Got it, the three P's" said Randall. "Big picture stuff."

"Right. Quantum physics," Dan continued, leaning forward, "also known as quantum theory or quantum mechanics, is the physics of the building blocks of matter, namely, atoms and subatomic particles. Quantum physics lies within classical physics but exhibits behavior that is not well explained by classical physics. To make it even more difficult, quantum behavior is often counterintuitive. It requires a completely different way of looking at our reality."

"I get what you're saying. Remind me: who was the physicist who proposed our classic picture of the atom?" asked Randall. "I knew it at one time."

"That was Ernest Rutherford around 1911," said Dan. "Kind of coincided with Einstein's relativity theories. Once we go subatomic, we're in Quantum-land. I'll honor your request and oversimplify. Imagine that we take Newton's apple, the one that fell off the tree, and keep dividing it until we get to its smallest part. That would be the atom. The term *atom* initially meant the smallest unit that matter could be divided into but, as you well know, if you could use an imaginary atom-sized micro-knife, you can divide the atom still further into subatomic components." Dan mimicked a tiny knife cutting his baseball.

"Kind of a picometer sized X-ACTO knife," remarked Randall.

"Right! One trillionth of a meter. About as far as I can run." Dan grabbed a large eraser and some tacks from the drawer. "The three basic subatomic particles are electrons, protons, and neutrons. This eraser represents the nucleus." He placed the tacks at the edges of the desk. "These tacks represent the electrons, which have a much lower mass. The negatively charged electrons orbit around the nucleus. The nucleus is made up of positively charged protons and neutrally charged neutrons, both with much larger masses than the electron."

"It's coming back to me now," said Randall. "Wasn't Rutherford from New Zealand and dubbed the Father of Nuclear Physics? Oh, and wasn't he the first to discover the emission of a subatomic particle?"

"Very good recall," Dan pointed at Randall. "Yes, in 1917 he bombarded nitrogen nuclei with alpha particles and found the emission of protons. But that's kind of going off on a tangent. What I was aiming for was that he determined that the atom is mostly empty space between the positively charged nucleus and the negatively charged electron."

"So is this where quantum theory comes in?" asked Randall with a frustrated head scratch.

"Just about," answered Dan. "The unit *quanta* means the smallest-possible discrete unit of any physical property such as matter or energy. Heisenberg and Pauli coined the term 'quantum mechanics' in the early 1920s. So you could say that the study of the micro-world has been around since then."

"It boggles the mind that this has been studied for just the last fifty years. And that raises a new question," said Randall. "If all matter is made up of atoms, which are mostly empty space, how can matter be solid?"

"Yes, but that's a bit off topic. Stop being tangential," scolded Dan. "Keep all your electrons in orbit! Now if we continue cutting the subatomic components of Newton's apple with an even smaller X-ACTO knife, we find there are smaller parts that make them up, called quarks. I could confuse the heck out of you by naming all the quarks, but that would be overkill for our purposes."

Randall shifted and kicked his shoes aside. "I get it. Alright, so we go from elements to atoms; from atoms to subatomic particles; and from subatomic particles to quarks," summarized Randall. "Is there a bit smaller than quarks?" Randall was well out of his depth at this point, although something familiar from his reading was resonating in his gray matter.

"Yes," said Dan. "That brings us to so-called string theory." Dan surprised Randall by bringing a rubber band out of his desk drawer. "It's called that because it's thought that inside each quark is a sort of vibrating string of energy." Dan stretched the rubber band between his hands. "Imagine a violin string being plucked, and the frequency of that vibration of energy determines the characteristics of that specific quark."

Randall reached up and plucked the rubber band, creating a resonant *twang*.

Dan smiled. "The math developing that theory is still evolving, but for it to work out it seems we need to make some significant leaps."

"How so?" Randall *twanged* the band again.

"First, it looks like there is not just one vibratory frequency attached to each quark," said Dan, stretching the band a little more. Randall plucked it again. This time the pitch was higher.

"The strings can modulate their shapes and each modulation changes the vibration pattern. There may be multiple, if not an infinite, number of variations possible."

As Dan stretched and released the rubber band, Randall plucked out a simple tune. "Perhaps the vibratory changes modulate what the quark does without altering what it is. Maybe it's a quarky language for communicating information. We don't know yet."

Randall raised his arms, as if conducting. "The music of the universe? *Hmm*, very interesting. This is starting to make me dizzy."

Dan started tapping his toes to the rhythm. "The symphony of syncope! Take a breath and stay with me. Second, and perhaps the biggest leap, is that for the math to work out, some string theorists posit that there are up to ten dimensions, not four. But the extra dimensions are not 'out there,' but enfolded upon each other inside each quark."

Randall grabbed the rubber band, stretched it between two fingers, and plucked out another tune, sounding vaguely like "Old McDonald."

"Dang, I never thought of it that way. That almost makes sense. And here I thought we had just three dimensions."

Dan snatched his rubber band back. "Stop plucking around! Trust me on this, there are actually four proven dimensions," said Dan. "I could show you, but then I'd have to . . . stray too far from our garden path. Keep on track, Dr. B."

Randall put his hands in his lap and rounded his shoulders. "So what do you think? Where are these extra six dimensions? Are they out in the universe somewhere or folded inside the quarks?"

"Good question!" Dan grabbed a piece of paper and scrunched it into a ball. "Most believe they are folds within folds inside the quarks."

Randall looked more closely. "Looks remarkably like a human brain."

Dan took a flat piece of paper and placed it precisely in the middle of the desk. "Some have proposed parallel or multiple universes." He placed a second, then a third, paper on top of the first. "Each universe is almost identical but slightly different and separate. It's all still on the table."

Randall let out a big whoosh of air. "Or the desk, in this case. So there could be infinite reams of universes! And that's just on THIS desk. Wow, this is some spooky stuff," said Randall. "Now I can see why it's been a pet subject of yours."

"You calling me spooky?" asked Dan with a quirky smile. "Now that we've dissected the atom to bare bones, it's time to cover how the quantum components behave. That's where the real spooky stuff happens. Before we start, I am going to point out that, for simplicity, I may refer to subatomic components and quarks as particles. However, most physicists today believe that a better description of them is not as particles but fields of energy. You'll see why as I go along. So think of the term *particles* as just a shorthand."

Bathroom Break

"You know," said Randall. "I need to visit the used coffee depot for a few minutes. Can we take a break and resume when I'm back?"

"No problem," said Dan. "I need to join you. And I think I need a coffee refresher to finish the story."

"Sounds good, let's go," said Randall and he led the charge.

Randall and Dan quick-stepped down the hall to the only men's room near the department, which was also used by patients and mostly staff from both Engineering and Physical Therapy. There were two wall-mounted urinals and two stalls, one with an enclosure and one without, for disabled patient access. To open the sliding door, a wall-mounted switch-plate had to be pushed. When the pair got to the door, a man was yelling from the inside of the men's room and pounding on the door. On quick inspection, Dan noted the sliding door had come off its top rollers and ground itself into the floor.

"Holy cats," said Randall. "I think there's a patient trapped in there. Let's see if we can slide the door open."

They both grabbed the door edge and pushed hard left. The door grudgingly moved enough to let them get through the opening. Inside they found a patient, in green-striped pajamas and robe, lying on the floor next to an overturned wheelchair. Randall checked the man out and found him to be unhurt. On questioning, the patient was a paraplegic down from the ward for PT. He'd gotten in the john alright, but the door had jammed shut on closing, and he'd fallen out of his chair trying to push the door back open. Randall and Dan got the wheelchair upright again and hoisted the man back into his chair. The door opening still wasn't wide enough to fit the wheelchair through, but the patient started banging the wheelchair against the door as if that would open it.

"*Whoa* there," yelled Randall. "Stop that or you'll really break the door. Just a second and we'll try to open it further, but right now I've got to pee like a racehorse, so you're gonna have to wait a sec."

"Me too," echoed Dan, who unzipped as he shuffled to the wall urinal. Randall, who suffered from a severe case of "shy bladder," even when at overload, instead chose the enclosed stall and almost didn't make it. While the two were relieving excessive hydraulic pressure, Bob Guarino, one of the draftsmen from Engineering, squeezed through the door opening and hastily made his way to the open urinal next to Dan. Bob surveyed the situation as he let go.

"Well, piss on it!" Bob yelled loud enough to cause midstream shutdown for both Randall and Dan. "I just fixed that son-of-a-bitching door two hours ago."

Dan dribbled in his pants and didn't hold back a verbal response.

"Well, it looks like you did your usual piss poor VA job," Dan yelled back. "That patient got trapped in here, and we had to rescue him. Dr. B will be filing an incident report, right?"

"You bet," Randall shouted from inside the enclosure. "Bob, maybe with your help we can open the door wide enough to get the wheelchair out. That might mitigate the need for a report."

The cantankerous old vet held up his arms. "Hey! Would you pansy ass doctors quit your whining?! I've been stuck in here for forty-five minutes, and I gotta tell ya, it was better lying keester-up in the air on that disgusting tile floor than listening to you three yapping in this god-forsaken echo chamber about your ivory tower problems!"

Bob paused, mollified mid-complaint. "You're right, sir. I bet this has been awful for you, I'm sorry you got stuck in here." Bob zipped up and turned to Dan. "I had to order a part for the door. Can't fix it until the part comes. We don't have another functioning john on this side of the building, so I didn't want to shut it down."

"Why not leave the door open until it's fixed?" asked Dan. "Disable the switch until it's repaired. None of us are so shy we can't use it with the door open for a few days."

"Quite logical," said Bob. "Have to clear it with the chief though."

"Just tell him that you did it on his behalf, so he doesn't have to run upstairs to relieve himself."

"Yeah, sounds like a plan," said Bob.

The vet rolled his chair up to Bob, hitting him in the shins. "You guys done yet!? Open this sucker!"

The three ambulatory men leaned on the door, heaved, and got it to slide open another two feet. At that point it was firmly stuck. Bob offered to return the patient to his ward. The vet wheeled himself down the hall with Bob trying to keep up. Randall and Dan laughed their derrières off and trundled back to the department to resume their quantal dissection.

They settled back in Dan's office with fresh cups of coffee. "Now where were we before we got pissed off?" asked Dan.

"I think we were about to start on the odd behavior of quantum entities," said Randall.

"Right!" Dan held up his hand, waggling each finger as he made his points. "In summary, we're going to briefly cover five subtopics: one, wave-particle duality, two, quantum superposition, three, quantum tunneling, four, quantum spin, and five, quantum entanglement. I can't go into each in any depth, but I'll try to give you the broad brushstrokes."

"Crikey," said Randall. "Sounds dicey."

"By the way," added Dan. "I think I'll use the electron for the illustration of the five behaviors. And I am not going to discuss questions like 'how do we know?' right now. You'll have to accept it as proven."

"Makes sense," said Randall. "The electron is the basis for how we make radiation with the Linac. I don't mind a bit of mystery."

"Good," said Dan. "Let's start with number one. Some think *wave-particle duality* is the quantum world's defining feature. As I've said, all the stuff around us and in us is composed of discrete particles, but these particles can also behave like waves at the quantum level." Dan drew a wave on the stack of paper. "It's like waves in the ocean with peaks and troughs or the flowing of ripples in a pond. The electron can behave both ways. By the same token, energy, like photons of light, travels as waves, but can also behave like particles." He drew a sun with rays shining down on the waves.

"How can one thing behave two different ways?" asked Randall, screwing up his face. "But wait. Einstein's $E = mc^2$ basically says that mass and energy are interchangeable. Is that it?"

"Essentially," said Dan. "In addition, when the electron is orbiting its nucleus, it behaves as a wave." He demonstrated with the eraser and one of the tacks. "Its location at one point in time is only a probability, and it's only in that probable spot as a particle when it's observed. Don't ask what observed means. That gets complicated. This leads directly to the next property: *superposition*."

"Is that in the book of *Kama Sutra*?" asked Randall.

"Very droll," Dan grimaced. "It means our little wavy electron particle can be in two places at once or do two different things simultaneously."

"The ultimate multitasker, our little guy," remarked Randall. "You're right. Neither of these behaviors is intuitive. Alas, they defy our observations of what happens in the macro world. Although I would love to figure out how to get quantum mechanical myself and be simultaneously at work and at home."

Dan gave Randall a disgusted look. "Indeed. Stay in your orbit, Randall. The next one, *quantum tunneling*, is related to superposition. Let's say our little overachieving electron is traveling along in wave form and encounters a wall made up of copper atoms, for example." Dan held up the coffee cup and a tack. "The likelihood of the tack getting through the cup would seem to be the same as you walking through a concrete wall. But there is a finite chance that the electron will disappear on one side and reappear on the other side."

"Dude, that is so awesome," enthused Randall. "I could have used that function a few times."

"Couldn't we all?" agreed Dan. "But like I said, these behaviors do not manifest, except perhaps indirectly, at the macro level. We'll come back to that. Next up to the plate is *quantum spin*. As we've noted, electrons can be described by their mass, charge, and particle/ wave behavior, but there's another feature they have that's important at the subatomic level. The electron is not just floating in orbit like a knuckleball pitch."

Randall grabbed the baseball with a knuckleball grip. "So the electron has spin?"

Dan nodded, intent on the ball. "Yes, it also has a spin, but not like the spin of a baseball. The mathematical description of the spin is complex, but let's just say that it either spins clockwise or counterclockwise. Physics guys just say *spin up* and *spin down*." He flipped the tack point up and point down to emphasize.

"Phil Niekro would disagree about the importance of spin," mused Randall.

"Who's Phil Niekro?" asked Dan with a crook of his head.

"Best knuckleball pitcher ever. Played for the Milwaukee Braves back in the day," recalled Randall. "Old Knucksie could throw the ball with absolutely no spin. It floated unpredictably and even his catcher had no idea where the ball was going. Had most batters flailing their bats in the air."

Dan soldiered on despite the baseball history lesson. "Early models of the atom pictured the electron as a particle orbiting the nucleus independently and had little notion of spin," said Dan. "But the type of quantum spin I'm talking about has more to do with two quanta that are bonded by how they are created. They display a *paired spin* behavior."

"Paired electrons?" asked Randall. "Now you're losing me."

Dan suggested Randall focus on the tack as an electron surrogate. "Look, if one electron of a pair is *spin up,* the paired electron is always *spin down.* The two are bonded in this way. Other particles, like a proton and neutron, can be similarly paired."

Randall squinted. "So all of this is just relevant at the subatomic level, right? It doesn't actually have any bearing when it comes to life on earth?"

Dan chuckled. "Ah, the innocent mind of a child. Actually, the spin behavior for an electron is an important function for chemical covalent bonding and biologic functions like photosynthesis, bird migration, odor detection, and enzyme activity."

Randall's eyes got big, as if a door in his mind had opened a crack and let in a breeze. "Geez, I never really associated that a quantum process like electron spin would matter in my own body." He rubbed his belly and sniffed, as if trying to assimilate the information in his body senses. "So these quantum behaviors take place in biology too?"

Dan smiled at Randall's slow learning process. "To be sure. We're made up of the same stuff as inanimate objects. Why wouldn't quantum mechanics apply to biology as well?"

Randall looked like a kid discovering new wonders in his own backyard. "I guess I never really thought of it. At the subatomic level, we are all made of the same stuff. We think we are separate and unique, but we are really built of the same energy. Are there actually people studying quantum biology? Is that even an area of study?"

"There are! It's not a big field yet, but I think it will be soon." Dan seemed to be enjoying Randall's fascination. "It's as simple as the human eye responding to one photon of light. Think about it."

Randall smacked his forehead with the heel of his hand. "Of course! I mean, I knew this already, I guess, since cells respond to even micro-doses of radiation. I just never thought about it at this level. It must have a powerful effect on all animal behavior. Like how deer know when it's time to mate or something."

Dan was on the edge of his seat. "Exactly! I know of some studies of bird migration that believe there's a quantum reaction in the robin's retina that helps the bird follow magnetic field lines when it migrates south for the winter. It's a good segue to the fifth quantum behavior, *quantum entanglement*."

"Goody gum drops. I'm salivating already. Unwind it for me." Randall rubbed his hands together.

Dan put down his coffee cup and picked up a tack in each hand. "Think about a pair of electrons spinning in mutual orbit. One is *spin up* and the other is *spin down*. The two are *spin neutral* together and are linked to each other, or *entangled*." Dan rotated the two tacks in an imaginary orbit around each other. "If one electron is kicked out of orbit, say by a photon of radiation from our Linac, it leaves the atom of origin one electron short." He puckered his lips and blew one tack out of orbit. "Now it has a net negative charge. That's what you and I call a free radical."

"Speaking of that, I think the President should free all the radicals," said Randall. "There's too many stuffy right-wing conservatives running the country."

Dan pointed at Randall with a tack. "Off topic, as usual! Get back in orbit, you hippie! Now back to brass tacks. The free radical electron, let's call him Malcolm X, just wants to find a negative charge to combine with and become neutral again. Malcolm X longs for his entangled mate Betty S, but what if the photon knocked Betty S clear to Pluto? Then what if our Malcolm, who spins up, finds a closer electron, Angela, but she also spins up. He likes the look of Angela, but the only way to attract her is to reverse spin; so he goes for it, switches to spin down, and he hooks up with Angela. But since Malcolm is still quantumly entangled with Betty, now on Pluto, Betty is shocked when she looks down and finds herself suddenly spinning up. By the way, it happened simultaneously to Malcolm's spin reversal, despite the distance."

"How's that even possible?" asked Randall. "Does Malcolm still love Betty? How could Malcolm do that to her? Was she pregnant?"

"Biedermeier . . . for Pete's sake," said Dan. "Sometimes you're such a juvenile. May I ask what stimulated your interest in quantum theory?"

QUANTUM BIOLOGY AND DUNG BEETLES

Randall's gaze wandered to the ceiling. "My interest was first triggered by the story about the atom walking down the street minding his own business when another atom accidentally bumps into him and knocks one of his electrons out of orbit," said Randall with mock seriousness. "The atom that knocks him down helps him up and asks him, 'Are you okay?' The atom replies, 'I'm not okay. You knocked out one of my electrons!' The other atom asks, 'Are you sure?' The atom replies, 'Yes, I'm positive!'"

"*Ugh!* That's the last straw!" said Dan. "I think we're done here."

"Sorry, I couldn't resist," said Randall. "I was pretty sure you knew that one and would stop me before it got that far."

"Alright, but one more of those, and we're done," said Dan, trying to hide a smile. "Let's continue, but without the walks down the garden path."

"Well I've done some reading about quantum theory, but it was mostly about the physics aspect," admitted Randall. "It led me to start wondering about its relation to biology. You alluded to a connection when you were explaining quantum spin and entanglement. You know, the stuff about bird migration and enzymes. What I've read says that this stuff only happens in controlled systems, like in a vacuum at extremely low temperatures so there's no disturbances from the relative heat and chaos in a living cell."

"Yeah, that used to be the thinking," Dan nodded. "But now we think biomolecules, like DNA and enzymes, which are also made up of subatomic particles, have interactions governed by quantum mechanics. Walking, talking, eating, and sleeping depend on quantum forces just like your car or toaster. Some believe quantum actions are behind human consciousness, but we're a ways off from proving that yet."

"It seems like the entanglement thing, with the paired electrons instantaneously switching spin, could work like a quantum switching device," imagined Randall. "Like maybe it could account for the switching on and off of genes or other biological communications. If you can have action at a distance, why couldn't a neuronal impulse in one brain signal a neural response in another brain, perhaps one genetically linked to the first?"

"Interesting." Dan considered the possibility. "I see where you're going. There's been some rumblings about a connection with telepathy, but that's been mostly debunked. Don't even think about communication with the dead. That's viewed with scorn as well." Dan shifted in his chair, tapping the pencil on his desk in contemplation. "But now that I think about it, an electron shifting spins could be considered a quantum electric switch. That, along with entanglement, could allow it to happen at a distance. In that way, the brain could act as a quantum computer with more computing power than a binary computer that codes by ones and zeros."

"Yeah! The most powerful computer on earth could be right between our ears! What about that multiple dimensions deal with string theory?" asked Randall. "You combine that with some of these quantum behaviors and it makes me wonder if we can get entangled glimpses into alternate realities."

"Now you're getting beyond the pale," thwarted Dan.

"As I recall from my reading," Randall pushed on anyhow. "Einstein and others postulated quantum entanglement in the thirties as a direct result of his relativity work. His famous equation $E=mc^2$ is a part of our lives now, but it blows my mind that he came up with it less than a century ago. It was only in 1905 that he examined something as unfathomable as the speed of light and was able to clarify it in a simple formula."

Dan motioned for Randall to move things along. "Yes, Randall, I know what $E=mc^2$ is. I don't need the lecture."

"Don't stop me now, Dan, I'm on a roll. My wheels are spinning, and I gotta lubricate the cogs in my cognition. So 'E' stands for energy. 'm' is mass, and 'c' is the constant speed of light, right? Right. So in short, energy is mass and mass is energy."

Dan zipped his lip and nodded. He enjoyed watching the smoke coming out of Randall's ears.

It didn't stop Randall from further expostulation. "But Einstein had a bigger concept of mass. Most people think of mass as something simple and solid, like a rock. But, really, with relativistic mass, the closer something gets to the speed of light, the more mass it has. Even photons, which have no mass, gain mass at the speed of light. And nothing can move as fast as light, according to Newtonian physics."

Randall reached the end of his breath and paused to refuel. Before Dan could say anything else, Randall zoomed on to lap two. "Who's to say further research in quantum biology won't lead down some pathways we can't even imagine today? Maybe higher-level communication with other beings and other worlds is within our grasp if we explore it further." Randall paused, making more neural connections in his speculation. "Maybe love itself has a quantum basis."

Dan pulled back, surprised. "Have you been sandbagging me about not understanding quantum theory?" he asked. "Don't push the science beyond its scope. But I do see where you're coming from. Could this have anything to do with the Swindell incident?"

"Got me on the sandbagging and Swindell," said Randall. "There's been some other stuff I've been trying to sort out that I don't wish to discuss, at least not yet. Sorry, I was just trying to get it from a fresh perspective, and your explanation really cleared up a lot of questions I had. I know I'll probably not get a quantum answer to my questions any time soon. But it's enough to know that a connection could evolve over time. Do you think it's possible?"

Dan shrugged. "Well, if electrons can go through walls and be in two places at once, why couldn't there be more . . . on closer inspection? Just don't start in about God or the Big Bang. My head's already swimming. Good grief, look at the time. I've got to finish the report, and you've probably got stuff to do too."

Randall shook his head and his shoulders sagged. "Dang if this whole quantum thing isn't both exciting and confusing at the same time. It seems like it'll take me another lifetime to wrap my head around it."

Dan clucked his tongue. "Don't worry about it too much. When Einstein and Bohr were postulating quantum theory in the 1930s, the concepts confused even Einstein because it flew in the face of the classical physics he knew. Einstein called the idea of quantum entanglement 'spooky science at a distance.' Richard Feynman, in the 1940s, probably understood quantum theory as well as any atomic physicist and, to paraphrase him, if you claimed to understand it, you didn't really understand it."

Randall smiled. "That makes me feel a little better. At least now we have the benefit of years more basic physics research that have validated the quantum theory concepts. But they still seem so foreign to everyday experience that they are hard to accept as real."

Dan nodded in assent. "Exactly. What you may have missed in all this is another mind-bending truth about quantum entanglement. If it's real, as we now assume it to be, for the spin reversal to occur simultaneously when the two electrons could be millions of miles apart, what must be true?"

Randall grimaced and pursed his lip for a long moment then raised a finger in triumph. "For the reversal to happen at exactly the same time, the communication between the two electrons would have to occur faster than the speed of light!" Randall got even more fired up with inspiration.

"Exactly!" Dan jumped on the excitement roller coaster.

"And that means it would take light a finite amount of time to travel that far. To date, we don't know of anything that's faster than light.

Therefore some thus far undetected subatomic force must be faster that the 'c' in $E = mc^2$. Holy moly!"

Dan gave Randall a high five. "You've got it, space monkey. The further implications of that are that space time is altered at speeds exceeding light speed. It could be the answer to time travel and worm holes. But that's another story."

Randall froze for a few beats, then shook his head again. "It feels like I bit off more that I can chew. How about we just back up to quantum entanglement for a while?"

Dan nodded his agreement. "I propose that, for the time being at least, we provide you with a personal theory of relativity. How about $E = RB^2$, where E = evolution, and RB = Randall Biedermeier."

Randall laughed. "That's a good one, Dan! $E = RB^2$, like I'm not an egghead anymore! I'm a square!"

"Think of it as Relativity 102. That will allow you to evolve further, either in this lifetime or future ones, so that you can exponentially expand your horizons. Einstein would approve, because most of his theorizing was done with thought experiments, of which this is an example."

Randall got up and walked in a circle, taking it all in. "I like your concept. I think I understand. Take it step by step. Build up to it, and let it percolate."

"Precisely," said Dan. "Like a good coffee."

"*Mmm* . . . coffee. Come to think about it, I think I have too much blood in my caffeine stream." Randall raised his hand. "Hey, teach, may I be excused? My brain is full. And I'd better get back to what they pay me for. I'll bet Grace is on the warpath."

As Randall walked to the door of Dan's office, Dan had another thought. "Oh, here's an additional factoid for you. Perhaps you can regale your kids with this tidbit at bedtime."

"Oh, yeah? What's that?" asked Randall.

"The lowly dung beetle uses the Milky Way for navigation," said Dan. "Entomologists think that's how the beetles find old dung that's lost its odor, but they're still sniffing out the details."

Randall groaned. Dan was giving Randall's attempt at atomic humor payback. The Milky Way reference was an odd coincidence.

"I guess turnabout is fair play." Randall waved goodbye to Dan and went back to his office with two empty coffee cups.

On his desk a stack of charts and reports awaited his review and signature. There were no paperwork holidays at the VA. Randall checked the time and was amazed to find it was already 3:30. He was tempted just to abandon ship early so he could make it to Chelsea Andretti's office in time for her second session with Kyle that was scheduled for 5:00.

However, Randall flashed back to his father showing ten-year-old Randall how to saw wood and sand it. Randall had attempted to leave the workshop without cleaning up when Joe hauled him back by the shoulder and pointed to the mess he'd made. Joe hammered in the first rule of woodworking. "If you call yourself a Biedermeier, you never leave a project without cleaning up and putting your tools away. If you don't, your task will be much harder when you come back. Got that?"

Despite Randall's disgruntlement with his father's fastidiousness, the dictum had proven to be a wise one with application beyond woodworking. Now he followed his father's sage words as a general practice. He found early on that procrastination only increased the degree of difficulty. He'd have to hustle to get the paperwork done before leaving, but he would invoke hyper-mode and make it happen. The other downside of leaving it until the next day was that he'd have to face the wrath of Doris. She hated putting things off worse than his father did.

Randall shifted into high gear and made like a papermill. He swept out the final dust of details and was out the door with time to spare. Randall chuckled to himself. *I see, said the blind lumberjack, as he picked up his hammer and saw.*

The traffic was favorable for the drive home to pick up Zelda and Kyle. They were soon Chelsea-bound.

RUNNING MARE

CHAPTER 27

———

DREAMLAND

"Trust in dreams, for in them is hidden the gate to eternity."

— Khalil Gibran

CHELSEA REDUX

Things were pretty quiet in the car on the drive to Chelsea Andretti's office. Zelda was anxious, Kyle acted sullen, and Randall was just plain pooped out. Everyone seemed lost in their own thoughts.

Randall tried to break through the wall of silence by commenting on the weather, but Zelda shushed him with a gritty "not now." Kyle began to whine that he was thirsty, but he got no traction. No one talked about the elephant in the car, namely, Kyle's aborted trip to Grandma's house via the snowy freeway. The smell of peanut breath hung in the air.

Randall, Zelda and Kyle discussed the first Chelsea visit and the Kyle runaway several times at home to make sure Kyle understood everything. Addie was included in some of those discussions. Yet, on the car ride to Chelsea's office for the second session, there was a deadly silence. No one chose to speak.

Kyle headed for the toys. Randall's palms were sweating. He wiped them repeatedly on his pants. Zelda kept readjusting her skirt.

Zelda leaned over to Randall. "How are we going to bring up Kyle's runaway?"

431

Randall put a calming, albeit clammy, hand on her knee. "Don't worry, I'll do all the talking."

Zelda pushed his hand away and dabbed at the sweaty spot. "No, you will not. We share the blame. We've got to do it in a way that Kyle won't get angry. We can't screw this up, Randy."

Randall rolled his eyes. "I get it. I just meant I'll start it off, and then we can both go through it. Maybe it's best if we just bring it up, and let Kyle tell it his way. That way we're not setting ourselves up as the bad guys."

Zelda nodded. "Could work. Let's play it by ear. Maybe Chelsea will lead Kyle into it."

After what seemed like hours, Chelsea emerged from her office with an older woman whose red eyes and hanky gave clear evidence that she'd been crying for more than a few minutes. The woman was shaky as she walked, and Chelsea supported her with one arm.

Chelsea guided the woman to the only empty seat next to Randall and sat her down. "You wait here, Mrs. Armbruster. I'll call your son to come get you. Hello, Biedermeiers. I'll be with you in a flash."

The woman continued to cry, and Randall asked if there was anything he could do to help. The woman reached out and took Randall's wrist firmly. "My Eddie is gone. My husband is gone; it's just not right. Can you get him back for me?"

Randall lamented his tendency to care-give in places he shouldn't. He tried to pull his wrist back, but her grip was firm. "Did your husband leave you?"

The woman laughed hollowly. "Of course, he did. He's dead. Just up and died. Bit the dirt. Doornail city. Ain't nothing anyone can do, including you, so stuff your lame offer to help." She let go of his wrist and almost threw his arm back at him. "Now leave me alone."

Zelda looked over at the pair with wide eyes and whispered, "Randy, it just may be that she doesn't want your help. You think?"

Randall rubbed his wrist. "Great observation, Miss Obvious. No good deed goes unpunished."

Chelsea came back out of her office and told Mrs. Armbruster her son would be by in fifteen minutes to pick her up.

Mrs. Armbruster harrumphed. "Rotten brat. Late again. Never was any good."

Chelsea just nodded in response and turned to greet Randall and Zelda. She motioned for them to enter her lair. She retrieved Kyle from the play area, and he brought along a Sikorsky helicopter toy. When everyone was in their places, Chelsea leaned back on the front of her desk and surveyed the "happy" trio.

"Sorry about Mrs. Armbruster. She can be difficult. She's got quite a grip, doesn't she, Randy?"

Randall raised a reddened wrist. "No kidding. I thought it was the Vulcan grip of death. My fingers went numb. She must eat her spinach."

Chelsea laughed, and Kyle chimed in from the play area. "Yeah, she's just like Popeye."

Now everybody laughed, and the room's atmosphere seemed a bit lighter.

Chelsea continued. "Didn't really mean to sic her on you, but that was the only chair available. Most folks would have just ignored her, but not you, Randy. The old doctor gene just can't be turned off, *eh*?"

Randall laughed. "Guess not. You got me."

Chelsea segued nicely. "So tell me what's happened at the Biedermeiers' since our first meeting. Have you accidentally or purposely talked about what we went over last week?"

Zelda raised her hand like a kid in class. "Well, we had a few sit downs at the kitchen table. Addie sat in for a few of those. Randy and I have had some one-on-ones with Kyle. And Kyle has had a pretty good week except for one little incident."

Chelsea just looked thoughtfully at Zelda for a minute while Zelda twisted a tissue in her lap. "Anything more? How have you been feeling?"

Zelda looked at Randall for answers, but he was watching Kyle play helicopter. "Since you ask, I've been a bit upset about how Kyle may be affected when Randy and I argue and go into one of our not-talking modes. It hurts me to think it might make Kyle act out to get our attention, even if it's in a bad way. It just confuses me."

Chelsea nodded. "You're right. A child's behavior can be very confusing, even for intelligent adults. We adults haven't been kids for a long time, so we forget what it was like."

Zelda's eyes began to leak. "I know. This week I started to think back about what it was like when I was a kid. My parents would fight until a Cold War broke out. Then it was like walking on ice around the house. The slightest misstep could spell disaster. Then my dad would come down on us. But it was better to get that attention than none. And now I might be doing it to my own kids?" She could not continue.

Chelsea put an arm on her shoulder. "We parent with the patterns that we learned growing up. There's no guarantee that our parents were any better at parenting than we are now."

"I just didn't realize . . ." Zelda reached her arms out to Kyle.

He threw down his helicopter and ran to his mother. While she repeated that she was sorry, Kyle let out a huge sigh of relief and leaned into her chest.

Randall connected the dots. "So Kyle has been acting out to get our attention?"

Chelsea did her best to normalize the situation. "Perhaps, and it's probably for a lot of other reasons too. It may not be a conscious process—we have to be careful not to assign adult reasoning to kid actions. You've both mentioned some conflict and frustration for both of you, and in your relationship. It's fairly common for the child to become the barometer for what's happening in the family."

"So it's not him, it's us?" asked Randall.

Zelda put her hand to her forehead. "More like it's me. I've screwed up everything. Just like my father always said."

Randall felt like climbing the walls whenever Zelda started this downward spiral. It could go deep and fast. He knew how to handle a cobalt rod emitting 1.1 MeV gamma rays but was flummoxed by Zelda's rapid decay.

But Chelsea didn't panic. "Look at how much Kyle trusts you. Like I said, there are a lot of things going right in this family. You are all here, you all want to get along better, and you are all learning better ways to care for yourselves. Right?"

Chelsea turned her attention to Kyle. "So little buddy. How was your week?"

Kyle zoomed the helicopter around in attack mode. "It was cool. I ran away from home in that big snowstorm. A cop car found me, and I got to ride home in it. The cop even turned on the siren for me."

Chelsea was nonplussed. "Oh, that sounds like a good time. I wonder what happened that made you run away?"

Kyle looked at the ceiling. "I don't know."

"Were you angry about something?" asked Chelsea.

Kyle hesitated a bit. "Yeah. I think so."

Chelsea walked over to Kyle and picked up a jet plane. She zoomed her jet to fly with the helicopter, and Kyle machine-gunned her jet. Chelsea flipped her jet in the air, diverting its path toward the floor. "I'm hit! I'm going down! It burns!" She smashed the jet down.

Kyle looked surprised. "I didn't mean to shoot you down. I was just playing. Man! I just cause trouble for everyone. It would be better if I wasn't around." He punched his fist into his head.

Chelsea looked down at the crashed jet. "I was just playing too. I know you didn't mean any harm."

Kyle was still agitated. "No, no. I hurt people, and I don't want to. When I ran away, I thought that if I left, maybe Mom and Dad would be happier. I knew Grandma would let me live with her. And she makes good pie. I love her rhubarb pie."

Randall and Zelda got up and hugged Kyle, evoking tears all around. Chelsea handed out tissues and set a trash can nearby. It took a bit of time to cry everything out, blow noses, and return to some semblance of normal.

Randall thought to himself that he shouldn't have worried about how to broach the running away topic. Chelsea did seem to have a knack for breaking through the barriers and opening tear ducts. The three B's settled in together on the couch at the side of the room and held hands. They shared the runaway story in detail with Chelsea.

Chelsea summarized. "The words we say have a lot of power. They make us do funny things. But the words aren't always what's important. We all say and do things we don't really mean when we're upset, right, Kyle?"

Kyle waved an arm. "Boy, howdy. Like how I told the dog he was annoying, and I wanted him to die. I didn't really mean it. I just didn't want to pick up his poo."

Chelsea was again quick on the draw. "Exactly. You didn't cause the dog to die just by wishing it." Kyle nodded slowly, taking it in. "Any more than you can MAKE your parents argue."

Chelsea looked at Zelda. "Kids can handle honesty better than bitter silence."

Zelda squinted at her. "I'm not so sure about that. See what good it did to be honest last week? Kyle walked on the friggin' freeway at night in winter!"

Chelsea nodded agreement. "It's easy to believe that it was the honesty that did that. Rather, all that frustration was already there, pushing against a dam of denial. We just opened the floodgates. Better now than when they're teenagers with driver's licenses!"

Randall smirked. "Or adult children in parent suits!"

"Exactly." Chelsea touched her nose. "And parents don't have to be perfect to have good relationships with each other and their kids. In fact, all relationships are a cycle of connection, rupture, and repair. These challenges leave us room to practice repair. You wouldn't want to burden your children by being perfect."

Zelda looked relieved. "So I'm doing him a favor by being imperfect?"

Chelsea nodded. "I prefer to think of it as being a perfectly imperfect mere mortal human. That's the beauty of repair—you're teaching your child how to be human. You're not leaving him a stranger in a strange land without a map."

Zelda took the cue. "Kyle, I admit I wanted to be a lot older than I was before I had kids. But that didn't work out. I didn't really mean it when I said I didn't want kids. I just wasn't ready to stop being a kid yet when I got pregnant. But I'm learning. I really love being your mother.

You teach me every day. I am not perfect, and you don't need to be either. When I lose my temper, can you be patient with me? I will do my best to apologize and make it right."

Kyle looked shocked to get this unexpected "Get out of jail free" card.

"Me too, Buddy," said Randall. "I get so busy at work that I'm not always very patient when I come home. Sometimes I just disappear into the garage to clear my mind by grinding rust. That must feel like I'm not noticing you."

Kyle nodded, looking exhausted and relieved.

Chelsea leaned over to Randall like an angel on his shoulder delivering a message. "As Wordsworth once said, 'the child is the father of the man.'"

Randall's eyebrows knotted up, as he cogitated on the quote. "You mean Kyle is teaching me to be a dad?" Randall had a sudden realization. "And I just figured out that I might be part of the problem. It isn't fair that I get to do all the fun things with Kyle and sometimes we kind of break the rules Zelda tries to set. I'm so sorry. I know she values good food and schedules. Sometimes I just lapse into being a big kid. It's not fair to you."

Zelda teared up, finally being seen after so much time feeling hidden.

Chelsea sat back and allowed the family space to take it all in. She glanced at the clock, needing to finish up. "Kyle, I think it's fair to say that you have a very important job."

"I do?" Kyle's voice raised an octave, like he had just jumped in a pool with freezing water.

Chelsea nodded with vigor. "Yep! You have the job to be a kid. To explore the world, to learn, to play, and to see what works for you."

"I can do that." Kyle smiled.

"I'm sure you can. You are off the hook, Buddy. And I have even better news: you are not responsible for your parents. They are both adults, and they will take care of adult stuff, like money, marriage, your sister, and the house." Chelsea looked at the shell-shocked parents.

Zelda and Randall nodded.

Chelsea turned her gaze back to Kyle. "Kyle, you are a great kid.

How about you and I work together to figure out how you can get what you need to feel safe? And how to act so you can get what you need, and people can understand you better?"

Kyle nodded enthusiastically. "Great!"

Chelsea continued. "Would you be willing to put the cars and blocks away while I talk with your parents alone for a little bit?"

Kyle started herding the cars with no resistance.

Chelsea motioned Zelda and Randall to meet with her just outside the door into the hall. "Great job, you two. It takes a lot of courage to see how a child's issues are usually a family's issues. There is so much love in this family! I just know that you are both open to seeing how to support Kyle and Addie as you work out the tough balance of parenting, jobs, and self-care."

"So he's okay?" asked Zelda.

"My prognosis is that he will live." Chelsea joked. "Even better, he is already thriving. I recommend some individual and family sessions just to make sure you all stay on the right path."

Zelda needed a little more reassurance. "What about the night terrors? That was so scary!"

"Well, as we said before, Kyle seems to be processing the stress of the family. That can happen during the day as behaviors, or at night in his subconscious state."

Chelsea had a way of making it all seem like normal childhood stuff. "For the most part, kids don't remember the night terrors and it's best not to try to wake them. Just keep him safe until he settles down to sleep again."

"Isn't there anything we can do to stop them?" asked Randall.

"Well, there are some factors that can lead to a greater likelihood of night terrors, such as being ill, stressed, or not getting enough sleep. Having a regular sleep routine can help stabilize his sleep pattern."

"We can do that! Right, Randy?" Zelda nudged him with her elbow.

"Yes, Mom." Randall hung his head in mock shame.

Chelsea laughed. "You may think I'm kidding, but you two are so cute together! You're different from each other for sure, but you work well as a pair. The love is clear."

Randall choked up and Zelda blew her nose with a honk. Everybody laughed.

Chelsea gave them both a hug and finished up. "Okay, kiddos, our time is up. Actually past time. So one last thing. You probably saw this coming. I think it would be very helpful if each of you had a therapist to talk to. Zelda, I see your hesitation, but let me finish. Like I said before, this parenting thing is tough as it is, and you didn't have the chance to be as ready as you'd like. A therapist can support you to learn how to honor yourself, process the big feelings you have, and also come up with parenting strategies that work for everyone. I wonder if there are some patterns you learned from your parents that maybe you don't want to pass to your children."

Zelda didn't answer . . . it was a lot to consider, and perhaps hard to admit it was a lot to accept.

"And Randall," Chelsea continued. "You have an inhuman amount of stress with your job. I bet you didn't have a lot of time to wander through your own psyche in med school. You showed on your paperwork that you are the first in your family to finish college, so I wonder if any of your family members would really be able to understand the kind of pressure you have. There must be a lot to unpack in that mind of yours."

Zelda piped up, "And Randy, you have been having those, *um* . . . , experiences lately. Maybe Chelsea is right." Zelda's eyes searched his. "I think I would be open to it. If Randy goes, I'll go. Different therapist though. I can't tell my secrets to someone who will also know yours!"

Randall was shocked. He had been considering seeing a therapist, but never in a million years imagined it would be Zelda encouraging him. She was always so secretive and distrusted any medical professionals. At first he was tempted to protest, but then he surprised himself by saying, "I think that would be a great idea!"

Chelsea smiled. "You're taking brave steps! I will have my secretary give you the names and numbers of some of my colleagues. You do your due diligence to find the right match for you."

Zelda and Randall agreed, feeling surprisingly better than they had expected. They fetched Kyle, who had already put away the scattered toys. They finished up with Chelsea and walked hand in hand in hand down the hall.

Kyle spontaneously hugged Chelsea.

Chelsea kneeled down to make eye contact with him. "Would you be willing to choose one of the match box cars to take care of at home? I would really appreciate your expertise, and I know it would be in good hands."

Kyle jumped up and grabbed the Corvette. He ran ahead to the front desk, yelling, "Mom? Dad? When are we coming back?"

Kyle Rates Chelsea

On the drive home from Chelsea's, Randall reflected on the contrast between this experience and the night after their first session with Chelsea. That night, Randall and Zelda had decided it was perhaps best to let the session marinate in Kyle's head overnight before discussing it with him further. Only then would they include Addie in disclosing what had happened in Chelsea's office. That night, dinner had been quiet and awkward, but without incident. If anyone had read the script of the evening, there would have been nothing of note. For the folks there though, the tension in the room had been palpable.

This night at dinner, after the second session, Randall and Zelda decided to leave any discussion of therapy up to Kyle. It was, after all, his to share. But Kyle had remained fairly quiet during dinner. The only sounds were clinks of silverware on plates and chewing as they all dug into the evening repast of chicken enchiladas. There was also the persistent mewing of two cats begging for table food.

Without verbal competition from Kyle, Addie held court during dinner on all manner of details about her stuffed animals and plastic horse collection.

Kyle mimicked gagging on his spoon several times, but otherwise didn't speak.

Addie finally changed topics. "Daddy, what happened at work today? Did you have a good day?"

Randall looked up from his plate in surprise. Usually, the kids had no interest in what he did each day. "Well, thanks for asking, gumdrop. Looking back on my day, I'd give it a B-plus."

Addie sucked in a breath. "I am not a gumdrop! I'm a rosebud."

Zelda put a calming hand on Addie's shoulder. "Don't get upset. Daddy didn't mean anything bad. He just meant you were sweet to ask about his day. So Randy, why just a B-plus?"

Randall squinched up his face. "I had this one patient. He was a weird one. He was sent down for treatment of a skin cancer, but I couldn't get him to stay on point. I'd ask him a question about his skin cancer, and he'd tell me about his bowels. Then I'd try to redirect him back to skin cancer, and he'd go on and on with a sad story about his strange headaches."

Zelda nodded in sympathy. "Sounds like a lot of tangential thinking."

"The man sounds loony," added Addie.

"Indeed," said Randall. "The symptoms he described to me were so mixed up, they didn't relate to any disease I ever heard of. So I went back to his chart and reviewed his past history. It seems he'd done this for years, you know, complaining about a bunch of stuff, all of which led to extensive workups with nothing found."

"Isn't that called Munchausen syndrome?" asked Zelda. "I saw a thingy on TV about that. You know, where a person plays sick so that people care for them, and they become the center of attention."

"By gumdrop, I think you're right," said Randall. "One of the consultants on his case, when he worked up the patient's bowel complaints, made the comment in his notes that the man 'has a classic case of whatever it is.' By my count, he's had at least seven different such classic cases. But so far, nobody has mentioned Munchausen. Zel, you're a medical whiz."

Zelda got all puffed up and looked proud of herself. "I resemble that."

Kyle finally spoke up. "I think the man was just lonely and loony."

"Well, welcome to the conversation," said Zelda. "How was your day, young scout?"

Kyle rolled his eyes a bit and then perked up. "Oh, I remember. A kid in school made up a funny calendar with new names for each month. He was passing it around in class, and Miss Andrews caught him and consecrated it. She sent him to the principal's office."

"I think you mean confiscated it," said Zelda. "She took it away from him."

Randall chuckled. *Maybe he actually burned it.* Randall decided it best not to say that aloud.

"*Duh*," said Kyle. "That's what I said. Before she took it away, I copied it down. I've got the paper in my pocket. Wanna hear?"

"Why not?" said Randall. "Let's see what creativity flourishes in the fourth grade these days."

Kyle produced the paper and read out the new months of the year. "Januworry, Februwooly, Mitch, Apehill, Maybe, Gin, Jewelry, Assgust, Septober, Octember, Noremember, and Dismember. There were pictures for each month too, but I didn't have time to copy them down."

"I can imagine," said Zelda. "I bet the pictures are what got him in trouble. Are you sure the kid wasn't you? Am I going to get a note from Miss Andrews?"

Kyle shook his head vigorously. "For sure, no. It wasn't me."

"Those are funny names," laughed Addie. "I was born in Dismember!"

"Am I in trouble?" asked Kyle.

"Not unless you want to be," said Randall. "Now it's getting late. Let's all help Mom clean up the dinner dishes and then get upstairs for your bath. If there's time, we can do a bedtime story."

"Can we pick it?" asked Addie.

Randall made a grand gesture. "Of course, one for each. I am at your service.

After story time and tucking Addie in bed, Randall and Zelda turned their attention to Kyle's bedtime routine. After getting him settled in bed, they both sat at his bedside and asked what he thought of Ms. Andretti.

Kyle twisted up his face before making a pronouncement. "She's real pretty, and she's got great Legos."

Randall looked askance at Kyle. "Hey, Buddy, was that a joke?"

Kyle grinned widely. "Yep."

"Excellent!" said Randall. "There may be hope for you yet."

Kyle reached over to his bedside table and grabbed the model Corvette Ms. Andretti gave him. He tucked it under the covers next to him. "And I love the 'Vette. I'm sleeping with it."

Zelda approved. "Sounds like a plan."

"It wasn't as bad as I thought it would be," said Kyle. "She's pretty nice, and no one got mad at me for talking about my stuff."

Randall nodded. "Yeah, sometimes it just feels good to get things out in the open. And if it stops the bad dreams, so much the better. Can't hurt, and it might help."

"Boy, I sure hope the dreams stop," said Kyle. "They make me afraid to sleep. Then when I miss sleep, I get real nervous, and it gets even harder to get to sleep."

"That's what we call a vicious circle," said Zelda. "We need to break that negative cycle, and create a new one. One that replaces the negative with positive. You know, out with the bad, in with the good."

"It's kind of like the proverbial Ouroboros," said Randall.

Zelda nodded agreement. "Yeah. Your dad is right. That fits too."

"What the heck is that?" exclaimed Kyle.

"It's an ancient symbol that shows a snake eating its own tail," said Zelda.

Kyle made a sour face. "That's weird."

"Yeah, a bit," said Randall. "It's a symbol that means the snake is renewing itself by eating away the bad. A symbol is any object that means something other than what it is."

"Okay, I think I get it," said Kyle hesitantly.

"Wait!" said Zelda. "I think I have a picture in my art history book. I'll get it and show you."

Kyle shook his head. "I'll never get all the weird stuff you guys do."

Zelda returned with the text. "Here you go. Have a look."

Kyle studied the picture showing a snake swallowing its tail, and shook his head. Kyle got out from under the covers and reached down for his right foot. "I could never do that. Look, I can't get my foot in my mouth."

"What a comedian," said Randall. "You don't have to actually do it, just think it. Now climb back under the covers and get to sleep."

Zelda kissed him on the forehead once he was settled in. "There you go. That's my *Good Housekeeping* seal of approval. It guarantees you'll have a safe regenerative sleep with no dreams."

"Yeah," said Kyle. "I'm really tired. Don't try to explain what you just said until tomorrow."

Randall and Zelda said goodnight to Kyle, left the room, and got ready for bed, exhausted.

"Randy, I need a break from this house and the kids real soon," moaned Zelda as she slipped out of her clothes. "Maybe a date with someone who's not a kid."

Randall perked up a bit. "Do I qualify as not a kid?"

Zelda grinned. "Mostly. I need to call Julie Miller, up the street, and ask who she uses for a babysitter, She's got two kids about the ages of ours."

"You have my blessing," murmured Randall as he dropped into bed. "Sooner rather than later."

Zelda joined him under the covers, kissed his cheek and promised to make it so.

Paranoia Deep in the Heartland

When Randall arrived at work the next morning, he was pleased to find a patient had brought in fresh donuts. He grabbed one before they disappeared and tucked it in his desk drawer for later. He wiped his sugary hands on his lab coat, then padded quietly into Doris's office to get filled in on what lay ahead for the day. She was busy listening to dictation on her headphones and typing.

"So Doris, what does the menu hold for us this fine day?"

She hadn't heard him come in, so when he spoke, she jumped up in her chair. "Great sufferin' succotash, Dr. B! You just spooked one cat year off my life. Can't you make a little noise when you come in?"

Randall hadn't been trying for that effect. It was just his supervisor-bred habit. "Sorry, Doris. Didn't mean to scare you. Is there something you feel guilty about?"

Doris tore off her headphones and slammed them on her desk. "Well, I never . . . I'll have you know that I am so pure that I have no reason to ever feel guilty. Heaven already has my chair waitin'! Plus, I just went to confession, and all my sins have been wiped away."

"Aha! So you admit you have sins," said Randall. "How many Hail Marys?"

"Never you mind," Doris shot back. "Now since you asked, you have a very unusual consult up next, one Stanley Dobleman. You ready for the summary?"

"Shoot," said Randall.

Doris made a pistol gesture and pointed at Randall. "If only this were real. I'd show you some holiness. We have a thirty-five-year-old young man with Stage 2 lung cancer. He's here with his brother, Sam, who is his guardian."

Randall raised an eyebrow. "Guardian? Why does he need one? Is he dangerous?"

Doris shook her head. "Only to himself. Apparently, he's a paranoid schizophrenic and has a problem separatin' reality from his delusional thinking. Sam helps him with all his important decisions. Stanley can sign consent, but Sam has to cosign."

Randall scratched his head and shifted his feet. "I sense there's a bigger issue."

Doris nodded. "There is. Stanley does not believe that he has cancer and has thus far refused surgery. He told the surgeons that, despite the fact his name is on the X-rays showin' the tumor in his right lung, the X-rays are not his. He is convinced that the government is dead set on capturing him, because they believe he is a traitor and they faked the imagin' to get to him."

Randall grunted and let out a breath. "I get it now. Why should he get treatment for a tumor he doesn't have? Makes sense once you buy into the delusion. I'm betting the surgeons didn't try hard to convince him otherwise. I bet as soon as he put his foot down, they sent him our way."

Doris smiled. "And that's why *you* are the big boss. Now it's up to you to convince him he has a tumor and needs radiation for it. Good luck with that! Here's his records. He was sent up from North Chicago VA. Oh, and here's his film jacket."

Randall grimaced and took the pile of loosely arranged papers. "Looks like the usual NCVA dump. Why do we always have to be their garbage bin?"

Randall mumbled to himself as he trundled off to his office to review the paper salad. He sorted things out and found the key ingredients. The chest X-rays were sparse, but clearly showed a right lung mass that had grown from two to four centimeters in one month. The needle biopsy showed a squamous cell carcinoma. Once armed with all he could sift out of the mess, he went to the hall where Stanley and Sam were waiting, then escorted them into the exam room.

Sam was a normal and healthy-looking young man, and his older brother looked like the sick one, somewhat haggard and exhausted. Sam may have looked normal, but trying to have a logical discussion with him was nigh unto impossible. His train of thought was often derailed by tangential thinking, free association, and reiteration of a complex delusional conspiracy ideation. No matter where the conversation started, it always circled back to the paranoid scheme against him.

Randall decided to hold off on talk for a few moments and turned to concentrated study of the X-rays and paperwork, as though the answer lay hidden there. Both Stanley and Sam became agitated and asked what he had found. Randall demurred and said he needed to do a more thorough chest examination. He spent ten minutes listening to Stanley's chest, percussing it, and having Sam repeatedly say the "e" sound while he listened with his stethoscope.

Randall finally sighed and gave out several loud *hmm* sounds. The room was heavy with tension.

Stanley broke the silence. "So, Dr. B, what did you find?"

Randall shook his head but didn't speak. Instead he went back to the view box and looked carefully at the images again. Then he pointed to the name imprinted at the bottom of the film. "So, Stanley, could you repeat the spelling of your last name for me?"

"Sure," said Stanley with a shaky voice. "It's D-O-B-L-E-M-A-N."

Randall made another loud *hmm* sound. "You sure it's got only one *O?*"

"I'm sure," said Stanley. "Been that way all my life."

"And your Social Security number?" asked Randall.

Stanley recited the number, and Randall made the *hmm* sound again.

Sam had had it. "So what is your conclusion, Dr. B?"

Randall stood up tall, put his thumbs in his belt, leaned back, and made his pronouncement. "You, sir, Mr. Stanley Dobleman, do indeed have Stage 2 lung cancer, and it needs immediate radiation treatment or it will soon kill you dead."

Stanley did not hesitate with his response. "That is a lie. You are in on the scheme with the government. I will not take any such treatment. I don't have cancer and don't need anything done. Sam, let's get out of here."

Sam put up both hands. "*Whoa*, Stanley. Why would this nice doctor try to hurt you? What if I sign the consent for you?"

Stanley stood up. "You go ahead, but no one can make me go in that room and lie down."

Randall knew when he was defeated. His little stratagem had backfired. "I understand, Stanley. I am not going to force you into treatment. That does neither of us any good. But do me a favor and just hold up for a moment longer. I have another expert I would like to review your case. It will only take another few minutes. Would that be okay? If you don't like what she has to say, no one will stand in your way if you wish to go home."

Stanley rolled his eyes and thought for a moment.

Randall added a sweetener. "Look, I'll give you both fresh coffee and donuts while you wait."

Stanley raised his eyebrows. "Got any jelly filled?"

Randall nodded. "I think I can make that happen."

Stanley smiled. "Yeah, I'm pretty hungry from all this talk. You've got a deal."

Randall scooted out and found only three donuts left in the Ortho Room. Luckily, one was filled with strawberry jam. He grabbed that one, plus a glazed, and took them to the exam room. Randall went to get them coffee and asked Doris to page Elisa Angeles, ASAP. Fortunately, she answered the first page.

Randall explained the situation and asked if she had any ideas. She had nothing off the top of her head, but promised she'd have something by the time she got there. Randall hoped that was true. He went back to Doris's office to wait.

"So I gather you struck out?" observed Doris.

Randall nodded abjectly. "Well, I fouled off a few good pitches in the strike zone, worked a few balls, and got to a full count. But then he threw a knuckleball, and I swung and missed."

"So now you're calling in your best pinch hitter?" asked Doris.

"You bet," said Randall. "I'm hoping she can at least get an infield hit."

"Well, you are certainly no Hank Aaron!" Doris shook her head and chuckled.

Elisa appeared in the doorway to Doris's office. "Is the patient still here?"

Randall smiled weakly and nodded. "I stalled him with donuts. Maybe he's in a better mood now. You come up with a strategy?"

Elisa pulled up a corner of her mouth and looked upward. "Maybe. Good old college try and all that."

Doris gave her an encouraging smile. "Godspeed."

"May the road come up to meet you and not smack you too hard," offered Randall.

Elisa smiled back. "Thanks, I think. Off to see the wizard."

Doris gave Randall a look. "What do you think?"

Randall shrugged. "Any storm in a port."

Elisa was in with Stanley and Samuel for about fifteen minutes before she came out with the two men. They were all laughing and grinning. Elisa directed Doris to set Stanley up with a simulation appointment. No other questions were asked until the duo left.

Randall put hands on hips and gave Elisa a quizzical look. "Okay, out with it, Houdini. How did you wriggle that one out?"

Elisa gave a small hand wave. "Simple. I told him that since he had a fake tumor, we would give him a fake treatment to fool the government conspirators. We'd go through all the motions to make them think he was being treated, but that we would actually be using invisible X-rays to treat him. And we would make sure that the tumor got disappeared on all his subsequent chest X-rays."

Randall was amazed. "And he bought that?"

"He did once I promised fresh donuts at least once a week," said Elisa.

"Is that even legal?" asked Doris. "Did he sign consent? Did the brother cosign?"

"They did," said Elisa. "And the brother understands the little game we're playing. He's good with it as long as his brother gets treated. He's really the one with guardianship. We just needed a way for Stanley to cooperate willingly."

Doris still wasn't quite convinced. "What about when he starts gettin' radiation side effects? How do we explain that away?"

Randall rubbed his chin. "That won't be until we're four weeks into treatment. We'll tell him up front that by four weeks, patients usually complain about trouble swallowing and get a red rash in the treatment area. He's going to have to complain about those symptoms to fool the government agents. With his thin line between reality and imagination, we could be okay."

Doris frowned. "So play it by ear is your best plan?"

Randall smiled broadly. "Improvisation makes some pretty fine music. Listen to the master."

Elisa looked offended. "What am I? Chopped liver?"

Doris pulled the last thread. "Perhaps. But very finely chopped."

"Very fine indeed," retorted Randall. "*You* are the master I'm talking about, dear Elisa. I'm the backup band!"

It had been a day of revelations, but Randall was way frazzled and happy it was TGIF time. He was looking forward to a long weekend of, hopefully, "normal" family activities. It was a slightly tentative anticipation of peace and restfulness. Normal had a way of being redefined at Creekside Place.

Organize a Posse

Just as Randall was ready to bolt for the exit, he decided to take a few minutes to call Joe Shepard and see how the plans for the study group meeting were going. Good fortune was with him. He found Joe still in his office and he had already done his homework. Joe had contacted a respectable number of possible participants and Joe went through the list with Randall.

The core group included Randall, radiation oncologist; Joe, child psychologist; and Dan Graham, Randall's new radiation physicist. They had also added John Bingham, MD, PhD, an adult psychiatrist friend of Joe's. John was also a Freemason member of the Fellowcraft Degree. Another added member was Ruby Cosgrove, a former Catholic nun turned yoga instructor and close friend of Joe's wife. Ruby had recommended a friend of hers, Chase Medley, a Christian Science practitioner who also dabbled in other belief systems such as Universalism, Multidimensionality and Transcendence, with a dash of Edgar Cayce tossed in for a spicy tang.

All study group members had been contacted and agreed to a three-hour kick-off meeting as soon as they could arrange a meeting place. Joe and Randall set up an agenda for the meeting, which would start with an opening presentation of the issues, led by Joe or Randall, followed by a fifteen-minute response by each invitee, addressing how their expertise might shed light on the possible mechanisms of non-verbal communication. This would be followed by a coffee break and a one hour roundtable discussion. They envisioned follow-up meetings with deeper dives into each perspective, aided and abetted by recommended readings.

When the call was finally finished, Randall gathered his gear and beat a hasty retreat to the parking lot and zipped home.

As Randall and Zelda were preparing for bed that night, Zelda winked at Randall and announced she was going to take a hot bath so she could get "nice and clean" for "a little bit later." She said she had been thinking about some cuddly time all day. She suggested Randall wait patiently in bed for her, and she would come out wearing her Zen robe.

Randall licked his lips and gave her a thumbs up as he got into bed. When his head hit the pillow, his eyes slammed shut, and he dreamed he was making mad passionate love.

Randall awoke at sunrise the next morning and tried his best to remember if his recollection of lovemaking was real or a dream. As he struggled to recall, he also couldn't quite remember who his partner had been either. He looked over at Zelda. She was soundly asleep. He pulled up the covers a bit and found she was naked. He still couldn't recall. He decided he'd go with "it happened even if it was only in his brain."

Despite Randall's terminal fatigue when he had hit bed Friday night and the opportunity to sleep in this Saturday morning, when he awoke early, he couldn't go back to sleep. *What good was the opportunity to sleep in if you didn't make use of it?* he asked himself. Then he thought of all the chores that awaited him, and he heard his father's voice again reminding him to clean up his mess before it got worse. There was snow to shovel, oil/filter change on the Scirocco, and something else. But he couldn't remember what the last thing was.

Then Randall recalled another disturbing task he hadn't done. The battery on the VW van kept dying. Zelda had gotten stranded at the mall parking lot. He'd have to at least charge the battery if not replace it. She'd been using the dead battery as the basis for buying her a Volvo station wagon, pointing out how sturdy and reliable they were. Randall countered with noting how boxy they were and the only doctors that bought them were gynecologists.

Zelda's riposte had one upped him: "The VW microbus is the epitome of boxy. The Volvo would be a step up!"

Randall panicked when he remembered that Zelda had to go

shopping with the kids and haul Addie to a ballet lesson. *Who needed ballet lessons anyhow?* The kids were growing out of most of their clothes and needed new shoes. Something about ballet slippers too. If the van wouldn't start, Zelda would have to take the Scirocco. Plus, the whole Volvo debate would restart. Then how could he change the oil and filter? When did days off get so complicated? One thing was clear. If he didn't get Zelda's wheels rolling, there would be no Saturday night roll in the hay. So he leapt out of bed and got cracking on his tasks. Completing them was no guarantee he would get lucky, but the alternative was an ice-cold shoulder.

Wheels were further greased that night by Randall taking the family out for a cholesterol replenishment feast at Big Boy's. This had put everyone in a compliant mood. Having wheedled his way into Zelda's good graces, there had been no need to beg for "cuddling" that night. Afterward, the exhausted parents had fallen into a sound sleep. That is until they were both awakened at 2:00 a.m. by screaming coming from Addie's room.

Randall and Zelda leapt out of bed and ran to the hallway where they found Kyle, who had been awakened as well and was on his way to check on his sister. The lights went on in Addie's room just before they all entered. Addie was sitting up in bed with the covers pulled up to her neck. Randall rushed to Addie's side, and she grabbed him around the neck.

"Daddy!" gasped Addie. "I heard breathing, and my eyes popped open. I was a-scared. Then I heard a voice and it said, 'You don't belong in this house, you little whippersnapper!' At first, I thought it was a dream and I tried to shake my head awake. Then something grabbed my leg! Right here, on my ankle! I turned on the light, but no one was there."

Randall felt an instant anger build inside of him toward anyone or anything that would dare scare his little rosebud. He surveyed the room and saw nothing suspicious. Addie started to sob into his shoulder.

Zelda looked suspiciously at her son. "Kyle, you weren't trying to pull a fast one on your sister, were you?"

Kyle put his hand on his chest, the other still rubbing his sleepy eyes. "Me?! What the heck? I don't go in her girlie room. It stinks like unicorns in there. I bet it was the Big Boy bobblehead. We should throw them all out."

Zelda sat on the other side of the bed opposite Randall, and Addie reached out her little hand to hold her mother's hand. "It didn't sound like Kyle's voice, Mommy. It was more like a witchy woman, all high and creaky, like a door in a scary movie. The breathing sounded like gusts of wind with wheezing like when I have an asthma attack." Addie started to shake.

Zelda held her tight. "That must have been so scary!"

Kyle tugged on Randall's sleeve. "Do we need to hire one of those stiff white-collar guys to come to the house and do his exercises? You know, to get rid of a devil woman in the house?"

Zelda stifled a giggle. "No, honey, we can take care of it ourselves. We can make sure there are no bad things in the house."

Addie sniffled. "Good. I don't want to be a snapperwhipper. I don't even know what that is. Mommy, can I sleep in your room?"

After Addie finally calmed down, Randall took Kyle back to bed and tucked him in.

"You're not scared are you, bud?" asked Randall.

"I don't think so," said Kyle. "I'm pretty sure it was just a dream. Maybe like the ones I get. I told you Big Boy milkshakes give Addie the jeebs. You can go back to bed, Dad. I'll be okay."

"Did I ever tell you what a good kid you are?" asked Randall.

"I think so, but you can tell me again," said Kyle.

Randall gave him a little head rub and kissed him on the forehead. "Good night, little dude."

"Good night, Dad dude."

Randall went back to Addie's bedroom, where Zelda had crawled under the covers with Addie. The two were all snuggled up. Zelda whispered to Randall that she'd stay with Addie until Addie fell asleep.

Randall kissed both girls on the forehead, went back to bed and collapsed into a deep sleep. Randall's last conscious thought wandered through his mind. *At least Addie waited until consummation was achieved.*

CHAPTER 28

SUNDAY MORNING STRING ME ALONG

"You know everybody is ignorant, only on different subjects."

— Will Rogers

Magnetic Electrons

Despite Addie's scary early Sunday dreams, everyone was up early. The kids usually liked to sleep in, but this morning they were hanging a little closer to their parents and asking for pancakes and bacon.

Nobody mentioned anything about Addie's dream, but thoughts of it were in the air. When breakfast was finished, the kids actually volunteered to clean up the dishes. In a rare showing of sibling camaraderie, they asked to go upstairs to listen to the new Steve Martin album on their record player. They loved the King Tut song and often annoyed each other by trying to outsing one another.

"Looks like we will have a relaxing day, Randy," said Zelda. "There's nothing really pressing. We did our chores yesterday. I think I may get to that painting I've wanted to do!"

The phone rang, and Zelda dried her hands to answer it. "Wow, seems like a lot of folks are up early for a Sunday."

She talked for a few minutes. Randall watched her body get more and more tense. When she hung up, she announced that she was going out to talk to Mrs. Miller up the street.

"No worries, take your time," said Randall. "I'll keep watch on the striplings."

Randall had been hankering for a little quiet reading time. He went to his den to read the paper, but mostly to study the comics. After finishing with "There Oughta Be a Law," he had a brain memo flash and got out the newly published 1978 edition physics textbook. One of the departmental perks was to provide the staff with new editions of reference texts. His new physics tome had arrived earlier that week.

Physics research was changing understanding of the physical world so rapidly that, these days, it was hard to keep up. He thought he remembered seeing a chapter near the end of the new text regarding string theory. Since it seemed to have little relevance to his daily work when he initially scanned through the new edition, he'd just skimmed the contents. However, Dan's reference to string theory stuck like a bug in his brain, and he was now very curious about it.

According to the text, string theory traced back to 1907 when German mathematician, Theodur Kaluza, attempted to expand on Einstein's unified theory of nature's forces. Einstein had been able to describe gravity in terms of warps and curves in space-time. Kaluza thought he could do the same for the other known force at that time: electromagnetism, which included electricity and magnetic attraction. Kaluza posited a fourth dimension, in addition to the known three, to explain electromagnetic force and complete a unified theory of everything.

Kaluza's theory seemed so far out at the time that it wasn't taken seriously by most scientists. But in 1926, Oskar Klein, who was intrigued by the idea of additional dimensions, suggested that, besides the dimensions we can see, there might be tiny, curled-up dimensions so small that, despite being all around us, they can't be seen by any direct means. Many physicists tried to verify the theory of additional small dimensions through the '40s and '50s, but could not make the math correlate with observations. Thus the additional dimension concept was temporarily abandoned.

Somewhere around the '60s and '70s, a new unifying theory began to emerge from the data coming from particle physics. Much of the new data came from the use of accelerators that bombarded various atoms and atomic particles at high speed from which emerged new particles. This work clarified how the atom was made up of electrons, neutrons, and protons. Looking still deeper, it was found that even the subatomic particles were made up of something smaller called quarks. Conventional physics concepts proved inadequate to explain quarks and, from this deficiency, emerged string theory.

String theory posits that inside each quark is a unique dancing filament of energy that behaves like a vibrating string. Some string theorists believe the string vibrates like a single string, such as on a violin, but most believe the string is looped upon itself and vibrates in different patterns and frequencies, much like musical notes, each defining the nature of the particle it makes up. Herein was the unification sought for nearly a century, since matter (made up of electrons and quarks) and radiation particles (made up of photons and gravitons) are all built up from one entity, the vibrating strings.

"I think I get it!" exclaimed Randall out loud. "It's just what Dan was explaining to me the other day. He knows his stuff."

Randall felt energy moving through him. The concepts were starting to take hold. He sat up taller, excited about what he'd learned. He felt a summary coming on as he read further.

The chapter went on to describe that matter and the forces of nature all have these unique vibrating strings making them up. Ironically, to make the math work for string theory, one needs to invoke more than just three dimensions of space. The way the strings vibrate is affected by the geometry of the extra dimension(s). Some suggested as many as ten dimensions are required, which led right back to Kaluza and Klein.

Randall found himself in a kind of timeless dimension of wonder, his brain vibrating with the thrill of exploration. *I'm a happy physics nerd, I am, I am.* For him, it wasn't just words on a page, it was more like a symphony of images, creating loops of electromagnetic energy, emerging in a double helix spiraling in space.

Randall had been studying science and physics for a long time and had the strange sensation that his foundation was shifting beneath him. Until now, physics was just a necessity for his job, but this new information allowed for exploration at a grander level. He was filled with an invigorating and disorienting bewilderment. It was time for some internal realignment.

The chapter finished with the strange phenomenon of quantum entanglement, mirroring the conversation that Randall had recently had with Dan Graham.

If all matter and energy were interchangeable, as Einstein showed and, if the basis for all of it were vibrating strings in multiple dimensions, could that possibly explain some of the unusual phenomena I have experienced?

Randall shook his head to try to settle some ideas into place. Certainly, Einstein's relativity theory did not explain the reappearance of the dead or psychic communication. However, string and quantum theory seemed to open a new door to the way the universe worked that might leave room for some of the imponderables. Could vibrating strings effectuate the manifestation of spirit beings, telepathy, telekinesis or even love—action at a distance from pure thought energy? Vibrating energy? Sending and receiving?

Man, this is some heavy stuff! I want to share this with Dan and Joe. They would get such a kick out of it. I think I finally understand what Dan was talking about. I wonder who wrote this chapter? Was it one of the physics gurus from MIT?

Randall flipped back to the beginning of the article.

Well, hog my hooter. The chapter was authored by Dan Graham, MS, medical physicist. That's my guy.

Babysitter Bad News

From the den, Randall heard Zelda come in the back door. Usually she was whistling or singing, but all he heard was the door closing and a flumping sound against the wall. He sensed something was amiss, so he went to check. Zelda was leaning with her back to the wall, barely moving, and looking dazed.

"Zelda, what's wrong? You look like you've seen a ghost."

"Huh? Give me a second. I'm still processing," said Zelda in a pained voice. "You remember last night when I mentioned Julie Miller?"

Randall frowned. "Remind me. I was pretty wasted last night."

"Julie is the neighbor up the street I was going to call about using her babysitter. She called me a few minutes ago. Can you imagine that? Right when I was about to call her!"

Randall raised both eyebrows. "Yow. That's one for the books. What did she want?"

Zelda's eyes watered up. "Here's where it gets even spookier. She called to tell me that something terrible happened to her babysitter, Alexandra. She is, *er* . . . was a freshman at the high school. She's been sitting for Julie's kids for the past three years. She actually watched Kyle and Addie a few times a couple years ago, remember? It didn't go well. Kyle put a frog in her purse. And poured my favorite nail polish in her shoes."

"Oh, man, I had purposely forgotten about that. And now I remember why we haven't had a date night in a while. But I do remember Alexandra. Her dad picked her up in that '69 Mustang Mach 3. Lime green."

"Oh Randy, of course that's what you remember. Alexandra was a tender soul. Julie taught her how to plant flowers. She had one of those little yappy dogs with the squishy face. Alex loved that dog, even though it pees on the kitchen floor." Zelda's voice drifted off.

Randall cupped Zelda's elbow and led her to the living room where he sat her down on the couch. He sat down beside her and draped a blanket over her shaking legs.

"Tell me what happened."

Zelda choked back a sob. "Julie said that Alexandra was found dead in her bedroom. Julie said the news has been all over the neighborhood. We're not Catholic, so we weren't in the grapevine. Apparently it was a suicide. There was no information shared about how she died."

"Oh, wow. That's every parent's nightmare. Why would a kid do that? Did she leave a note?"

Zelda shook her head slowly. "Julie was more in shock than I am. There was no note."

Randall held her shoulders. "I wonder if she had been planning it . . . how would we even know?"

Zelda shrugged. "I asked that too. But there was no indication that the girl was planning on doing something that drastic. Julie said Alexandra had a garden she was growing and had drawn up plans to build a greenhouse in the backyard. She talked all the time about what she wanted to study in college."

"I can't imagine that happening. I mean, how could parents miss the signs?" Randall shivered, imagining himself missing any signs in his own kids.

Zelda started to cry. "But Randy, maybe there wasn't any clear sign. I feel so bad for her parents! I'm sure they feel responsible. I know I would. I always feel an attack of FTM when I hear stuff like this. Like this could happen to me."

Randall tilted his head. "FTM?"

"You know, Failure to Mom. Missing the signs, not seeing the burning forest. Oldest job on the planet, and I'm failing at it."

Randall held her tighter. "Then I'm guilty of FTD, and not the kind that delivers flowers to the door. Sometimes we are so close to the day-to-day that we don't see the larger trends. Wow, so they don't know much about what may have led up to it?"

Zelda sighed. "I got the feeling that Julie knew more, but she had to get ready for Mass. One more thing she did share, though. The funeral is today, this afternoon, right after Mass. She said we could come, but Randy, I don't know . . ."

Randall felt his skin crawl. He had been to more funerals than he cared to count. Many had been family, so other elders were in charge. He wasn't sure how he would handle a funeral for Alexandra, though. And what would they tell the kids? Should they bring them? Go and leave them home alone?

As if she were reading his mind, Zelda decided the issue. "Oh Randy, I don't think Kyle and Addie would truly understand what's going on if they went. They probably don't remember Alexandra all that well. I do, though. She was a shy girl, always hiding behind her hair. But I still feel like I need to go and support Julie."

"Zel, then you should go. What time does Mass start?"

Zelda recoiled, as if scalded by holy water. "Oh, I don't mean go to mass. I had enough trouble going to your parents' Lutheran church for our wedding, and I'm not going to convert anytime soon! I'll just go for the service. It starts at 12:30. I'll meet Julie and Chris there. Julie is pretty torn up. I don't know how Chris will handle this—even though he's a pretty stoic guy! I bet he'll just take the kids home after Mass and skip the funeral. You know how some guys hate funerals?"

Oh boy, thought Randall, *count me in the same camp as Chris!*

Kid Query

After Zelda left for the funeral service, Randall wondered where Kyle and Addie had gone off to. It was quiet; too quiet. That didn't bode well. He thought it might be an opportunity to catch them at some mischief, so he crept quietly up the stairs and found the doors closed to both Kyle's and Addie's bedrooms. Randall slowly opened Kyle's door and found him playing quietly with his *Star Wars* figures.

Randall poked his head in the room. "Whatcha doing, Bud?"

"Planning an attack on the Death Star," said Kyle somberly.

"What's the plan?" asked Randall.

"I know Darth Vader already killed Alexandra," said Kyle. "But someone needs to rescue the body and bring it back to Earth for a proper burial. She was a nice girl. Why did she have to die?"

Randall was slightly taken aback. "So Mom told you she died?"

"Yeah, but she didn't tell me much. She just said to play in my room until she got back from the church. I know Darth actually told Alex to kill herself with the phone cord."

Randall's gut tied up in knots. *Time to change the subject.* "*Hmm*, tell you what, let's play a game. Why don't you go downstairs and get out Monopoly and set it up in the kitchen. I'll get Addie from her room and join you in a few minutes. We can talk about stuff while we play."

"Jumping Jack Flash!" said Kyle. "We haven't played Monopoly in forever. I love that game. I always win." Kyle put down the *Star Wars* gear and ran off downstairs.

Randall knocked on Addie's door and asked if he could come in.

"Yes, Daddy, come in," said Addie quietly. Randall found her lying on her bed, holding her replacement stuffed unicorn and stroking its head. Big Boy was on the nightstand with its curly forelocked head still bobbling.

"Whatcha doing?"

"Being sad," she murmured. "Alex used to read me bedtime stories. She was almost as good as you. Now she'll never read to me again."

"Was Uni helping you?" asked Randall.

"Yes," said Addie. "He told me not to be scared."

"Were you scared?" asked Randall.

"If it could happen to her . . . ," said Addie, her voice trailing off. "But why did it happen, Daddy? It's not fair."

"I don't know, Sweetie," said Randall. "I asked Kyle to set up Monopoly downstairs. We can play the game and talk about this together."

"I don't feel like playing anything! Do I have to?" Her little eyelids drooped.

Before Randall could answer, Kyle was back upstairs and ran to Addie's door.

"Hey, what's taking so long?" yelled Kyle. "Everything is set for Monopoly. Hurry up and get downstairs so I can beat the pants off you guys."

The brazen challenge emboldened Addie. She squinted her eyes with resolve. "I feel like playing Monopoly now. Let's go give him a Boardwalk wedgie."

After thirty minutes of play, Kyle was, as predicted, well vested in prime property, and Addie was steaming.

"Why does Kyle always win?" griped Addie. "And why did Alex have to die? I loved her. Why does everything we love have to be taken away?"

Randall was gobsmacked. Addie rarely burst out with anger at the inequities of life. And so much for Kyle and Addie not remembering Alexandra.

"Yeah, Dad," said Kyle. "You said you'd explain it while we played. I win at Monopoly 'cause I have the force with me. But I don't know why Alex died. Was she sick? Did she have an accident with the cord? Did Darth get in her head?"

The moment of truth had arrived, and Randall couldn't think of a way around it except to be honest. He wished Zelda was present to help him, but sometimes the posse is not in time.

"Okay, let's stop the game a minute and, Kyle, if you don't mind, I am going to put the bank money out of reach while we chat," said Randall.

"Dad, I wasn't cheating," protested Kyle.

"Didn't say you were," said Randall. "Just saving us all from temptation."

Randall shuffled his feet, rearranged himself in the chair, and cleared his throat.

"There's no easy way to say it," began Randall. "Alexandra wasn't sick with a physical disease. It looks like she took her own life."

"*Duh*, Dad, I knew that." Kyle crossed his arms and his eyes.

Randall ignored him. "For reasons we may never know, she decided she didn't want to live anymore. She didn't leave a note or anything to explain why she did it. For reasons we don't completely understand, young teenagers sometimes get depressed."

"What's depressed?" asked Kyle.

"That's when you start feeling like life is not worth living, and nothing interests you anymore," explained Randall. "For young teenagers, sometimes they feel like they can't ever please their parents. Other times it's from kids picking on them at school. Some doctors think it's because of all the changes teenage bodies are going through. Sometimes it's all those things together."

"But why did Alex do it?" asked Addie, starting to cry.

"I don't know, Rosebud," said Randall weakly. "She didn't leave a note and her parents didn't have a clue it was coming. That's the sad part. Many times, we just never know why."

"How did she . . . was it tied to something high? Or did she just tie it too tight?" asked Kyle.

Randall didn't know what to say. He didn't understand why Kyle kept alluding to a cord and strangulation. "I don't know," said Randall. "Her parents didn't say, and that's their business. I have to respect their privacy."

"Well, then how do kids like Alex usually do it?" continued Kyle.

The runaway train was threatening to derail. Randall shuffled his mental deck, looking for the right cards. He didn't want to plant any ideas in their heads but decided to play the honesty card again.

"Well, it isn't a pretty story, but if you really want to know, and if Addie is okay with it, I'll give some examples," said Randall.

Addie thought for a moment and decided that she wanted to hear. The truth was never as brutal as what the scared imagination could conjure.

"Once kids, or adults, decide on suicide, they usually pick a way to do it that's the least painful," said Randall. "At that point they're not afraid to die, but they are afraid it might hurt. So they pick ways that are the quickest and the least painful."

"Like shooting or jumping out a window?" asked Kyle.

"Exactly," agreed Randall, wishing his son didn't have that insight.

"Sometimes people take too many pills or use poison. My aunt did it by hanging herself with a rope. She got up on a chair, put the rope around her neck, tied the rope to something high up and jumped off the chair."

"Your aunt suicided?" asked Addie with a gasp.

"Yes, my uncle came home from work and found her hanging in the basement," said Randall. "The rope cuts off your breathing or can break your neck. There are many other ways you can kill yourself, but they all mean that you die, and you never get a chance to live the rest of your life. You never get to find out what you're meant to be. Plus, all the people who love you lose you forever and are very sad for the rest of their lives."

"I would never do it," said Kyle. "You and Mom don't make me feel that bad. Sometimes the kids at school are mean to me, but I just get meaner right back, and they leave me alone. Plus, all those ways to die don't sound so great."

"I wouldn't do it either," said Addie. "But sometimes I get really sad about stuff, and if I got ten times or twenty times sadder, I think I might think about it, but I would be afraid 'cause I'm sure I'd miss you and Mom too much. And I know it would make you and Mom really sad too."

"That's good, you two," said Randall, feeling like he was still treading deep waters. "That's exactly the way I feel about it. Life is precious, and it's already too easy to lose it from disease and accidents. So we should take it as a gift that we've been trusted with to protect until it's our time to give it up."

A pregnant pause lasted a few beats. "Dad, this is heavier than a thunderstorm, and it's getting hard to breathe." Addie shivered. "I want to stop talking about it. Can we finish Monopoly? I think the force is with me now, and Kyle is going to lose!"

"No way, José," rebuffed Kyle. "Bring it on, Sister."

"Okay, you two, settle down," urged Randall. "I never win anything, but pretend I'm wearing a shirt with black stripes, and I've got a referee's whistle around my neck. If there's any rough stuff, I may call a penalty." Randall was glad to be back in shallow water.

The three resumed playing Monopoly and Kyle gradually began to lose his property holdings. Addie was in early gloat mode, and Randall was rapidly approaching bankruptcy when Zelda came in the back door rather quietly. She took off her coat and hung it in the closet, then slowly approached the gaming table. The three players were so engrossed in the game, they didn't notice her until she put her hands on Randall's shoulders and kissed him on top of his head.

"What was that for?" asked Randall, rubbing the kiss spot into his scalp.

"For being a good dad," she said.

"Hey, Mom," said Kyle. "How was the church thing for Alex?"

"Very sad," said Zelda.

"We were feeling pretty sad too," added Addie. "That's why I'm holding Uni. I loved Alex."

Zelda sighed. "I've had enough sadness for one day. I don't want to talk about it anymore. You know, it's been a while since I last played Monopoly. That looks like fun. I'd like to join in when you finish this round. From the size of the money pile in front of Rosebud, she's cleaning up."

"Yeah," grumbled Kyle. "Right after Dad explained about how to kill yourself, I lost the force, and Addie started winning."

"Randy! You did what?" gasped Zelda.

CHAPTER 29

———

MEMENTO MORI

"Nothing in life is to be feared; it is only to be understood."

— Marie Curie

MONOPOLISTIC BEHAVIOR

Unexpectedly, Addie and Kyle did a good job backing up Randall's explanation of the suicide discussion they had during Monopoly. Zelda seemed quite mollified. In fact, she was secretly relieved that Randall had done the heavy lifting. She put on a big smile and clapped her hands.

"Alright," said Zelda. "Before you finish the game, I want all three of you to stand up and come over here right now."

They did as commanded, and Zelda enfolded them in a group hug. She squeezed so hard the kids almost came unglued.

"I'm so glad I have all of you, right here and right now, in my arms," said Zelda, maintaining her hold. "Randy, you're such a good man. I'm so grateful for you. Kyle, you are important to me. Please remember that. Addie, please know that you can always talk to me and Dad, okay? We love you."

Both kids soaked up the honey, but then got fidgety. Finally, Kyle pulled himself away.

"Geez, you're being weird, Mom," said Kyle. "I want to finish the game."

"Me too," said Addie.

"The attention spans of a flea," muttered Randall. "Okay, guys, take your places, and let's draw final blood. Your mom can probably use the time to freshen up."

"Great idea," said Zelda. "I could use a change of clothes and some liquid refreshment , not necessarily in that order. I'll be back."

Addie continued and completed her conquest in short order. When Zelda came back downstairs, Kyle proved to be a very sore loser and declared a complete lack of interest in playing another round. Addie excused herself to go back to her room. Zelda was happy to have Randall to herself so she could do a debrief about the funeral service.

"The service was lovely, Randy. At least as lovely as a funeral for a young lady could dare to be. I could barely bring myself to look at her parents—they were so distraught! The church was full. They invited people to stay and connect afterward. Julie and I just stood around together talking about how Alex could be anyone's kid, really. Maybe even our own someday." Zelda looked down at her hands. "It got me thinking about when I was that age and had similar thoughts."

That was news to Randall. He couldn't think of a thing to say and just put his arm around her shoulders. He thought about the silence in his family after his aunt's suicide all those years ago.

"I'm glad you're here now, Zel." He really didn't know what else to say, so he chose the wiser path of closing his mouth and opening his ears.

"Come to think of it, Randy, those thoughts weren't really that long ago. How did I even make it through adolescence?"

Randall shrugged his shoulders and put on his best Chelsea Andretti "tell me more" face. Zelda sighed and continued. "There was food at the reception, but I couldn't eat anything. Julie and I overheard a lot of conversation about how on earth anybody would choose death as the best way out of any situation. A student in Alexandra's class told us that her best friend's younger sister was also considering suicide after hearing about Alexandra."

Randall decided to try some reflection skills. "So it really rippled through the community, huh?"

Zelda nodded. "Julie and I eased over to the teens' conversation. You know how teens don't really talk to their own parents but sometimes talk to other adults. We figured we're both moms, maybe we could take the opportunity to have a positive influence on the girls."

"Good idea. I bet it helped." Randall sighed.

"Julie and I encouraged the girls to open up. All the other adults were huddled around the food and drinks. Why wasn't anyone talking to the kids? Once we listened for a while, the older girls shared a little more. They said that there was a rumor that Alexandra had strangled herself somehow."

Randall couldn't contain himself. "Oh my gosh. How?"

Zelda looked relieved. "That's what I was wondering too! But I didn't want to fuel the rumor mill. I wanted the girls to know that these things are not for kids to handle alone. We talked about how situations could feel overwhelming and life-threatening, but when you look at them in perspective, nothing is really worth a permanent solution to a temporary problem."

"Sounds like you and Julie made a good team."

Zelda shrugged. "Yeah, well, Julie seemed to be a bit more level-headed than I was. I just followed her lead. She spoke at their level, and we got to the important stuff pretty fast. We talked about how to handle someone's suicidal ideation, and who to call if you hear about it. Since kids are more likely to tell a friend or classmate than an adult, it seemed like the perfect way to have an indirect impact on anyone thinking about it in the future."

Randall stared and sighed. "Wow. This is such a daunting topic for teens to handle. How can we prepare our sprouts to deal with this big stuff?"

Zelda looked overwhelmed. "Someday, Randy. All I know, is I don't want to deal with it today. I think I just need to pretend Kyle and Addie will be little kids forever."

"Fair enough!" Randall was relieved. He didn't feel ready to go any further with Kyle and Addie yet either. "Zel, sounds like Julie had a handle on this. I wonder why she wanted you to go with her to the service?"

"I was wondering that too. She seemed to know a lot of people at the church, since they've been going to Mass there for ages. At one point, she pulled me to the side, away from the crowd. She asked me, 'what do you think happens after we die?' I was surprised, because I thought the church had a pretty clear message on those kinds of things."

"Really? So do you think she's questioning her faith?" Randall cocked his head to the side.

"I guess so. We talked about it for a while. After she encouraged me a few times, I told her my beliefs. I told her I believe we have a spirit given by the universe. That spirit is part of the universal oneness and each one of us endeavors to learn lessons with each incarnation. Then we choose a body and situation that will provide it the chance to learn. We may decide to inhabit a body for a while, whether it's a person or an animal, or even a tree. We live the life of that body, encounter teachers, learn the lessons, and return to the universe to decide our next lessons."

"And those teachers are often the ones who challenge us the most?" Randall suggested.

"Right! Like my dad, who often told me 'In China, they drown girl babies.' That hurt so much. And my struggles with Kyle. He may get my goat, but I know that he's my teacher."

Randall nodded, understanding. "Yeah, the people we want to change or seek their approval. Or the ones who challenge us and raise our bile . . . they are the teachers?"

"Yeah. They show you where you have a trigger or a hot button. If you didn't have that trigger, the challenges wouldn't bother you. Your job is to find and fix your trigger spot."

Zelda was prone to moments of insight when she wasn't feeling defensive. Randall had not expected a pearl of wisdom to emerge.

Zelda continued. "Of course, that's hard to remember in the moment. My emotional reactions just explode up out of me. It's like there's a part of me that's still a hurt kid, and she's the one reacting to Kyle's defiance! And of course, hurt feels powerless, so it activates a part of me that wants to protect the hurt kid. It turns to anger in a red-hot flash."

Randall had often been the recipient of those red-hot flashes. "Yeah, I know what you mean!"

Zelda looked into the distance. "That's when I take off for a while, like outside on the deck or for a walk or a drive. I'm trying to listen to that part and ask it to give me some distance. I'm trying to reconnect with ME, with the spirit part that's timeless. When those parts of me are in an internal bonfire, I have got to walk away from the fuel and find myself again. It's like the spirit self has direct access to universal peace and wisdom."

Zelda paused to let the thought sink in.

Randall suddenly had a cascade of insight, linking all the times Zelda seemed so angry and just stormed away. He had always thought it was something about him, a rejection or abandonment. Again, his mother had said it best, back when he was a little kid: "Randy, other people's storms are almost never about you. Don't take on their fury—just come in out of the rain."

Randall stared down the hallway as though he could see the past more clearly there lurking in the shadows.

"You with me so far?" asked Zelda, noting the faraway look in his eyes.

"Yep, present and accounted for. Just integrating. Carry on."

"So it seems perfectly natural to me that spirit can communicate with spirit, even if it has no physical form. I have experienced spirit in ways I can't explain—like how I felt my grandma at her house after she died."

Randall nodded, recalling the incident when baby Addie had mysteriously choked on her blanket bunting.

"Remember how we seem to communicate when it's important, even if we don't pick up the phone or see each other?" said Zelda, continuing the line of thought. "We have to see and listen differently and be open to the messages, I guess. That's what I shared with Julie. All she said was 'that's not what my church taught me.' She didn't say much after that. Just looked really thoughtful and kind of spaced out, like she was following a misty path into her own mind."

Randall was awestruck at the depth of Zelda's mind, when she wasn't hiding behind her brick wall of defense.

"Thanks for your talk with the kids," said Zelda. "I think it was a good start for them to understand. I'll reinforce it at bedtime. What did you already cover?"

Randall recounted his conversation with the kids and the depth of their understanding of the issue. "At first I wanted to gloss over it to spare them the pain. But they got down to the nuts and bolts right away. I like what you said about not using a permanent solution to a temporary problem. That's going to be tough to put into kid language, but I have faith in you!"

Zelda looked down at her hands. "*Hmm*, no pressure, please. I think I can make the point with the Polluto story."

"Good one. That will strike close to home." Randall paused. "I am surprised you told Kyle about the strangulation with the cord. He told me he knew all about that."

Zelda pulled back. "Randy, what are you talking about? I didn't find that out until the reception!"

Randall's mind whirled, putting all the details together. *What threads did Kyle have access to?* He made a mental note to explore this with Zelda. But later. She was pretty full right now.

Zelda popped up from her chair, like something lit her pilot light. "Enough of this. Right now, I'm going to call a babysitter that Julie uses. She gave me the number after the service. With any luck, we'll have a date night next Saturday. Julie said her sitter can only stay until 11:00."

"Good. That will give us more time to . . . you know."

Zelda just shook her head with a quasi-disgusted look on her face.

POKING FUN.

10/22

RB

CHAPTER 30

———

OUT, OUT DAMNED SPOT

"We are all like the bright moon, we still have our darker side."

— Khalil Gibran

RELIGION 101

Sunday morning the following week the family gathered for Sunday brunch at 11:00. Randall and Zelda had decided to make it a weekly ritual so the family could have one unrushed meal a week to spend enough time to share their thoughts. Chelsea Andretti had recommended it as a "no fault" family safe time together at which the kids knew they could raise any issues of concern without fear of parental reprisal. Randall and Zelda were good with it since it still allowed them one morning to sleep in.

Kyle poked his fork at his Sunday morning pancake and frowned. The rest of the family was chowing down. Randall looked over at Kyle while chewing his last bite of bacon. He swallowed and washed it down with a slug of coffee. "What's the matter, Mr. Vader? Your light saber batteries need a recharge?

Kyle's receiver was not quite on the correct wavelength. "What?"

Zelda joined the query. "Earth to Kyle. Do you read me?"

"Oh, yeah, sure, Mom," said Kyle, coming out of his daze. "What's up?"

"Yeah, Kyle, you're usually trying to steal a pancake from me by this time," added Addie.

Kyle rolled his eyes. "I think I put too much syrup on my pancake. It's way soggy."

Randall feigned a sad look and stuck out his lower lip. "Come on, big boy. How can you ever have too much syrup? But there's some batter left, if you want a fresh pancake."

Addie softened a bit. "I'll share my last one with you."

Kyle whined again. "You put grape jelly on it. I hate grape jelly."

Zelda took a different tack. "Kyle, is something else bothering you?"

Kyle made a face. "Well, maybe."

Zelda put a hand on his arm. "So out with it. You know we have free speech at Sunday brunch."

Kyle hemmed and hawed a bit more, then spoke. "I was outside this morning to get the newspaper for Dad. Charlie and Claire Ichner were walking down the sidewalk toward the path on the Parkway, all dressed up and carrying some books. I asked where they were going. They said, 'Sunday School.' I laughed at them and said they were silly 'cuz there was no school on Sunday."

Kyle paused. Randall looked at Zelda, and they both felt a bit of tension coming on. Randall prompted Kyle to go on.

Kyle continued, "They laughed at me right back and told me I was a moron. They said they were Catholic and going to St. Juice Church for Bible study. Then later they go to church with their parents. They said all the kids on our block are Catholic and go there too. Charlie said we must be aceyists if we don't go to church. Claire said they weren't allowed to play with kids that weren't Catholic."

Randall had to stifle a laugh before he could respond.

Kyle noticed the not-quite-successful effort. "It's not funny, Dad! Why are we different?"

Zelda, who had kept a straight face, kicked Randall's leg under the table. "Honey, you're right. It's not funny. Dad wasn't laughing about us not going to church. He was laughing because you didn't get the name of the church quite right. It's called St. Jude's. Jude is the Catholic patron saint of lost causes."

"What's a saint?" asked Addie. "And what's an *aceyist*?"

Randall had another laugh attack. Addie looked at him with a deep frown. Zelda kicked Randall again and spoke. "Last one first. The correct word is 'atheist.' It means someone who doesn't believe in God. A saint believes in God and does lots of good throughout his or her life. Then after they die, the Catholic Church gives them that title of saint to recognize their good life."

Randall made a face. "Yeah, kids, but around here, you guys can achieve sainthood while you're still alive by helping with the dishes."

Zelda scowled at Randall.

Kyle smiled broadly. "You mean I wouldn't even have to be Catholic or go to Sunday school to be a saint?"

Randall patted Kyle's shoulder. "Nope, you don't. We are an equal opportunity sainthood denomination."

"For me too?" asked Addie.

"You too," said Zelda.

"Wait a minute . . . does that mean I HAFTA help people?" asked Kyle.

Zelda gave no leeway. "Yes, you do, sonny boy."

Kyle took the high road. "Alright then. But for that I'll need two fresh cooked pancakes."

While Randall warmed up the pan, Addie still seemed a bit confused. "So, Dad, if we're not Catholic, what are we? Is there a church we belong to?"

Randall let out a big breath and demurred. "I'm cooking. Ask your mom."

Zelda gave Randall the finger under the table. "You coward," she chirped. "Alright, here's the scoop according to me. There's lots of other churches out there besides Catholic, which go by lots of different names, called religions. So many, it gets confusing. I'll just name a few. Most of them believe in some kind of God, a super being that created everything. But they all have somewhat different rules of how they operate."

Kyle looked surprised. "They have rules? And they're all different? How did there get to be so many, and why are they different? Wouldn't God make the same rules for all the religions if they all believe in Him?"

Addie was perturbed. "Why does God have to be a him? Don't girls get any say so?"

Randall plopped two hot pancakes on Kyle's plate. "Both excellent questions, kiddos. And you've hit on exactly why your mom and I do not currently attend any specific church. We think most religions started out okay many years ago, but men, mostly, have changed the rules over time for their own benefit. We believe that there is a kernel of truth in each religion, so that all should be studied and learned from. We don't believe that any one religion should be forced upon anyone, especially kids. It should be something you study on your whole life and decide what feels right in your own heart."

Kyle looked troubled. "How do I know what's right?"

Zelda took over. "Sometimes it's not easy. But when you look inside yourself, really hard, you'll know what is right and true for you. No one else can tell you."

Kyle nodded his head. He seemed to get it. "Dad, did you or Mom ever go to a church?"

Randall responded. "I didn't go to church until I was ten years old. Then my mother decided we had to get some religion and announced that we would all be Lutherans."

"What the heck is Lutheran?" Addie slapped the table. "There you go with all the big words again!"

Randall didn't want to go too deeply into the layers of Christianity and world religious beliefs, especially with the kids' miniscule attention spans. "I wondered that too! My mother, your Grandma, chose the Lutheran church simply because one was close enough to the house that we could walk there. So I went, but I wasn't happy about it. It meant getting up early on Sunday and going to Bible study and catechism class. Even in the winter. And I wasn't sure I really believed any of the stuff they taught there. But I did it all. It never set well with me, and I found it hard to continue. It was like it wasn't my choice to start with."

"Yeah, I hate to do stuff 'cuz I have to," said Kyle.

"Or just because somebody says so," added Addie.

"You're not alone on that score." Randall chuckled and continued,

"I stopped going to church after high school, but when your mom and I were married, we picked my parents' Lutheran Church because it was important to them. But I still didn't feel comfortable about it."

Addie looked at Zelda. "Mom, did you ever go to a church?"

"Sort of," said Zelda. "My dad didn't believe in churches, but my mom did. She was a Christian Scientist. They don't really believe in God like most Christian churches do. That's a whole other bag of worms. The Christian Scientists believe that prayer can heal our ailments and that doctors are to be avoided."

Randall interjected. "Yeah, to me they're not very Christian, and not at all scientific."

Addie went into a huff again. "More grown-up talk. I need the kid version." She crossed her little arms and gave them each "square eyes."

Zelda laughed. "You're right, Rosebud. It's all confusing—even for grownups. Let's just say that what all the religions have in common is that they believe in some kind of Higher Power. You know, a big guy in the sky who made everything there is. He, or She, goes by many names, like God, The Great Spirit, Yahweh, Allah, Jehovah, and probably hundreds more."

Kyle interrupted. "Ha, see, there's no girl names."

Addie huffed once more. "I'll bet there are!"

"Addie's right," said Zelda. "In India, there are at least five goddesses, like Parvati, Kali, Saraswati, and I forget the rest."

Addie punched Kyle's arm. "Told you so, Superman brain."

Kyle tried to punch back, but Randall caught his arm before he could let loose. "Dad! She punched me first. I get to punch her back."

Randall shook his head. "Not if you're a good Christian. You are supposed to turn the other cheek."

"But she punched my arm. What's my cheek got to do with it?" whined Kyle. "And I still don't get what Christian means. Where does that come from? There's a kid at my school named Christian, but he's not very nice."

Randall nodded. "It is confusing! In the Bible, it says you should love your enemy. If they punch you in the right cheek, you're supposed to turn your head and give them the left cheek to punch to show your love and forgiveness."

Kyle shook his head. "That's bogus!"

Zelda took up the slack. "Well, the story goes that about 2,000 years ago, God was not happy with our behavior, so he sent his son, Jesus Christ, down from Heaven to straighten us out. Some people believed he was God's son, but most didn't, and wanted him dead, so they killed him. But he came back from the dead to prove them wrong. Those who believe Jesus Christ really rose from the dead are called Christians."

Kyle scoffed at the idea. "That's a load. Dead is dead. Croaked people can't do that."

Randall nodded. "Well, that's exactly the public relations problem that Christians have. They get around that by saying you just have to have faith that it's possible. So if Jesus can come back, so can the rest of us, but we have to really believe."

Addie looked at the ceiling for answers then stood up with a question. "Well, if it didn't work out for God when he sent Jesus, why didn't he send a daughter later on to remind us?"

Zelda was blown away. "That's an excellent question. I like your thinking. Actually, many believe other special people have been sent to repeat God's message, like Mohammed and Mahatma Gandhi. And maybe Mother Theresa, if you want to throw in a girl."

"Sounds like a lot of gobbledygook to me," concluded Kyle. "That's probably why you have to go to school on a Sunday to learn it all. Yuck."

Addie snorted. "Yeah. I'm not interested in learning more. I just want to know what all this talk has to do with anything?"

Randall looked at Zelda for a long moment. Zelda shrugged. "You want to start, or should I?" she asked.

The Elephant

"I'll start," said Randall. "Have you kids ever heard the story about the elephant in the room?"

Kyle's eyes widened. "No, Dad, but I bet the room was stinky."

Addie chuckled as Randall tried to keep a straight face. "Well, imagine there's a bunch of people in the room, talking about stuff, but none of them are willing to talk about the big smelly beast in the room."

"I bet they pay attention when the elephant takes a big dump in the corner," observed Kyle, chuckling at his own brilliance.

"That's not the point," said Randall, stifling a laugh. "The point is, why didn't anyone say anything about what was so obvious before it started to stink?"

"'Cause they were fraidy-phants?" offered Addie.

"Exactly," said Zelda. "Each person was afraid to bring it up, because they wanted to avoid being responsible for it. They all convinced themselves it wasn't really there, and if they all ignored it, it would just go away on its own."

Addie screwed up her face in puzzlement. "Mommy, Daddy . . . do you mean there's an elephant in the room with us now?"

Kyle scowled and sniffed. "I don't smell peanuts or fartyphants. Are you goof nuts?"

"Stop calling me names," yelped Addie.

Randall intervened again. "*Whoa.* Slow down, kids. No need to get testy. Sorry to disappoint you, little dude, but your sister has it pegged. Addie, tell us more. What are you thinking?"

Addie squinted one eye and leaned forward in her chair as if to tell a secret in confidence. "If the elephant is a big scary thing we don't talk about much, my little goof nuts brain says it's all the spooky stuff happening around here. You know, Kyle's night terrors, the bad lady in my room, and . . . all that other stuff. It's pretty scary."

Addie started to cry a bit, and Zelda motioned her to come sit in her lap. Zelda encircled Addie's small frame with her arms and kissed her forehead. "I know it's scary, honey, but Daddy and I are planning to do something about it. That's why we're having this talk about religion. But it's more about what we believe, not what other people say we should believe. Once we get all that straightened out, then we're going to make a plan to stop the spooky stuff from happening anymore."

Kyle crossed his arms and struck a warrior's pose. "I'm not scared.

Maybe you guys are. But I've got my light saber and my TIE Fighters. No spooks are going to get *me*."

Randall looked at Kyle in amazement. "That's great. Can I be your sidekick? With you at my side, I'll always be safe. Explain to me how that works."

Kyle waved a hand like the solution was as simple as ABC. "Any time some problem comes along, I grab my saber and I sit in my special *Star Wars* chair in the corner. I close my eyes and think it real hard. Yoda comes to me, and I ask him what to do. He usually says the Force is with me to do whatever I need to. So I think about what I want to do really hard, and then I know what to do when I open my eyes."

Zelda looked at Kyle wide-eyed. "That really works for you?"

Kyle nodded. "Usually. It works better for getting stuff than fixing stuff."

Addie looked incredulous. "Kyle's making it all up. That can't work."

Kyle leapt to his defense. "No, it's true. Like when I needed a new bottom bracket for my BMX bike, I did that. Yoda said to just keep asking Dad for it, and it would happen. Same for the new headset."

Randall protested. "That's just pestering Dad until he gives in. You know I can only take so much pestering."

"That's what Yoda said in my head," replied Kyle. "What's the difference? It worked."

Randall nodded weakly. "Well, I'll give you that. Bottom line, when you needed an answer, you had a talk with yourself."

"No, Dad!" exclaimed Kyle. "I asked Yoda."

Zelda interjected. "Where was Yoda?"

"In my head, silly! Where else?" shot Kyle, looking frustrated at his mother's failure to grasp the obvious.

Zelda and Randall looked at each other with satisfied smiles.

Kyle stood up from his chair, as if to leave.

"Where are you going, Buddy?" asked Randall.

"I'm tired of explaining what I do," said Kyle. "Besides, I have to pee."

"Well, hurry back after," said Zelda. "Your turn is over for now. When you get back, it will be Addie's turn."

Addie frowned and rolled her eyes.

When Kyle returned, he slumped on the chair and crossed his arms. He put on a very convincing bored face. Zelda resumed the discussion. "So, Addie, is there anything you do when you need to solve a problem? Is it anything like what Kyle just told us?"

Addie shrugged her shoulders helplessly. "I don't know . . . well, maybe. But I'm not anything like Kyle. I'm not into *Star Wars* stuff. It's kind of lame."

"We know you're different, honey," said Randall. "Everybody has a different way, but that doesn't matter. Whatever gets you to where you need to go is what's right for you. If you're not comfortable talking about it, that's okay."

Addie thought for several more moments while Kyle drummed a pencil on the table. "Stop that, Kyle!" squeaked Addie. "I'm trying to think!"

Kyle smirked. "What's the matter? Nothing happening?"

Addie banged the table with her hand. "Okay, I'm gonna try to explain. No laughing." She stared daggers at Kyle.

Kyle held up a hand and made a lip-zipping gesture.

Addie pointed a menacing finger at Kyle and continued, "I talk things over with my stuffed animals and my Breyer horses. But the leader of the group is my Uni, my new unicorn. She is a goddess. She's smarter than the one Polluto chewed up. When all the talking is over, whatever she says goes."

Randall nodded quietly. "Do you have long meetings?"

"Sometimes," said Addie. "If the animals don't agree, we have lots of arguments. But then Uni takes over and tells me what's what. Then that's what I do."

Kyle interrupted. "I thought you said Uni was a boy."

Addie was quick to defend her companion. "Uni can be anything I want!"

"So you really trust Uni?" asked Zelda.

"Well, sure," said Addie defiantly. "She's never wrong."

Kyle was looking rather sullen. Randall asked him what he thought of

Addie's process. Kyle looked around for a moment. He gave his reluctant approval. "I guess it's okay. I've got Yoda. She's got Uni. Whatever works."

The room went quiet for a long moment with both kids finally staring at Randall and Zelda expectantly. Randall cleared his throat loudly, and Zelda coughed a bit.

"Well, kids," said Randall. "Receiving your signals loud and clear. All frequencies are in sync. I must surmise it's our turn to reveal our innermost stuff-dealing techniques. We're guessing you now expect us to do the great reveal."

Addie gave a knowing nod of her head. "If that means you're going to tell us how you do what we just explained, we're waiting."

Zelda raised her eyebrows. "Randy. You go first."

"Why, sure thing, fair wife," said Randall. "Before I start, I want to remind us all about something we mentioned earlier. There are many different names for what people think of as God. To me, that means every person knows God in their own particular way, and each way is alright as long as it leads to the place we all need to get to."

"And it doesn't matter what name we call Him?" asked Addie.

"I don't think so," said Randall. "Look, your given name is Addie, but we also call you Rosebud, honey, sweet pea, and other nicknames. But all of them are still you. Just different aspects of you. Understand?"

Addie nodded.

"So whether I refer to God as Yahweh, Jehovah, Great Spirit, or even Yoda or Uni, it's still Him. Or Her. And God made everything. Even us thinking about God was made by God."

"I get it, Dad," said Kyle. "But where is God? Is He up in Heaven somewhere? Does He take long-distance phone calls?"

Zelda took over. "Good question, sonny boy. The Bible is like the owner's manual for Christians. It says God is everywhere and in everything. To me, that means God is in each of us already right from birth. When they say God is in Heaven above, they could really mean He's in our brain, above our shoulders. No need to wander around looking for Him."

"Or Her!" squeaked Addie.

"Exactly. That's what I mean. To keep it simple, I'm gonna say 'He,' but you know it's He or She. Anyways, He's already with you, waiting for you to ask for help. He may even be talking to us, but we may not be listening. Or we may hear His words but disagree and try to argue with Him."

Kyle nodded his understanding. "That's probably why it takes so long sometimes to get it straight."

"Good call," said Randall. "Christians say that praying is the way to talk to God. But instead of just having a chat, some people pray just when they want something or are in trouble. If God doesn't provide them with what they want, they say God doesn't hear their prayers. But really what happened is that they didn't like God's answer."

Zelda took over. "Or they didn't listen for the response at all. I say praying is just talking with the God that's already inside of us . . . in our brains. And it has to be a two-way conversation. Not just an *ask* and a *give*. No need to run around like a chicken with its head chopped off looking for the answer or the solution. We have to be open to the receiving, to make space for the response we'll feel inside. It's right there inside us waiting to be found."

Kyle jumped up like he was poked by a cattle prod. "I get it! Yoda is the name I gave my God, and Uni is Addie's. What name did you give your God, Mom?"

"Atta boy!" exclaimed Zelda. "Someone has been paying attention. Well, I'm an equal opportunity worshiper. I mostly call Her God, but I use a bunch of the other nicknames as well depending on how I feel that day. Plus, I may add some choice adjectives and verbs."

"How do you pray, Mom?" asked Addie. "I never hear you!"

"Well, I don't do it talking out loud. I do it a couple of ways," said Zelda. "My favorite way since I was a kid is drawing. Like now, I go up to my art studio, close the door and lock it, put on some good music, and smoke a cigarette. Then I put a clean sheet of drawing paper on my easel, close my eyes, and recite some of my favorite Khalil Gibran."

Addie frowned. "What's a calillgi bran? Is that a breakfast cereal? You said no food upstairs!"

Zelda chuckled. "Khalil Gibran was a poet in the early 1900s. Even though he wrote a long time ago, his wisdom is timeless and speaks to my heart. For example, he wrote, 'You talk when you cease to be at peace with your thoughts.' So when I am not at peace with my thoughts, I draw whatever is bothering me and stare at it for a while. Then my drawing guru directs my hand, and a picture takes shape. The answer I'm looking for appears in my drawing."

Addie momentarily stared at Zelda. "Does it always work, Mommy? You can use my Uni if your way doesn't work sometimes."

Zelda smiled broadly. "You are so sweet! I will gladly use your Uni if I ever need to. I have learned that sometimes the answer comes right away, but sometimes it comes much later. The process is what gets things moving for me. Nobody ever sees those drawings, because I burn them to ashes out on the porch and smudge the smoke with a feather."

Kyle bounced up in his chair. "So that's the special smoke I always smell. That sounds way cool! I love burning stuff . . . I mean, I think I would love it."

"Is there something else we need to talk about, son?" asked Randall.

"No, Dad. I was just thinking about it. No harm in that, right?" stuttered Kyle. "Mom, are there some other ways you pray?"

"I've got some other ways, but we don't need to go into them now," said Zelda. "Maybe when you guys are more grown up."

"*Aww*, you always say that when it gets interesting," griped Kyle. "What about you, Dad?"

Addie got excited. "Yeah, Daddy! Do you smoke special stuff too?"

"So it's my turn, huh?" asked Randall, shuffling his feet on the floor, trying to ignore the question.

"Go, Daddy," sniped Zelda.

"All right, already," said Randall, clearing his throat loudly. "It all started with my imaginary friends, McGillicuddy and Agadaboo, in the basement of my house in Shorewood when I was just a kid. When I had a problem, I'd sneak down there and talk to them in the old coal bin. They weren't always trustworthy, and sometimes they'd get me into trouble."

Kyle plugged right into that. "Yeah, sometimes I get that too. Boba Fett is the worst. He got me in trouble lots of times."

"Care to share?" asked Zelda.

"Now is not the time," redirected Kyle. "It's still Dad's turn."

Randall continued. "It was after McGillicuddy and Agadaboo had gotten me in deep doo-doo several times that I turned instead to my best buddy, Winnie-the-Pooh. Of course, he was just a stuffed animal but, right after honey pots, he loved talking to me. He never steered me wrong."

Addie bounced up and down in her chair. "Holy Unicorn, you had a stuffed animal pal too?"

"Yep. Got me," admitted Randall. "Now keep in mind, I was just a kid, and when I got older, I traded up to different prayer pals."

Kyle looked indignant. "Whadya mean, you switched? This is getting confusing! Which one of the religions is the right one?"

Randall looked like he had won the lottery. He had been waiting for someone to ask this question. "To paraphrase the wise words of the ancient Chinese prophets, 'There are many paths up the mountain, Grasshopper, but the view from the top is just the same.'"

Addie couldn't roll her eyes high enough. She was tired of the highfalutin adult talk.

Kyle's head tilted to the side. "Do you mean that every religion has its own way, but really they all get to the same place?"

Randall pointed at Kyle enthusiastically. "Exactly! Every religion wants their version to be the true one. The one that leads to Heaven or Nirvana, whatever they think is our grand destination. Yet once we get there, we find each other."

Kyle nodded slowly. "So it doesn't matter which way you go, as long as you're true to your path?"

Randall felt proud of his son. "Ed Zachary. I can't believe you said that. Out of the mouths of babes. You can choose whatever prayer pal works for you, and that may change as you grow up. It's probably easier to find a prayer pal when you're a kid."

"Easier?" asked Zelda. "Why is that?"

"My theory is that our brains have parts in them that act like radio receivers and broadcasting equipment," explained Randall. "We can send out brain signals and receive them from others like us, especially when they are close to us, like family and friends. We operate on the same frequencies, so it's easier to send and receive the signals. When we're kids, our brains are not all cluttered up with new things we've learned, so it's easier to focus. When we're older, the daily life clutter and stuff we need to know causes interference with the signal, so we don't get a clear message back."

Addie looked intrigued. "You mean it's easier for us to get brain signals 'cause we're kids?"

"Exactly, honey," said Zelda. "Now here's the tough part to understand. Daddy and I think that we are what we think."

"Huh?" Both kids responded in unison.

"Open ears, shut mouths. So the essence of what makes you YOU is eternal. Dr Seuss might even call it the 'Who of You.' That Who that thinks and feels and experiences lives in your body and doesn't stop being you when your body stops. Our bodies die, but the energy that makes up our Who, our essence, continues on without our bodies."

Addie started bouncing up and down. "Yahoo! That means I have a You-Who too!"

Kyle looked startled. "Then when you die, where does the You-Who part go?"

"That's the big question, kiddo," said Zelda. "You-Who is a perfect name to call it! We don't have a real good answer on that one, but your dad thinks that the You-Who might have something to do with the way the whole universe is made up. It's something he's looking into with some friends, but it may take him a long time to get the answer. Maybe he never will until he's just a You-Who. It's kind of complicated."

"So Dad has a You-Who crew?" asked Addie.

Randall took over again. "I do have a You-Who crew, indeed I do. It's new. We are looking at a big something that we think may explain the You-Who. I'll try to put it in simple terms. The big something has a complicated name. It's called 'quantum biology.' Basically, it says that when you break down what we're made of into the tiniest pieces possible, we are all made from stuff that constantly shifts between being energy and solid matter. These smallest pieces of stuff are able to do some really strange things, like be here and there at the same time. Or go through a solid fence instead of over it."

"You mean we're not really solid?" Addie squeaked, a little scared.

"In a way, we're mostly empty space," said Randall.

"Like I could go through a wall if I wanted to?" asked Kyle.

"At the tiniest level, maybe," said Randall. "And maybe not our physical bodies, but our thoughts."

"So like our You-Who could visit inside another person's head?" asked Kyle. "I could know all their secrets!" Kyle scowled. "And they would be in my head. I'm not sure I like that idea."

"It's entirely possible," said Zelda. "Think of it the way Christians talk about it. They say that God is pure energy, and he's part of us all. That means we are all part of each other. When I go into my thoughts, God must already be there. If he's connected to everything, then my thoughts have to be connected to yours. When we talk to our Yoda or Uni or Winnie or the art guru, we are really talking to the God in our mind, but we have to focus to make the right connection."

"What do you mean by focus, Mom?" asked Addie. "Like a camera?"

"Kids, my brain hurts," said Zelda. "Randy, help me out."

Randall thought for a moment, frowned, and then had an idea. "Remember when we looked through a telescope at the moon? It wasn't perfect at first. We had to wait for dark, move the telescope around to find the right spot, adjust the focus, and then be still to get the full image. The light from the moon was all brought together in the telescope and enlarged so we could see the detail more clearly. That's what we do when we focus our mind. Some people call that prayer. Others call it meditation or contemplation. All it comes down to is looking quietly inside our minds to allow the answer to show up, because that's where it always was."

"Right," said Zelda. "What we're trying to say is that we don't need to pick a religion to do what Dad said. All it takes is a quiet conversation with yourself. If having a Yoda or Uni to help you focus helps you do that, go for it."

Randall looked at the two kids, and they appeared to be either deep in thought or totally confused. "So do you guys get any of this? We're in pretty deep waters."

"I . . . think so," muttered Kyle. "Addie, do you understand?"

"I want to go upstairs and get Uni pretty soon," Addie said softly. "But I sort of think I might maybe get it. It's just, how are we gonna use this stuff to get rid of the spooky lady? I'm getting scared, 'cause if your mind energy sticks around after you die, does that make you a ghost?"

"You are one sharp little cookie," said Randall. "That's a perfect segue into where this sailing ship is headed."

"What's a saggy way?" asked Addie, frowning.

"It's kind of like the on-ramp leading to the freeway," said Randall. "A segue brings us to the next place we need to be."

"Where's that?" asked Kyle.

"On the freeway to free a way from the spooky stuff that's been happening," said Zelda. "Now go grab your Uni, and we'll map out the road. Meet you in the Room of the Living in one hour. Your dad and I need to get the room ready and gather some things. We're going to have a ceremony to rid us of the spookies."

Kyle grabbed Addie's hand. "I'll go up with you, 'cause you look scared."

Addie held on to Kyle's hand tightly. "Thanks, Ky Ky. And you probably want your light saber too." Kyle looked relieved at the suggestion.

They headed upstairs while the adults started the downstairs arrangements.

Kyle lead Addie gently up the stairs. "What's with calling me Ky Ky, little Sis? You haven't called me that since you were two years old!"

"I don't know," said Addie. "I guess 'cause I'm scared."

Kyle patted Addie's shoulder. Don't worry. We're going to kick that witchy lady's skinny buttski."

CHAPTER 31

—————

WHO, ME?

"There is an extremely powerful force that, so far, science has not found a formal explanation to. It is a force that includes and governs all others, and is even behind any phenomenon operating in the universe and has not yet been identified by us. This universal force is Love . . . the most powerful unseen force. Love is light, that enlightens those who give and receive it. Love is gravity, because it makes some people feel attracted to others. Love is power, because it multiplies the best we have...Love unfolds and reveals this force, explains everything, and gives meaning to life . . ."

— attributed to Albert Einstein as a letter to his daughter on the universal force of love (later refuted as not written by Einstein)

Spooky

An hour later that day, as requested, Kyle and Addie ka-thumped back down the stairs, charged into the living room and plopped on the couch next to each other. They were ready to join Randall and Zelda in beginning their ad lib ceremony to eliminate any cohabiting disembodied entities from their residence. In other words, they were going to "despookify" the Creekside house.

Zelda sat near the window on "Rex the wonder chair." Rex was a Victorian armchair that Zelda rescued from a street corner years earlier. The front legs were carved on the bottom to look like lion's feet grasping a ball. The ends of the armrests were carved to match the legs. Zelda had disassembled the entire chair, stripped off the old finish, sanded it smooth, then polished it to a satin luster with tung oil. She found an old-fashioned floral print fabric and reupholstered the seat and seat back so that it looked 1920's new. Rex wasn't really that comfortable to sit in, but it looked like a throne, and made one feel like a king or queen when seated in it. Thus Rex was appropriate for the mistress-of-ceremony to begin the ritual.

Zelda sat forward in Rex and cleared her throat loudly to get everyone's attention. "Alright, travelers, we all know why we're here. Let's get started. We've actually been down a similar road before, so it's not a new trip."

"We have?" asked Addie.

"We have." Randall had started a fire and stood with one hand on the mantle. He was hoping to create a regal image of a man who "had the floor," a man in control, a father who would protect his family.

The fire crackled and sent a spark toward his already overheated derriere. He could not stop himself from jumping and barking like a lap dog. So much for maintaining a commanding demeanor!

The kids burst into a fit of giggles, and the tension eased dramatically. Perhaps the fire was a tool of God/Universe/Uni/Yoda in collusion to help deliver the night's message. Randall himself tried not to feel too much like a tool as he waited for his butt to cool.

For the gathering, Randall reviewed prior suspected visitations of Biedermeier homes by noncorporeal conscious entities. He noted "Harold the Unfriendly Ghost," likely the perpetrator behind the lawnmower incident in the Colorado Springs house. Then there was the unwanted presence in the rental house in Durham responsible for knocking down shelves and other mischief. Now it seemed possible that the spirit of a restless suicide victim, or two, was making trouble at the Creekside house. Randall didn't discuss his unusual communications with dead or dying patients at the VA for fear of further escalating anxieties, but he was hoping the pending ceremony would detoxify those specters as well.

When Randall finished, there was a long silence among the troops. He paused to refill his coffee cup and let their minds marinate the new data. When he returned, Addie raised a hand.

"Yes, Rosebud?" Randall asked.

"So are we going to say 'Aunts' to get the bad ghosts out of our house?" Addie asked.

Zelda looked puzzled. "What? Oh, you mean séance. The cute blonde girl wins the big prize! That's my little whiz kid. How do you know that word?"

Kyle looked irritated. "I'm smart too, Mom. I told her the word. I saw it in a movie. Then I dreamed we were gonna do a séance, all gathered around a table saying gobbledy gook. You know, where the table starts to wobble, and there's scary sounds and voices."

Zelda and Randall looked at each other wide-eyed for a beat. Had Kyle seen this on TV? Or was their little boy picking up foreign channels in his little boy neural network?

Kyle had no patience for the long silence that followed his question. "So is that how we're going to do it?"

Zelda was the first to recover her senses. "Yeah, actually. I've decided that's exactly what we're doing, but we're going to use the Chinese menu method."

Kyle interrupted. "But I'm not hungry!"

Zelda chuckled, then held up a hand. "Patience, child. It's like a menu for the rituals. We'll pick two from Column A, three from Column B, one from Column C, and maybe some from Columns D through G. Don't worry, there will be eggrolls."

"And fortune cookies?" asked Kyle.

"Exactly," said Randall. "There are many traditions with rituals, and since we don't follow any particular tradition, we get to sample them all and see what tastes best for our purposes. With our combined mind energy and a little help from Yoda, Uni, Winnie the Pooh, Khalil Gibran, plus a large cast of other players, we are going to decontaminate, no, *excoriate* the bad energy from this old house." Randall mimed raking his claws across his chest. "It will be The Great Excoriation! And before you ask, it means to 'get rid of' with great prejudice."

Addie and Kyle looked at each other, still somewhat puzzled, but then decided that what he said was a good thing and cheered. Randall and Zelda chimed in.

Zelda took a deep breath, held up a small metal bowl in her hand, and made a show of tapping it with a wooden stick. The sound rang through the room, drawing everyone's attention like a laser. She motioned for Randall to sit down while she took the floor, moving away from the fire. She figured her jeans were holy enough.

"Every sacred place has essential elements, whether it's a church, a synagogue, a mosque, a temple, a sacred circle in the forest, or your own special altar. It doesn't matter what the altar is made of, but more that it means something to the You-Whos who gather there. We are going to use this table for our sacred place."

Zelda pointed to the round coffee table in the center of the room. "As you know, your father made this table. There once had been a mighty oak tree on our property when we first moved here. The tree fell in a storm, so when the workmen were cutting it up, Randy asked for a round of it to make into this table. He sent you kids into the woods to find matching branches in the shape of a large Y to make the legs."

Kyle's hand shot up. "I remember that! I got the best ones."

Addie waved him off. "Why the Y, Dad? And why only three legs?"

Randall was impressed with his daughter's questions. "Your whys about the Y's are wise. Three legs are more stable and easier to balance than four. And Y reminded me of the word You. Makes even more sense, now that we're talking about You-Whos! And it symbolizes more than one You are working together for a common goal. Even in the Bible it says, roughly, that whenever people gather to talk to God, that's a church. So this is our sacred space, our gathering to understand our universe."

Addie nodded, seeming satisfied with that answer. "Now what, Mom?"

"Now we need to prepare symbols and talismans to put on our

sacred place," said Zelda. "We have lots of choices. Symbols are objects that you choose to represent something else. You can use fire, stones, books of wisdom, pictures, or anything that means something to you."

Randall could see the question coming. "Before you ask, a talisman is sort of like a symbol but with more power. It can be any object, but is usually something of greater value, like a gold ring or jewel, that you believe has magical powers to protect you from evil or to bring good fortune."

"Like my light saber?" asked Kyle.

Randall nodded. "Or Addie's Uni."

"Or my locket with a picture of Grandmother in it when she was a young lady," offered Zelda.

"What's yours, Dad?" asked Kyle.

"That's easy," said Randall. "The two of you."

"But Dad, you can't wear *us* around your neck," said Addie.

Randall lifted Addie into his arms and over his shoulder. "Oh, yes, I can!" Randall tickled Addie, and she laughed until she couldn't catch her breath. Kyle ran for cover.

When things settled down again, Addie asked if the fire in the fireplace was a symbol. Zelda answered her question. "Yes, honey, but we're also going to use candles. One thing that fire represents is light and illumination to better see our way when things are dark. We'll be using candles for that in tonight's ceremony. What do you think the big fire in the fireplace stands for?"

"That's easy," said Kyle. "To burn Daddy's butt!"

"No, dummy." Addie shook her head. "It's the source of all light, like warmth that never runs out. Something that protects us from the scaries at night."

Zelda's heart warmed with her daughter's insight. "Exactly, honey. It represents what's always there for us and something we have to respect."

Yoo Hoo

Zelda and Randall had prepared a tentative menu for the Great Excoriation. They assigned each person a list of séance items to find and bring to the round oak table. After long minutes of hunting and gathering, the table slowly accumulated a bevy of interesting objects: candles, feathers, sage, crystals, stones, crosses, a Bible, a Quran, and a mélange of other curious oddments the kids had decided were meaningful to them. These included a small ceramic *Star Wars* thimble and a lock of hair from a deceased pet. The potpourri included faded Polaroid pictures, a dried pinecone, and sand from a beach. Randall asked for everyone to bring a musical instrument. Kyle brought his starter Ludwig drum, Randall his acoustic guitar, Addie her ocarina, and Zelda her kazoo.

As the living room darkened near sunset, they began their home-grown liturgy with a candle-lighting ceremony. Zelda chose seven candles to represent the Native American prayer of the seven directions. Addie and Kyle took turns lighting one candle prior to each direction Zelda faced.

The first prayer was done facing EAST, the source of the sun. Zelda thanked the sun for offering new beginnings, hope and promise. Taking a quarter turn to the right, Zelda did a prayer to the SOUTH, the direction of warmth, growth, and fertility. Then she turned to the WEST, where the sun goes down, the direction of rest, dreams, and closure. With another turn, she faced NORTH, the direction of cold, winds, strength, and courage. Zelda took a long silent pause, just breathing.

With four candles now lit, the light in the room flickered eerily, further accented by a reddish light cast by the glowing embers in the fireplace. Addie shivered involuntarily. Kyle looked warily at the moving shadows on the walls that seemed to have a life of their own. Randall strummed a few minor chords on his guitar to further set the mood. He shivered too and felt his feet grow cold despite the warmth from the fireplace.

Finally Zelda resumed the seven directions prayer by turning back to the EAST and looking UPWARD. Here she prayed to Father Sky to remind us to look upward with mind, heart, and spirit for daily guidance. And to remember how small we are in this world. At a hand signal from Zelda, Addie lit the fifth candle. Zelda turned her head

DOWNWARD to pray to Mother Earth and promise that all we do will be to honor and revere her. Kyle lit the sixth candle.

Zelda put her hand to her heart to turn her attention INWARD. Addie lit the seventh candle as Zelda prayed, "May we all be true to the spirit of God and the Holy Spirit that dwells within us." With all seven candles lit, a stronger light was cast about the room, creating even more wavering shadows and a sense of other-worldliness.

Another long silence ensued until Randall tried to lighten things up with one of his patented off-the-wall remarks. "Say, ladies and germs, how 'bout we do a little song together?"

The kids rolled their eyes. Zelda looked like she was ready to do Randall in with a laser bolt from her left eye for spoiling the spiritual mood she'd so carefully crafted. "A song? A song? You're cracked in the head, Randall Biedermeier!"

Randall put up a hand. "No, no. You're going to like it. It goes something like this. In fact, it goes exactly like this: *I'm gonna scratch that ghost right out of my mind . . .*'" Randall stopped when he saw the immediate negative facial expressions of his family. "Okay. Not ready for levity, I see. How about we stay in the reverential mode Mom has so thoroughly set up. How about we do the random Bible passage read now instead?"

Zelda nodded. "You're getting warmer again, Randy. Remind us how that works."

Randall pointed to the vintage Bible he had brought to the table. It was a large tome and very old. Printed in 1876, it had belonged to his grandfather Peter. In it, Peter had recorded, in carefully executed handwriting, important family events, like weddings, births, baptisms, confirmations, and deaths. The leather binding was well worn, and several pages were loose. Each page was as thin as tissue paper and quite brittle. Randall figured if any Bible had gravitas, it was this one.

"I can do that," said Randall. "You kids get to help with this one. We'll start with you, Kyle. I will say a few words and then point to you. Then without looking, you just open the Bible to any page and put your finger down randomly on a page and read the Bible verse your finger is closest to. Think you can do that?"

Kyle nodded and tried to pull the Bible closer to him but was surprised by how heavy it was. "Dang, this thing weighs a ton."

"Sure does," said Randall. "It's full of weighty words. By the way, it doesn't matter what the words say or if we understand them. What's important is that we go through the process. Are you ready?"

"Yes, Dad," said Kyle.

"Before you start, Mom is going to burn some sage and do some smudging with a feather while she raises a crystal to the sky and invokes the name of the Great Spirit. When she finishes, I'll say some words and then I'll wave my hand to you. It's important we do it exactly that way and remain otherwise silent."

Everyone nodded. Zelda held a small bundle of sage into a candle flame and used a feather to waft the smoke in the seven directions. Zelda spoke. "Oh, powerful Spirit who watches over us, we beseech you to help us in our hour of need. Herein, we believe, dwells a presence that has not found peace outside the flesh. Please guide the lost presence to the peace we all seek, for there is little we can do for it here among us."

Randall took his turn. "Oh, Spirit Father, we summon your help with the reading of your Word." Randall waved a hand toward Kyle.

Kyle clumsily opened the Bible and put his finger down on a page. He looked down and exclaimed. "Someone already underlined the part I just put my finger on."

"Probably your great-grandfather," said Randall. "Go ahead, read it, my son."

"It says Ecclesiastes 12:7." Kyle had a hard time pronouncing Ecclesiastes but stumbled on. "... and the dust returns to the earth as it was, and the breath returns to God who gave it."

Randall nodded and went on officiating. "We have heard your word, but still seek understanding."

Addie commented, "Yeah, I don't get it either. Can I do the next one?"

Randall nodded agreement and motioned Zelda to perform another smudging. She did so and Randall made another request for help.

"Great Spirit who guides us, we honor you with another reading of your Word."

Randall waved a hand and pointed to Addie. Kyle had to help her open the book, but she put her little finger down on the page.

"Hey, look," exclaimed Addie. "Mine is underlined in red. And it starts with a man named John. It says, '1 John 4:4. Little children, you are from God, and you have conquered them, for the one who is in you is greater than the one who is in the world.' *Ummm . . . I don't get it.*"

Zelda nodded. "Don't worry about it, pumpkin. Think of it like a magician casting a magic spell. Like when he says '*abracadabra*.' It's all part of the process."

"The process?" asked Addie.

Zelda pondered. "You know, like saying a password to get let in a locked door."

"Oh, yeah, I get that," Addie said with a smile.

Kyle looked excited. "Can I do one more? This is fun."

"Sure," replied Randall. "Close the Bible back up and get ready."

After another round of sage burning, the room began to look and smell like a pothead den, but it added to the ritual ambience.

Randall gave another Bible passage send up. "Mighty one who shares spirit life with us, hear, once again, our plea for strength of forbearance. Grant us fortitude in the face of the unknown. Herewith, the reading of your Word by one of your children." Randall waved and pointed to Kyle. This time he was quite composed.

"This one's not underlined, but there's a checkmark next to it. Darn. It's another hard word I can't pronounce: 2 Corinthians 1:21–2. 'But it is God who establishes us with you in Christ and has anointed us, by putting his seal on us and giving us his Spirit in our hearts as a first installment.'" Kyle's face twisted in confusion.

Zelda looked at Randall with surprise on her face. "Randy, these Bible verses seem to be talking about roughly the same thing. And it kind of fits our purpose. That can't just be coincidence, you think?"

Randall screwed up his face and thought about it for a moment. The kids waited intently for his answer. "Well, I guess one might find some continuity in them, but the way the Bible is written in code, it all kind of sounds alike to me. Tell you what. Grab the Bible, and *you* do the honors with one last reading."

"I suppose that would improve the statistics," said Zelda. She burned, smudged, and wafted once more and Randall invoked the Word once more.

Zelda opened and pointed. Her finger landed on James 4:7. "Randy, you're not going to believe this. 'Submit yourselves, then to God. Resist the devil, and he will flee from you.'"

"Holy schneikies!" murmured Randall. "How about I read a passage from the Quran you brought, instead of the Bible, and you do some more advanced preliminary crystal and stone manipulation?"

"Yeah, and we all grab our talismans for good measure," suggested Zelda. She performed her sage-burning ceremony one more time. In addition, she held up a clear quartz crystal in her left hand and a finely polished piece of petrified wood in the right hand, raising them to the sky as an offering. She lit loose tobacco in a pipe and bellowed cherry-wood smoke. She took a handful of small stones, a marble, and a small diamond earring, shook them in a wooden cup and scattered them on the floor. She did some hand waving, a few belly dance moves, and flung a multicolored scarf around her neck. Bowing her head, she gestured to Randall.

Fortunately, the old Quran Zelda had purchased at a used bookstore was more manageable, but it also had a rather ragtag look to it. Randall held the book in front of him and looked to the East. "Honored Allah, the Master. Grant your mercy upon our humble request. We seek *baksheesh*. Now I read Quran 17:85. 'And they ask you about the soul. Say: the soul is of the affair of my Lord. And mankind have not been given of knowledge except a little . . .'"

"A little what?" asked Addie.

Randall shrugged. "I'm not sure. But it sounds like the soul is from the Lord. And that we have just a little knowledge from all that is in the universe. Seems to have lost something in the translation. But if we listen with our You-Whos, I think we'll understand."

Randall and Zelda again exchanged frowning glances. "Randy, I think now it's time for some song from the choir."

Randall agreed and took the floor once more. "Alright troops. I've composed a little ditty to help finish off our quest to oust our unwanted guest. I have adapted it from a Calypso song I've known since I was a kid."

Addie raised her hand.

"Whatever could you want to know, little pumpkin?" asked Randall, feigning ignorance.

"Calypso?" sighed Addie.

"Righto," said Randall. "I've written it down on a piece of paper. It's in my pocket here somewhere." Randall fumbled in his pockets while Addie got antsy. "Ah, here it is. 'Calypso: A style of Afro-Caribbean music that originated in Trinidad. It was sung, using an underlying African rhythm, by the native workers during tedious and laborious work, like picking or hauling bananas.'"

Addie put hands on hips and glared at Randall.

"What?" asked Randall. "That's what the encyclopedia says. Don't worry. You'll get the idea once you hear the song. Here, I'll sing a few verses of the original with guitar accompaniment."

Randall did so and soon everybody was nodding in recognition and singing along.

"I know that one!" shouted Kyle. "It's the 'Banana Boat' song."

"Yeah, I've heard it too, but I never get the words straight," said Addie.

Randall stopped after a few choruses. "Okay, now let's try my version. I have the words typed out and copied for you guys to sing along. Now where did I put them?" Randall made an exaggerated show of pocket patting and even looking down the front of his pants before Zelda waved the music sheets. Randy threw his hand up. "Oh, yeah. I gave them to your mom."

The kids laughed at the slapstick show. Zelda passed around the lyrics and the kids looked them over.

Zelda held up the sheet and pointed to the top. "The title of Dad's song is 'You-Who Be Gone'?"

"Singing it will make the ghost lady be gone?" asked Kyle.

"That's the idea," said Randall. "This will work because a ghost is just a You-Who of someone who has passed. We are inviting it to go wherever it needs to go. We're giving it a segue. I'll play a few lines on my guitar and Kyle can pick up the beat. Kyle, think you can keep the beat going on the drum and sing at the same time?"

"Sure thing, Dad," affirmed Kyle.

"And, Zelda, Addie," said Randall, "as long as you have instruments, when we finish the words, we'll continue the song as an instrumental. You two join in on the ocarina and kazoo."

"Can do," said Zelda. "You up for that, Rosebud?"

"I'll try, Mommy," said Addie, a bit unsure of herself.

"Great," said Randall. "Kyle, start giving us the rhythm on your drum, and I'll come in with some opening chords on the guitar. When I put my right hand up, we'll start all together. Everybody got it?"

Addie raised her hand. "What if the song doesn't work to get rid of the You-Who?"

Zelda tooted her kazoo for attention. "There's no room for negative thinking here. We can repeat the song if we need to until we know the unwanted You-Who is gone. Plus, we've got lots of little rituals to repeat another night. Altogether, they're bound to work. Now let's play the spooks away."

After a few false starts, they finally all came in together. The sound of music filled the house. But it was not your usual kind of music. There was enough dissonance to raise the dead.

"You-Who Be Gone Song"

You-Who, You Who-oo-oo-Who
Daylight come, wan' You-Who be gone
Who, me say who, me say who, me say who,
me say who-oo-oo-who
Daylight come, wan' You-Who be gone.

Pray all night and we beat the drum
(Daylight come, wan' You-Who be gone)
Wish you go back to where you're from
(Daylight come, wan' You-Who be gone)

Come see our Talisman and our sage
(Daylight come, wan' You-Who be gone)
Bring out the sacred text and turn the page
(Daylight come, wan' You-Who be gone)

Smudge six time, seven time, eight time more
(Daylight come, wan' You-Who be gone)
Turn round twice and stomp the floor
(Daylight come, wan' You-Who be gone)

You-Who could be a woman or a man
(Daylight come, wan' You-Who be gone)
Hit You-Who in de head with Mama's fryin' pan
(Daylight come, wan' You-Who be gone)

You-Who, You Who-oo-oo-Who
Daylight come, wan' You-Who be gone
Who, me say who, me say who, me say who,
me say who-oo-oo-who
Daylight come, wan' You-Who be gone.

By song's end, the whole family was hot and sweaty, shedding sweaters and wool socks. Wondercat and Milky Way had joined in the song, howling in what seemed to Randall like an alternate definition of catatonia, or perhaps catcophony. Meanwhile, the seven candles had slowly burned down to the nub.

The Biedermeiers continued strumming, drumming, kazooing, and ocarina-ing for several minutes once the lyrics were over. Zelda swayed, shimmied, and flourished her scarf in circles, swirling smudge smoke to the ceiling. An astute observer outside the front window might imagine seeing a shimmering, coiling spiral of energy escorting one, or maybe two, lost You-Whos who knows where. But with a shake of the head, the observer would probably conclude "looney family" and move on.

Another howl echoed the cats' as if they had called in reinforcements. The fire, which had been fading away in the fireplace, flared up as a huge downdraft thrust chilling air across the embers and into the living room. The shock of air silenced the hooting, hollering, and howling. The sage smoke dissipated, leaving only clear, cool air and shivering humans.

Silence finally settled over the room like a comforting blanket, and all four Biedermeiers caught their collective breaths and sat peacefully for a few beats. The cats had stopped their wailing and settled in front of the fire for warmth. They might have been spooked, but no self-respecting cat would admit to that.

Zelda looked around the room, taking in the whole scene. She tilted her head as if to refocus and find a comfortable way out of the collective trance. "Well, folks, I think our work here is done," she announced with an air of finality.

"Are you sure?" asked Addie, pulling an Afghan around her. "I do feel a lot better. I just don't want that witchy lady in my room again. Are you sure there's nothing more we can do?"

"I'm pretty sure we've performed every viable ritual we can to fix this," responded Zelda. "Don't you agree, Randy?"

Randall listened for any vibrations in the room. He didn't know the answer for certain. As a scientist, he liked things to make sense, to be measurable, to have replicable outcomes. This quest to find the deeper meaning to life; a connection between body, mind, and spirit; to heal his family and cleanse his home, was powerful. It went beyond his medical training yet seemed to have a deep connection to healing. The more he looked outside himself for answers, the more questions he had.

When he opened his mind, heart, and spirit to something beyond the logic of the brain, to some wider knowing, the more he realized that wisdom was inherent to BEING, not just DOING. That openness to what is, to the higher realities beyond what he could perceive with his physical senses, gave more clues about the universe. Not by seeking what may be "out there" in the physical world, but by being open to the wisdom in himself could he really begin to understand the universe and spooky science. *That's what the wisdom keeps telling me. The answer is in You. In the You-Who.* Randall wanted to hug everyone.

Randall made his own final pronouncement to put Addie's concerns to rest. "I guess we have to go by how we feel. If you feel, in your heart, at peace, then we have done the best we can. And we have each other as a family."

Addie sighed. "My You-Who feels really good, Daddy. I'm not scared of my room anymore. I know you guys will keep me safe."

Kyle put his arm around Addie. "I'll always watch over you, little sis. I know, let's start our own séance to remind lost spirits to stay away. Mom and Dad, can we put a candle on the dinner table every night?"

"Great idea, Kyle!" Randall turned to Zelda, and she nodded agreeably. "*Hmm*, you know, Zel, there is another little ritual we can perform later tonight after the kids go to bed, *eh*, what?"

Randall winked and nudged her with his elbow.

Zelda socked him hard in the arm. "Another gutter ball. Dream on!"

"Oh, come on. I know you want to go bowling." huffed Randall.

"What does Daddy mean?" asked Addie.

"Never you mind, little girl," said Zelda.

"I know what he means," said Kyle. "It's kind of naughty, and I'm not telling."

"No one ever tells me anything," yelled Addie. "Why am I always in the dark around here?"

Randall chuckled, picked up Addie, and whispered in her ear. Addie laughed and wrapped her arms around his neck. "My You-Who loves your You-Who too."

EPILOGUE

From the kitchen, Kyle yelled, "Can we have mac 'n weenies?"

Zelda looked at Randall with squinty eyes. "Now, see what you've started with your bad meal choices? How can we say no? We might undo what we just did."

Randall shrugged and nodded. "*Mea culpa*, but you're right. We should probably comply to reinforce today's lesson. Might stick better if we associate it with a good meal memory."

Zelda flailed her arms in submission. "I try so hard to help them eat right. By the way, before we start to prepare your sublethal concoction, I have a simple question for you, oh, husband of mine."

Randall felt his defense shields go up. No "simple" Zelda question was ever totally benign. "Go ahead, fire away."

"Now that we've conducted our Excoriation ceremony, are you still going ahead with your You-Who crew investigations? From what I heard you say this afternoon, it sounds like you've resolved things in your mind."

Randall pursed his lips in thought. "What I said today is an excellent working theory and good enough for the purpose of calming the stormy seas of childhood. But I'm kind of like Don Quixote when it comes to getting to the root of things. I'm not planning to tilt just any windmill. I've got one particular quantum windmill in mind. I'm happy with my theory of a quantal-neural connection, but I'll not be satisfied if I don't at least try to prove it. If, after all my tries are exhausted, I haven't proved it, it will still have been a fun joust."

Zelda shook her head. "Always the scientist! Is jousting all you ever think about?"

URK!
Not Jumping
Overboard
(Dropping
His
DRAWERS)
WOTTA
TRIP!
RB

ABOUT THE AUTHORS

ROGER BYHARDT is a retired radiation oncologist who lives in Brookfield, Wisconsin, with his wife Marilyn and his cat Hobbes, a largish and always-hungry orange tabby. Roger draws inspiration for writing from his "everyday" experiences with cancer patients and his "normal" family life. This comes seasoned with a fascination for the often-strange conjunction of reality and the unknown in our journey through life. He often takes reality with a grain of Nembutal.

LYDIA BYHARDT BOLLINGER is Roger's daughter and greatest writing fan. She is a psychotherapist who lives in West Linn, Oregon, with her husband Paul, their teenagers, Levi and Anya, and two fuzzy kitties, Sophie and Maeven. This book was born January 1, 2019, when Lydia called Roger and said, "Happy New Year! It's time to write your book. Tell me all the stories you've been telling me since childhood, with all the details you saved for my adulthood." Starting with Thursday afternoons together, the father/daughter, author/author collaboration evolved into this mystery novel, filled with "true" stories and creative liberties, pearls of wisdom, and the questions of life. And the father/daughter bond was transformed at a quantum level.

www.ingramcontent.com/pod-product-compliance
Lightning Source LLC
Chambersburg PA
CBHW022012300726
48970CB00003B/854